BLACK DUST

BLACK DUST

LYNN CHARLES

interlude ✦✦ **press** • new york

interlude press • new york

To E: in constant wonder of who you would have become.

"Like a diamond from black dust, it's hard to know what can become if you give up."

—Busbee & Geringas

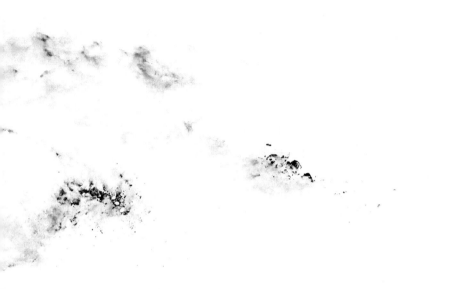

RIDGEVIEW, Ind.—April 2000

Falling in love with Emmett had happened so easily that Toby couldn't pinpoint when the fall started and the in-love finished. It was a constant swoop of his heart that softly landed in a love he never would have imagined for himself.

Toby Spence didn't make intimate connections with people. A military kid who moved every two years, he had quickly learned to make friends and evade enemies, and if the two ever merged, he would play a pretty song on the piano and avoid confrontation. Moving day would arrive soon enough.

But when Emmett Henderson came into his life Toby's heart not only swooped, it spun, swirled, hopped and leapt until it would never be the same.

"I know I saw those damned things on the bathroom sink," Emmett said, as he came back into his bedroom for the fourth time in twice as many minutes.

"Maybe they grew legs."

Emmett snarled and started toward the door to continue looking for the missing cufflinks that went with his prom tuxedo. But Toby grabbed at his wrist and tugged him back for a kiss before he could get away.

Emmett snapped his fingers and stepped back just when Toby was getting to the good part. "Mom and Dad's room." He was out in the hall before Toby could open his eyes.

The last place Toby's family had landed before he went off to college was where he now sat: Wayne County, Indiana. It was an agricultural county dotted with small towns and villages, each with a charm of its own—if you looked hard enough. Emmett lived in Ridgeview, a small college town that had an even smaller Christian university with an alarmingly good music program. Toby's family lived in nearby Xavier— the home of XACT, Xavier Area Community Theater.

And it was at XACT where, two years ago, Toby met Emmett during auditions for its summer production of *She Loves Me*. Emmett was sixteen at the time; Toby was eighteen and the accompanist for the production and preceding auditions. Emmett hopped onto the stage, told Toby his selection—"Try Me"—and without any further direction, launched into the complicated, lyric-heavy, comedic song that landed him the role of Arpad, the character who sang that song. Toby was so taken by the boy—young, confident, handsome and innocent, with a talent that defied his age—that he felt the need to indeed... try him, as the song suggested. Or at least try getting a slice of pizza after rehearsal.

Emmett moped back into his bedroom. "I'm beginning to think you're right; they grew legs." He flopped onto his back on the floor and made a noise not unlike that of a very old dog.

Toby feigned checking the bedside table. Again. "You honestly thought your dad would *wear* Fenrir cufflinks?"

"Well, no. He's not into Final Fantasy so much." Emmett sighed, stood up, rummaged through his desk drawers for the umpteenth time and gave Toby a quick kiss on the cheek. He lifted a forefinger. "Guest room." Then he disappeared into the hall.

Once rehearsals had started for *She Loves Me*, Emmett agreed to get a slice of pizza, but it took Toby until the next season to make a move. Eventually, a slice of pizza turned into a movie, and then a kiss or twenty, followed by phone calls and emails that filled the miles between them when Toby had to go back to college in New York.

For the first time, Toby had understood what it meant when people spoke of being grounded. Of having roots. Of knowing that no matter where they roamed, they had a place to call home. And now, two years later, Emmett was home.

Emmett returned empty-handed and huffed. "You're not helping me."

Emmett had a point: Toby hadn't moved from the edge of the bed since the search began. "I most certainly am." He tugged Emmett closer by his belt loops. "I'm your voice of reason."

Emmett tilted his head and cocked an eyebrow. "You have not come up with one good place to look."

"Reason states that your Fenrir cufflinks, while definitely misplaced, are not a required accessory for our enjoyment of your prom tomorrow night." Toby began dotting Emmett's chest with kisses, and Emmett's body relaxed beneath his touch. Reason. Relaxation. Whatever. He was helping.

"They are if Mom finds out I've lost them." Emmett's anxiety buckled when Toby lifted Emmett's shirt enough to tongue at his navel. "She'll boil me for dinner and use you as a table decoration. Do not unsnap my pants, she's *home*, for Christ's sake."

"It would be a delicious and beautiful meal." Toby hiked himself back onto the bed to avoid cupping Emmett's visible erection through his pants. "Let's go get a boring pair at the mall. No one cares as much as you do."

Toby's phone buzzed in his back pocket.

"I bought them special… "

"No one will notice but you."

Emmett took a deep breath and crawled onto the bed. "Kiss me first."

3

Toby grinned at the incoming kiss, and at each press of Emmett's lips, as his fingers toyed with the little curl over Emmett's right ear, the only curl in his otherwise nondescript head of brown hair. Unfortunately, his phone continued to buzz.

"I've decided I really hate—" Emmett stood up and dragged Toby with him, whining as Toby continued to trail his lips down the curve of Emmett's neck. "I really hate that phone of yours."

Toby pulled back with a grin. "You're jealous because your mom thinks they're cancer magnets and won't let you have one." He flipped his phone open and answered. "Whaaat?? You're interrupting important things here, dude."

"My dad's being a dick."

Toby lowered the phone and spoke to Emmett. "Scotty's dad's being a dick."

"What else is new?" Emmett asked from his new position on the floor, as he peeked under his bed. "I'm surprised his feet haven't turned into testicles by now."

"Gross." Toby went back to the phone. "Need a rescue?"

"Actually, yeah. I need to get to work. He won't take me because I missed baseball practice for theater practice—which I'd already cleared with the coach."

"So now you're going to miss work."

"Are you guys headed into town? Hot pre-prom date or something?"

Emmett and Toby rerouted their trip in order to get to Brighton, the closest thing to a big "city" within a twenty-mile radius, via Scotty's house. And before Scotty had completely closed the door, the trio started up their go-to car shenanigans, reciting classic *Saturday Night Live* skits.

Emmett had mastered Opera Man. Toby and Emmett did a mean Sweeney Sisters tribute. And Scotty's best characters were the melodramatic ones: The Master Thespian, Dieter and Stuart Smalley.

"And doggone it, people like me."

They'd spent hours in cars, in basements and onstage after rehearsals making general jackasses of themselves and entertaining anyone who would listen. Usually, they only entertained themselves.

Today, it was time for Scotty's best, and most infamous, beloved character: Matt Foley, motivational speaker. Scotty's voice work was spot on and he somehow, even while buckled in, twisted and turned as if hiking up pants under a belly. He pitched a line up to the front seat. "Now young man, whaddya wanna do with your life?"

Emmett was too busy laughing to answer, so Toby took the next line as he slowed at a familiar crossroads. "Actually, Dad. I kinda wanna be a writer!"

"Well," Scotty answered, elongating the "el" sound with great drama. "La-di-frickin—" Scotty gasped. His hand slammed against the door. "Toby?"

"Yeah, man?"

"TOBY!!!"

THE CACOPHONY OF SQUEALING BRAKES, crushing metal and his own screams echoed in Toby's head as he took an uneasy breath and pushed the airbag away from his face. He hissed in pain. His chest was tight from the blow; his knuckles were reddened and raw from the chemicals and impact of the airbag.

"Em… Emmett? Scotty?" His voice was hollow and muffled, as if speaking in a dream. "Everybody okay?"

He reached out and flexed his fingers to ease the burning sensation in his hand. Pushing Emmett's airbag back, he rolled his head to the side and tried again. "Emmett?" He touched Emmett's shoulder and shook it gently. "Oh God, please, Emmett! Wake up. Wake—"

Everything went from slow motion to hyper speed and back again. Emmett stirred and looked at Toby, offering a sleepy smile. He lazily patted around for something and when he connected with Toby's hand, he brought it up to his lips. After a soft kiss, Emmett slipped into a doze again.

Toby eased his body into motion, stretching his legs and elongating his back, and began to hunt for his phone. "Scotty? You okay back there, man?"

Scotty never answered. His face was peaceful. His body was contorted amidst the shattered glass, twisted metal and blood. So, so much blood.

Toby's fingers shook as he dialed 9-1-1. Tears filled his eyes, and the dispatcher answered. "There's—there's been an accident. At the corner of um… shit. Where are we again?"

Emmett smacked his lips as he tried to speak. "Liberty… had to get Scotty first." His eyes drooped closed again, and his head lolled to his right; shattered glass crunched under his neck.

"Liberty. Liberty Road and Route Three. My life… " Toby brushed Emmett's hair from his brow and pulled in a deep breath. "My friends are hurt. There was—I think? There was another car. Silver?"

Emmett nodded. "Silver pickup."

"Yes. Silver. Please hurry!"

"Toby… " Emmett patted for Toby's leg, his sleepy tone suddenly urgent. "Toby! Oh God, Toby!"

"Yes, ma'am. I'll stay on the line." Toby turned to Emmett and grabbed his hand. "What, baby?"

"I can't—I can't feel my legs. I can't move—Toby!"

"They're on the way, Em. Can you hear the squad?"

Emmett didn't remember falling asleep. His eyes were too sticky to open, but Toby's hand covered his own with soft caresses. Emmett tried to focus, to hear the squad, but all he heard was Lenny Kravitz singing away from the car stereo.

I belong to you.

You belong to me.

He was a favorite of theirs. They had made love to his songs, the slow, sensual rhythms, the hard, driving pulse.

You light my way in the dark.

Emmett slept again until he heard Toby's voice. "I'll see you there." Sensing Toby standing over him now, Emmett forced his eyes open. Toby's blond curls were tousled and his eyes were huge with worry and love and a promise that, even through the worry, everything would be okay.

His body was jostled and moved away from Toby, and the deafening whirr of an engine took over all of his senses. Nausea engulfed Emmett like a tidal wave. Instead of throwing up, he slept and slipped into a dream.

"No, Emmett. You can't come in. It's not ready yet."

"Oh come on, Scotty. Let me see." Emmett crawled closer and tried to push himself past his stubborn and mud-covered friend under the porch. Scotty had been building a fort. "You said we could play in there!"

Scotty slammed his hand down on Emmett's Tonka dump truck and glared. "It's. Not. Ready. You have to go back."

"Go back where?"

"Go back, Emmett. I promise when it's done, I'll come get you, okay?"

Emmett was confused, but Scotty was practically pleading, so he stood up, dusted off his knees and turned back toward his own house.

He woke briefly inside a giant tube.

"Hello, Emmett. Don't be scared and do NOT move."

He slept again until he was moving under blinding fluorescent lights. "Toby? Can I see—" People talked around him as if he wasn't there. Maybe no one heard him over their own barked words: *blood pressure, internal bleeding, three pelvic breaks minimum, fixator, update his parents.*

He slept again. It was the best sleep he'd had in the entirety of his eighteen years. No dreams. Just peace and quiet.

When he awoke, he felt sick. He puked, and the vomit ran down his cheek, and he cried at the grossness and the sickness and the fear that surrounded him.

And when he woke further and saw more fluorescent lights overhead and strange faces coming in and out of his vision, he wanted to scream, to shout. "Hey! I'm here! I'm scared! Where's Toby? Where's my dad?" Strangers spoke his name as they cleaned him and reassured him. A redhead who could have been Scotty's sister raised his bed a little. "If you feel sick again," she explained, lifting his hand so he could feel an empty bowl on his lap, "you've got this, okay, sweetheart?"

And then he heard himself say, "Toby." She smiled at him, but said nothing as she looked over his head, made notes and pushed a few buttons on a box next to his bed.

His dad arrived at his bedside. He kissed Emmett's forehead, tucked his fingers in Emmett's curled hand and sat. Emmett didn't feel sick anymore.

When his mom blustered in, she brought a whirlwind of questions and anxiety. She fussed and tucked his sheets and kissed his cheek and called him "sweet baby." She cried as she sat on the other side of his bed, mumbling about how pale he was, that he blended into the pillow.

She squeezed his hand as she spoke, and it hurt. He pulled away. "I'm trying to comfort you," she said in her typical impatient tone. He put that hand on the plastic bowl on his lap and turned to his dad's calming, steady presence.

After what seemed like ten thousand more naps, Emmett mustered enough energy to attempt a full sentence. However, his mouth was too dry to speak. His dad swabbed it with a small sponge and lukewarm water.

Finally, "I need Toby."

"Emmett, I don't think—" His mother grabbed for his hand again, and he pulled away, shooting what he hoped was one of his better glares at her. The kind she had taught him to cast.

"Miriam, let him see the boy."

When Toby arrived, his eyes were still huge with worry and love and promise. His face was scratched, and he winced whenever he took a deep breath. He was perfect and brave. Once Emmett's parents left the room, Toby too began to fuss and pet.

But his touch was soothing and welcome. He looked at the contraption bolted to Emmett's hips, at the cast swallowing Emmett's right leg, and back up to Emmett's face. Some of the promise had slipped away.

"I'm so sorry, Emmett."

Emmett smiled to reassure him. There was nothing to be sorry for.

The doctor had visited between Emmett's naps and said that the external fixator, an apparatus of steel rods and large screws attached to his hips, would keep Emmett in place until he healed.

Toby looked down again and took in a huge gulp of air before asking, "Do they think you'll walk? Again?"

Emmett nodded and smacked his lips. Toby swabbed them and Emmett said, "They think so. I'm young—"

"And fearless. And strong."

"And I have you." Emmett wanted to say more, to tell Toby how much he loved him. How sorry he was for—well, he didn't know what he was sorry for, but he felt so tremendously sorry. Because Toby's ever-present light was clouded and dimmed as he looked at Emmett's damaged body.

"You have me. You'll always have me," Toby promised, and then broke into a sob that cracked through his lungs like a loose ember jumping from a burning flame.

Emmett brushed the tears from Toby's face. He resolved, then and there, "We'll get me up and on my feet again, Toby. If I know you're there—"

"Always, Emmett. We'll get you home."

Teenager Killed in Crash
18-year-old dead in two-vehicle collision

RIDGEWOOD TWP—A tragic two-car accident on Liberty Road Monday evening left one person critically injured and one dead.

The incident occurred around 7 p.m., when a westbound 1992 Lexus sedan driven by Tobias Spence, 20, originally of Xavier, Indiana, slowed but failed to stop at the Route 3 intersection, resulting in a T-bone collision with a southbound 1987 Ford F150 driven by Ronald Fischer, 37, of Clifton, Indiana.

A passenger with Mr. Spence, Scott Barnes, 18, of Ridgewood, was pronounced dead on arrival at Brighton General Hospital.

A second passenger with Spence, Emmett Henderson, 18, also of Ridgewood, was flown to Brighton General Hospital where he remains in critical but stable condition.

Mr. Spence was treated and released at the scene. Mr. Fischer was treated and released from Central Medical Center with no apparent serious injuries.

The crash remains under investigation. Neither alcohol nor excessive speed appear to be a factor in the crash.

Liberty Road was closed for approximately four hours during the rescue and preliminary investigation.

1

SEATTLE—October 2015

Tobias checked the time before entering his favorite coffee shop, his last stop before catching a flight back to New York.

Continuing the nomadic life of his youth, Tobias never stayed in one city for long. But after a vaguely successful workshop of a musical in Seattle—a workshop fraught with strife, overblown egos and a director whose vision was muddied at best—he was ready to head back where the familiarity and chaos of the city could engulf him again for a few months.

He opened the door for a young mother whose arms were loaded with a squirming toddler, an overstuffed diaper bag and a stroller that looked large enough to seat a small preschool. She scurried inside and thanked him.

He didn't miss the parallel of their lives: the juggling, the constant harried pace, the yearning for a moment of quiet ultimately spent trying to corral a clear thought. While this mother carried her world with her, Tobias visited his. He left chaos in one city only to pick it up again in the next.

A Broadway musician who spent more time off-Broadway than on, more time away from the city than in it, Tobias played piano for readings and workshops all over the country. He arranged scores to accommodate smaller theaters and casts than shows had been written for. He played piano wherever they would pay him and directed music for venues just getting started or gasping their last respectable breath.

If he wasn't working, he was en route to or from work. So these few stolen moments in a coffee shop that smelled of Sunday mornings with *The New York Times* were a treat.

A young redheaded man popped up from behind the counter, obviously retrieving something he'd dropped. He smiled at the young mother.

And Tobias couldn't breathe.

The ghost of Scotty Barnes stood in front of him, dressed in a black apron decorated with a dancing coffee cup.

Tobias glanced at the line that had formed behind him. If he made a quick exit now, it would be more than indiscreet. He swore under his breath and focused on the scuffed laminate floor while taking a few deep breaths.

A tap on his shoulder zapped through him like lightning. "You're next, honey. We're all in a hurry here."

He took a step forward and smiled nervously at the young man.

Tobias opened his mouth. Nothing came out.

The barista cocked his head to the side, and when he smiled, the resemblance to Scotty was striking: friendly and freckle-faced, he had thick, frizzy, rumpled red hair that made you wonder if he styled it that way or had missed his alarm and didn't bother.

"Come on, Shirley. A line's forming." His voice was spot on, too, a raspy, jovial baritone with a natural flirtatiousness.

When Tobias didn't answer, the barista sighed and looked beyond him. "Lady in the blue scarf. I'll take you while he sails on the Good Ship. What'll it be?"

Tobias had the sense to step out of the way. He scrolled through news feeds on his phone. They reported the same things they had the last time he looked: Middle Eastern crises, election scandals, racial tension, battles over religious freedom.

"All right, Shirley. You ready now?"

Tobias raised his head and looked at the kid's name tag. Justin. Ordinary. Common. Every fifth male on the continent was named Justin. He could do this.

He plastered on a smile and took a step forward, pulling a few napkins from the dispenser on the counter. "Shirley. As in Temple?"

"Well." Justin blushed and swirled his fingers around his own hair. "I mean—you know. The hair."

Tobias chuckled and felt himself relax, if only a little.

It wasn't new, the Shirley moniker. Between the hair and what this barista didn't know—many years in tap classes—it was a clichéd reality. The spiraled ringlets of Tobias's youth had relaxed into large, loose curls as he aged. When he was being completely honest with himself, he acknowledged that they'd thinned a little. Imperceptibly. Mostly.

"I'm surprised you know who Shirley Temple is." Tobias fluffed his not-so-thin hair and pointed to the larger cup displayed on top of the espresso machine. "Large hazelnut latte, dry. You like old movies?"

"I do. Did. I used to watch them with my grandmother." Justin blushed at the admission and quickly punched Tobias's order into the cash register. "She really preferred horror movies, though."

Justin grinned, and Tobias sucked in a breath, trying to smile but probably looking more like someone had stepped on his toe. Scotty's horror movie collection, particularly the classics, had been renowned. He would bring selections to XACT cast parties and sit like a predatory bird surveying its potential kill as everyone watched through spread fingers, curled up with their favorite people.

And Emmett hated them—sort of.

"Why is she going in there?" Emmett would always ask. "She's going to get—"

"Killed," Toby would say and pull Emmett in closer. "She's going to get killed. Why are you scared if you know what's going to happen?"

At Justin's quirked brow, Tobias cleared his throat and tried conversation one more time. "N—now, if you're going to watch old horror movies, you need to see them at a theater with a live organ."

Justin gasped. "Oh my God, that would be *awesome*."

Tobias nodded and grabbed more napkins. He looked down and grimaced; he had about forty in his hands already. "Paramount has a Wurlitzer. See if they don't show classics now and then."

"Thank you. I'll look into that."

Tobias stepped aside and went back to his phone. He deleted text messages sight unseen, voicemails without listening to them. His email inbox was full of unread follow-ups, requests and confirmations. It was as though his phone was screaming at him to keep moving.

This quiet moment was only a mirage.

"Shirley? Is there a Shirley here?"

"Yeah. Shirley. That's me."

A pink-haired barista looked at the name scribbled on his cup and back at Tobias. "Whatever."

Tobias offered her a pinched grin and found the condiment bar.

It had been a few years since Tobias had seen a doppelgänger, and none of them had been as close to Scotty as Justin was. Usually, the boy would be too tall or too thin, or his voice wouldn't have Scotty's distinct rattle. With a second glance, something would be so off that Tobias would be set right again.

Except that "right" had always been a little "wrong" since the day Scotty died. Tobias was the lucky one that day, the one who lived. The one who wasn't injured. And still, the things he had loved with such ease, that he had loved with all his heart—Emmett, composing, long drives along winding country roads—became impossible to love any longer.

He had hung onto the slippery, crumbling edges of his life for as long as he could, but eventually he lost his grip. He left Indiana for good. He left Emmett. He walked back into the life he had been making for himself as if nothing had ever happened.

Tobias was able to keep the dark days surrounding the accident deep in the caverns of his memory. They did not factor in, anymore. Or, more accurately, he didn't give them room to factor in.

Tobias finally sipped his coffee and choked on the syrupy-sweet hazelnut atrocity. He had placed Emmett's coffee order.

Fucking hell.

"Is something wrong with your order, Shirley?"

"Yes." Tobias took a shivering breath and looked at Justin. "My fault. Could I get a house blend, French press, please?" He couldn't return Justin's smile. He couldn't look the kid in the eye.

Scotty had been Emmett's friend, mostly—Tobias's by virtue of dating Emmett. When you loved Emmett Henderson, you loved the whole of him, and Scotty was part of the Emmett package.

The trio had become a force of nature at XACT. Both onstage and off, their roles remained the same: Scotty was rhythm, a steady friend with comedic timing; Emmett was melody, sweeping emotion and lyrical beauty—the lead; and Tobias was harmony, a support system that tied it all together in a rich soundtrack.

But mostly, Tobias was Emmett's. His favorite role was being Emmett's.

And now, fifteen years later, he was channeling his long-lost sweetheart. *Hazelnut latte, dry, please.* Had he been channeling Emmett completely, he probably would have caught himself checking his reflection in a mirror and singing Sondheim under his breath.

Justin remade Tobias's order himself. As he plunged Tobias's coffee he looked back, worry creasing his brow. "Did I do something wrong, Shirley?"

"No, Sc—" Tobias smiled faintly and shook his head. "Justin. You did nothing wrong." As if to punctuate this truth, he dropped a few bills into the tip jar.

Justin poured the coffee into a cup, handed it over and offered another apology. "For the confusion, go pick a treat out of the case. On the house."

"No, thank you. It was my fault." At Justin's look of disbelief, Tobias looked around and saw that the line had dwindled to nothing. "I'm sorry I've been weird," he said. "It's just—you remind me of someone."

"Oh. Well." Justin smoothed his apron down his chest and shoved his hands into its front pockets, where straws and napkins rustled under his fingers. "I hope it's a good memory."

Tunes from Sondheim's *Company* floated through Tobias's head in Emmett's silky, smooth voice, personalized with Emmett's own lyrical touch.

Someone is waiting, cool as Michael, easy and loving as Toby...

Tobias popped the lid off his cup and let the smell of the dark roast overpower the memory of Emmett's voice. "It's complicated."

Justin nodded and went to the pastry case as he talked. "My grandmother always told me that if the past comes back to visit you, maybe you should invite it to tea."

Tobias chuckled, imagining a silver-haired woman with an apron, a flowered teapot and Alfred Hitchcock's *Psycho* playing in the background.

Justin slid an oversized cookie across the counter. "Maybe it's a sign?"

Tobias hummed and sipped his coffee, settling back into his skin as the bitter heat slid down his throat. "Maybe it's just Wednesday."

"I hope not. I don't give away free cookies on just any Wednesday."

Tobias took the cookie and tossed a forced but gracious smile over his shoulder. "Thanks, Justin. Have a good afternoon."

Someone is waiting, warm as Justin, frantic and touching as Emmett...

◆◆◆

NEW YORK CITY—October 2015

Tobias caught the tumbling stack of unanswered mail before it fell to the floor. He had been back in New York for twenty-four hours and he was already grousing about the condition of his office. He had been grousing and growling since he walked out of that damned coffee shop in Seattle.

As far as organizational prowess was concerned, Tobias was not, by any stretch, the nation's top expert in ClosetMaid storage systems. Thankfully, he was also nothing like the creepy weirdo from back home who kept naked baby doll parts on his front porch.

Every few weeks there would be a cardboard sign by Mr. O'Day's gravel driveway advertising a yard sale. In reality, the guy was trying to make a buck from the junk that littered his property: old truck parts, plumbing fixtures—including but not limited to the kitchen sink—tires, said doll parts and probably creepy-guy sauce sold in Mason jars. No one ever bought anything. Or shopped. The only reason Tobias knew about the guy was because he lived up the road from where Tobias and Emmett would sneak off to make out—

Tobias growled and stood up from his crouching position.

The six-hour flight from Seattle to New York had about killed him. Stillness. Quiet. Solitude. The three worst things for his mental health. The only time Tobias stopped was to sit in a vehicle that was taking him to his next gig.

He tossed a stack of sheet music onto his desk and growled again at the paper disaster around him. It was reaching the level of creepy baby doll parts. "How do I leave this place clean and come back to such utter chaos?"

"Because your ideas of clean and chaos change when you're gone two months at a time."

Tobias spun around to his doorway, where his friend Malik stood against the doorframe sipping at his coffee as if he had paid admission to watch the show in Tobias's office. "How long have you been standing there listening to me talk to myself?"

"Long enough to know that you hope *Rent* never makes a comeback, that Disney will stop cranking out musicals, *and* that you have a firm belief that sheet music and paperwork have copious amounts of reproductive sex while you're off making music in some exotic location."

"Seattle is hardly exotic."

"Does it smell like piss and rotting meat?"

"No. No, it does not."

"Exotic." Malik moved a stack of papers off the chair by the door and sat down with the pile in his lap. "What the hell are you doing, anyway?"

"I was looking for the score for *Company*, but then I started unearthing all sorts of shit—" Tobias sighed and looked around at the mess, which included a pile of show freebies, most oddly a felt, stuffed gingerbread man from *Shrek the Musical*. "And now I'm standing here wondering where I put my coffee."

Tobias and Malik Nagi had been friends for a number of years. Malik called himself *The* Melting Pot. He was a blend of European, African-American and Arab, with, if his Auntie Talia was to be believed, "A nice handsome spot of Spaniard named Biel, but that's our little secret." He rented studio space down the hall from Tobias's office and made intricate and bizarre wire, metal and glass sculptures. In addition to Malik's being a competitive racquetball partner, having someone around who wasn't in Tobias's business but who *got* the business was a perk of their friendship that Tobias particularly enjoyed.

Malik pointed to a mug on the credenza. "*Company*? I thought you were doing a new show next month."

"That's empty. And crusty." A shrill violin chord rang through the office. Malik startled and lost the papers perched on his lap. Tobias ignored the commotion and stepped over a stack of junk in search of his trash can. "And I am doing a new show. I just—I wanted to look something up."

Cacophonous piano chords clanged through the small space, and Malik groaned. "What the hell is that? I've been hearing it all day."

"My phone."

"Answer it maybe? Who puts that ugly shit as their ringtone?"

The atonal Schoenberg piano concerto finally stopped, and Tobias shoved a stack of papers into the trash. He looked up at Malik and grinned. "I put that ugly shit as my ringtone so I will answer it and make the ugly shit stop."

"And yet today… "

"Today, this flaky producer I have no intention of working with has an impressively persistent hard-on for me and won't stop blasting my phone. Deleting his messages isn't getting the hint across."

"Silence it?"

"I can't *find* it."

Malik laughed and stood to go, but the violin screech ripped through the office again and stopped him in his tracks.

"Fucking *hell*." Tobias followed the sound around his office while Malik smirked and watched all the stacked piles of papers splay across the floor.

"Keyboard."

"Keyboard, thank you." Tobias flung a score of *Candide* off the keys and unearthed his phone. Just as he answered, he noticed that the call was from an unknown number. "Fucking hell. Yeah, what? This is Tobias."

There was a long silence and then, "T—Toby?"

Tobias felt the blood drain from his head. A rush of heat flushed down his body and out his fingers and toes. "This is Tobias." He stumbled to his desk chair and sat down with an uncoordinated *thump*. "Emmett?"

Malik stepped forward, concern furrowing his brow. "You okay, man?"

Tobias nodded numbly and grabbed for his coffee.

"Yeah. It's me," Emmett said. "Did—did I call at a bad time?"

"No. No, you—" Tobias gulped and wished for the smarts to have stashed a flask of something stronger in his desk drawer. He shook his head and dumped his cold coffee into the trash. "No. This is fine. Um. Can you—can you give me… maybe two minutes?"

"Sure. I'm sorry to just—"

"No. No apologies. I want to go somewhere more… less… "

He looked helplessly up to Malik who asked one more time, "You're okay?"

Tobias stood and walked toward his door. He tripped over a stack of playbills and covered his phone. "I'll explain later." Without another word, he headed down the hall to the elevator, remembering he'd left Emmett—*Emmett*—hanging on the line. "Hey, sorry. I'm getting in an elevator. If I lose you—"

"Let me call you back then."

"NO!" Tobias cleared his throat. "No. Please." He sighed at himself and hit the button for the basement. "How are you?"

Emmett chuckled, and Tobias closed his eyes, remembering his dimpled smile and shining green eyes. "I'm good. I hope you don't mind. Ms. Lipman from XACT gave me your number."

"I don't mind at all." The elevator bell rang and, as expected, Tobias temporarily lost the connection for the eight-flight ride down. The hardwood grain of the elevator walls, the insipid Muzak playing overhead were welcome diversions to help him gather his wits.

It was Emmett. On the phone. And he sounded *terrific*.

TOBIAS EXITED THE ELEVATOR AND flipped on a couple sets of lights in the small theater.

Hiking himself onto the edge of the stage, he laid back and looked up into the light riggings just as he and Emmett used to do before and after rehearsals, squeezing in every possible moment together.

They had talked about living and working in New York together. About Emmett taking over the light opera scene, or, if that didn't work, how he would become the most sought-after recital performer, traveling the world to bring Mozart and Schubert, Vaughn Williams and Fauré to new audiences. About Tobias writing the next great musical, and how they would have to build larger and larger mantels over their West Village flat's fireplace to make room for all of his Tony awards.

In a place just like this, Tobias had begun to understand that the fall into love was the sweetest fall of all.

But that was then. Before all of their youthful promises and dreams of forever, fame and fortune turned to dust. Now, he held Emmett's voice in his hands after years of silence. Tobias wasn't twenty years old anymore, he wasn't in love anymore, and he most definitely wasn't quixotic enough to wax sentimental about the past.

"Okay, I've landed. Sorry about that." Tobias swallowed thickly. "I just—my office can be Grand Central at times."

"I understand. 'I hate to intrude, but…' is my least favorite phrase."

Tobias chuckled and then went silent. He wanted to hear Emmett laugh, too, as if time hadn't passed. As if Emmett were lying next to him on the hard wooden floor.

There was a long pause and then, "It's really good to hear from you, Em."

"Yeah? I, uh—it took me three days to build up the courage to call."

"I'm sorry."

"I know. Plenty of time has passed, I just—" Emmett stopped and sighed. "This is ridiculous. Look, I'm bringing my a cappella group to New York for an exhibition at the Hudson Theater next month."

"Oh yeah? Where are you teaching now?"

"Morningside. Been here for a few years."

"Morning—Emmett. You *wound* my little Xavier Buccaneer's heart."

There was Emmett's laugh. Tobias's heart flipped in his chest.

Emmett's voice was a touch deeper than when they had last spoken. It still had an earthy, rich timbre. Emmett was a true Tenor II, who could dip into baritone range and then soar into the purest falsetto with little to no effort. His voice was always stunning and musical, especially when it twisted with the ribbons of laughter.

"Oh come *on*, Toby. That was basketball. You were more of a football man."

"A rivalry is a rivalry. So, who beats whose ass nowadays?"

"Morningside is on top, honey, or else I wouldn't be here."

Tobias laughed, and the sound cracked and echoed throughout the empty stage. "Of course. So, how does Morningside A Cappella Ensemble land a gig in New York City?"

"A colleague's friend's... uncle's dog. Hell, I have no idea anymore. I know we're coming—"

"You wanna meet up for drinks?"

"And I'd love to see—" Emmett stopped and paused a moment too long for Tobias's comfort. "Yes. That's exactly—yes. Will you be in town?"

"I'm here through January."

"Good, then. So... "

The wind blew out of the conversation, as if the tension of what Emmett could possibly want was all that held it together. Tobias longed to say something beyond setting a time and goodbye, but all he could do was breathe into the phone and stare at the steel trusses and lights over his head... and remember.

Remember their first date to the Brighton Art Museum for an exhibit of children's book illustrators—Van Allsburg, Bemelmans, Sendak, DePaola—and how Emmett's childlike wonder lit up the already lively displays. Remember how Emmett's words, Emmett's voice used to make him laugh even in sadness:

"Mom keeps trying to hook me up with the new neighbor girl. It's so awesome; I get to come out again. Because apparently she didn't hear me the first time."

How that voice used to make him sing:

"Please tell me it's not too soon to tell you I love you. Because I love you. And I'm going to explode if I don't get to say it."

And, of course, how it made him ache:

"Leave me alone! Don't you see I want to be left alone?"

Tobias sucked in air with a gasp and sat up, hearing Emmett's voice in the phone pressed to his ear. "I'll let you go, Toby. I'll call when I get into the city."

"No, wait!" Tobias scrabbled his hands through his hair. "I'm sort of overwhelmed—hearing your voice again."

"Yes, I'm—where are you anyway? I hear an echo."

"Oh." Tobias chuckled and motioned as if to show Emmett around. "I'm in this little theater we have in the building. Can you hear me okay?"

"I can hear you." There was another long silence, and finally Emmett broke it with a heavy sigh. "I was hoping this wouldn't be awkward. Maybe this is a bad idea."

"Emmett, please. I want to see you." Tobias held his breath and waited.

And then, with another sigh, Emmett admitted, "I guess I'm a little overwhelmed too."

"It's to be expected."

"Besides, I went to shameful lengths to get a choir mom to agree to cover for me if we could work this out. I can't bail now."

"Oh? Did you sell your soul to the devil?"

"My soul is a long-lost cause," Emmett said. "It's worse. I'm going to have to give her daughter a solo."

"Ooh. Promise me you didn't just make a deal with a Lexi Moore clone."

Emmett cackled. "Oh God, I almost forgot about Lexi! Her crush on me was frightening."

Tobias chuckled with him—the poor girl was shameless and clueless. "I wonder if she ever recovered from your Seven Minutes in Heaven."

"Wait, back up now," Emmett said, still laughing. "That was *her* Seven Minutes. I was there under protest, and, if I recall, about three shots of tequila. I experienced no 'heaven' in that closet."

"Yes, but she didn't need booze; she was in *love*." Emmett groaned, but Tobias pushed on. "I still wish you could have seen the look on her face when you unearthed yourselves."

"Stop. You wouldn't kiss me the rest of the night because I had Lexi juice all over my face."

"I *said* I wouldn't kiss you. You know I was always unable to resist—" Tobias shut his eyes and flopped onto his back again. "Shit. Sorry."

"No, these are fond memories," Emmett said. "I—Toby?"

"Is it okay to tell you that I miss you?" Tobias said, before he could stop himself.

"Yes. I miss you too."

The silence draped comfortably between them until Tobias realized Emmett was talking again, about setting up a time to meet; it didn't take nearly long enough. Finally Emmett said, "I'm really looking forward to seeing you. Gotta find out which one of us has less hair."

"Oh! Is *that* what this is about?"

"We had a bet, Mister," Emmett said. "I believe we had twenty-five dollars riding on it."

Like a refreshing spring warmth after the cold of a harsh winter, everything was coming back: the jokes, the laughter, the little whispered conversations in the dark as if time had stood still and waited for them.

Except for that receding hairline. "Well, this *is* a stressful business…"

"Yeah, yeah. Save your excuses for next month." They shared one more silence, and Tobias got up and killed the backstage lights, leaving the stage illuminated with a dim, golden glow.

"It was wonderful to hear your voice, Em. I'm really looking forward to this."

"Me too. Take care."

Tobias tossed his phone onto the piano in the middle of the stage as his mind swirled with memories of Emmett. The offstage moments they had shared held the everyday comforts of a love that was young and full of promise. But the stage was where they toyed with fantasy and reality.

The stage was where kids like Tobias and Emmett thrived. They were the kids who took tap and piano lessons instead of playing Little League, the kids who made mix tapes of Broadway shows and old standards. They were the kids who danced—*actually* danced—at parties. Scotty had also played and excelled at sports, and Tobias and Emmett cheered him on, but their hearts were where their imaginations played, where their voices soared, where life lessons were learned through memorizing lines, conquering tough piano licks and finding truth in a playwright's words.

Standing on this empty stage, Tobias recalled one of his fondest memories.

He and Emmett had been dating for a few months, but living in two separate cities much of the time. Tobias was home for the summer; rehearsal had ended. And just like the theater he stood in, the house was dark, and the stage was lit in muted gold tones from two haphazardly directed spots. Ms. Lipman, the theater's director, had known their time together was rare and precious. She gave Tobias a pointed look and reminded him of his place.

"Don't make me regret leaving you two here," she said as she left. Steel met steel as the backstage door slammed closed behind her, leaving them in stark silence.

"You said you wanted to go over something in the show?" Toby asked as he uncovered the piano and tossed the quilted fabric onto the floor.

Emmett nodded and walked to him, running a finger along the piano's curved edge. "Could you play 'De-Lovely' for me? I'm having some trouble with the steps."

"Is that why we're here?"

"Yes. Partially."

Toby started the song, a gentle lilting melody that was perfect for a light-hearted couple's dance. Emmett danced and sang with an imaginary partner, but he knew the steps. He didn't need the work. He stopped and sighed while Toby kept playing. "It's not me; it's Lexi. Come be my partner."

Toby stopped and laughed. He could tap. He could sing. But his home was behind the keyboard. He looked at Emmett, at his wide eyes and pouty lips, and in a moment he was away from the piano and in Emmett's space.

"I already am your partner," Toby said. He kissed Emmett with a soft brush of his lips. "Besides, you dance side by side for most of it."

"Shut up and dance with me." Emmett slid his arm around Toby's waist and took hold of his hand. With one forward step that Toby instantly followed, they were off in a silent foxtrot. The only sound, but for an occasional phrase Emmett sang from love songs written before their time—"The Touch of Your Lips," "Cheek to Cheek," "The Way You Look Tonight"—was the scuff of their feet on the stage floor and the creak from an occasional loose board.

Scuff scuff, creak-step.

Emmett was confident. Agile. So comfortable in his skin, even at age seventeen, that Toby could follow. He was swept away in the wisp of air that encircled them as they quarter-turned. In the warmth of Emmett's temple, tenderly placed against Toby's cheek. In the delicate whisper of lyrics Emmett breathed into his ear.

They were magical together.

"I don't want to go home tonight." Emmett walked his fingers around Toby's back and held him tighter. Their foxtrot dissolved into a junior high slow dance with their bodies pressed close and their breath intermingling as they kissed and spoke secret wishes.

"We have time. I'm not going anywhere."

"You leave in six weeks."

Toby cupped Emmett's face in his hands. "I might leave Indiana. I'm never leaving you."

Emmett nodded and stepped back to start a proper foxtrot again. He hummed the tune of "Five Minutes More."

Toby laughed as they spun. He knew the truth then, even at age nineteen: he would need an eternity of "five minutes more" to satisfy his desire, his longing for this beautiful young man.

Tobias moved across the stage alone now in a disjointed foxtrot. He spun once and bumped into the grand piano, which was covered in black quilted fabric. He didn't remember hanging up his call with Emmett. He flipped off the lights and headed back to his office, flushed and scattered.

When he got there, Malik was sitting behind his desk waiting for him. The piles of scores and fake sheets, invitations and invoices were still scattered all over the room.

"Don't you have something to solder?" Tobias asked as he spotted the score for *Company* peeking out from a pile of playbills.

"From the look on your face when that call came through, I was afraid it might need to be your senses." Malik kicked his feet up onto Tobias's desk. "I've never seen anyone go that peaked that fast and not pass out."

"Shut up. I was surprised. And get your fucking hipster boots off my desk."

"Hipster? These are Doc Martens. Everyone wears Doc Martens."

"Did you buy 'em at Urban Outfitters?"

"No." Malik dropped his feet from Tobias's desk and stood up, his full six-one frame matching Tobias's inch for inch. "Yes." Toby smirked, and Malik flicked at his labret stud with his tongue before plowing on. "So, are you going to tell me who the hell *Emmett* is, or am I going to have to get you shit-faced and humiliate it out of you?"

"Has your coffee iced over yet?"

"Sufficiently."

"Fresh coffee. Emmett's a long story."

2

MORNINGSIDE, Ind.—October 2015

"So?" Emmett's cracked door opened and his co-worker Mac peeked in. "How'd it go?"

Emmett's smile curled at his lips before he could stop it. He didn't want to smile. She had been teasing him about his anxiety over making the call to Toby, and a smile admitted she was right about its significance.

To her students, Estelle MacIntyre was an imposing force. She was head of the music department at Morningside, a twenty-six-year veteran of their instrumental program, and she had a reputation for being tough. Forthright. A champion for her students' right to a quality music education who wouldn't let the students get in the way of that right, no matter how hard some of them tried.

"If you marched yourself into band to get an easy A, you might as well march yourself right on outta here. This ain't no study hall with a soundtrack."

Six years earlier, when Emmett worked in Fulton, Indiana, he met Mac when they both attended a dreadful music educators' convention. They were opposites in many ways: his tall and slender build to her short roundness; his newness and lack of passion to her seasoned, singularly-focused drive to make new musicians at every opportunity; his almost embarrassingly sheltered whiteness to the strong sense of history, tradition and culture that made her stand out in this very white community—proudly stand out. Still, they had bonded over a couple of six-packs of hard cider, a drunken run-through of the entire musical score of *Dreamgirls* and two dozen of her infamous oatmeal-butterscotch cookies.

"Close the—"

Mac closed the door and sat down as Emmett turned his laptop to face her.

"November sixth, ten p.m.: Toby. Davenport Theater," she read. "Well look at that. I told you he wouldn't hang up."

"You did. He didn't. Now I have three weeks to freak out all over again."

Over the years, Emmett had told Mac about Toby. About how, at age eighteen, he *knew* he'd met his forever; about Toby's blond curls, piercing blue eyes and tall, sturdy frame that held him up, held him close, held him dearly; about Toby's mastery in making music more beautiful, more meaningful than he ever imagined it could be.

About how Toby had loved not only who Emmett wanted to be, but also who he was in each moment.

"You're flushed, love. And avoiding eye contact. Start talking."

"He was… " Emmett tossed his glasses onto his desk and leaned back in his chair. He could make her work for this, but really, he had been pretty annoying about the whole thing. "He sounded so *good*. It was weird as hell. And then it wasn't."

"I still don't understand why you thought he'd hang up on you."

"Hey. He walked out on me and *never* looked back. Hanging up was certainly a possibility."

"Fif-teen years ago, Emmett," she said. "Fifteen. Half of your freshman choir hadn't been born yet."

"Don't remind me."

"I will remind you. You ruined one of my favorite shirts with your snotty-assed sob fest over the guy." Mac sat firm, as if she'd won an argument he wasn't in. Yet.

"That was *years* ago. And I was drunk."

"You spent most of your time drunk back then. Because of him."

"Are we going over this again? I was not drunk because of Toby. I was drunk because—"

"Because you were a *miserable* teacher." Her tone was melodramatic and mocking, as if she'd heard his woeful tale time and again.

She had.

"Let's see, what else?" she continued. "Oh yes, you were a miserable son. You would die alone and forgotten—"

"And would never see the stage again. Yes, yes, I know. See? Not. All. Toby."

She wasn't completely off-base. He had been a miserable teacher at Fulton because he had never wanted to teach in the first place, especially not for a poor district with an administration that didn't care any more about the arts than it did the stock market. If it weren't for a failed school levy that gave the district a kinder way to lay him off, Emmett's stupid behavior would have cost him his first teaching job.

"It all trails back to him, and you know it." They stared each other down, and for once in their history of stare-downs, she caved first. "So, you have a date."

"It's not a date. It's *on* a date." He stopped and put his glasses back on, hoping to evade any further questioning. Her arched eyebrow indicated otherwise. "Uh… I'm meeting him after some off-Broadway gig he's doing… " She circled her hand in front of her. "And Hailey Foster's mom is going to cover my hall at the hotel while I'm with him?"

They eyed each other, and Emmett calculated what else he could tell her. And then it dawned on him. "You want to chaperone. You *hate* these things."

"I hate them with the heat of all nine fiery rings of hell, but there is no way my old black ass is waiting until you get home to tell me the details you want to tell. I want a front row seat."

"You have lost your mind."

"Baby, please. You want my help and you know it. Corralling thirty-five kids, ten obnoxious parents and your broken heart is not something to leave to a rookie."

"Okay, first? My heart is not broken."

Mac started to argue, but stopped. Emmett held her gaze firmly, because no matter how well-intentioned she might be, this was *not* a matchmaking journey. He wouldn't be going if his heart were still broken. Or marred with the tiniest of splinters.

She tried anyway. "Anyone who had that much anxiety about making a goddamned phone call—"

"Second," Emmett said, "I have been teaching for *eleven* years. I am not a rookie."

"Ten. You took a year off to get your shit together from your days of drunkenness and debauchery."

"Well, if you're going to be that way, nine. I took a year after college because I was pouting."

"And probably drunk. Nine, then." She pointed to herself. "Twenty-six. *You* are a rookie."

Before a good retort came to him, there was a knock on his door.

"I hate to intrude, Mr. H, but... " Emmett sniggered. He hadn't been kidding when he told Toby this was his least favorite phrase.

"You already have, Tori. What is it?"

"I can come back if—" Tori looked nervously at Mac. "Hi, Ms. MacInt—Mrs. Mac—"

"Mac is fine, darling. Do you need to speak with Mr. Henderson alone?"

"No, she does not." Emmett's smile was more polite than genuine. "She's already intruded without waiting for me to answer my *closed* door."

Victoria Graham was a blonde, wide-eyed and occasionally compulsive soprano who, in her junior year, was the most talented student Emmett had ever encountered. She reminded him of Kristin Chenoweth: slight, giggly and, by outward appearances, flighty. But in reality she could slay dragons, not only with her voice, her acting prowess and her comedic timing, but also with her drive, determination and fantastic work ethic.

She was a popular girl, a former cheerleader who frequently had a football or baseball player on her arm and, with her expert skills in coercion, had almost single-handedly made choir cool again at Morningside High.

Some days, Emmett wasn't sure if Tori were a blessing or a curse. Come to think of it, he had the same question about Mac.

"I'm sorry," Tori said. "It's just—my demo stuff? You said we'd talk about it before we head to New York."

"And I have you on my calendar for... " Emmett looked at his computer. "Tomorrow after seventh period."

"I'm impatient."

"I'm aware." Emmett motioned to Mac and back to himself. "And I'm busy."

"Yes. I wondered if I should go with something unusual, or something more tradition—"

"Tori. Tomorrow. You'll have plenty of time to put something together from your *vast* repertoire." Emmett side-eyed Mac, who stood and feigned interest in a stack of choral music. "But today, I'm having a conversation with Mac. And your mother will be here soon. You know better than to make her wait."

"Yes. I'm going. So. Traditional then?"

"Goodbye, Tori. I'll see you in women's ensemble bright and early tomorrow."

"Right. Bye, Mac."

Tori left, and Emmett swatted at Mac's backside. "I could *hear* you snickering over there."

She shrugged and picked up a copy of "Ride On, King Jesus." "You doing this in New York?"

"Yes. Classic competition number. Prep it now, and spring contests will be easier."

Mac nodded and sat down again, shaking the sheet music in front of him. "You know, Mr. Miserable Teacher, they wouldn't be doing any of this if it weren't for you."

Emmett took the sheet music from Mac and fanned through it. "What? You don't think Mr. Cayman could have handled this one?" Emmett winked. The irony of Emmett's position at Morningside was that he had replaced someone much like who he had become in Fulton. Mr. Cayman's excuse was that he was old and burnt out. Emmett's was that he was an angry son-of-a-bitch because life had been gloriously unfair.

But, as Mac had reminded him when her recommendation got him the job, if he played it right, building Morningside's program back up could be redemptive for both him and the district. Add a blonde, overzealous talent named Tori, and the road to redemption was well paved.

Mac took the music and tossed it onto his desk. "You know I don't dollop out the praise, but—"

"So don't. I don't need it, and no matter how you say it, it sounds like a Lifetime movie."

"Fine. Who you planning on giving Tori's demo tape to in New York?"

"I don't anticipate giving it to anyone." At Mac's raised eyebrow, Emmett pressed on. "We'll make the demo, she'll have it for college auditions, everyone's happy."

"Tell her to sing 'Memory.' Casting agents love that one."

"I will do no such thing. I want her to *leave* Indiana so I will have some peace." He grabbed a pen and sat back, clicking it open and closed in the rhythm of the overly familiar song. "Are we done? Or are you still prying?" *Click... click.*

"I'm still prying. We left off with you, me and Toby in New York."

"Let it go, Mac. Toby is a blip in the New York trip." *Cli-cli-cli-cli-cli-click... click.*

"Then we circled around your year of forced chastity and sobriety after a decade of promiscuity and wretched excess."

Cli-cli-cli-cli-cli-click. Click.

"And how I saved you from it all by getting you this job in spite of your stupid self." She yanked the pen from his hand and tossed it back on the worktable.

"Hey!" He looked longingly at the pen, caught her stern expression and sighed. "It was not a decade, *and* who the hell said I was chaste that year?"

"Just—leave me to my fantasies. When do we leave?"

"I thought your fantasies involved me with—"

"Not you, you jackass. Gorgeous men."

"I'm not gorgeous?"

"Gorgeous men I do not work with. With other gorgeous men I do not work with." Mac scowled at Emmett's smirk and stood with a huff. "It's not polite to tease people for what turns them on."

"Does your husband know you fantasize about gorgeous gay men?"

"What my husband doesn't know won't hurt him. He's been getting it really good for over twenty-three years." She smoothed her hands over her full bust and smirked. "When do we leave?"

"Lucky Mr. Mac." Emmett grabbed a copy of their itinerary and handed it over. "And I think I lost the thread on how my previous stupidity relates to you chaperoning this trip... unless you think I'm going to go off boozing and boffing all over New York City."

"That's always a possibility."

The truth was, having her along for the ride was a good idea. He had no problems corralling and controlling his kids, but Mac never put up with the parents' dramatic, overblown bullshit. She could divert them; he could deal with the kids. And Toby.

But mostly the kids; Toby was going to be a simple chat, a drink and a goodbye.

"You're paying your way, Mac. I've already turned in the money."

"When do we leave?"

He pointed to the paper. "November fifth. Ass-crack o'clock."

"My favorite time of day. And tell Hailey's mom she's fired."

"You're going to be waiting outside my hotel room door when I get back from seeing him, aren't you?"

"No. We're getting connecting rooms and you're going to come visit me like a gentleman, with a knock on the door and a full bottle of wine in hand." She leaned over and held his chin before kissing the cleft of it. "We're having a slumber party. New York City-style."

"Fabulous. You'll be wearing a pink, fur-lined hooded robe and slinky lingerie too?"

"Bring Madeira. Dark chocolate is always nice too."

♦♦♦

THE WEEK BEFORE LEAVING FOR New York, Emmett's a cappella group had been rehearsed within an inch of their lives. Chaperones had been assigned, shoes had been polished and robes were at the dry cleaners for a final press.

All that was left to handle were teenaged meltdowns:

"Mr. H! I lost my packing list. Do you have extras?"

"Mr. H! How are we going to keep our phones charged on the twelve-hour bus ride? I will *die* without my cell phone!"

"Mr. H! Since Mrs. Coleman isn't going to come, can I bring my boyfriend? He's twenty-two, so he's an adult."

From the moment one period ended until the following began, a parade of students marched in and out of the choir room with demands and questions. If it wasn't a student breathing pimple-faced anxiety all over him, it was a parent blowing up his phone with more.

"Will the children be left unattended at any time?"

"Will the boys be allowed in the girls' hall?" Emmett always loved that one. Separating by gender in no way prevented sexual improprieties; it occasionally encouraged them.

"Have they had proper training on how to avoid pickpockets?"

"How often will they be stopping to eat? Jimmy has a *condition*."

Emmett had reached the end of his patience. He needed to de-stress, decompress and drop any pretense of being "Mr. H" in the best way imaginable: with his pants at his ankles and a sexy man on his knees in front of him.

So he hadn't completely rehabilitated from his days of stupid. His definition of stupid had changed: Drunkenness was stupid; consensual sex was not.

Before heading home, Emmett made a pit stop at the art room.

"I can't go home with you tonight, love. Kitten Kabooty is playing at Eclipse." Gino smacked a handful of paintbrushes on the side of the sink and spread them out on the counter.

"Kitten Kabooty," Emmett said with a grunt. "Please tell me she doesn't wear cat ears."

"She wears *pierced* cat ears. She's a precious six-five, three hundred-pound goddess of pure drag royalty."

"And Brighton is where drag royalty is born. Right," Emmett grumbled.

Gino Agostini and Emmett were not friends. They weren't enemies either, but they most definitely were not friends. Gino was every kind of gay man that Emmett typically avoided: flamboyant, flighty, flaky and, if you, God forbid, had on last year's shoes, flippantly rude.

To the non-art students, he was known as Gina Fagostini, and if Emmett were honest, he would admit to muttering the name under his own breath from time to time. He didn't like *not* liking Gino—everyone deserved a place at the proverbial queer table—but Gino seemed to delight in expressing himself through every negative gay stereotype that crossed the scene.

It drove Emmett mad.

But when Gino wasn't trying to be Mr. Fabulous 2015, he could be mildly appealing: Italian-handsome, always single and, as of the last year, Emmett's good-and-reliable when he needed a nice stress-relieving fuck.

Gino collected bottles of acrylic paint, hitching his hip as each bottle landed in the cradle of his arm. "Funny, I don't recall you being such a bitter puss about the drag scene back in the Anita Mann days."

"I was making cash running sound for their gaudy shows, Gino. Any relationship I might have had with Anita doesn't change that."

Gino hummed and sauntered across the room to his closet. His ass jiggled as he put the bottles away. "I seem to remember you were hired for three shows. You stuck around for nine months, didn't you?"

"I'm kind-hearted. And his name was Derek, not Anita."

"Kind-hearted, my ass. Derek was easy, and you… " Gino closed the cabinet door and sashayed back in front of Emmett, limp-wristedly pointing a finger at him. "You are a slut."

This was partially true. Emmett really had liked Derek. He enjoyed the drag scene and found great pleasure in mixing music for their shows. It was the year between Fulton and Morningside, and for an in-between-jobs job, it served Emmett well.

"Yes, I am a slut," Emmett admitted. "And apparently an ineffectual one today." Emmett opened the door to leave and tossed his own pout over his shoulder. "Tell Kitten I said hello."

"Say hello to Kitten yourself."

Emmett was even less interested in three hundred-pound drag felines than he was in going home to an empty house. He accepted Gino's kiss, full of tongue and a promise for another time.

By the time he got home, numerous text messages lit up his phone.

Toby: Checking in to confirm for Friday. Got called for a little jazz thing that night and don't want to double-book.

Wonderful.

Mac: Is that Kyle Trentnor kid still in your group? He had this weird thing with my necklaces and I'm thinking maybe I shouldn't pack so many.

Emmett had no idea what she was talking about and was afraid to ask. Kyle was generally creepy anyway; knowing him, it was a surreptitious route to touching her chest. Regardless, Mac would blow up his phone all night if he didn't answer.

And then there was:

Mom: Call me before you leave. You never know what could happen.

Irritated, Emmett hung up his hat and coat. He sifted through his mail and threw the junk in the trash with a little more force than was absolutely necessary. He changed clothes, pulled a steak out of the freezer and shoved it into the microwave to thaw. And then he sat back down to deal with... *them.*

With a quick reply, he told his mother he would call the next day after work. She would probably call him tonight anyway.

Mac was next. He wished he did not *need* Kyle Trentnor and his rich, soaring tenor voice.

Emmett: Kyle is still in my group. Maybe if you set up some sort of electrical zapper that you could remotely control?

Mac: I'll electrocute myself.

Emmett: In all good things there is risk, my friend.

Mac: You could talk to him about inappropriate touching.

While finishing dinner, he mulled telling her about Toby's text, but decided against it. It seemed like a passive-aggressive ploy to get out of their meeting—Toby used to be good at that, but Emmett had outgrown the game. If he timed his response right, maybe it would be show time and he wouldn't hear back until after he had gone to bed.

Okay, maybe he hadn't outgrown it completely.

EMMETT: We can cancel.

TOBY: No. That is not what I said. I won't do the other gig if we're still on. I want to see you.

Toby wasn't supposed to have answered so quickly. Emmett washed his few dishes, threw in a load of laundry and scrolled through Netflix while he debated his next move. He could cancel and save himself the potential disappointment. He could leave Toby hanging. He could— novel as it sounded—not be an asshole and take the man at his word.

EMMETT: Right. So, I'll be at Davenport at ten on Friday night.

TOBY: Excellent. I didn't want to do this other thing anyway. The club owner is a dick.

EMMETT: You could have said no.

TOBY: I could have. This way I got to talk to you again and make him think I'm more in demand than I really am.

EMMETT: Well, that night you're in demand.

Oh God. Emmett deleted the words, then tapped: Sneaky. I'll see you then.

For the first time in… well, in fifteen years, Emmett had an overwhelming desire to watch something of Joss Whedon's. Halfway through the puppet episode of *Angel*, Emmett zoned out. He began imagining not only his life, if kids' brains had been sucked out—probably no different than usual—but how all his fellow teachers would look as puppets.

With the clear image in his mind of Gino being controlled by someone's hand up his ass, Emmett's phone rang.

"Hi, Mom." Miriam Henderson would make an interesting puppet. The puppeteer would have to work out just to have the strength to hold the thing upright, with all of her over-teased, over-styled, over-sprayed hair.

"Tomorrow," she was saying. "I wanted to hear your voice before you took off for The Big City."

"Yeah, yeah. Tomorrow's the big day."

"Tomorrow? I thought you were leaving Thursday." *Shit.* "Were you listening to me?"

No. "Yeah, sorry. I have the, uh—" he paused the show and went to the kitchen for a bottle of beer. "The television was too loud, I guess." He snapped the cap off and took a quick swig before continuing. "How are things?"

"Are you drinking?"

"Yes. Why do we do this every time?"

"Because I don't like you drinking."

"And I don't like hearing your opinion on things that are none of your business. Is there a reason for this phone call?"

"I wanted to touch base with you before you leave. You know I don't like you flying."

"Mom, you don't like much of anything."

"That's not true. I like the flowers your dad gave me on our anniversary last week."

And so it went, as she launched into the story of the flowers and how much he had paid for them. "They were all out of season, of course," she said. "Someday someone will explain to me why I thought a fall wedding would be perfect."

And then he endured the story of their anniversary dinner. Before he knew it, forty minutes had passed, his bottle was long empty and she was waiting for an answer to a question he wasn't sure he had heard her ask.

"Are you listening to me?"

"Yes, I am. Tiramisu. Statue of Liberty."

"I *asked* if you were going to see The Statue with the kids."

"Oh. Yes. The kids aren't real hot on the idea, though."

Another long-winded lecture about the importance of "our history" kicked in and, if for no other reason than to shut her up, Emmett interjected, "I'm also going to see Toby."

For a moment, she forged ahead. "Freedom from oppression—" The silence was louder than any moment thus far. "Did you say…"

"Yes. Friday evening. I figured it was time, and since I'll already be in New York... "

"I never understood why you stayed with him after the accident. He killed Scotty. He could have killed you, too."

"Yeah, except he didn't. He didn't *kill* either of us, Mom. I want to touch base with him and move on. That's all."

"After everything he did to you? Emmett, I can't believe you don't love yourself more."

"Oh, for God's *sake*, Mother! He didn't *do* anything to me!"

That was the irony with Miriam Henderson. Emmett never met her expectations, and yet she accused him of not loving himself. She never caught on.

"Okay, so forget the accident, since we've never seen eye to eye on that. Tobias left you, Emmett. He left you lying in a pile in our hallway, unable to get up by yourself, while he traipsed back to New York to become rich and famous. You are worth more than that."

"He left because I was horrible to him. No one would have stayed for that."

"You were in pain, Emmett. Your life had been taken from you."

"And yet here I am. A viable member of society, living a pretty damned good life."

"He left you at your weakest."

"Maybe, Mom... maybe he left me at his weakest."

Finally there was silence again, and Emmett waited it out, hoping against hope that his words had sunk in, not only through his mother's thick skull but, more importantly, through his own. Toby's departure had not been graceful, kind or easy to overcome. But enough time had passed that it seemed fit and right to say goodbye with a little more dignity.

"It was still cowardly."

"It was fifteen years ago, Mom. If I can let it go, maybe you should too."

"I never liked him anyway."

"Okay. That's enough. I'm hanging up. I'll send you a text when I arrive in Manhattan."

The problem with what his mother said wasn't that it was untrue. It was that it hadn't changed in tone, intensity or insistence over the years. Toby did walk out on Emmett and leave him in a pile of weakened limbs on the floor of their foyer. That was a fact.

What time had revealed, however, was exactly what Emmett had pointed out to his narrow-minded mother: Emmett wasn't the only person weakened by the tragedy of the accident. While Emmett spent his months of physical recovery becoming angrier and angrier at his circumstances, Toby spent them trying to be supportive, fighting every urge to run away all the while. And since he had never learned to sit still and handle stress, conflict, heartbreak, Toby's urge to fly eventually superseded his ability to stay.

Toby had come home that weekend just to be with Emmett. Every visit had become more and more tense, as Emmett grew more and more resentful of the life Toby lived in New York while he was stuck rehabilitating with his mother breathing down his neck at every turn.

Each blind to the other's pain, they barely got along anymore. Toby had warned that day, after offering to help him out of the car, "If you smack my hand away one more time... "

To Emmett, it was an empty threat, offering no consequence.

Emmett was in extreme pain that day; therapy had been especially difficult, and he was reliant on his walker again. He hated his walker. Still, they made the best of it and snuggled on the couch to watch *Angel* until Emmett's mom made them separate.

"Sit up, Emmett." She tapped his foot. "You know I don't like when you—"

Emmett was too exhausted to fight with her. Toby dared to speak. "Yes, of course, Mrs. H. It's just that his hip is sore."

"Just sit up. It's inappropriate."

Emmett got up to use the bathroom, and when he came out, he caught the walker on the leg of a hallway table and fell. The fall was almost a relief, letting his limbs land where they may and his body rest on the cold tile floor. The split second of silence that followed became a blissful peace.

Toby ran to his side, interrupting Emmett's peace. "Are you okay, sweetheart?" He offered his hand for Emmett to grab.

Emmett looked at Toby's hand, at the scar that ran down the length of his index finger, which was Toby's only physical marker of that tragic day. He glared up at Toby, into his pleading eyes, and missed Toby's exhaustion, Toby's pain. Blinded by his own turmoil, he missed Toby altogether.

He smacked Toby's hand away and glowered at him. "No. Leave me alone."

Toby waited there another moment, his breathing heavy, his glare pointed, challenging Emmett's. Finally Toby nodded and stood erect.

"Get yourself up, then," he said, in a voice free of the exhaustion that had consumed them for so many months. "I'm done."

And even with Emmett's whimpered pleas to stay, to come back, to give him one more chance, Toby walked out.

Dramatically speaking, it was a great exit scene. Unfortunately, it wasn't the stage, it wasn't drama for entertainment's sake; it was Emmett's heart. Toby's heart. Their everything had crashed right along with Toby's car, and there was no getting it back.

Promises of love and forever, dreams of fame and a glorious life in New York were not enough. They were too young, and ill-equipped to bear the breadth of their grief and loss.

Emmett understood that now, even though the ragged edges of pain and loss still lingered. His knee-jerk reaction to Toby's potential cancellation proved they did, and made him wonder if meeting really was a wise idea.

Before heading to bed, he sent one more text.

EMMETT: I'm sorry I snapped earlier. I'm unreasonably nervous about this.

TOBY: It's not so unreasonable. I can be pretty scary.

Emmett smiled at the words on his phone. At the root of it all, Toby made everything so damned easy.

EMMETT: See you soon.

3

NEW YORK CITY—November 2015

"You sure you don't want to join us tonight?" Monica, Tobias's double bass for the little off-Broadway production, squeezed by him on their way out of the theater.

"Yeah, I'm sure." He took her hand before she could leave for the train. "Sorry, by the way. I'm—I was distracted tonight."

"Are you okay?"

"Yeah… " Tobias looked over her shoulder to the small parking lot next to the smaller theater. "I'm fine. Or, I will be."

"Good, because if I have to guess when the hell you want me to come in after that interminable flute solo again—"

"Yeah, yeah. You won't come in at all," Tobias said. "Except we both know you will, because you're more of a perfectionist than I am."

"Not possible."

Tobias grunted. "You okay to walk alone?"

She shot him an irritated look and hiked her bass up onto her shoulders again, almost cracking herself on the head. "You think someone's going to mess with me with this contraption on my back?"

Tobias waved goodbye and listened to the click-clack of her shoes fade as she disappeared down the quiet street. And then he took a deep breath, shivered and turned back to the parking lot.

At first glance, it was empty but for an old jalopy that probably belonged to the lot's attendant. But there in the shadow of the back wall, with his hands stuffed into the pockets of a trench coat, stood Emmett. A scarf fluttered at his sides, and a fedora sat cocked atop his head. Old Hollywood. Classic.

He looked amazing—even in silhouette.

A breeze swept into the small lot and kicked up leaves littered between them. Tobias bristled and hiked his coat to his neck, letting the waft of air propel him to speak and step forward again. "You been waiting long?"

"No, just a few minutes." Emmett pushed himself away from the wall and grabbed something from under his arm. As he stepped into the faint light of the tiny parking lot, Tobias gasped, a quiet "Oh shit."

Emmett walked with a slightly hobbled gait; his cane made an arrhythmic click-pat-click against the asphalt.

Tobias stopped walking. He stared at the cane as each step Emmett took cracked through Tobias. He wanted to run, but was frozen in place. And all the while, Emmett walked confidently toward him, completely unconcerned with the extra beat in his step.

Emmett stopped in front of him. Tobias was still transfixed by the cane.

"Hey." Emmett tapped Tobias's foot with the walking stick. "Up here."

Tobias closed his eyes, but with a deep breath, he lifted his gaze and looked up into Emmett's eyes, which crinkled with the slightest smile.

"Hi," Emmett said.

"Hi." Tobias swallowed, trying to find his breath. He didn't know what he had been expecting; the cane ripped any ideations right out of his head. "I'm—I'm sorry." He shook his head in embarrassment and pointed to the cane. "I understood you were well."

"I am well." Emmett lifted the cane and, steady and sure on his feet, did a quick shuffle-ball-change. "It's precautionary when I do a lot of walking." He twirled the stick like a baton and offered it to Tobias. "My students bought it for me."

Tobias stared at it and back at Emmett. The years had been kind to him. Long gone were the random acne scabs and gangly limbs, replaced with a graceful maturity and assuredness. The most notable change was the addition of stylish wire-frame glasses.

Emmett wiggled the cane, and Tobias finally took it for a proper inspection. It was beautifully crafted, with a swirled wooden handle and pewter collar. "Your students have great style."

"They wanted me to fit the New York image."

Tobias laughed and handed the cane back with a small bow. "I was afraid it meant you couldn't foxtrot any more."

Emmett's smile was instant. He hooked the cane on his arm. "I can still foxtrot." Emmett opened his arms and motioned for him to step in closer. "It's been too long, Toby. Come here."

"Of course." He stepped into Emmett's arms, into a slow hug that drew him in tighter. They embraced and relaxed a little, walking their hands farther across each other's backs to hold tighter again, as if catching up on fifteen years' absence in a single embrace.

Emmett smelled of sandalwood and something spicy and warm. He was taller and a little thicker in build than when they had last seen each other. Instead of Tobias having a few inches on him, Emmett was now just shy of meeting Tobias eye to eye. "You've grown."

Emmett laughed, then, squeezing him before stepping away. "A little." Emmett studied Tobias's face and his gaze felt comfortable, a reintroduction without judgment. "You look really good," Emmett said.

"So do you." Another gust of cool air swept through their space, and they shuddered. "Let's get a cab." Tobias tentatively slipped his arm into Emmett's and leaned into him when Emmett's hand covered his. "I know a great place for drinks."

"Quiet?"

Tobias led them toward Eighth Avenue to catch a cab. "Yes. A little soft jazz okay?"

"Perfect."

WHEN THEY ARRIVED AT THE Carlyle, Tobias quickly paid and tipped the driver. He shot out of the cab and scurried around to Emmett's curbside door before Emmett could get his hat and cane situated.

Tobias reached in to take his hand and Emmett's shuffling stopped. He didn't come out of the car.

"You okay?" Tobias peeked in. Emmett was staring at Tobias's hand. "Em?"

"Y—yeah. Sorry." Emmett grabbed Tobias's hand and scooted out of the car, looking at their surroundings rather than at Tobias. "A hotel? I'm not a floozy, you know."

Tobias chuckled and hooked his arm into Emmett's. "You sure you're okay?"

"Yeah. Yeah. Not used to cabs, I guess."

Tobias tended to forget how treacherous a cab ride could be—until he had a newbie with him. Emmett had white-knuckled his cane the entire way; he'd finally relaxed when Tobias had placed his hand over Emmett's.

"Sometimes it's easier if you don't look out the window," Tobias had told Emmett. That had eased him enough to get to their destination. But he couldn't help but poke a little fun anyway. "I'm surprised at you, Em. Cab rides *are* New York. You used to think this city was Mecca."

"Well… some things change."

They entered the bar, and Tobias slid Emmett's coat from his shoulders. Excitement thrummed under Tobias's skin; he had been to this bar several times over the years, and every time he had thought of Emmett.

The walls of the classic bar were covered in muted yet colorful illustrations. It wasn't until Emmett stepped in past the grand piano and really looked around that his eyes lit up.

"Bemelmans! This is… " Emmett brushed past Tobias to the wall nearest the bar to get a closer look. "Toby! It's *Madeline!*" He glanced at the shades on the table lamps, which were decorated with more of Ludwig Bemelmans's work, and, his eyes bright with childlike awe, looked back at Tobias. "Toby… "

"This is exactly the reaction I was hoping for."

"Yeah?" The crowd was thinning, and Emmett stepped around the bar to take in as much as he could. He seemed as enamored now as he had been with the exhibit Tobias had taken him to on their first date.

"My sister used to read these to me." Emmett straightened and blushed. "Of course you know that already," Emmett said. "What you don't know is that I took them to college to read when I got homesick."

"You always wanted Genevieve, the dog."

"I did. Still living a Genevieve-free life, sadly." Emmett stopped gawking at the walls and fidgeted with his hat. "I'm sorry. We should— do we seat ourselves?"

Tobias pulled out a chair that faced one of the larger murals, and Emmett sat down and fussed with a place to put his hat and cane.

"You're not used to having that, are you?"

"No." Emmett finally laid the cane on the floor and looked at it one more time as if it might walk away by itself. "I hate it," he said, handing his hat to Tobias to put on the bench seat next to him. "I hate needing it."

Emmett used to say the same thing about his walker. "Feels more like a burden sometimes, huh?"

"Yes," Emmett said. "I'll grab it for after school rehearsals and then get pissed off I can't use both hands to direct. I end up tossing it aside and then go home wondering why I'm such a cocky S.O.B. Those days end with Advil. And whining."

"Now why doesn't that surprise me?"

"Because while *some* things change, not everything does." Emmett looked around the bar. "So, what's good to drink here?"

Tobias sat back and massaged his chin while he sized up Emmett. "You look like a… "

"Oh, stop. You have no idea what I drink."

"An Old Cuban." The bar was known for it: rum, champagne and muddled mint—like a mojito after prom night sexcapades. Perfect.

"You saying I'm old?"

"No, I'm saying you're Cuban." Tobias picked up the small menu on the table. "You want a cheese plate too? I haven't eaten in hours."

They ordered and smiled at each other. Tobias fidgeted with the cocktail napkins. Emmett picked up his cane and put it on the other side of the table. Twice they started and stopped conversation at the same time.

Emmett finally chuckled and adjusted his glasses. "I feel like I need a script."

"You always preferred it that way."

"And you always preferred to improvise."

"I did. Besides, I'm too busy staring to care," Tobias admitted. "You haven't lost a lick of hair, have you?"

Emmett cracked a laugh. He took off his glasses and leaned in to inspect Tobias's hairline. "Mr. Spence, I do believe you owe me twenty-five dollars."

Tobias grunted and tugged a tuft of hair to cover his forehead. "I blame my father."

"Mmm." Emmett ran his fingers through his ash-brown hair, still thick as ever, complete with that confounded curl just over his right ear. He heaved a melodramatic sigh. "I blame my mother. Fortunately, I didn't inherit her proclivity for bad dye jobs and perms."

"Always the fashion maven, Miriam."

Their drinks arrived, and Tobias lifted his glass. "To old friends?"

"To *old* friends."

"Hey now... " Tobias took a sip of his drink. "So, how *is* your family?"

"Really? We're going to start with small talk about my family?"

"I'm improvising... playing to your strengths. I figure you'll have a perfectly scripted answer."

Emmett took a much too large gulp of his drink, but smacked his lips in delight once the taste hit his palate. "I owe you an apology—you *do* know what I like to drink."

"Would you prefer not to talk about Mama Miriam?"

"Actually, she's *Grandma* Miriam now."

"You have children?" Tobias teased.

"Fourteen, if you must know. Ten different mothers. Natural conception."

"Well, aren't you the little stallion?"

Emmett waggled his eyebrows and a piece of cheese before popping it into his mouth.

"No, really. How many grandkids?"

Emmett held up two fingers and rolled his eyes. "If two-point-five were a possibility, I'm sure good old sister Molly would manage that," Emmett said. "But, no. Two. A boy and a girl—yes, they stopped after the second because they had one of each."

"Gross."

"She met hubby in college, they live in Baymont Springs with their purebred Pekinese and attend the local Methodist church."

Tobias was never sure who was less impressed with Emmett's mother and sister, Emmett or himself. "Sounds like the perfect Stepford life for Miriam's perfect Stepford daughter. Do they have a white picket fence, too?"

"No fences." Emmett imitated his sister's occasionally haughty tone and flipped his hands as if fixing shoulder-length hair. "'We want to encourage community spirit in the neighborhood.'"

Tobias squinted. "Dear God."

"You dodged a bullet turning that one down."

"She was relentless." Tobias laughed and swirled his drink on the table as a chuckle bubbled up along with an awkward memory. "Until she walked in on us in the bathroom."

"Oh God." Emmett's cheeks reddened. "I swear my left ear *still* rings from all of her blood-curdling screams."

"Always made me wonder if she was a screamer in—"

"Stop. Just. No. My sister does not have sex."

"Your sister is a mother, and unless she adopted… "

"They're bots. All four of them. That damned dog too." Emmett went for the cheese plate, but lifted a warning finger in the air one more time. "I mean it. Let me have that one thing. It helps me sleep at night."

"So, something tells me you and your mom never kissed and made up?"

"Things are better. I know she lives in her little cubicle of convictions about how people should think and behave, and she is resigned to the fact that I do not live inside of that cubicle." Emmett stirred his drink with its garnish of skewered lime. "In all fairness to her… " He looked at Tobias with a sadness in his eyes. "You weren't the last person I hurt."

"Emmett."

"You weren't. My anger got a lot worse before it got better. So, we've met on this really awkward road in the middle." Emmett took the final swallow of his drink and caught the server's eye for refills. "Since we're on the subject—your folks? They split, right?"

"Right before I graduated. Something about their son being tried for murder—"

"Toby… "

"Emmett, that's what was happening. The woman wanted me in prison for the death of her son."

"*The woman's* name is Karen, and she had lost everything."

"Right. And it destroyed—" Tobias looked down and mumbled. "Many things."

Anxious heat flashed through Tobias's body. The memories were reigniting faster than he could process them from hearing his childhood name, from their easy, snarky conversation, from the Bemelmans art and Emmett's giddiness over it. But while the evening had started out warm and cozy, with a slightly prickled edge of expected nerves, tonight wasn't the night for this conversation.

Tobias wasn't sure he ever wanted it to be the night for it.

With a firm set to his jaw, as if he'd been reset, Tobias looked up and offered Emmett a sad smile. "Can we not do this tonight? Please?"

The server arrived with two fresh drinks. Tobias took the drinks and handed Emmett's over; their fingers grazed as they dared to look one another in the eye again. Tobias lifted his glass.

"What are we toasting this time?" Emmett's smile was tender. Understanding.

"A new beginning."

Emmett's studied gaze was less comfortable; the pause was too long. "Sure. Yes. A new beginning."

The history they shared was far too intimate for a truly new beginning. But as they drank, each with his gaze never shifting from the other, Tobias warmed to the idea.

Beginnings always seemed to start in the middle anyway.

EMMETT RETURNED FROM A BATHROOM break and inadvertently kicked his cane when he sat down. He grumbled, and Tobias offered to put it on the bench next to him.

"You know, if you'd have taken it with you… "

"I don't *need* it," Emmett said. "Besides, I never know what the fuck to do with it when I'm peeing."

"If you can foxtrot with it, surely you can pee."

Emmett finally laughed, tossing one more comically dirty look at the cane lying beside Tobias. "I'm tired. It's been a long couple of days."

"When did you guys get in?"

"Around eight o'clock last night. The kids wanted to see Times Square, so we did that, called lights out, which takes about an hour to accomplish, and we were down for breakfast at seven this morning."

"Tell me you did something exciting today, because all I've heard is Times Square and shitty hotel breakfast buffet."

"Well, my *big* excitement of the day was when I had to visit room 1752 for excessive noise. One of the guys answers the door and there's Tommy Ryan's seventeen-year-old bony naked ass dancing on his bed with his underwear on his head. Bikini underwear. Purple zebra-striped bikini underwear."

"That's not exciting; that's traumatizing."

"Worse, they caught me snickering before I threw down the gauntlet. The potential for a repeat performance is very high."

"I have a feeling that kind of sightseeing wasn't on your itinerary."

"No, but we made up for it. I think we covered every mile on this damned island today." Emmett shot a glare at his cane.

"Not possible. Tell me you're at least seeing a show while you're here."

"I couldn't convince the parents to raise the extra money for it."

"Don't you have some theater kids in your group? It seems such a waste to be here and not—"

"A couple. It's—we're rebuilding. The experienced parents are gun-shy and the rookie parents are oblivious. I'm trying to turn the ship around very slowly."

Tobias sat back and popped a hunk of cheese into his mouth. "I have an idea," he said. "I'm at Helen Hayes Theater. Bring the kids by for rehearsal tomorrow."

"I thought you were at… " Emmett pointed towards the street.

"I'm helping out a buddy there for a few nights. I'm really in New York to get *Hit Men* opened." Tobias emptied his glass and pointed to Emmett's. "Another?"

"No, thank you. I'm the grown-up on this trip."

The prickled edge of nerves and the unknown had smoothed, and Tobias sensed a lightness around them. He saw it in Emmett's eyes whenever he smiled and heard it in his voice when he spoke of his students.

"So, I wasn't kidding. What are you all doing tomorrow before your competition?" Tobias asked.

"I think we're headed down to World Trade. The Statue."

"Oh come *on*. Did you guys hire a touring company for this or something?"

"As a matter of fact… " Emmett chuckled.

"Fucking hell, Emmett. Skip World Trade and come to rehearsal."

"But we've paid for—"

"Free tour, a real Broadway rehearsal, free… " Tobias paused to consider if it was doable and shrugged it off. "Free lunch. Besides, what good is the Statue going to do you in class once you all get home?"

"Toby, I don't know."

"Come on. The show is still rough as hell. It'll be educational."

"I always love rehearsal," Emmett said.

"Let them see it when it still belongs to the performers." Tobias grinned. This was a conversation they used to have: how performance was rewarding, of course, but nothing could match the high of a rehearsal or of owning the piece as a cast and crew until an audience came to redefine it. "Maybe we could get you all on the stage to do a number for me. Any of your kids into sound or lighting?"

"Yeah, a couple." Emmett tossed back the last drops of his drink. "Toby, you don't have to—"

"Perfect." Tobias picked up Emmett's hat and put it on his own head. "When should I expect you?"

"You always looked good in hats," Emmett said as he grabbed for his wallet.

"Thank you." Tobias put his hand on Emmett's arm and shook his head. "My treat."

"I invited you."

Tobias shook his head again. "I've always wanted to bring you here." He held Emmett's gaze until Emmett broke it to look around the magical room one more time. He nodded. "Excellent," Tobias said. "What time tomorrow?"

Emmett heaved a sigh and grabbed for his cane. "You still don't take no for an answer, do you?"

"Not when yes is in everyone's best interest."

4

THE EVENING WITH TOBY HAD been everything Emmett had hoped. And now, as he stood in front of his mirror readjusting his tie for what might be the eighth time, he had to wonder if they should have left the night as it was.

By the end of the evening, their conversation had filtered down to Wayne County legends, like Mr. O'Day, his junkyard and the more recent news of his penchant for aiming his shotgun at young drivers who slid onto his property on snowy winter days.

"Like... an *actual* shotgun?" Toby had asked, incredulous. "Get off my lawn or I'll put a hole in your head?"

"An actual shotgun. Happened to one of my seniors my first year at Morningside."

"Does he still have all those creepy doll heads all over?"

"Not that I've seen," Emmett said. "Now he has two beat-up rusty school buses."

"Maybe the heads are inside... like little imaginary schoolchildren."

It had been easy. Comfortable. Sure, Toby spent a ridiculous amount of time staring at Emmett's cane, asking if he was okay to walk more.

They dodged any deep, meaningful conversation, which didn't seem appropriate anyway.

Emmett huffed at his reflection in the mirror and loosened and redid his tie. They should have gone to the damned Statue. He would be wearing a sweatshirt and jeans, not fiddling—

"Mr. H!" A frantic knocking at his door followed. "Mr. H!! Kelsey can't find her name tag!"

Emmett was never sure if Kelsey Kennedy could find her way back home from school every day. He gave up on his just-a-little-too-long tie, grabbed his coat and cane and slipped into the hall to be Mr. Henderson.

TOBY GREETED THE STUDENTS AND handed out mock-ups of the playbill so they could follow along. *Hit Man* was a story about a hitman—a struggling songwriter by day who was also a man paid to off people by night. It included all of the requisite bad puns, dorky humor, catchy music and convenient plot devices that led up to the big number at the end. The musical arrangements were full and lush, both comedic and, when necessary, poignant.

Emmett wasn't sure what he enjoyed more—the show itself, or how everyone interacted with Toby after the rehearsal, showing him equal amounts of respect, good humor and sarcasm. Toby was home here. In New York. At the piano behind the stars, making them better than they could ever be on their own.

This would be, without question, the highlight of the trip for Emmett's students. At the end of the tour, Toby invited the kids up to sing for him. They crushed the anthemic "Seize the Day" from *Newsies*, earning a standing ovation from the cast and crew, who had all graciously lingered to hear them.

After a backstage tour, Mac led the group to a conference room for a catered lunch. Emmett looked for Toby to thank him, but between the constant interruptions of his delighted students, and the fact that Toby obviously wasn't there—

And then he was, standing just outside the doorway, shoving his phone into his pocket. He still had that boy next door-smile, but his face was more angular now, and his body was thick and sturdy, confidently housing the beautiful man within. He was the kind of handsome that turned heads on the street and made Emmett's heart swell until he almost forgot what he was doing in this room with a bunch of weird teenagers.

Toby caught his eye, and Emmett pushed his way through the hungry teens and swallowed Toby up in his arms. "Thank you so much! So much! These kids are just—this meant the world."

Toby clung to him tightly, laughter gusting from him with each new squeeze. "You're welcome, you're welcome." Toby pulled back with a distracted expression. "You've got a great group there. Amazing kids, I, uh... " He peeked in the room and a couple of students caught his eye. He waved politely, but stayed firmly planted outside the room. "Emmett, I got a call and... I'm sorry. I have to take off."

"Oh. I thought you were going to join us. You arranged for such a nice lunch."

A great time, an interruption, a hasty escape. Indeed... some things *didn't* change.

"I know. I thought I would too, but I can't get out of it. I'm sorry." He looked at his phone, grimaced and looked at Emmett. "I'm sorry."

"No, no. It's fine. I understand, you're a busy man. This has been—I'm so glad I got to—" Emmett tried to hide his disappointment, but this stank in every possible way. "Thank you, Toby."

Toby turned to leave and stopped. "We'll, uh—" He turned back to face Emmett again, shoving his phone in his pocket. "We'll keep in touch, yes?"

Emmett nodded, afraid he was making a promise neither of them would keep. "Yes. Yes, of course. Thanks again."

And with a nod of his head, Toby turned and was gone.

"Eyes on me. Eyes on me." Emmett looked around at the wide-eyed group of students. They gathered for a pre-performance pep *whisper* as the previous group finished their set. "Mr. Ryan, eyes on *me*. You already have two detentions, and we're not even in Indiana."

"Yeah. Sorry. I was—"

"Not paying attention and wasting everyone's time." With one more pointed look, Emmett began his spiel. "Bright eyes, lifted palates and chests, relaxed necks. Go out there looking like you give a damn and you'll sound like you give a damn."

He reminded them of the song order. The theater filled with applause. Emmett stood taller, lifted his hand and sang his next words. "On an 'ooh,' please, ooh."

They obediently matched his pitch and sang back to him, following his hand motions up and down the breadth of their ranges, all meeting back on the original pitch. "Now let's go show 'em how it's done."

From the hum of the pitch pipe for "Ride On, King Jesus" to the final notes of "Nellie Bly," they did just that. Emmett not only taught his students how to sight-read music and sing with proper technique, but also how to grab and hold an audience by growing the music from two-dimensional notes on a page to a performance with meaning.

Emmett beamed as his students filed offstage. Mac helped corral them into their post-performance powwow. And then, just as Emmett was about to congratulate his students and thank them for making the trip memorable, enjoyable and meaningful, he spotted him.

Toby. Smiling. Waiting patiently until Emmett could free himself from his responsibilities.

Emmett ignored him—visibly, anyway—and gave his singers the congratulatory speech they deserved. And as they circled and celebrated each other, he slipped away to the cocky blond jerk standing off to the side, rocking on his heels.

"You bastard." But Emmett was still beaming from pride in his students, from relief that the educational point of the trip was over.

And from the thing his heart was doing in his chest as his eyes rested on Toby's.

"They're amazing," Toby said.

"I thought you had a meeting."

"I cancelled. And you need to focus on what I'm saying to you." Toby narrowed his eyes and slowed his words. "They're amazing."

"It's all them. I'm just the monkey up front."

"They're amazing because of you."

"Thank you. Why did you cancel?"

A stage manager came by and curtly escorted the group into the depths of the theater, where their scores would be posted. Emmett lost track of Toby in the fray.

And then he heard Tori squeal.

"Really? You'll actually *listen* to it?"

Emmett shot a glare in her direction, but she was so enraptured by Toby's presence she never felt its heat. "Morningside!" Emmett called. "Find a chair and wait quietly until our scores are posted."

"Can we look at our phones?"

"School rules apply." He turned his attention to his impudent soprano. "Tori—"

Toby stopped Emmett's charge with a hand on his arm. "Em, it's fine."

"It is *not* fine," Emmett said. "I specifically told you, Tori." He looked at the panda-shaped flash drive in Toby's hand. "How do you have a copy of that demo?"

"You gave me one for my parents."

"For your parents. And are they here?"

"You know they're not; Mom can't handle the bus."

"Emmett, it's fine," Toby said.

Emmett ignored Toby. "Tori, you are taking advantage of my friendship with Mr. Spence, and I will not have it."

"Emmett. It's *fine*. I don't mind."

"I mind. I don't want to be—" Emmett stopped himself. The truth of what he didn't want was not for a conversation in front of a student. "You're being disrespectful of Mr. Spence's time. And disregarding my simple request."

"*You* weren't going to ask him… "

"Ms. Graham. Walk away and do not say another word." He shot a look at Mac, who took Tori to the women's room for a breather. "I'm sorry. She was out of line."

"To you. To me, she's driven."

"Toby, I understand where you're coming from, but I specifically told her—"

"You've said that. What exactly was supposed to happen?"

"I thought… " Emmett scoffed and rolled his eyes. His hip was sore. He looked around for his cane and cursed when a student noticed and got it for him. "I thought if it came up in natural conversation, I'd ask if you knew of anyone we should send it to. *Not* to give it to you herself. It's imposing. It's rude. It's—"

"It's *fine*."

"Toby… "

"Is she good?"

"The best I've had in eleven years."

"NINE years!"

Emmett shot a look across the room, where Mac stood with her hand on her hip and her supersonic hearing apparently firmly in place. "Nine. I had a sabbatical for bad behavior."

"Someday I want to hear about this bad behavior."

"Mmm, not likely," Emmett said.

"What sets Tori apart?"

"Classically trained from a young age. Great comedic timing. Can crank out a pop tune, a Sondheim ballad and a Mozart aria with equal grace."

"So, better classical or Broadway?"

Emmett tapped the tip of his cane on the linoleum floor. "She'd say Broadway."

"I'm not asking her."

"The eye of the opera needle is smaller."

"It is. I'll give it a listen." Emmett started to argue, and Toby lifted a finger to stop him. "But—it's probably going to be *months*. Is she a senior?"

"Junior," Emmett said. "Is this what you do?"

"Yes. And no. But I'll put her in my pile. She's going to go through the ranks like everyone else. Is that a fair enough compromise?"

"It'll do. Thank you again for coming by."

"I didn't like running out like that."

Emmett chuffed and then wanted to kick himself.

"But, I do have to get moving to the Davenport. You were amazing. They were amazing."

The double doors to the room opened, and an usher in an ill-fitting tux entered and whipped out a Sharpie. With flair and a flourish, he added Morningside's score to the board. *Superior*: the highest possible score. The kids erupted.

Toby shouted over the commotion. "It's been so good seeing you."

Emmett nodded and welcomed the incoming hug. Before it had registered, his students swarmed him.

And, like so many times before—Toby slipped away and out the door.

◆◆◆

EMMETT LOOKED IN THE HOTEL room closet for the fourth time. He checked the shower, which was preposterous, and under the bed— discovering that there was no "under" because the bed rested on a screwed-down box. He knocked on Mac's door and was shooed out because, "No, I promise you, your very special, important,

I-bought-it-at-a-haberdashery-in-Chicago fedora is most certainly not in my room. And you can't have the last cookie either."

It was almost lights out. Students littered the hallways as they packed, re-exchanged articles of clothing and swapped last-minute cell phone pictures. They were generally loud and reckless and *so* ready to head home.

And Emmett couldn't find his fucking hat.

This was not the sort of "keeping in touch" he thought he and Toby would do.

EMMETT: You still have my hat.

TOBY: Oh. Shit. I do. I meant to bring it today.

TOBY: Is there any way you can come and get it? I'm in my office. 520 8th Ave between 36th and 37th.

Emmett decided he hated text messaging. He couldn't hear Toby's tone. Was it clipped? "Come and get it, I'm busy, you bother me." Or did he have that glint in his eye, knowing that slipping away from the kids would be impossible—that glint that made the corners of his eyes crinkle a hair's breadth, so slightly that those who didn't know him would never notice?

It was the glint that made Toby horrible at Bullshit, the card game that was more of a constant presence in XACT's theater than the rats that ran under the stage. Emmett always caught his tell. Girls who chose not to believe the "gay" thing? Not so much. It had been a trump card Emmett loved to hold.

He didn't hold it anymore. Especially not when it came to texting.

EMMETT: Can you possibly bring it here and leave it at the front desk? I sort of have minors I'm responsible for.

TOBY: Right. I'm leaving within the hour. Hope your concierge doesn't look good in snazzy felt fedoras.

EMMETT: Thank you.

Goddammit. He knocked on Mac's door again. "Toby has it."

"And?"

"And… he's bringing it to the reception desk."

"Okay?"

Emmett huffed and turned on his heel to close their connecting door.

"Stop, Emmett. What were you wanting from me here?"

Mac looked ridiculous. She was one-third of the way through a facial treatment that had somehow oozed into her left eye. Her eye was twitching and her brown skin was partially covered with a green, slimy—Emmett sniffed and coughed. "Is that safe for your face?"

"Go get the damned hat, Emmett. This is why I demanded to chaperone."

"So I would remember my hat?"

"Get out of here. And in an hour, I'm sending Mr. Foster to drag you back by your shirt collar—assuming you'll still have a shirt on."

"Mac. This is not about—"

"You came here to make the goodbye better; go make it better."

"I love you." He moved in with puckered lips.

"Do not kiss me; this stuff tastes like rotten cheese. Also, if anyone asks, you have a migraine."

"Right. Thank you. Again."

Emmett stared at his phone all the way to the street before he was completely convinced he should be doing this.

EMMETT: Stay put. I'm on my way over.

The desk clerk at Toby's building couldn't have been more than twenty years old. Announcing visitors seemed to make him feel important. "Tobias, there's a tall-and-good-looking down here asking to see you." He sported a green pompadour and more rouge than Anita Mann had worn during her entire tenure at Eclipse.

Toby's laugh snapped through the staticky speaker. "How good-looking?"

"Dimples. Green eyes like an Irish hillside. Dapper-as-fuck cane. He seems a little skittish though."

"Send Mr. Henderson on up, please."

The young man handed Emmett a key card. "You'll need it for the elevator. Number 825. Don't break him, sweetheart. He's a favorite around these parts."

"Oh, I'm sure he is. I'll be gentle."

"Oh God, you *are* precious… "

Emmett waved and turned the corner to the elevator. He rested on his cane and then hooked it on his arm. He unbuttoned his coat and re-buttoned it. *Don't want to look like I'm staying for tea.* He untied his scarf and checked his hair in the warped reflection of the silver walls. He needed a script.

Following the signs to room 825, he relaxed, his anxiety quelled by the sounds of activity that filled the hall so late in the evening. Singers arpeggiated, electronic pianos synthesized, actors emoted and, in one studio, he swore he heard the screeching whirr of a jigsaw.

Toby's door was open. Emmett heard the tinkling sounds of a piano beneath the murmur of two male voices. He peeked in and almost stopped breathing.

One of the most beautiful men he'd ever laid eyes on stepped toward the door with his hand extended. "Emmett! It's so good to meet you!"

"Um. Hi." Emmett hooked his cane on his arm and shook the gentleman's hand. Dreadlocked hair framed the man's sculpted face, and his body was—breathtaking. "And you are?"

"Malik. Malik Nagi. Toby's been telling me all about you."

Emmett looked at Toby, who was still turning musical phrases on his keyboard. He wore a ridiculous grin… and Emmett's fedora. "I'm sure it's half true. I, uh—I didn't mean to interrupt."

"Nah, we're shooting the shit. I'm gonna head home, Toby. Racquetball tomorrow at eleven, right?"

"Right. Goodnight, Malik." Toby finally met Emmett's gaze and motioned for him to shut the door. As soon as he did, Toby busted out laughing. "Oh my God, I *knew* he was your type."

Emmett's mouth was still hanging open. He shut it. And reopened it to form, he hoped, a complete sentence. "Please tell me he's gay. And that he has more interesting piercings than the labret, because that thing is—"

"Bi. Actually."

"Oh God." Emmett sat in the chair by the door. "I'm good with bi."

"And dating one of the most beautiful, sensual women to grace this godforsaken planet. Simmer down."

"Damn. That is one pretty man."

"Sculptor."

"Works with his hands…"

Toby laughed and turned off his keyboard. "Works with his hands, yes." He pulled Emmett's hat farther down on his head and brushed at the feather in the band. "What do you think? I might keep it."

"I think you need to go find your own. That's a favorite."

"Hmm." Toby turned his keyboard back on, rose from the small bench and flapped back imaginary coattails before sitting back down again. "I think it might look good in the pit, don't you?" And then he began to play.

Toby's touch on the keys—even on the electronic keyboard—was smooth and flowing, as if his fingers were made to dance over them. He turned his head to look at Emmett with a flirty smirk, clearly knowing the control he had over a room when music flowed from his fingers like water sluicing over rocks in a stream.

"You are so fucking cocky," Emmett said, but the smile never left his face.

Toby kept playing. It was clear he was making up the melody as his fingers moved surely and confidently from one note to the next. And yet the tune also sounded vaguely familiar.

"Are you still writing?" Emmett asked.

"I tinker." Toby twisted the melody and ramped it up from flowing to bouncy, lightening the conversation with a simple rhythmic change.

Toby had been "tinkering" since they'd met. Since before Emmett knew who Toby was, when he was the cute blond boy who would quietly sit and play on cue for rehearsals.

He'd been tinkering with *this* melody.

"Don't look at me like that," Toby said.

"I will. You studied composition in school."

"I dropped it. After… " Toby's melody faltered, and he spun it into an intentional bridge.

"The accident. After the *accident*. Just *say* it."

"Besides, I meander. I improvise, remember? It's not meant to be permanent."

Emmett imagined multiple responses that interlaced with the melody singing from Toby's keyboard. He opted to remain silent. He was not going to fuck up this goodbye.

With two leading chords, Toby moved his song into a solid, structured chorus. "I do have one asshole producer who's been blowing up my phone."

"So maybe if you answered it, he'd stop blowing it up."

"You sound like Malik."

"Pretty *and* smart. He's getting more appealing every minute."

Toby stopped abruptly and turned off the keyboard. He stood and grabbed his coat and bag. "I'll walk you back."

Emmett took note: This was another topic not up for discussion. He motioned for Toby to lead. "It was nice to hear you play again."

"Thank you." Toby shouldered his bag and flipped off his lights. "I don't have time to stop and focus like I'd need to."

"As someone who was forced to stop once upon a time—there *can* be strength in it."

"I seem to remember there was great trauma in it, too." Toby avoided Emmett's gaze and closed his door with a solid click. "You want to catch a cab instead?"

"No. One more walk before I go?"

Toby smiled and hooked his arm through Emmett's. "I should slow down and walk more often. This has been a nice little break."

"You also need to give me my hat back."

When they got to Emmett's hotel, they tucked themselves against a brick walkway separate from the sidewalk traffic of Thirty-fifth Street. In spite of the chilly November air, neither made any motion to leave. Toby still wore Emmett's hat. He still looked amazing in it. Emmett still wanted it back.

"So, when do you leave tomorrow?"

"I think the bus pulls away at ten," Emmett said, calculating a swift move to yank the hat from Toby's head. "I want to thank you again. For everyth—"

"What's next for your choirs?"

When they spoke at the same time, Emmett chuckled, and then Toby blushed as their eyes met. A few more minutes wouldn't hurt. Besides, it was nice to have someone other than Mac to talk to about his work. "We have a preliminary adjudicated event right before Thanksgiving, and then we'll toss together a holiday program for the parents."

"You sound less than excited about that."

"I don't see how the annual sing-along of "Hallelujah Chorus" teaches them anything, especially when all the alumni do is try to out-sing each other."

"Ew. No. But a happy crowd means money for the program, no?"

"Yes. So, He shall reign forever and ever, and I will be a professional about it."

"I have complete faith in you."

"You always did." It seemed like a good place to close. Emmett looked up at the lit-glass hotel overhang and sighed. "And I really have to go. Thank you again."

"I'm so glad you called." Toby tilted the hat off of his head and inspected it, played with the weight of it before placing it on Emmett's head.

When Emmett opened his eyes, Toby was right there, close; his blue eyes were bright in the golden glow of the hotel entrance.

And with a quick intake of air, Toby's lips were on his, soft and tentative, but insisting on more than a friendly peck. In spite of every ounce of common sense that teased the edges of the moment, Emmett kissed back, his cane and a soft moan escaping his grip before he could catch either of them.

As Toby's lips caressed his, Emmett could be sure of one thing: They were *lousy* at goodbyes.

5

Tobias didn't know how it happened. He wasn't sure who moved first, but in light of how he had been fighting the urge every time he was near Emmett, Tobias feared it was probably him. Thing was, Emmett kissed back. He *deliciously* kissed back.

Until he stopped. His breath was visible in the cool air, shallow and stuttering as his voice. "Why did you *do* that?"

Tobias flushed with regret and stepped back. "I'm—I'm sorry. I don't know." Unable to meet his eyes, he picked up Emmett's cane and quickly handed it to him. "I'm sorry. I just—it felt like the natural thing to do."

"You know that's not why I came, right?"

"I know. Me either." Tobias readjusted his bag across his chest and glanced toward his train station. "I'll—I'll go."

"No." Emmett tugged Tobias back by his bag's strap and kissed him again. His lips were wet and demanding; his hands were warm on Tobias's cold cheeks. Tobias clung to Emmett's scarf, losing himself as Emmett deepened the kiss with parted lips and the soft seeking of his tongue.

Emmett pulled back with a smack and took off his glasses. His eyes were huge with wonder, and he licked his lips. "You—you taste the same."

"That's ridiculous," Tobias said. "You don't know that." But Tobias kissed him again to taste for himself.

And when he found it to be true, he didn't let up, even when Emmett tried to speak again. "Remember coming back for my senior homecoming?"

Tobias kissed him between words, catching his lips, his cheeks, the cleft of his chin.

Emmett kept talking, kissing, giggling. "Game night was crisp and clear, like tonight. We were in the courtyard—" Emmett stopped long enough to rest his cane against the wall. He looked at Tobias with the sweetest smile and went right back to nibbling at Tobias's bottom lip before continuing his disjointed story. "Mmm, seriously you taste—"

Tobias knew he tasted like whiskey, mint and cheese, but he wasn't about to interrupt.

"In the courtyard after the football game," Emmett continued after another smoldering smirk, "up against that dying sycamore tree. The band played the fight song while the team rang the victory bell." He worked his way across Tobias's cheek to his ear.

Tobias moaned. "Right. We'd missed the game. Why did we miss—" Tobias gasped at Emmett's hot breath in his ear.

"You remember." Emmett's teeth grazed Tobias's earlobe.

Tobias pulled back as their breath ghosted between them. Emmett's eyes were dark; a rim of green was visible around his blown pupils.

Tobias remembered: Emmett's wanton gaze, sweat-slick skin, their bodies twined and satiated and so, so in love. "Fucking hell."

Emmett kissed him again, tongue first, and sucked at Tobias's bottom lip before finishing his story. "You teased me for knowing all the words to my alma mater."

Tobias pulled back completely. "Who the hell knows the words to their alma mater?"

"Choir kids, you delinquent."

"I don't *like* to sing—"

Emmett shut him up with another kiss. "Can't you smell the bonfire at Mr. Forsythe's?"

Tobias pointed back over his shoulder. "I think the halal guy burned his peppers." But he couldn't hide his smile or his desire for Emmett to kiss it right off of his face.

Emmett's eyes danced. "See? You do remember..."

It wasn't that Tobias had forgotten, not really. Seeing Emmett here, bright-eyed and swollen-lipped, his words caught under his breath and so comfortable with these memories, reminded Tobias how *good* everything had been. "I remember the hayride the next day," Tobias finally confessed. "And you wore those jeans that pissed your mother off."

"She never understood why we paid for holey jeans."

Tobias stepped close again, his lips brushing Emmett's as he spoke. "I remember why I liked them."

Emmett chuckled deep in his chest and kept on with the story. "What was that stupid song everyone was singing on the hayride? We were doing all the motions to it and Scotty fell off—"

Tobias gasped and jolted back two steps as his eye caught Emmett's cane, where it was propped against the brick wall. He closed his eyes and took a deep breath, willing his breathing to steady. It was ridiculous after all this time. The utterance of a name should not—

This was why Tobias didn't let himself remember. He felt as though he was suffocating.

"Off the wagon." Emmett reached out for him. "Toby?"

Tobias never spoke of Scotty. To anyone. Until Emmett called those weeks ago, he had never spoken of Emmett, either. The elation of loving Emmett was too closely attached to the pain of everything they lost that day.

"Toby. Talk to me. You're swaying. Do you need to sit—"

"Do you still miss him?" The words poured from him like a flood, a confession that would never earn forgiveness.

Emmett took Tobias's hand. "Of course I do."

"I—I forget. And then all at once I remember."

"How can you forget?"

Tobias looked into Emmett's eyes, unsure how Emmett didn't understand. "I haven't had a *choice*."

Emmett sagged back against the wall. He looked defeated. Tobias still couldn't fathom Emmett's lack of understanding. "Is that why you flinch?" Emmett asked. "Because I'm making you remember?"

"I flinch?"

"When I say your name. It's for a second, but… I've noticed."

"I didn't know. I—I'm sorry."

"I'm not asking for an apology. I didn't think… " Emmett took Tobias's hand again and tugged him closer. He brushed his thumb along the line of Tobias's jaw. The concern in his eyes seeped into the parts of Tobias's heart that he had shut down the day he walked out of Emmett's life. "I didn't think it would be so *raw* anymore."

Tobias wanted to sink into the ground. "No one calls me Toby now." Tobias shook his head and hated the worry he saw in Emmett's eyes. "I'm not that boy anymore… "

"I never expected you to be." Emmett's gaze was like fire through Tobias's skin. "I'm not that boy anymore either."

Tobias wanted to look away, but was frozen. In spite of the whirr in his ears and the urge to run vibrating in his legs, he was held in Emmett's gaze.

"Would you prefer I call you 'Tobias'?"

"No." It was out before Tobias even considered it. And as he heard it, he meant it. *No. This man. This* man who knew everything, he had every right to the darkest corners of Tobias's past. "No. It wouldn't feel right. Not from you."

Emmett nodded and grabbed his cane. Tobias winced and looked away from it, his anxiety unreasonable to him in light of Emmett's calm. But when he dared to look back at Emmett, he saw the mischievous twinkle that he knew well, the one that could quiet the whirr and convince him to stay.

"So... " Emmett lingered on the vowel and pushed his glasses back on his nose. "If you're not *that* Toby anymore, and I'm not *that* Emmett anymore... who was it that couldn't resist kissing me?"

Tobias closed his eyes and chuckled with pleasure. "Just... me."

Emmett kissed Tobias again. It was familiar, soothing, the kind of kiss that could crack Tobias wide open.

But even in the swell of Emmett's lips on his, in the warmth of Emmett's tongue brushing his, Tobias knew that this was temporary—an interlude that stretched the limits of Tobias's will. It was all he could do not to drag Emmett back to his apartment and keep him there until the years of separation were unwound between them.

And Emmett must have been aware of this, because, with soft pecks to Tobias's lips and cheeks, temple and curls, he put a gentle end to it. "Toby, I *have* to go." He tapped his cane against the concrete. "My cane turns into a serpent after midnight."

Tobias laughed and fidgeted by fixing Emmett's scarf and collar and running a finger along the brim of his hat. "Call me?"

"Is that what you want? You want to hear from me again?"

"Of course. I've wanted to hear from you for—" Tobias sighed at their joint stupidity. "I just—I never knew how to make the first move."

Emmett kissed him one more time, a soft lingering press. "I'll call you."

Tobias started toward the sidewalk, but stopped and turned back. "Em?"

Emmett walked toward him; his visible confidence was the inverse of Tobias's anxious heart.

"Call for something stupid? I think I've missed that the most."

Emmett adjusted his hat and pointed his cane toward the top of the hotel. "I have thirty-five teenagers supposedly asleep up there. It's quite possible you're going to hear from me before the night's over."

"I could manage that."

◆◆◆

Two weeks after Emmett's bus disappeared into the Lincoln Tunnel, out of New York and onto the road to Indiana, Tobias heard from Emmett again.

That did not mean that two weeks passed before he thought of Emmett. Before he caught a whiff of sandalwood and spent too much time trying to figure out the other half of Emmett's cologne's essence. Before he stirred restlessly through many sleepless nights in a row with his mind a cacophonous symphony of emotions that had broken through his years of silence the moment he saw Emmett standing in that parking lot with that fucking fedora cocked on his head.

Emmett's first contact came through an email. Tobias closed his office door and put on some Vivaldi.

Toby,

I've been trying to come up with a way to thank you again for not only meeting with me, but for reaching out to my kids. They haven't stopped talking about their day at the theater. In fact, I'm about to have a rebellion on my hands from my other choirs wanting to go to New York too. I know your time is precious, and it meant the world that you gave it so freely.

You and I, we've come a long way, haven't we? From my starry-eyed dreams of stepping off a plane at LaGuardia only to land the lead in Così fan tutte *with one audition and a recommendation from you, to your more realistic dreams of working your way up, even if it meant celebrating an off-off-Broadway gig substituting for the triangle player.*

Friendship always seemed the root of everything between us, and I hope I'm right in thinking maybe we can have a glimpse of that back. Because you're right, it was the silly things that were the best. We laugh so well together, Toby. And laughing with you is something I hope never to lose again.

So, thank you. Thank you for meeting with me, for making a few of my kids' dreams come true and for balding faster than me. That's especially important.

As Hit Man *opens, break a leg! Except, I really don't recommend that. It absolutely sucks, a broken leg.*

—Emmett

Tobias read the email at least three times.

He refilled his coffee and devoured a stale bagel from the break room down the hall. And then he sent Emmett a text. It picked up an old silly argument about which operetta role better suited Emmett: Ferrando in Mozart's *Così fan tutte*, or Nanki Poo from Gilbert and Sullivan's *The Mikado*. Silly was all he could summon.

TOBIAS: I always thought you'd make a better Nanki Poo. Ferrando's aria is a snoozer.

Hours passed before he got a response.

EMMETT: We're still doing this? Ferrando's aria rested in my voice like it was written for me. Nanki Poo requires comedic timing... of which I have none.

TOBIAS: Lies. You're just resistant because *Mikado* has no sweeping arias. Egomaniac.

EMMETT: You caught me. Hook me up with a kimono and I'll be your Poo.

TOBIAS: See? Comedic timing. Also, I'd like to remind you that my first gig in New York was on the stage crew. I opened and closed the curtains. They didn't trust me with instruments.

EMMETT: My apologies. You didn't get the triangle gig until your second year, did you?

TOBIAS: I did not. I also choked on our second night and dinged when I should have linged.

EMMETT: Ha. Gotta run.

That night, after dinner with Malik, Tobias led a Gilbert and Sullivan sing-along at The Duplex and drank three too many whiskey sours. The next morning, Malik made fun of him until he finally sobered up enough to kick his ass in a sweaty, profanity-laced racquetball match that lasted well over an hour and quite possibly cost Tobias's left deltoid its life.

The next day, after a meeting had been cancelled, and Tobias couldn't concentrate on anything other than Nanki Poo's opening number from *The Mikado—A wandering minstrel I/ A thing of shreds and patches—*he decided that, if his past was going to insist on interrupting his present, he might as well invite it to tea, as the barista's grandmother suggested. Symbolically speaking.

After some digging around in an old filing cabinet down the hall from his office, he found what he was looking for: a spiral-bound pad of manuscript paper. Its pages were yellowed and curled at the corners from years of being shoved into backpacks and messenger bags. The metal spine hung loose from nights of raking a pencil up and down its coiled edge in creative contemplation.

Emmett had asked Tobias, "Are you still writing?"

And Tobias had fudged, "I tinker."

For much of his life, Tobias had toyed with the intangible. Melodies played through his head as readily as storylines play through an author's. But when he and Emmett started dating, when everything was easy and filled with promise, Tobias began in earnest to write a specific piece to express what Emmett meant to him. This masterpiece was, of course, unbeknownst to Emmett, lest his unquenched curiosity alter the course of Tobias's own ideas.

Their love made writing easy for Tobias. Simple rhythmic structures and smooth harmonies melded together with ease.

Years after they parted, Tobias continued to write. He tried to fill the gaps where guilt and grief lived with the kind of music that brought Emmett near. It was a safe constant when his mind wandered into darkness.

In time, other people's music drowned out his own. He filled the silence with more work, longer to-do lists, more everything, until any lingering song had no space to grow. He fiddled with a melody or a chord passage from time to time. He played with a rhythmic bounce that resonated in a coffee shop or at the turnstile in a train station. Little got written down. Less was recorded. He barely tinkered anymore.

But then, Emmett called. And after spending a little time together, Tobias had found himself whistling a familiar melody.

Tobias sat at his keyboard and propped open the notebook. The pages were covered with faded, penciled staves and jotted musical thought. He found a section of solid score, squinted, and as if sight-reading a complicated Rachmaninoff piano concerto, he slowly began, testing it until muscle memory kicked in.

"Ah, yes. Quick. Snappy. Here we go."

The song fell into place under his fingers. like the tunes of his early piano lessons: "Für Elise," "Jackson Street Blues," "Moonlight Sonata"; a little clunky at first, but quickly easing, as if he'd known it forever.

It was Emmett's song, left in fragments and scraps just as they had been. But maybe, with a little work, a little love and pruning, it could come alive again.

◆◆◆

IT WAS ANOTHER WEEK UNTIL he heard from Emmett again. *Hit Man* had opened to mediocre reviews, which was better than Tobias had expected. They loved the music and hated the story. Tobias had just come out of a production meeting when his phone rang.

His heart skipped a beat as Emmett's face smiled back at him from the screen. Tobias had snuck the shot at the Hudson while Emmett's students surrounded him in their victory celebration. In it, Emmett's head was thrown back in laughter at some exuberant proclamation from an ecstatic student. It was Emmett at his natural best.

Tobias closed his door and moved paperwork from his chair before sitting down. "Hey."

"So you'll never guess what happened today."

Emmett's voice was confident and sure in Tobias's ear, as if it belonged there. "Please tell me it was stupid."

Emmett chuckled. "Remember Tori?"

"Vividly." Tobias, ready for a fantastic story, propped his feet up on his desk.

"Caught her in a practice room tipping the velvet with our Alto II section leader."

"What?" Tobias yanked his legs off his desk, not giving two cents about the slew of papers that fluttered to the floor. He couldn't decide what was funnier, the scene itself or Emmett's "it's another day in Indiana" attitude about it.

In the midst of his own laughter, he could hear Emmett giggling too. "Toby, goddammit. It's not that—" but the hilarity of the scene could not be denied.

They finally composed themselves, and Tobias kicked his feet up onto his desk again. "Okay, okay—you have to set the scene. Tell me *everything*."

"Toby. There was vagina. Everywhere."

And that sent Tobias off into another peal of laughter, imagining Emmett's horrified face, the squeals of panic from the girls scurrying for clothing and gathering what little dignity they had left. "Have you never *seen* a vagina?"

"I—what? Yes, as a matter of—why?" Emmett huffed and Tobias bit back another snort of laughter. "Yes, I have. I was drunk and there were two of them and it was very confusing. I don't see how—" Emmett paused while Tobias chortled away. "Okay, Mr. True Confessions. Have *you?*"

"Have I what?"

"Vagina. You now know more about my sordid past than is necessary."

"Ha. No, sir. Gold star gay." Emmett grumbled, and Tobias soothed, "I don't think it counts if you're blotto."

"Whatever. I'm traumatized here, and you're laughing at me." Of course, Tobias wasn't laughing alone.

"So, what? They were sprawled out on the floor, or... "

"Oh, *worse*," Emmett said. "They were on the fucking timpani in one of Mac's practice rooms."

"Oh, God. She doesn't seem like one who would handle that gracefully."

"I went in there to get some extension cords, which is an entirely different conversation about budgets and jocks breaking into the band room and Mac's control issues—"

"Not yours, I'm sure."

"We're not talking about me. And I waltz in there with my mind on nine hundred non-vagina-related things—"

Tobias started cackling again. He could very clearly hear, "Tobias Cole Spence, I swear to God... " He tried. He really did try to gather his wits, but with this imagery—now with the addition of a timpani and Mac glaring over Emmett's shoulder—control was not a viable option.

Emmett laughed with him and tried to tell more of his story. "And Tori's on her back on the damned thing. Do you know how much those sons of bitches *cost?*"

Tobias answered, with all manner of control in his voice, "A set of two is going to set you back about three grand."

Before Emmett continued his rant, Tobias was cackling again. Emmett joined him.

"So, was the Alto II naked too, or was this just—"

"What are you doing, drawing a fucking picture for the *Brighton Beacon*?"

"I'm not very artistic."

"You are an asshole," Emmett said.

"You are beautiful."

"I couldn't believe—what?"

The laughter stopped. The story stopped. Tobias's heart seemed to stop. But Emmett was waiting, prodding. "Toby... don't do this."

"You are. Laughing like this. I'm imagining you standing there slack-jawed and speechless. But, yes. I apologize." Tobias cleared his throat and stood to pace around his 175 square-foot office, which now seemed about three square feet. "We were talking about vaginas invading your practice room."

At that, Emmett snorted and then groaned. "The other girl is Mac's lead percussionist, too. I hope their orgasms were worth it, because they have totally fucked our holiday programs."

"I have a feeling you sort of prevented any orgasms."

"I'm blaming you for this, by the way."

"Me? What the hell did I do?"

"They were roomies in New York."

"Okay, here. Let me check my calendar. I *believe* your trip to New York was planned with your choir long before Tobias Cole Spence was ever a part of the picture."

"Mmm. Well. Anyway." Emmett laughed again. "Is this stupid enough for a phone call?"

"You know, you don't have to call for *only* the stupid stuff. But yeah. I think this qualifies. I guess this means it's my turn next."

"I can't imagine anything stupid happens in New York." The laughter in Emmett's voice made Tobias want to tell him again that he was beautiful.

Instead, he blurted, "You could come back and visit me. Find out for yourself."

"I—what? When? I don't think—"

"Last I remember, teachers get about two to three weeks off over Christmas. And I have it on good authority that Christmas in New York is magical."

"Toby."

"Emmett." Tobias pulled his chair over to his keyboard and turned it on. He put his phone on speaker and rested it on the control pad as he started playing a wintry melody.

"Oh, you're being rude now." Emmett was silent for a moment. "That's not a recording, is it?"

"No. It's not. Come see me. Just a couple of days. I know Miriam won't demand that much of your time over the holidays."

"Miriam can suck it; she's not my concern."

"What's your concern?"

"You called me beautiful." Tobias ramped up his tune, weaving in a lick of "Silver Bells" as if it belonged in his original composition. "And I get really stupid when I hear you play."

"I think those are two perfectly good reasons for you to come."

"Money."

"Stay with me. I have an extra bed. I'm in the Village. December. New York. See my show. We'll find something playing Monday and see one together."

"Toby."

"Emmett."

Emmett sighed, and Tobias imagined him running his hand through his hair in exasperation—and maybe, just maybe, caving a little. "Let me think about it."

"Should I trash Tori's demo?"

"Oh God, I forgot about that. No. Yes? Shit. You know what, do what you want with it. She'll have to suffer the consequences."

"Em, I have no concern who she spreads her legs for or where. Just so she doesn't think that will get her a better opportunity here."

"On the *timpani*, Toby."

"I know." Tobias chortled and played a line of "O Come all Ye Faithful." "Impulse control is an issue when you're seventeen."

"Did you just play… "

"Maybe."

Emmett was quiet for a moment and Tobias continued to play.

O come ye, o come ye…

"You're going to hell," Emmett said.

"Hopefully."

"Were we ever that stupid? Taking risks like that?" Emmett asked.

"Blowjob on your staircase before Mr. Peterson's wedding. Your dad was in the adjoining room watching the Hoosiers."

"Shit."

Tobias laughed and sighed at the memory, the crazy panic after Emmett came and they had to tuck him in and zip him up and get out the door. They still missed the wedding. And as they stood outside the church doors, watching the receiving line through the glass, all Emmett could say was, "I thought the time on the invitation was for the organ music!"

"You think about my offer, Em. I'd really like to see you again."

"I'll think. Thank you. Break a leg tonight."

6

NEW YORK CITY—December 2015

Two nights. Three days. That was all Emmett would agree to. And even then he was pretty sure he'd lost his mind deciding to go at all. Mac couldn't disagree with him.

"I thought you were satisfied with how things ended. What are you hoping to accomplish?" she'd asked.

"I don't know. Can't it be just a holiday?"

"Will it be *just* a holiday?"

He didn't know. He didn't know. He did not know. But now he was on a plane, and according to the pilot, he was already thirty thousand feet in the air.

He had spent the night before his flight at Eclipse flirting with a guy named Breslan. In hindsight, it had been as ridiculous as it sounded. The kid might have been twenty-one. Maybe. Probably. Fortunately, Kitten Kabooty, who actually was a damned amazing drag queen, showed up onstage. Breslan got so entranced with her that Emmett had been able to make a quick escape before he brought the kid home and took out his confusion on the poor boy's pert little ass.

As he left the dance floor, Gino had blocked Emmett's escape with a drink in one hand and Emmett's waistband in the other. "Leaving so soon? I thought maybe we'd—"

"No." He had removed Gino's hand, taken a drink from Gino's glass and kissed him hard. Dirty. "When I get back. Promise."

"It's Christmas," Gino pouted. "You're always home for Christmas."

"I'm going to New York for a few days."

"What the hell for?"

He didn't know. He didn't know. He *still* did not know.

When he spoke with Toby, it all made perfect sense—two adults taking time to catch up after years apart. No expectations, no agenda. It was clear they still had much in common, much to laugh about. At the root of everything, they had a friendship that really shouldn't be neglected again.

But, it wasn't that clear. Toby had kissed him. Kissing back was the most natural response. Had it not been for his students upstairs, there was no telling—

Emmett grabbed for the *SkyMall* magazine in the pocket of the seat in front of him and tried to think about anything but Toby.

Toby had called Emmett beautiful. *Toby* was beautiful. Still. More so than Emmett ever imagined: tall and striking, the kind of handsome that would turn the eye of any reasonable man or woman; the kind of handsome that smiled back at you from a Rolex ad or—Emmett slammed the catalog shut—a *SkyMall* magazine.

Emmett had no idea why he had agreed to come. He had no idea why he had agreed to stay with Toby and he had no idea why, with all of this confusion, he was still giddy with excitement. He wasn't so different from his hormonal students, who had decided to have oral sex on a three thousand-dollar timpani in a public practice room.

There was only one way this could end—in epic disaster.

Upon landing, he was greeted by a man holding a small white board that read: "E. Henderson." After another death-defying drive from

LaGuardia, they crept into Midtown, cars bumper to bumper, inching along, jerking forward into every free space.

Standing at The 520, Emmett looked up at the disproportionately small wreath hanging over the gigantic numerals on the building. Then he looked back at his driver, who was patiently waiting for him to make a decision. He had no idea how the hell to tip someone who'd cut in front of so many people without so much as a turn signal that he wondered how he was still alive.

Five dollars for not killing him? Two for the sheer panic? Fifteen for the promise to send a different driver for his trip home? He pulled out a five, offered a pinched smile and stopped after his first step away. "My luggage?"

"Will be waiting for you at Mr. Spence's, if that's okay."

"Yes. Thank you." Emmett removed his hat, hooked his cane onto his arm and walked in.

Mister Green Pompadour was now sporting a plum-colored quiff with the letter "B" shaved into the stubble at his right temple. He had replaced the rouged cheeks with lavender and lime eye shadow.

"Ohhh, look at you! Tall-and-good-looking came back."

"I missed you, darling."

Plum Quiff handed over a key card and blew him a kiss. This kid needed an agent. Or a date. Or both.

The eighth floor was as cacophonous as it had been during Emmett's first visit. He suspected it would be at any hour of any day; creativity knew no clock, after all. Emmett rapped on Toby's closed door with the hook of his cane and broke his own cardinal rule to peek in before Toby could answer. "I'm ready for my audition, Mr. Spence."

"Emmett!" Toby stood and stepped over a stack of papers. His heel caught the top of it and he slid a few inches forward before finding his balance again. "Hi! Welcome! Watch your step."

Emmett talked through the hug Toby offered. "What *is* all of this?"

Toby squeezed him and kissed his cheek. They pulled apart. "I'm organizing."

Emmett looked around. It didn't seem as though there had been any improvement since his previous visit. "Looks like you need a secretary."

"I'll have you know—" Toby scooped up a stack of scores. "These are scores from 2005 to 2010." He looked at the stack, plopped them on his desk and flipped through them. "2010 to the present, actually. I think."

Emmett hummed. "Your system seems quite foolproof."

"No, see, I remember in seasons." He picked up the score for *Urinetown* from another pile. "I was second keyboard on this for the previews in 2001. Then 9/11 happened, Broadway went dark and we opened a few weeks later." He plopped it onto the 2000 to 2005 pile. "And then I directed it in Chicago in 2006."

"So, shouldn't it go into the 2005 to 2010 pile?"

"No?" Toby looked at it. "Maybe."

"You do have a database, right? In case you can't remember when you performed it?"

"No." Toby scratched his head and scrunched his nose, and Emmett remembered all the reasons he had told himself he shouldn't have come. "Maybe."

"Is that why you invited me? To get your shit organized?"

"No. Definitely no." Toby looked around his office and sighed before grabbing his coat. "I'm afraid three days won't be enough time for that."

"You're a hot fucking mess."

"Yes, but this really isn't new information now, is it?"

Emmett looked at Toby, at his stupid beaming face. He plunked his fedora onto Toby's head. "No." Toby's hair puffed out from under the brim, and Emmett couldn't resist flicking his fingers through the wavy tendrils. "I seem to recall your dorm room had alternate life forms living in the crevices."

"Now *that* was the roommate. Science major. Experiments."

"You went to a music school, you ass. He played French horn." Emmett opened the door and tapped at the back of Toby's calves with his cane. "I'm craving dim sum."

"He played lousy French horn. Probably would have been a better scientist."

"Feed me, please."

Toby turned back to him and cocked the fedora to obscure his left eye. But his right eye… "I'm so glad you're here."

And with that, Emmett tossed all of his questions about the wisdom of this trip to the wind. He'd deal with them later. "I am, too."

EMMETT WAS BEGINNING TO UNDERSTAND the concept of a New York minute. One minute he was in nice, quiet, peaceful Indiana, and the next he was walking across the street for dim sum and dodging a pissed-off cab driver careening around the corner. As they ate, Toby talked about the show, and Emmett talked about Tori and the fallout from her indiscretion in the practice room.

"It's been a parade of meetings and counseling sessions with her and her parents."

"Are they upset?"

"They're trying," Emmett said. "I want them to stop worrying about *who* she's with and start focusing on *where* it's safe to figure this stuff out."

"Maybe providing that place for her."

"Wouldn't that be a novel idea?" Emmett cracked open his fortune cookie and flicked the fortune to the table unread. "What is it with parents' insistence that their kids be asexual?"

"Hey now." Toby picked up the slip of paper and read it. He handed it back with a stern look. "Fortunes are never wrong."

Emmett yanked it from his hand and read. "'Traveling more often is important for your health and happiness.' Ha. I needed a two-week hibernation period after my last trip here."

"That's because you were corralling teenagers and traveling in a bus. With corralled teenagers." Toby cracked his cookie open and grinned. "'No distance is too far, if two hearts are tied together.' Aw, isn't that sweet?"

"Don't forget to add 'in bed.' Even sweeter."

Toby snorted, and they argued over who was paying the bill. Toby won, Emmett grumbled and they headed back uptown for Toby's show.

The show was as ridiculous in its run as it had been in rehearsals. The jokes were stale, the acting was over the top, the costuming was beyond cliché and yet, by the second act, Emmett couldn't deny his enjoyment. The music sealed it all together and proudly trumpeted its off-center nature. By curtain, Emmett was disappointed that he wasn't going to get to see it again before he headed home.

He waited for Toby, meandering around the crushed velvet seats. He walked to the orchestra pit and smiled down at Toby's podium. The score was still open, and his baton rested along the top edge of the stand.

It wasn't exactly what Toby had dreamed of, all those years before. But from what he had told Emmett, Toby had a good life. He had made an easy move from stage crew to playing for community theaters in every borough, in every niche house that would have him. He played in touring companies as third backup to the second keyboard player; he played for readings and workshops, saying yes until his calendar was filled with music, rehearsals and show after show after show.

He deserved it all.

Emmett looked back into the house and breathed in the musty, woody scent of the theater. The smell was familiar and comforting. A smoky haze covered the first few rows, left over from the final scene of the show.

Suddenly, music came from the house piano—the light-hearted opening vamp to "Try Me," Emmett's audition song and big solo in *She Loves Me*. It was the song that had started it all for them, and the show where Emmett spent every opportune moment shooting discreet looks of longing over to the piano. He thought Toby would never notice him, much less fall in love with him and dream dreams with him.

He turned to the stage. Toby sat at the piano with Emmett's hat perched on his head and a smile that could always render Emmett stupid.

"Come up and sing for me," Toby said, holding the chord that cued Emmett's entrance.

"No."

With a few chord changes, Toby moved the chorus into the sappy love song "All Through the Night" from *Anything Goes*. He was playing hardball now. Every song from this musical brought Emmett right back to the summer when they fell in love and made earnest promises that they were too young to keep.

"Toby."

"Broadway stage… " Pushing Emmett's buttons with a coy smile and a song, Toby slid into the bouncy, flirtatious "De-Lovely" from the same show. "Do you remember the dance?"

"Pieces of it."

Toby nodded toward the empty stage. "Let's see. Does your hip feel okay tonight?"

"It's fine. And no thank you." Emmett leaned back onto a chair to listen. He could listen to Toby play all night.

"Come on." Toby almost whined, playing meandering chords from the song. "We were so good together."

"We were. But like you said, we're not those boys anymore."

Toby started the melody to "Day by Day" from *Godspell*, and Emmett stood tall and stomped his foot to get Toby's attention. "Toby, *please*." The melancholic prayer of the song scratched at Emmett like sandpaper. *Godspell* was the show he never got to perform because his body was held together with bolts and screws while his heart began slowly to unravel.

Toby lifted his hands as if he had lost control of what was coming out of his fingers.

"What are you trying to accomplish?" Emmett asked, his tone softer than the simmering anger inside.

"Nothing, Em… nothing. I thought it might be nice."

"Can't we just pick up where we left off, instead of dwelling on—"

"On what brought us together?"

"Is that what you want?" Emmett asked. "You want us together?"

"I want to make music with you, that's all. We were so good." Emmett was frozen to the spot, frozen in Toby's pleading eyes, until Toby broke their gaze and looked down at the keys. "How's this instead?"

He began the trilled opening to Bach's "Sonata in A Major," a piece for one piano and four hands. It was a piece they had messed around with for the two short years they were in each other's lives and never quite perfected.

As if propelled, Emmett rose from the seat and joined Toby onstage. He sat to Toby's left to take the secondo part.

"Do you remember it?"

"I'm not sure," Emmett confessed. "We'll find out."

Toby began again, and, to Emmett's surprise, the notes and fingerings came back to him as if he'd never stopped playing it. Toby nudged Emmett's shoulder—a silent "I told you so." They continued and slowed, as one forgot and the other reminded, "B minor here, yes, yes." It all came apart at the end of the first movement with missed notes and much laughter.

"So close!"

Emmett futzed around with what he could remember of the second movement, lingering over the notes to see if Toby would join him. He didn't. Emmett nudged this time, and Toby stilled Emmett's hand with his own. "Thank you."

Emmett stopped his failed attempts at the rondo and picked up the chords of "De-Lovely" as Toby stood to retrieve the quilted piano cover. "You're welcome." His students had performed the number back in Fulton. It was one of the few decent songs in their very small repertoire, so it was familiar to his fingers: a ghost with a different face than that in Toby's memory.

Toby hummed the tune until Emmett finished, ending with the first chorus. "Drinks?" Toby asked.

"Home—I mean… " Emmett blushed and hid it by helping him place the piano cover. "Back to your place? I'm exhausted."

"My place it is." Toby hopped off the stage and took Emmett's hand. "I don't know where home is anymore, anyway."

◆◆◆

UNLIKE HIS OFFICE, TOBY'S APARTMENT was immaculate. Of course it had to be, or he would drown in his own clutter. The place seemed smaller than a hotel room, but otherwise everything one would want in a city flat: brick walls, contemporary furnishings, a functional kitchenette, living space and a bedroom partitioned off by a floor-to-ceiling, frosted glass sliding wall.

It was odd, existing in Toby's living space. It was so Toby—a print of "Map" by Jasper Johns hung over Toby's bed, and a Keith Haring piece decorated the living room wall. Both were bright, colorful and abstract. And yet, the turquoise leather couch was so impractical and peculiar; it showed a man Emmett no longer knew.

Being here—stepping out of the shower while Toby smeared bagels with cream cheese and called into the bathroom about Emmett's cream and sugar preference—seemed to Emmett as if he'd stepped into an already-occupied hotel room and decided to room with the stranger anyway.

"You know I like my coffee sweet. Just lay it out and I'll get it." The sensation was familiar and unfamiliar. Finding relics of their past in a land they had never traveled together.

They had a full day and night, so they took in as much of the city as possible. Touristy Christmas highlights were anchored by visits to

Toby's favorite restaurants. They strolled Fifth Avenue to enjoy the Christmas windows. At Rockefeller Center, Emmett found himself ridiculously giddy over the size of the tree—such a cliché for a local, he was sure—and completely taken with the wonder of New York that had never really left him.

After dinner, they went Uptown to Barneys. Emmett lit up with childlike wonder at the colorful animated window displays. He clung to Toby, as if they both might float away into the winter wonderlands and infinite toy shops.

"Take me to Lincoln Center?" The Lincoln Center had been Emmett's moon—the focal point of his goals. At eighteen, just like Tori now, he was oblivious to the rarity of actually making it there. He didn't dream it anymore, of course, but his fascination had never wavered.

Increasingly comfortable with the constant presence of it, Emmett spun his cane like a baton. Toby still glowered at it like an intruder upon their perfect day. "You wanna walk across the park or grab a cab?"

"Let's walk. "

"Yes, let's walk." Toby said as he readjusted Emmett's hat on his own head. "Thank you, by the way."

"I don't care if you did buy me a new hat today, Toby. You're not keeping my fedora."

Toby laughed. "No, I mean for this. Today. Christmas is one big blur for me every year. I barely remember to call my folks, I don't exchange gifts with anyone, I'm usually working… "

"But it used to be your favorite."

"You've reminded me why." Toby chuckled on a sigh. "So many lost opportunities between us, you know?"

"Toby… we changed."

"Did we, though? Everything feels so comfortable, and I can't help but be a little—"

Emmett's phone buzzed. He tried to ignore it, but reflex caused him to pull his arm from Toby's and reach for it. "Sorry—go on."

"No. Get it. I'm rambling anyway."

Emmett looked at his phone and then at Toby. "It's Tori?"

"She has your phone number?"

"I give her private lessons, yeah." He stared at the phone for another moment and finally answered. "Merry Christmas."

"You're not home, Mr. H."

"Um… how do you know this? And hello."

"Hell—Merry—" Tori sighed, and Emmett followed Toby to sit on a bench. "You're supposed to be home."

"Well, I'm tremendously sorry. Calling ahead is usually a preferred practice. And coming to my home is typically not."

"It was supposed to be a surprise!" Tori huffed. She sounded as though she was on the verge of tears.

"Okay, okay. What's going on? Are you all right?"

"Yes, I'm fine. We're fine. All of us. Um." She mumbled something to someone else away from the phone and shuffled back. "Can you FaceTime?"

Emmett shot a look at Toby, who had been listening. "Uh… sure? I'm not really in the best place for this, but… "

"It's New York. No one cares," Toby whispered, and motioned for him to get on with it.

Tori's smiling face appeared on Emmett's screen, and he couldn't help but smile back. She was bundled for the cold and her upturned nose was Rudolph red. "Good evening—you've been out in the cold too long."

"So have you. Your nose is red. And you have a new hat!"

Emmett grinned. "I do!" He pulled the newsboy down a little lower to show her the fabric. "Can you see it? Do you approve?"

"I do." She turned to someone else, smacked an arm and chastised, "I know! Give me a second." Back on the screen she offered a huge grin, and all Emmett could do was laugh at her and whomever she was with, whatever they were up to. "So, we came to see you. To sing to you.

Carols. For Christmas." She groaned and tried again. "I had a speech all ready, and you're not here."

"You came to my house to sing for me?" Damned kids. "How many of you are there?"

"I don't—here." Tori lifted the phone to show the group behind her. "I don't know. Thirty? Whoever could make it. And parents because, you know. The cops think minors don't know how to behave after eight p.m."

"That's because most of you don't know how to behave *before* eight p.m." Emmett settled back onto the bench, ignoring the chill it sent up his back. He did not, however, ignore the pressure of Toby's hand as it slowly rubbed across his shoulders. "So, this isn't what you had planned, but will you sing for me anyway?"

"Yes! We're cold and it will probably suck, but… "

"It's Christmas carols. Have fun. If I wasn't in public, I might join you."

"You should anyway. Wherever you are." She shouted back to the group, "Who has the pitch—" A G4 buzzed from a pitch pipe. She mimicked the pitch and sang, "Starts on *sol*," and they were off with a rousing rendition of "Hark, The Herald Angels Sing."

After the first phrase, they split off into two and occasionally three-part harmony. Some songs worked better than others. All were charming. And delightful. And inviting enough that a few people slowed to listen as they walked by.

Somewhere between songs three and four, Toby got up and paced, eventually disappearing around a bend. But Emmett stayed planted, a little shivery, but completely warmed by the thoughtfulness of his students. The kids finished awkwardly, with one student starting a new song, quickly shushed by another.

"Mr. H! Are you there?" Tori's chill-reddened face filled his screen.

"Yes, I'm here. Thank you *so* much! I'm sorry I wasn't there for the live show."

"It's okay. This was sort of fun. And weird."

"Do me one favor while you're there? Mrs. Danville—some of you had her in elementary school?"

"Yes! Best art teacher ever!"

"That's the one. She lives in the brick house next door. Can you go sing for her before you pack up and go?"

"Sure! We won't scare her or anything?"

"She's old, not senile," Emmett said. "She'll be thrilled."

"Okay. Merry Christmas, Mr. H!"

"And to all of you. Thanks again."

Emmett sat back and stared at his phone. He finally pulled out of his reverie when he realized Toby hadn't returned. A quick flush of panic washed over him, but as he fetched his cane to start looking around, Toby sauntered back.

"Hey. I thought you'd left me." Emmett hoped his tone was more jovial than his remaining panic would indicate.

Toby's hands were stuffed in his pockets; his nose, pink from the cool December air, now matched Tori's. It was his smile that was hard to read. "I wouldn't leave you."

Emmett met Toby's eyes; there was a sharp intake of air between them. They both knew it to be untrue. "Of—of course. You okay?"

Toby smiled, then. Brightly—too brightly. "Yep. That was beautiful of them. I wanted to give you some space."

It wasn't until after they'd started walking again, until after Emmett had relived a few of the songs—"I think Kyle belched in the middle of 'Silent Night'"—and a few of the faces and smiles and cold-bitten noses, that Toby spoke again.

"They love you."

Emmett nodded and hooked his arm in Toby's. The cold air made him melancholy. "It's not until recently that I've been able to admit that it's mutual."

Toby's smile didn't reach his eyes. "That's good." Toby pointed to the right fork in the walkway. "You've obviously found your way."

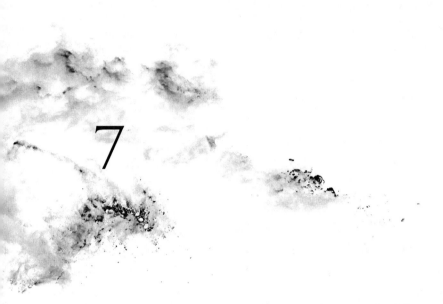

7

A PEACEFUL QUIET SETTLED BETWEEN them as night fell over the city. They crossed Broadway on Sixty-third with synchronized steps; Emmett's cane gave a lilt to the rhythm. Tobias found himself mentally articulating a musical pattern until Emmett's step hitched, and they stopped cold.

Before Tobias could register what was happening, Emmett had taken hold of his hand and was tugging him across the street. "Oh my—Toby, my God, look! It's stunning! Huge! The stairs are lit up with—"

Emmett stopped again and squinted at the words illuminated across the shallow staircase that led up to the main courtyard of Lincoln Center. "Welcome, Willkommen, Benvenuti, Salve." He read and read until the words changed to titles of upcoming shows. Emmett squeaked in glee.

"The tree! Come on, Toby. Come take my picture by the tree. And the fountain, and the—" Emmett stopped again and spun around to take in the enormous space, made more remarkable by its setting in such a cramped, tightly packed city. "Why are you still *standing* there? Come *on!*"

Emmett had been alight all day with the wonder of the city decked out for the holidays, but after the call from his students, his joy had elevated to enviable proportions.

Tobias had plenty of friends and colleagues; no city found him alone. But no one popped by unannounced to sing Christmas carols to him. No one came to him for advice on how to navigate the maze that is society's view of non-default sexuality. No one waited up for him, to hear about his evening—whether he brought a bottle of wine and freshly-baked chocolate chip cookies or not.

From an outsider's point of view, Tobias lived The Life: jet-setting, creative work, private parties and plenty of men to keep him warm whenever he might want that sort of companionship. But Emmett's life overflowed with real riches: respect from his students, close friends, a job that he was not only excellent at, but that he also loved. He had a comeback story that he wore as comfortably as a well-loved cardigan.

Tobias couldn't deny that Emmett's joy was contagious. He jogged up the awkward stairs and took pictures from afar as Emmett posed in front of the fountain, his silhouette changing shape with each position. They walked around the complex, past The Met and across the plaza back to Sixty-fifth Street.

"Do you miss it?" Tobias finally asked.

"Miss what? I never had it."

"The dream. Do you miss the dream?"

"No." Emmett stopped and looked back at where they'd walked, at the multicolored glow peeking around the buildings. "I think I like it best as a dream."

Tobias assumed the night was winding down, but Emmett dragged him into a cupcake shop and insisted they share a peppermint twist. They squeezed into two wrought-iron chairs scaled more for elves than for grown men in winter coats. By the time they finished, they were covered with crumbs; a smudge of icing smeared Emmett's cheek.

When they walked back outside, Emmett twirled his cane in his fingers, took in a deep breath and sighed. "I want to go dancing."

"What? We've been on our feet all day, are you sure?"

"I'm sure. A small place, maybe? Live music and… " Emmett closed his eyes and swayed to a song in his own head. "Maybe a cover band? A little Prince? Lenny?" He closed his eyes and hummed an unknown tune, and his sway turned into a private dance right on Columbus Avenue.

"What's gotten into you?" Tobias was grinning, of course he was. Emmett's joy *was* contagious. And he was beautiful. He didn't dare utter that thought aloud, but nothing would stop him from thinking it.

They left Christmas behind and grabbed a Downtown B to enjoy one of Tobias's favorite house bands in a bar near his apartment. The drinks were generously poured, and the sensual pulse of the bar wrapped around them like a cat twisting and purring at its owner's feet to welcome him home.

Emmett's Columbus Avenue dance was spot on for the place, a close, slow sway with Emmett's hands smoothing Tobias's back like a warm waterfall. When Emmett spun away to get another drink or to move with a different man, Tobias felt cold and rigid, uncomfortable in the bar he had frequented for years. Emmett always came back. He never stopped dancing, except to take a swallow of his drink or drape an arm over Tobias's shoulder.

It was after Emmett returned with the drink that was two drinks past Tobias's limit, and they had toasted to Santa's magic—of all things—that Tobias set his drink down, stepped into the curve of Emmett's neck and brushed his lips over Emmett's sweat-salty skin.

Emmett made no move to stop him. If it weren't for the poorly mixed bass that rang in their ears, Tobias could have sworn he heard a bit of a moan. He felt the shift when Emmett stretched his neck to invite him in closer.

Tobias was no longer envious. He was intoxicated. Booze and beat pulsated in his veins, muscle and movement twisted under his fingers, sweat and… Emmett teased at his lips. Tobias pressed a kiss under Emmett's ear then pulled him closer when he felt the vibrations of Emmett's chuckle at his chest. "Let me take you home."

Emmett kept moving and didn't respond. Loose from drink, he stepped back and fingered the damp hair over Tobias's ear. Emmett had left his glasses at the coat check, so Tobias had an unaltered view of his eyes, dark and focused on Tobias's. "No."

This was so clear and decisive that Tobias felt foolish. But then Emmett scrambled. "I mean, if you *want* to leave, yes, but… " He smiled tenderly, as he continued to play with Tobias's hair. "I'm having a really great time. Just like this."

Disappointment slumped Tobias's shoulders. The reality that this was no more than a nice dance at a neighborhood bar was all too clear. But Tobias nodded and smiled back, taking Emmett's hand to kiss his palm. "I'm sorry. I got caught up."

Emmett didn't say anything for a long while. But then, as if mulling a way to pry, he finally blurted, "You don't do this very often, do you?"

"What 'this' are you talking about? I go to bars."

Emmett pulled him in when the band cranked up their next tune; his breath was warm on Tobias's neck as they moved to the slow seductive beat. "No. Dance. Like this." Emmett grabbed Tobias's waist. "Let the music take you somewhere."

Tobias shivered. His head was heavy with booze and Emmett's conflicting signals. "N—no. I don't." Emmett moved them together, their hips a left-right-left sway that brought them closer than before. "You do, though."

At that Emmett stepped back; his apologetic smile brought home the truth of the moment. "Yeah. I do." That's all this was—something Emmett did.

Tobias nodded and tossed back his drink. "You ready to go anyway?"

"Sure." When they were outside and almost to Tobias's apartment, Emmett stopped him. "Toby."

Embarrassed that he'd let the music take him to a place Emmett wasn't willing to go, Tobias found it hard to look at him. But he swallowed his shame and met him eye to eye. "This has been a fantastic day," Tobias said. He flashed a bright grin and stepped forward again.

Emmett hesitated but came along, darting one more look of concern Tobias's way. "The best. Even that lumpy sofa bed of yours sounds really inviting right now."

TOBIAS COULDN'T SLEEP. HE WAS drunk-ish and Emmett was one frosted glass door away. Emmett, who danced and hummed the sultry rhythms of the bar band their entire walk home. Emmett, who was going home to Indiana in less than twelve hours.

He flopped to his side and faced the living room. Emmett didn't seem to be faring any better.

Tobias headed to the bathroom, just to have something to do with his legs. He pretended he didn't notice Emmett's restlessness as he snuck past his bed, but when he came back, Emmett sat up. "Mmm, hi." His hair was ruffled, his shirt was slipping off of his shoulder and his smile was lazy-sexy.

Fucking hell.

"Too tired to sleep?" Tobias asked as he tucked the edge of Emmett's blanket back under the mattress.

Emmett nodded and ran his hand over his hair, mussing it more. "Maybe. I was thinking of pulling up a movie on my laptop. Will the light bother you?"

"No." Tobias looked into his room, at his bed and the large screen television on the wall opposite it. "I, uh. Have a—why don't you come in here and we can watch together?"

Emmett glanced into Tobias's room and smirked. "This is starting to sound like bad porn."

"We have some hot delivery boys in this area—I could call for pizza."

Emmett smiled and stood, rearranging his pants around his waist. "Maybe a plumber." He walked into Tobias's room and pointed to the far side of the bed, the side that had always been his. He propped himself against the pillows with a flirtatious grin. "Clogged pipes, sir?"

Tobias turned to slide the divider closed. "There's always the sexy teacher story." He hitched his hip and looked over his shoulder. "Mr. Henderson, I need to talk to you about my grades."

Emmett choked and tried to look scolding. Instead he patted the bed and said, "How about we watch a movie, young man?"

They flipped through the choices and decided to watch old episodes of *Angel*.

"Maybe I can finally convince you that Angel and Wesley's love was real," Tobias said as he tossed the remote down between them.

"Are we really going to do this? Wesley loved Gunn. Character arc trumps everything."

"Because Wesley grew a pair of balls—"

"This has nothing to do with balls," Emmett explained. "It has to do with the fact that Gunn would make any warm-blooded man's loins ache."

"Which sort of has something to do with balls."

Before the first episode was over, Emmett had tucked himself in and was only listening. By the end of the second, he was asleep. Finally, Tobias turned it off, nestled against Emmett's back and fell into a peaceful sleep.

TOBIAS STIRRED A FEW HOURS later and had to pee. So did Emmett.

"I drank more than you," Tobias said.

"So you should suffer and wait." And with that, Emmett was up and out before Tobias could get his heavy head off the pillow. When Tobias returned, Emmett was already snuggled back in, mumbling and half asleep. "This is much comfier than that couch. You need an upgrade."

Tobias didn't answer; Emmett's breathing had already slipped into a steady rhythm. Tobias was awake now, unable to focus on anything other than Emmett's body, warm and loose, sleeping next to him. Or how the faint scent of Emmett's cologne, now embedded in his pillow, tickled Tobias's nose every time Emmett shifted in his sleep.

"Cardamom!" Tobias meant to think it, whisper it at worst, but his voice startled Emmett onto his back to stare at Tobias with a less than friendly glare.

"Pardon?"

"Go back to sleep." Tobias dared a glance at his clock. It was a little after four a.m.

"Do you need to make a grocery run?" Emmett's giggle was laced with sleep and residual alcohol.

"No, I—" Tobias ran his hand over his face. "Go back to sleep, Em. I'm sorry I woke you."

"Suit yourself."

"It's your cologne," Tobias said as Emmett turned to his side again.

"Mmm?"

"It's mostly sandalwood, but I keep getting a hint of something else and it's… " Tobias looked over; Emmett's breathing had evened out again, so he kept talking in a whispered hush. "It's been bugging me. There's this bakery near my old train stop. They made the most amazing cinnamon rolls—not so cloyingly sweet. I finally asked. They said the secret was cardamom."

"Mmm… love cardamom."

"It would appear that I do too." Tobias began to stroke Emmett's head. He considered stopping—considered Emmett's words of the night before. *"Can't we pick up where we left off instead of dwelling on… "*

It wasn't that Tobias was dwelling. He was remembering. And it was the first time in years—the first time since the day he walked away from Emmett to live his life in New York—that remembering didn't hurt quite so much.

The summer after the accident, Emmett had started to give up. His body had been healing as quickly as they had predicted, but it wasn't enough for Emmett. Leaving for New York in the fall was not going to happen. Emmett's mother had become more and more controlling of his time, his independence. He wanted out. The options dimmed with each passing day.

Tobias had sat with Emmett at these times and let him sleep and temporarily ignore the new world he faced: hours of painful physical therapy, a life without his best friend, the realignment of dreams that had filled their afternoons months before.

He sensed Emmett pushing him away during those days, but this, this kind of simple massage of Emmett's scalp with Emmett's cool soft hair slipping through his fingers, was always something that could anchor them together. Tobias couldn't make Emmett heal any faster, but he could comfort. He could console. He could believe he was doing *something* to make up for all the hurt he'd caused.

And, just like tonight, Emmett would slip into sleep under Tobias's fingers.

He brushed Emmett's hair up and over his ears and smoothed it down the back of his head as Emmett snoozed beside him, unaware. He massaged his neck for a few strokes, stopped and then started again.

Emmett moaned and pressed his head back into Tobias's.

"Does that mean stop or keep going?"

"Keep going," Emmett said, his voice rough and slurred. "That feels so good." He leaned back to give Tobias a better angle. "You should sleep, though."

"I'm fine." But he did lie down and prop himself up on his elbow to soothe Emmett all the way to sleep.

With a sleepy moan, Emmett stretched his body to press back against Tobias's. His ass rested in the crook of Tobias's hip; his legs twined with Tobias's to pull him closer. His neck was bare; his exhalations were a breathy plea that could not be ignored.

Tobias continued to run his fingers through Emmett's hair and kissed the tender skin under Emmett's ear. Emmett groaned and rolled his hips back as if asking for another. Tobias kissed him again, slowly and deliberately, nudging his nose against the shell of Emmett's ear.

"Yes?" Tobias kissed again in case the answer was no.

"Yes."

With one word—igniting the desire that Tobias had been fighting all day, that had twisted tighter and tighter as they danced in the bar and the sounds of their glory days seeped into his veins—everything shifted. Charged.

He surged forward and folded Emmett into his arms.

Emmett melted into the embrace and pulled Tobias's arm around to guide his hand up his shirt. They moved together, undulating slowly, with no purpose other than finding a rhythm. No matter how aloof Emmett might have seemed earlier, Tobias could no longer believe that their seductive dance was simply "something he did."

Tobias rid Emmett of his shirt and then took off his own, taking Emmett in his arms again, his front to Emmett's back, the rolling motion of their bodies barely missing a beat. He slipped his hand down to Emmett's waistband—"Yes?"— and Emmett's deep, raspy moan, "Yes," hit him low in his belly.

The combination of foreign and familiar splintered Tobias's mind. The body in his arms was new: adult, sturdy, thick with muscle and age. The voice uttering moans and sighs of pleasure was deeper, more mature and raw than the soft pleas and moans that rang in his memory. And yet it was all Emmett, the boy who stilled Tobias's heart, the boy who quieted Tobias's scattered mind so the music inside of him could sing.

Tobias took Emmett in hand, thick and iron-hard, to stroke and coax more out of him. He swirled his palm over the head of Emmett's it; his motions were slicked with pre-come.

"Lips… God." Emmett curled his arm around to sink his fingers into Tobias's hair, arching his back as if chasing Tobias's crotch. "Pants. Please."

Tobias smiled against Emmett's shoulder and chuckled, following Emmett's delirious order to remove his pants. Emmett continued to beg, "Mine too… mine too. Want to feel you," and he removed Emmett's as well.

They groaned in unison as their naked bodies landed again, back to front. Emmett pushed back, and Tobias's cock nestled into the crack of Emmett's cheeks. He would have been satisfied with this; feeling Emmett surrender in his arms like this again was a bliss beyond his wildest imagination.

Tobias's cock slipped between Emmett's cheeks and thighs, caught at his hole again and again until Emmett was whimpering. "Please. Toby, just… *please.*"

"Yes?"

"Yes. *Yes.*" Emmett reached around to take Tobias in hand and guide him there to stroke and tease. "Please."

Tobias quickly gathered lube and a condom. Emmett writhed and prepped himself with lubed fingers, tossing salacious, needy looks over his shoulder. Tobias crawled back into bed behind him as before. "Like this? You want me like—"

"Yes. Yes. Love this. Love—" Emmett hitched his leg and arched his back, ready. Begging.

"Fucking hell, Em. Look at you." Tobias ran his hand up and over Emmett's shoulder, down his arm and across his stomach, muscles flexing under his fingers.

Emmett gave in to the pace, but then reached back and pled for Tobias to get on with it. With a slow push, a stop and start and soothing words and grunted guidance, Tobias sunk into Emmett's slick heat. Emmett rested his head back on the pillow and his eyelids fluttered shut as Tobias pulled out and pushed back in again, as though sinking into the heart of Emmett as well.

Again. Still.

Slowly, steadily, Tobias's hands traveled everywhere, then stalled to take in the tight drag of his cock, the warmth of Emmett's body molded against his, fit there as if it belonged. Taking in the lines of Emmett's neck as he stretched to wrap his hand back and bring Tobias in. "Kiss," Emmett breathed. "Your mouth. Want more."

Tobias gave more; he took his time, he made it last, with long deep kisses and long strokes to Emmett's cock that matched his own thrusts— sleepy, lazy, with a peace surrounding them that belied their history of hurt and brokenness.

Emmett's hummed a plea for more, more, more. Tobias's thrusts grew shallow as Emmett's breath quickened. "Yes. Toby… " His eyes stayed wide as Tobias's in their awkward pose until the air cracked with a shout. Emmett jerked, hot and wet over Tobias's hand and up onto his own stomach. He reached back again for a kiss as his ass throbbed around Tobias's dick.

Tobias whimpered with the memory: Emmett always wanted an anchoring kiss before he landed, always begged for Tobias's lips on his skin so they'd never miss a moment. So Tobias would know it was always them—never one over the other.

He hiked Emmett's leg a bit more, his orgasm coiling within. He heard Emmett call his name, "Toby," as if in wonder that it *was* them. That it was Tobias. That things could be, if just for one night, as they once were.

Tobias buried his face in Emmett's neck with a deep groan as his orgasm crashed through him. The scent of sandalwood and cardamom was faint on Emmett's skin. He held on tight, slowing, stilling, curling his body around Emmett's as they had been. Their legs intertwined, and Tobias rested comfortably against Emmett, spent and sweaty, so blissed the idea of cleanup seemed a chore, and sleep was the only resolution.

"Emmett… "

"Oh God."

Emmett's voice was shattered and shaky. He let go of Tobias's hand that he'd grasped and clung to, as if suddenly realizing he had been hanging on.

Tobias pressed a kiss to Emmett's shoulder and rolled out of bed. "I'll be right back."

He cleaned. Emmett cleaned, and when Tobias returned from putting the wet cloth back in the bathroom, Emmett was still gloriously naked, on his stomach and fast asleep.

Tobias couldn't name what he was feeling as he tucked himself under the sheets and nestled himself hip to hip with Emmett's warmth, but it stretched beyond the scope of satisfied, or satiated.

He feared he could get used to it.

◆◆◆

WHEN HE AWAKENED, TOBIAS WAS surprised to find Emmett already nursing a cup of coffee. His hair was sleep-mussed, and he had dressed again. As on the night before, the neckline of his shirt draped over his shoulder. His eyes were dark with morning and a slight hangover.

"Where did you get this coffee?" Emmett asked. "I'm going to steal it."

"Only if I can steal your hat." Tobias hopped into his lounge pants and poured himself a cup. "And, I bring it back from Seattle." He opened his freezer: half was filled with bags of coffee, the other half with frozen dinners.

Emmett shook his head and stood to rinse his mug. He had yet to look at Tobias. "I think I'm going to head out a little earlier than I planned."

"We'd talked about going out for brunch… you going before that?"

"Yeah, I think so." Emmett stayed at the sink and quickly washed the few items there. "I overdid things yesterday. I'm going to have to take my time at the airport."

Tobias stood to help, but Emmett shook his head and kept working. "I've got it."

"What's going on?"

Emmett didn't turn around. The walls of Tobias's tiny apartment closed in.

"I don't know what you wanted from this trip, Toby." When Emmett finally turned, his eyes were dark, not with a hangover, but with worry, sadness and maybe a flash of anger.

"I wanted to spend time with you."

"Okay," Emmett said, drying his hands. "But see, now I'm going home. *Home,* Toby." He tossed the towel onto the counter and pulled his bag out of the closet. "I'm not leaving New York for my next job, to turn around and come back like you do."

"I understand that. I never thought—"

"I'm going home. Where I live and work and exist on a day to day basis."

Tobias tried to respond again, but he wasn't sure Emmett was listening. The act of packing had taken over. He stomped into the bathroom and back to the couch's side tables where he had kept his glasses and pocket items. He angrily unzipped pockets and shoved various articles of clothing from one divider to the next.

"Emmett, what is going on?"

Emmett didn't answer. He pulled the pillows from the sofa bed, removed their cases and tossed them back onto the bed.

Tobias hadn't asked for any promises. He was pretty sure he hadn't made any. He might have wished for some, but he couldn't figure out why Emmett was so agitated. Unless, maybe in his drunken haze, he'd misread Emmett's desires.

Tobias got up and tossed his coffee in the sink. "Emmett, I gave you every opportunity to stop what happened last night."

Emmett yanked the sheets and blankets from the mattress. "That's the problem, Toby. I didn't want to stop." He continued stripping the bed.

Tobias desperately needed him to at least slow down so they could talk and not throw out angry words they'd both regret.

But Emmett kept talking. "And now I'm fucked in the head again because of you. Because of how I feel in your arms."

Emmett's voice broke, and Tobias went to him, but he took a step back and shook his head.

"It's all back and you're not," Emmett said. "You're not back. You're still here living the exact life you always dreamed—*we* always dreamed. And I'm leaving to live my life somewhere else."

"There's no reason we can't—"

"It's a good life, Toby. I'm not giving up how far I've come to have you roll over on top of me and fuck it up again."

"Is that how you saw that? That I rolled over to blow my load?"

Emmett closed his eyes, and Tobias waited, waited for his attempt at composure to break against whatever horrible thing blazed through his mind. "I'm going to get in the shower. And then I'm going home."

"No."

"No?"

"We're not done yet."

"Toby, don't be an ass. I need to get moving." Emmett dug into his bag again and pulled out clothes to wear.

"I am not going to be held responsible for your discomfort. You wanted something when you called me. I didn't care what it was; I was so fucking happy to hear from you again. But you wanted something to make that call."

Emmett tossed his clothes into the bathroom, but he didn't go in. He didn't close the door.

"You kissed me back like you wanted something," Tobias continued. "You laughed and played and smiled like you *wanted* something. You rolled back into me last night like you wanted something."

"I wanted to—to close the door. We had so much and then it was gone, and I felt—after all this time, it felt unfinished."

"Is that why you're pushing me away again? Do you want to be finished with me?"

"Obviously not." Emmett leaned against the doorframe to the bathroom and wiped his face with his hands, more confusion in his eyes than before. "You're *everywhere*, and I don't know what to do."

Before Tobias could say another word, Emmett stepped into the bathroom and closed the door.

8

MORNINGSIDE—January 2016

When Emmett had emerged from the shower, Toby was gone. He had, however, left a note this time.

> *Emmett:*
>
> *Got called to an unexpected meeting. Let me know when you get home. Talk soon.*
>
> ~~*Tobias*~~ *Toby xoxo*

The fact Toby had actually corrected his name should have made Emmett laugh. Except he sort of wanted to punch a hole in the wall, signed: *Emmett xoxo.*

He didn't let Toby know when he arrived home, and Toby never asked after him. School started, and, within a few weeks, Emmett was deep into competition season: solo and ensemble contests, various and sundry exhibitions and performances throughout the state.

His life was back on track, as it had been. Without Toby.

Except it wasn't. And that? *That* was worse than another one of Toby's infamous departures.

Oh sure, Emmett's life *was* on track. His students were succeeding. His principal continued to be happy with the invigorated program, the growing numbers and the attention that the success brought to his school. Emmett had been invited to speak on the use of technology in the choral classroom for the state music educators' conference. Things were fine. Excellent even.

Except that Emmett hadn't been exaggerating: Toby *was* everywhere.

There was not another man alive who could make Emmett hop on a plane for a visit. With each press of his lips, with each caress, with each imploring whisper, Toby had cracked Emmett open and laid him bare.

"Yes?"

"Yes."

Emmett couldn't shower without remembering Toby's tiny bathroom, and how he would sneak in to wipe down the mirror for Emmett. He couldn't tie his tie in the morning without feeling Toby tug on it to pull him close when they danced on his last night in New York. He hadn't worn his fedora since he got home. He hadn't worn the newsboy hat Toby bought him either.

Toby reminded Emmett how it felt to crave again. Not want. Not need. *Crave.* Cell by cell, kiss by kiss, Toby had awakened Emmett to the intimacy he had stopped longing for the day he realized Toby was never coming back.

It was absurd. He hadn't the time for that sort of emotional bondage. And most definitely not with a man who actually had to look at his phone to remember his own address.

Emmett needed a diversion. Someone to tear him apart without cracking him open. He could put himself back together afterward with a hot shower and glass of wine. Which is how he found himself in Gino's classroom, strapping on an apron and collecting miniscule flecks of clay from worktables. He and Gino worked together in silence until Gino tied up the last bag of potters' clay and smacked Emmett's ass on the way to the cabinet. "Where are we going?"

"My place is fine," Emmett said. "You hungry?"

Gino tossed a smile back. Hungry indeed. No pretense here. Gino knew what Emmett wanted and was happy to oblige: quick and dirty, hot and mind-numbingly good sex. No post-coital snuggles. No "what are we now" conversations.

Emmett left first and got lost in his playlist as he worked his way through afternoon traffic. Lenny Kravitz cycled around, haunting him with too many memories of his last night with Toby. He turned the music off and drove in silence. And in the silence all he could hear was his former therapist chastising him for his penchant to use sex to drown out the ugliness of life.

"You need to find some closure to this relationship. To your loss of Scotty."

Emmett hated the word, the concept of it, the idea that with one simple act every wrong thing, every loss, every inexplicable shift in life would suddenly be behind him. Grief time was over. Hurt time was over. Time to get up and forget anything had ever happened.

She never had any valid recommendations for how to achieve this elusive "closure" outside of visiting Scotty's grave or writing a goodbye letter to Toby that he would never send. So, while he pulled himself together professionally and behaved like a reasonable adult around alcohol, serving his libido remained a healing balm.

He let his garage swallow both his car and his therapist's nagging voice and pushed himself to the task at hand. Upstairs, he hung up his waistcoat and slipped off his tie. Within minutes Gino's keys clanged on the kitchen island and his shoes clattered onto the foyer's tile floor.

And like every time, Gino called up to him. "Honey, I'm home!"

The asshole.

Gino landed on the top step and stood at the threshold to Emmett's room as Emmett tossed his tie onto his valet. Gino's eyes were almost black with lust; his strides were long and intentional as he unbuttoned his shirt and walked in.

They met in a frenzied kiss. It could have been rote if Gino wasn't so good at diving in, cutting to the chase, making this about unrepentant satisfaction. Gino's hands fumbled with Emmett's belt as he mouthed down Emmett's jaw and latched onto the soft skin under his ear.

Emmett sucked in a breath, and Gino seemed to take it as encouragement. He pulled and grasped at Emmett's shirt, and Emmett slammed his eyes closed. All he could see were blond curls, blue eyes and long, expressive fingers on black and white keys.

"Gonna be so good," Gino mumbled against Emmett's skin. "I've missed you."

Gino's words ghosted in Emmett's ear, deep and resonant and… *wrong.* "No, wait." Emmett stopped Gino with a firm grip on his wrists. He felt paralyzed… foul, as if he was breaking a promise he'd never made.

"What? What'd I do?" Gino stepped forward again and tried to cup Emmett's jaw, but Emmett held him firmly away.

"N—nothing. You didn't do—" He swallowed, his mouth so dry he almost choked. Gino's shirt was twisted and unbuttoned down to his navel; his lips were ripe and raw. "I need you to leave."

"What? What the fuck, Em. You can't just—" Gino pointed to his crotch, pants tented as if all Emmett owed him was some relief.

"Yeah, I'm—I'm sorry. " Emmett let go of Gino's wrists and, in a fog, headed toward his bathroom. "Show yourself out." He shut the door, walked in a circle in the dark room and opened it again. "I'm really sorry. Please go." He slammed the door closed and braced himself on the counter. His breath came in fits and spurts.

He could hear Gino gather his belongings to leave, and then, "Don't expect me to be on call for you if this is the game you're playing, asshole."

Emmett didn't respond. He reached up to his neck and rubbed the skin under his ear, and trailed down his chest with the memory of Toby's hands on him only weeks before.

He started the hot water for a shower and, after standing under its heat until it chilled, he poured himself a glass of wine and reminded himself that this wasn't the first time images of Toby had interrupted an otherwise satisfying encounter. He just needed some time. Some space.

He was fine before. He was going to be fine now.

◆◆◆

EMMETT THREW HIMSELF BACK INTO his work. Solo and ensemble contests were a success. The students worked hard and earned quite a few medals, as well as the respect of those from other schools who were told by their own directors, "Go check out anyone from Morningside. Learn from them."

Emmett had found a rhythm again, a balance of work and play during this busiest season of the school year. Granted, it had cost him an entire night's worth of drinks in apology for the blue balls, but he was fine.

Two weeks had passed since the encounter with Gino. Emmett sat alone in the choir room, going over the recording of the latest bass sectional's rehearsal. Headphones covered his ears as he jotted notes into his score of "Die Nacht," a competition number by Franz Schubert he'd selected for his men's ensemble. It was the first song this group had done in German, and while it was hymnodic, it wasn't coming very easily to them.

He sang the boys' part, over-enunciating as if to help their recorded voices get it right. "*Wie schön bist du.* Oooh, oooh, boys." His phone vibrated loudly against the metal music stand, and he mindlessly grabbed it, still singing along with his students. "Lift those palates now. Oooh."

TOBY: A new city, a new theater; I miss you.

Attached was a photograph taken from the stage floor, looking up into light riggings whose red and yellow beams flared into the shot.

Fuck.

He turned off the recording and stared at the picture again.

"Language, Mr. Henderson. Do we need to have a discussion with the principal?"

Emmett tossed his headphones onto the music stand with his phone. "You a mind reader now?" He smacked Mac's hand as she started sniffing through the music he'd been studying.

"I *am* a mind reader, but this time your mind was audible, love. And," she continued as she grabbed the piece of music in front of him, "I'm the head of this department. Someone has to keep an eye on you."

"Hmmm. Where have you been, anyway? I was beginning to think you'd quit to join the circus or something."

"It's contest season. This is the circus." Mac pulled up a chair and spun it around to straddle and scrutinize. She never straddled without scrutiny. "What's up?"

"Nothing," Emmett sighed. "Tired." Mac shot a look at the cell phone still alight with Toby's name. "He misses me."

She narrowed her eyes and looked back at Emmett again. "You've been off since you got back."

"I'm fine."

"You've been off." She lifted a finger as if to say something, stopped herself and picked up the phone to shake at him as if it was to blame for everything that had made him "off." "You slept with him."

"I don't see how that is any of your business."

"It isn't."

He didn't feel judgment from her, which was oddly unsettling. She judged. Hard. She was invested in him. She had put herself on the line to get him this job when he was at the lowest point in his life. And, tough act or not, he knew she loved him and only wanted the best for him. Her silence, her waiting for him to come out with it said as much.

"I slept with him. It didn't mean anything. I'm fine."

"If it didn't mean anything, you wouldn't have dropped a hefty f-bomb in the middle of your planning period when any number of students could have been around to hear you."

Emmett tossed his pencil onto the music stand and sat back in his chair. "You were right. I shouldn't have gone back. We had the perfect goodbye, and now it's all… " Emmett flapped his hands around. Words were inadequate.

Mac put the sheet music back on the stand and tapped at the bass line. "What do you do when the guys can't get their part?"

"Some days I yell a lot."

"You yell a lot when they act like jackasses."

And sometimes, when they acted like jackasses, he sat down and waited for them to realize that the entire room was watching them. It was surprisingly effective; boys who wanted to get laid didn't enjoy girls looking at them as if they were jackasses.

"When you go over and over a part and no one's grasping it," Mac continued. "When the rhythm won't become their heartbeat and the melodic line won't seep into their soul. Work with me, Emmett. What do you do?"

"I go back to what we know. We reacquaint ourselves with the song."

Mac smiled and smacked her thighs before standing up. "Maybe. Just maybe—" She draped the headphones back over Emmett's neck and looked him square in the eye. "You should work on what you already know."

And what Emmett knew—what he could no longer avoid—was that he missed Toby too. He had never stopped.

◆◆◆

EMMETT DIDN'T WRITE A REPLY to Toby's text for two days, and it was three before he actually considered sending the reply he'd typed.

EMMETT: Maybe if you'd have waited for me, we could have—

He couldn't finish the sentence. After letting it stew for a day, he deleted and typed again: I miss you too and I'm pretty fucking angry about it.

The bell for his last class rang. He hit send before reconsidering again. Toby's response came that evening as Emmett slipped into bed.

TOBY: Come see me.

Emmett yanked off his blankets and got out of bed like a shot. He dialed Toby's number and poured himself a glass of whiskey.

"I'm in Houston for six weeks," Toby answered as if he had been sitting there waiting for Emmett to call.

"I have a *job*, Toby."

"So do I. It's in Houston. *Camelot.*"

"You fucking walked out. Again."

"I—" Toby sighed and Emmett could hear ice tinkling in a glass.

"What are you drinking?" Emmett didn't know why he cared, why he wanted an image to go with the call, because he already had one: Toby had arrived home after his show. His hair was orchestra conductor-messy—as if it hadn't been combed in a week. His nose was still red from the cold, and he probably had his shirtsleeves unbuttoned and rolled. The left sleeve was lower than the right, because his drink was in his right hand, keeping it pinned in the bend of his elbow.

He looked amazing, and it was only Emmett's memory from his first night in New York, a permanent imprint to add to the old and yellowed memories of their younger days.

"Old Fashioned. And I'm sorry. I didn't know what to say to make it right again."

"Because walking out worked so well the last time. Jesus, Toby." Emmett took a drink, grimaced and dumped the rest of his whiskey down the sink. "I need bitters."

"You need to meet me in Houston."

"It's the middle of competition season. I have two conventions to speak at. My seniors are auditioning for colleges." *I have no resources left to fall for you over and over again.*

"Boston then. *As You Like It.*"

"I can do Boston as I like it? Or is Shakespeare offering me a date?"

"I miss you." The ice in Toby's glass rattled again and Emmett opened his laptop. "Look, I'm trying here. I don't date. I barely have friends—"

"Oh, stop it. I saw you with your cast after your show. Those people love you."

"Yes. Yes, they do. But I don't know them. Once we wrap, I'll only see them again if we work on another show."

Emmett stared at his calendar and, as suspected, found a swath of blank space in April. "What am I supposed to say to this, Toby? Are you asking me to be your traveling fuck buddy?"

"What? Fucking *hell*, Emmett."

"I'm not sure what you're asking. I'm tired. I'm stressed. I'm working sixty hours a week right now and my mother has to have some procedure... thing." Emmett pinched the bridge of his nose. "Second week in April."

"I do not want my life to go on the way it has been. I'm sick of bouncing from city to—what?" Emmett heard Toby rummage around, mumble for him to hang on and then: "That's my last week in Boston."

"So it's Shakespeare then."

"Men are April when they woo, December when they wed."

"Love is merely a madness." And while this wasn't love, it was most definitely madness. "Since when is *As You Like It* a musical, anyway?"

"Since some dude made it one a few years back in L.A."

"Toby, if I come, we're going to talk. We're going to label this. I'm not going to—"

"Yes, yes. We'll use a fucking script. Whatever you want," Toby agreed. "You'll send me the dates?"

"I haven't agreed to anything yet, but I'll send you the dates."

"Sounds to me like you just agreed."

Toby's smile was clear in his voice. And, while Emmett wanted to deny it, he was smiling too. "I miss you too, Toby."

"We'll be fine. Call me for something stupid again, okay?"

"This wasn't stupid enough for you?"

"No. This was genius."

It felt stupid. Which is why Emmett started looking up flights instead of going to bed.

9

NEW YORK CITY—March 2016

Tobias learned at a very young age to pack light and carry only necessities. It's how he lived his life: he didn't bring home souvenirs from different locations, and other than Malik, he didn't maintain long-term friendships.

His carry-on was always packed with a good set of headphones and an outfit for one extra day in case his luggage ended up in Boise instead of Boston. He had a small bag for all of his necessary electronic paraphernalia, he kept money in various places and he always had an umbrella.

On a quick pit stop in New York between Houston and Boston, however, Tobias stopped into his office to add something new. Actually, it was something old. He had been carrying around his manuscript notebook ever since he unearthed it those few months before and he had played around and jotted down new notes, but not much was being formed from his efforts.

Then he remembered the box of musical scraps he had kept over the years: It was filled with slips of hotel paper covered in hand-drawn staves and jotted notes, floppy disks and CDs of poorly recorded efforts of different voicings and attempted orchestrations and diner napkins with notes like, "add cello for depth in the second movement," and "remember how his mother used to sound like an out of tune oboe when she got angry?"

The piece he was looking for didn't have a first movement, much less a second. It wasn't even a "piece." It had no structure beyond the melody that wafted through Tobias's head whenever he least wanted it to.

He pulled out a CD labeled "2011," shoved it into his computer and chose the third track. Sharp staccato notes with a heavy bass filled the room, an angry passage if there ever was one. He switched to a new track. The voicing was less strident—mellow strings first, then a more rounded piano setting. It worked, and then it didn't. Nothing resolved. The anger in the earlier track now seemed comical—as if it was the soundtrack to a children's cartoon and not the deep longing of his heart.

After Tobias invited Emmett to Boston, they had begun to talk more frequently. They shared ridiculous stories about their lives, about their families. About how, in Houston, Camelot's Lancelot had made to draw his sword at an audience member whose cell phone went off during "If Ever I Would Leave You." About Emmett's mother's minor procedure blowing up into such a huge fiasco that he had to cover for his sister and care for his niece and nephew for a weekend—a task Tobias would have paid admission to see. Emmett's distaste for young children was not a secret.

They played during those calls, enjoying a sort of suspension and tension as the stories unfolded, and then a peaceful resolution as laughter dissolved into the regretful admission: "I should probably go." It was easy. Light. Friendly and flirtatious. And it made Tobias want to keep the feeling near, keep Emmett near.

Now, Tobias skipped to a new track and waved at Malik as he peeked in on his way out for the day. "New show?"

"Nah. Futzing around." Tobias ejected the CD and slipped it into its paper sleeve. "I've gotta get moving, though. My flight's before dawn tomorrow."

"Let me know if you want me to come out. I need to get out of the city for a bit, man. I'm suffocating."

"Can you hold off 'til May? I'll be in San Francisco."

Malik smiled and hiked his coat onto his shoulders. "Emmett's coming out, isn't he?"

"For a bit, yeah." When Malik nodded and smirked as if he had it all figured out, Tobias reminded him, "I haven't seen him since Christmas. It's a visit."

"Uh-huh. You don't hear from this dude for fifteen years and now he's a quarterly booty call." He pointed at Tobias's old, beat up box of junk. "You got a song in there for that? 'Old and Gray; He's Still My Bae.'"

"Get the fuck out of here. I knew I should never have told you anything."

"Look, if I wasn't taken… " Malik thrust his hips up with a grunt. And another.

"But you are. Besides, your multiracial, multisexual self would break his mother's delicate constitution."

"All the more reason." Across the room, Tobias's phone buzzed in his coat pocket. Malik grabbed it for him and grinned. "Booty booty, rich and fruity."

"Give me—also, he's not gray." Tobias answered and tried to shoo Malik out of his office. "Hey! I wasn't expecting to hear from you tonight."

"Bootay, bootay!"

"Yeah, I know," Emmett sighed. "I've been thinking about this trip—what the hell is that?"

"Malik. Ignore him. He's leaving."

"Bye, Malik. Tell me that gorgeous man at least has a pimple or something."

"He has a boil the size of Indianapolis on his left oblique," Tobias said, staring straight at Malik. "Makes him look like he has a second, less attractive package."

"Hey!" Malik cupped himself and flipped Tobias off.

"And you're familiar with his more attractive package, I take it?"

"Racquetball. Packages happen," Tobias said. "Why? Are you jealous?" Tobias waved as Malik finally took his leave, wiggling and pointing to his ass as he went.

"As a matter of fact… " Emmett laughed and Tobias could hear his office chair creak as he leaned back into it. The stress in his voice disappeared. "Although I'm more of a yoga man."

"Mmm, bulges *and* bendy bodies." Tobias shoved the CD into his bag. "So, I'm assuming you didn't call to drool over Malik in my ear."

"No. I did not. It's about coming out to see you. I'm not—" Emmett stopped short. "Hang on a sec." He called to someone else, "Come in."

Tobias could hear snatches of a young woman's voice. She sounded a little uptight, concerned maybe. Emmett's voice was deep and comforting, yet firm. And then, "Toby, I'm sorry. Can I call you back?"

"I'm actually taking off—"

"Wait! Toby?" the girl's voice asked. "Is that Mr. Spence?"

"Yes. Yes, it is." Emmett sounded exhausted.

"Hey, Em. Let me call you back." Emmett couldn't hear him over the excited young lady begging, saying something that sounded an awful lot like, "Let me talk to him for a minute!"

"Toby, I need all my brain cells to wrangle someone—"

"Hey!"

"Can you call me before your flight?" Emmett asked.

"Who is it? Em? Is that, um… Tori?"

"Y—yeah. It's Tori." Tori squealed. "Who is officially one step away from a week's worth of detention."

"Let me talk to her."

"Toby. We've been over this."

"I'm here. She's there. Let me see what she—do you know what she wants?"

"Elphaba," Emmett said on a sigh.

"Well, that's not happening." Tobias laughed and overheard her correct Emmett; she preferred Glinda. "That's not happening either. Put her on."

"No."

"Mr. Spence," Tori interrupted in the background, her voice still crystal clear. "I just wondered, um… if you've listened to my demo yet."

"Tell her I haven't. Not sure when I will, either."

Emmett must have simply shaken his head because the next thing he heard was a very disappointed girl. "Oh. Okay, yeah. Well. I, uh… " There was a shuffling of papers and a moment of silence.

"Sorry. For all of that. She came in to give me applications for the state fair choir."

"I've told you I don't mind."

"I know you don't. I don't want you to think that I planned this—"

"Emmett. Really? Why would I think you got in touch with me to benefit a student?"

"Because it happened at the same time? Because… " Emmett sighed. "I have no idea."

"Okay. You called me? What's up?"

Emmett chuckled. "Never mind. It wasn't important."

Tobias waited a moment. Emmett didn't offer anything else. "Okay. I'll see you in a few weeks?"

"Yes. And I apologize for her interruption again. She has patience issues."

Tobias laughed—like teacher, like student. "If she gets itchy again, let me know. I really do plan on listening."

"Do not feel obligated."

"I'll see you soon, Em."

◆◆◆

BOSTON—April 2016

"All right, sweetheart. Go home and rest that voice." Tobias scrubbed his face with his hands and started scanning his mind for a name. A female name. A qualified, available, female name attached to someone who might possibly owe him a huge favor.

"That is not the face of someone who is having a good day."

Tobias looked up and grinned. "I think my day just turned around." He hopped off the stage to greet Emmett and shed the last few hours from his mind. "You look amazing, as usual."

"You look tired." Emmett kissed his cheek. He lingered there, hands still in his coat pockets, as if deciding what to do next.

Tobias wasn't sure either, but he knew what he wanted to do. He cupped Emmett's cheek and kissed him, a soft, slow press of his lips to Emmett's. "I am tired. My Rosalind is ill."

"Oh, that's not good. No understudy?"

"She *is* the understudy," Tobias said. "I think I get to call my lead and see if she is well enough to disobey doctor's orders."

"Pity I don't have the right cheekbones. This could be my lucky break." Emmett took off his hat and preened. "Do you need to make some calls?"

"No, I'm going to pass this to the director. He knew I had plans."

"I can wait, Toby."

Tobias stepped in and kissed Emmett again. "I can't."

Tobias took Emmett to a little Italian place in the North End. It was decorated in warm-toned wood, with high-backed booths and a second-rate mural of a Tuscany hillside on the back wall. The rumble of the small crowd was accompanied by piped-in Sicilian serenades. It was cheesy and cozy and perfectly intimate.

"Is this okay?" Tobias asked.

"Yes." A swell of violin filled their corner space and Emmett grinned up at the phantom speakers. "Although if Dean Martin starts crooning 'That's Amore,' I might change my answer."

"I think they save that for dessert."

Later, as if on queue, the waitress delivered their tiramisu and Dean Martin revved up. "You know," Emmett said, while spinning the plate to find, Tobias assumed, the perfect corner to eat, "you almost have to give it to him. Having the gonads to compare romantic love to a plate of pasta is pretty—"

"It's romantic."

"You're ridiculous. As is this song." Emmett took a bite of the dessert and moaned. "I have no further complaints."

Tobias laughed and dug into his pocket. He pulled out a panda-shaped flash drive and set it on the table next to the plate. He said nothing before taking a bite of cake.

Emmett spied the drive, lifted an eyebrow, forked a bite and dangled it in the air before eating. "That's Tori's panda."

"That is Tori's panda. I listened to it the other day."

Emmett put down his fork. "And?"

"Who did the recording?"

"I did, why? Is it poor quality?"

"Did you rent space at the college in Ridgewood?"

"No? We used a practice room."

Tobias nodded and handed Emmett's fork back to him. "Without timpani."

"Without—" Emmett grinned and ate. "What's your point?"

"I have two points, actually. One, I have never heard a demo tape of that high caliber before… "

"Never?"

"Well, not often. I want the story behind that."

"I tinker." Emmett winked, and, from two words, Tobias thought he understood completely. "Your second point?"

"She needs to change her songs. And go to college."

"I told her 'Out Tonight' was a bad choice."

"Why do you think it's a bad choice?"

"Because it's inappropriate for her age. Because it doesn't showcase her strengths, just her dreams of being a bad girl—"

"Is that why she was on her back on a timpani?"

"That—yes. Probably. She's working on it. But you still have a poker face. Why else shouldn't she have—" Emmett stopped and laughed. "You hate *Rent*. How could I forget?"

"I do not hate *Rent*!" Tobias broke into an embarrassed grin. He sort of hated *Rent*. "I will die a much happier man if I never hear anything from it again."

"You hate *Rent*. You used to mercilessly mock me if I ever had the CD in my car."

"I did not." He did. He hated *Rent* 525,600 ways to Sunday. Get a fucking job and make your stupid art after work the way every other starving artist has had to at one time or another. "And you're right. It doesn't fit her voice. She's good. She will never be Mimi."

"And 'Little Town'? I thought that fit her voice much better."

"It does. She could be a convincing Belle. And maybe paired with something else I'd have been more open to it. But, it's a song little girls have been singing since they could put words together. Show me something that's not from her preschool days."

"Ouch. That song's not easy."

"Nope. Just too familiar to her," Tobias said.

"So, what do you recommend?"

"I dunno—'Glitter and Be Gay,' maybe."

Emmett's face contorted into fifteen different expressions, none of them positive. "That's so overdone."

"It is, but she will have to work *hard* for it, and that counts." It was a beast of a song for a soprano, unattainable for most girls Tori's age.

Only the best, the most trained and disciplined girls should even dare to attempt it. But Tobias could hear that she just might have it in her.

"So, no 'Let it Go' then, either." Emmett shoved a huge bite of tiramisu into his mouth and grinned around it. "She could bring a little pretend Olaf as a prop. I'll dress up as the stupid reindeer."

Tobias hated *Frozen* more than he hated *Rent*. That Emmett correctly assumed as much was almost unsettling. "I should put you on a plane back to Indiana for that."

"Hey, don't knock it; a big Disney musical? That would be a hell of a gig if they called you for it."

"Pfft, Disney musicals. Done with 'em." Tobias put down his fork. "Write something new. Also... " The truth was, once he might have jumped at the chance to direct the music for something that potentially successful. But now... "They're monstrous. They take *years*."

"I would think a multi-year commitment would be a bit of a relief from all the running around you do."

"I like running. I don't want to be tied down."

"I thought I heard you say you're getting kind of tired of the race." Emmett wasn't supposed to have had heard that. They were words said in haste. They also had not been a lie. "Or are you no longer talking about a professional sort of commitment?"

"I enjoy my freedom, yes. And I'm still speaking professionally." Tobias pointed to the last bite of their dessert before stabbing it for himself, buying himself a bit of time. "It's more that I'm not interested in working for a money machine that'll make me creatively impotent."

"So," Emmett started, wiping chocolate from the plate with his finger, "This is coming from ignorance, not judgment, okay? Don't you sometimes feel creatively impotent doing other people's music all the time?"

"Do you?"

"No. I always worked from pre-existing music, so... "

"No, but you performed it. Now you're just the monkey up front, as you say."

"Yes, but it's still up to me to mold the music into what I want it to be, so no. I don't feel stifled."

"Fair enough. And I still compose… in a way. I write the vocal arrangements, I improv at readings and workshops. I get to flex my creative muscle now and then." He thought about his box of musical scraps at home, his disc in his work bag, and grabbed the bottle of wine to refill Emmett's glass before he confessed something he wasn't ready to reveal. "What's your point?"

"I'm not sure I have one," Emmett said. "When we were young, you were always shooting for the stars. It's sort of strange hearing you so opposed to the biggest and best now."

"Ah. Well. Haven't you heard?" Tobias lifted his wine glass and took a gulp. "Stars burn out. And then you're left with nothing to hang onto."

Tobias held Emmett's gaze. The sadness of the truth in what he said rested between them until Tobias couldn't take it anymore. He took hold of Emmett's hand, present, warm and full of life—not burned out in the least.

Emmett smiled, then, a sad smile that quickly turned professional as he slipped his hand out of Tobias's grasp. "So. Is that why you're telling Tori to go to college first? Because you don't want her to get hurt?"

"I'm telling Tori to go to college first because… " Tobias stopped and considered. "Yes. I suppose I am. You and I both know that going to school will prepare her for her dreams, not keep her from them. It's tougher out there now than it was when we were starting out. Showing up at a theater's doorstep with two hundred bucks and a smile isn't going to get you into the chorus anymore."

"How can you explain that to a seventeen-year-old, though? I sure as shit wasn't hearing it then."

Tobias shrugged. "She's going to hear what she wants. Just like you."

"Hopefully it won't take getting broadsided by a pickup truck for it to sink in."

"No. That would—" Emmett's crass words hit him right in the chest. He plastered on a good-natured smile before blindly grabbing for a credit card to pay for the meal. "Wisdom from a teacher like you would be much preferred."

10

"So, Tori asked if you were my boyfriend," Emmett said as they stood along the waterfront overlooking Boston's inner harbor.

"Mmm. Did she?"

Toby had grown frustratingly silent since they had left the restaurant. Emmett wasn't blind to what could set Toby on edge: mention of The Accident; Emmett's cane clicking on the sidewalk; the casual utterance of Scotty's name, as if they could just call him up for drinks.

Emmett didn't particularly want to have a "Kumbaya" moment about it all either. But if he was going to be in Toby's life, it stood to reason that they should at least stop pretending that everything was as it had been, with less hair and more corrective lenses.

"Toby, what's on your mind?"

"Mmm?" Toby pulled his attention from the Navy Yard across the harbor and finally looked at Emmett. "I'm sorry. I'm preoccupied with the show. I figured I'd have heard about a replacement by now."

Emmett nodded, and Toby caught up to what Emmett had said. "What did you tell Tori?"

"I told her it was none of her business. Which… was the wrong answer because, little did I know, that is how one admits to something nowadays."

"Who knew?"

"So, I had to set her straight," Emmett said.

"You told her no." Toby leaned against the wrought-iron fence and stared back out into the water.

"Of course I told her no. We're not—" But Emmett saw the pain of that answer pinch Toby's brow. "Toby?"

"It's not such a crazy notion."

"What? We haven't seen each other since Christmas. And once before that."

"It's not our first time at that rodeo," Toby said. "We used to go months between visits. There are better ways to communicate now."

"What are you suggesting?" Emmett tugged at Toby's wrist to make him face him. "And just because we have better ways to communicate doesn't meant we communicate better."

"Meaning?"

"We lie to each other."

"We do not," Toby argued. "When did we lie?"

"Oh I don't know, the *last* time we saw each other?"

"Oh. Yeah." Toby took Emmett's hand and started walking. "There was no meeting."

"I'm aware." At the weight of Toby's hand in his, the fingers that fit so perfectly against his as they always had, Emmett followed without question. And that was the entire problem. This was asinine. "You lied to me not five minutes ago."

Toby stopped in his tracks, looked at Emmett and opened his mouth with what seemed like a ready explanation. One Emmett was not interested in. "Right. Although I really am concerned about tomorrow's show."

"That isn't why you've clammed up."

Toby didn't offer another explanation. He kept walking. They were outside of the park, and, while the evening was beautiful, it was beginning to chill… just like the conversation. "I upset you in the restaurant," Emmett said.

"Yes." Toby sighed and stopped walking. "I don't want to do this in public," he said. "Do you want to get a cab? Or I think the T is another ten-minute walk?"

"Cab's fine."

Emmett wasn't sure why he did what he did next, but the desire was so overwhelming, it took very little effort to tamp down any doubt as to its wisdom. As Toby lifted his hand to hail a cab, Emmett took his face in his hands and kissed him.

Toby grasped Emmett's wrists to balance himself. He laughed as he kissed back, pressing soft, searching pecks to Emmett's lips and turning his face to let Emmett do the same on his cheeks and temple. And that's where Emmett stayed. His fingers scratched through the hair on the back of Toby's head. His lips lingered, and he breathed Toby in for a few moments more.

"What was that for?" Toby asked.

"Your kisses used to remind me that everything would be okay," Emmett said, convincing himself as he spoke. "I needed a reminder."

"I'M STILL A LITTLE COLD. Do you want some tea?"

"Sure," Emmett said. He pulled out the tin of shortbread cookies they had picked up earlier in the evening. "Not quite crumpets, but—"

"Not quite afternoon, either."

Toby's temporary residence in Boston was much larger than his home in New York. It wasn't decorated in any way that said "Toby," which Emmett found oddly unsettling. He was instantly at home in Toby's flat, but here, where the furniture and design read more like feminine colonial, he felt like an interloper. "I'm afraid to sit on the couch."

"Sit on the couch. Put your muddy feet on it if you want. The cleaning lady is annoying as hell."

"Well, I would be too if I had to clean this upholstery." Emmett swiped his hand over the garish floral print and scrunched his nose. "Although I'm not sure how the hell you could *see* mud on it."

"You like your tea sweet too, right?"

Toby dug for matching saucers and heated the water in a kettle rather than zapping the mugs in the microwave. Finally, he brought in a tray with the mugs of steeping tea, a carafe of milk and a silver dish of sugar.

Emmett laughed at the absurdity of the ceremony. "Should I put on an ascot?"

"I figure if I have to use the ugly china in this kitchen, I might as well go all the way."

"You're evading," Emmett said.

"Partially," Toby admitted as he set the tray on the coffee table. "A wise person told me not too long ago that if the past comes back to visit you, you should invite it to tea." He handed Emmett a mug and the dish of sugar. "So, tea."

Toby continued to fidget after he sat down: He ate a cookie in silence, took a few slurps of tea, readjusted the sugar and cream. One false start and then another.

Emmett stirred his tea and waited.

"Here's the thing, Em," Toby took a deep breath and put his cup back on the coffee table. "I still can't talk about it… the accident. I still freeze." Toby groaned and rubbed his neck. "And you seem to make light of it, like it was another *day* to you."

"I—I don't mean to… it's just how I cope." The years hadn't lessened the fact that *everything* changed that day: their dependence on each other, their general outlook on life, on permanence, and on what "the future" meant now that the world spun in a different direction. There was no light to be made of it.

"How can you expect me to make jokes and reminisce about the worst fucking day of my life, Em? Of our lives?"

"I am so sorry," Emmett said, wishing for more meaningful words. "I never meant to be insensitive."

"I know you don't mean to be—"

"But, I honestly didn't think it would still weigh you down like this. You kept going. You never looked back. I assumed you'd shed it all—including me."

"Surprise." Toby suddenly looked as if he hadn't slept in a week. "I'm not sure how you can think that I could walk away from everything. From everything I'd done."

"Toby, that's what you did. You *literally* walked away." And then Toby's last words hit him—*everything I'd done*. Emmett took off his glasses and patted Toby's leg for him to face him. "Is that why you left? Because seeing me was like a gavel falling on your guilt?"

"Largely. And, honestly—" Toby blushed. "You became really fucking difficult."

Difficult wasn't the start of it. Emmett had become bitter and mean, enraged and combative. He was angry with his mother, with Scotty and with the God everyone thanked for saving his life, as if his life was more valuable than Scotty's. And then there was the buried anger at Toby.

"You never seemed to understand that you weren't the only person who lost—" Toby choked on his words and tears pooled in his eyes. "You were so strong, Em. So fucking *angry*, but so strong. I looked up to you—how you got better. You worked so hard, and I never could have done that."

"Yes, you could have." Emmett said as his eyes, too, clouded with tears. "Besides, I couldn't have done it without you."

"Bullshit. You had enough drive and anger to heal fifty people. I knew you'd be okay."

"But I wasn't okay. Don't you understand? I lost *everything*. You were all I had left, and then for you to leave—" Emmett let go of Toby's hands and sat back. "You *left* me there, Toby!"

"I didn't have a choice. I had to *try* to survive, and the only time I thought it might be possible was when I was in New York."

Emmett understood. He didn't like that Toby had felt more capable in New York, but in light of the tears staining Toby's cheeks, the plea for forgiveness in Toby's eyes, he had to understand. "It was all so much bigger than we were, wasn't it?"

"You managed. You picked up the pieces and became this amazing, beautiful man," Toby said. "And I kept running."

"But you survived."

"At a cost." Toby looked up, shame pinching his brow. "It haunts me. At first it was everywhere—Scotty, the accident… you. I'd get busy doing little gigs all over. I'd go out with people, date a little and then… someone I was with would accidentally find that spot—" He looked into Emmett's eyes, the most direct contact he'd offered since they left the restaurant, and put Emmett's hand on his right side.

Emmett ran his hand forward and back along Toby's waist with a slight scratch of his fingernails through the fabric of Toby's shirt. Toby's face softened at his touch. "I know the spot," Emmett said. He knew it intimately. Toby's right side was so sensitive that if Emmett lightly rubbed its curve, no matter where they were, he could wordlessly say, "I want you," or "I can still taste you," or "When we're alone, I'm going to *wreck* you."

Impulsively, he brought Toby's fingers to his own neck, just below his ear, to the spot that shut down his last encounter with Gino. "I hate when men kiss me here."

"Because of me?"

"Silly, isn't it?"

"No," Toby said in a hushed voice. "I missed you. I—" Toby smiled, clearly proud of what he was going to say next. "I even saved a spot for you."

It was absurd. Still, Toby rubbed the tender skin under Emmett's ear with his thumb, smiling confidently—a victor over the spoils.

"So, you're seriously suggesting… " Emmett said, chasing for breath, lost in the hope in Toby's eyes.

"Why not? Why not try again, Em? I mean… it's not like much would change, would it?"

But everything *had* changed. Emmett sat back and focused on a particularly weird floral design on the back of the settee.

"What are you so afraid of?" Toby asked, seemingly no longer afraid himself.

"This. How I feel when I'm with you. That it all comes back like nothing ever happened."

"I thought that was a good thing."

"It would be, except you're still paralyzed by any reminder that that day happened. And it happened. And I'm visible evidence of it, and you dismissing it with silence and quick escapes isn't going to change that."

" I don't *want* to run anymore, Emmett. Especially from you."

"Don't you see? I cannot lose you again," Emmett admitted. "It's—it's easier if I never have you."

A gentle smile spread across Toby's face and lit up his eyes with the slightest mischief. "Seems like it's a little too late for that now, isn't it?"

"Yes. Dammit."

When Toby kissed Emmett, a whimpered moan escaped between them. Toby pressed in again and again, his soft, dry lips caressing Emmett's mouth. "I know we don't have all the answers," Toby whispered, his lips still grazing Emmett's, "but can I please take you to bed now?"

"Yes. Take me to bed."

FROM THE DRAWN-OUT, TENDER KISSES they shared on the couch, to the quiet, blush-filled walk into Toby's bedroom, everything moved differently with Toby than with other men. They took their time. They held hands like two nervous teenagers about to see each other naked for the first time.

"Take off your clothes," Toby said as he sat on the edge of his bed.

A chill ran through Emmett's body.

For years, his sex life had been pared down to one of simple commands, necessary touch, cursory kissing and quick exits.

But here with Toby—his eyes bright and expectant on Emmett's, his hands sliding up and down Emmett's arms as though he were made of fine stone, his thighs spread wide to bracket Emmett's as Emmett stepped between them—that simple command was an invitation to so much more.

Let me see you.

Let me feel you.

Let me know you.

Let me love—

Emmett lifted his shirt off and went straight for his belt.

"No. Wait." Toby took Emmett's hands from his buckle and kissed his fingers. "I changed my mind."

"What?"

Pushing Emmett's hands aside, Toby began undoing Emmett's belt and pants himself. "The last time. It shouldn't have been like that."

"Toby, it was fine. It was—"

"Anonymous, almost." Toby gasped at his own words, as if saying them made it true. Dark now, rimmed with the slightest ring of blue, his eyes shot up as he lowered Emmett's zipper. "Wasn't it?"

And maybe it had been. Maybe that was the only way Emmett would have gone through with it. That was why Emmett had to leave so abruptly; Toby was not another nameless, faceless fuck. He never had been. He never would be.

"Is that what you wanted it to be?" Emmett asked.

"I just wanted you." Toby pressed soft kisses to Emmett's belly, brushing his nose over the coarse hair that trailed down from his navel. He shimmied Emmett's pants down over his hips. "I didn't work out the details."

The soft kisses continued up Emmett's thighs as Emmett stepped out of his pants and scratched his fingers into Toby's hair. His cock bobbed there comically, almost tapping Toby's cheek as he ran his tongue up the line of Emmett's oblique.

With a gasp, Toby stopped, his eyes focused on Emmett's right hip. "Em, oh my God." Toby's fingers brushed Emmett's hip bone, and he smiled as he looked up. "Where—when did you—what is it?"

Emmett chuckled and took a step back. It was odd, how he forgot about the tattoo. The sapphire blue would catch his attention in the mirror now and then, and the top of the three-swirl design occasionally peeked out of his underwear to remind him.

"I've had it a few years. It's—" Emmett blushed. Getting the tattoo wasn't his idea. He had agreed, but it wasn't his thing, the meaning of it. But then, once the design was on his skin—in his skin—the meaning had seeped into him right along with the ink. "It's a faerie symbol… for healing."

Toby traced the tattoo with his fingers, first one swirl and then another, and the third. His touch sent shivers up Emmett's back, sent blood back to his forgotten cock.

When Toby's fingertip brushed the colorless center of the design, Toby stopped. Gasped again. Pulled his hand away as if he'd touched a hot coal. "Your scar."

Emmett nodded and placed Toby's finger back on the permanent mark on his skin—the one made by the screws and fixator that had held his pelvis together until his body could do so on its own. "Over here, too." He took Toby's other hand to his left hip, unadorned with body art, to a raised circle of skin where more screws had brought healing and made permanent marks.

"It's beautiful."

Emmett swept his hand down over the tattoo, took hold of himself and stroked slowly, studying Toby. Toby's eyes never left the tattoo. His touch was reverent; his brow was pinched with worry.

Feeling Toby slip away, back to that horrible day once again, Emmett removed Toby's shirt and nudged him back onto the bed. "You have too many clothes on." His eyes rested firmly on Toby's as he worked Toby's pants off, climbed back onto the bed and straddled Toby's thighs, dotting kisses on his shoulder and into the curve of his neck. "Come back to me, okay?" He reached between them, took Toby's cock in his hand and worked him slowly, feeling him pulse and harden in his hand.

Toby hissed and bucked to meet Emmett's stroke. "Right here, fuck."

"Just us." Emmett lowered himself onto Toby's body, their cocks aligned and catching in a teasing friction. With soft, dry kisses to Toby's jaw, cheeks and mouth, Emmett dug in with one long thrust as his tongue swept into Toby's mouth.

Toby's nails dug into Emmett's back; their hips began a perfect rhythm. "You were right, you know," Emmett said as they moved. "We were always so good together."

11

It would have given Tobias performance anxiety if he thought too much about it—how good they were together, what Emmett might be expecting and wanting now. But as he rolled them over and lay between Emmett's legs, when he felt the adult man beneath him and not the young boy who had been as inexperienced as he was, Tobias took his improvisational skills to heart and lived in the moment. Every moment.

He moved deliberately over Emmett and along his body as they rocked together, and then as he slid down, mapping Emmett with his mouth and hands. He listened to Emmett's body, and to his voice as he relearned the ways to please him. Yes, that spot under his ear was a given, but the tender flesh at the inside of his elbow was new.

Emmett groaned and bucked at a firm grip to his cock, writhed and mewled when Tobias ran his tongue along the thick vein at its underside, and tugged on Tobias's hair when he bobbed over the head of Emmett's cock, collecting pre-come and tasting the silky skin of his frenulum.

Tobias celebrated when this move elicited that sound, when that touch opened Emmett up in a way Tobias had never seen before. *I never knew that would lead to...*

They giggled over a cold drop of lube that landed right in Emmett's navel. Tobias tore open a condom wrapper with his teeth and Emmett insisted on rolling it on for him. That wasn't new; Emmett's desire had always ratcheted up then. "I love you thick in my hand, ready for me."

But now when Emmett looked up through his lashes, torturously rolled the condom on and squeezed him at the base of his cock—unlike those youthful days of desperate urgency—Tobias could hold off. He could take his time sinking into Emmett, watching his body give, feeling his abs flex and coil under his fingers. "You good?"

"So fucking good." Emmett kept up a slow massage of his own cock, reaching under his balls to feel for Tobias. Emmett knew his own body better now. And Tobias intended to catch up. He curled into Emmett, feeling him everywhere in slow shallow thrusts and then sinking in deep.

Emmett clung to him, his breath hot, begging in his ear. "More, more. Fuck, yes." Asked him to sit back. "I want to watch you move," he said, and then slammed his eyes shut when the adjustment brought Tobias's dick right against his prostate, a persistent nudge with each rolling thrust.

"You can't watch with your eyes closed," Tobias teased.

Emmett laughed. His ass clenched tighter with each puffed breath, and Tobias thought he might burst from having missed Emmett, from having missed how good they could really be and from having it back.

Emmett pulled his thighs tightly to his body, hiding the sapphire ink under the bend of his leg, begging with his body. "Toby... please."

Tobias vibrated with the smooth, easy heat around him.

"Come on." Emmett grabbed at Tobias's ass and pulled him in. "Harder. I want to—" He let go and took hold of himself, eyes commanding. "*Fuck* me, Toby."

But this gentle pace was good, tender. Otherwise it all still seemed too fragile, too easily splintered and torn again. The pain of their conversation still bubbled at the surface, ready to bite; the unsteadiness of living in such different places, in coming back from all that had blown their life to dust, seemed dangerous.

Emmett took hold of Tobias's wrists where they curled around Emmett's thighs and pulled him down for a searing kiss, messy and a little demanding. "I can see your brain spinning," he said, the sweet smile curling at his lips made devilish by the need in his eyes.

That need, the desire in the rasp of Emmett's voice, pulled Tobias out of his head to try to listen. "I'm here. Just us."

Emmett kissed Tobias again, held him close by the back of his neck. "This is so good," he moaned. "You are so good." His eyes stayed dark, focused on Tobias's. "But, Toby... I'm not broken anymore." Soft puffs of air escaped between Emmett's parted lips as they moved together. "Please. You're not going to hurt me."

"Of course not." Tobias sat back on his haunches, hiked Emmett up one more time and held onto Emmett's thighs, feeling his firm, strong body under his hands. "I'm not going to hurt you." He sank in deep again with one solid thrust, convincing himself. Testing.

Emmett threw his head back, the moan escaping his lips so deep, so guttural it rumbled through Tobias's bones. Emmett wasn't broken. His strong, beautiful Emmett was whole and wanting beneath him.

Tobias let himself go. He moved steadily. Relentlessly. Trusting in himself, but mostly in Emmett to tell him what he wanted, what he didn't.

Emmett cried out with each stroke. "That's it! Yes!" He twisted in the sheets and wrapped his hand around his own cock, a blur of motion as everything coiled tight around them.

Tobias lost focus in the tight heat of Emmett's ass, the unabashed pleasure dotted all over Emmett's body in sweat and blotched skin, in ripples of muscles and the lines of his neck and jaw as he lifted for kisses and fell back into the pillow.

"Come on, sweetheart, let it go." Tobias's legs burned with effort, and with one long groan, Emmett stilled and then bucked as his orgasm flooded through him. Long ropes of come landed on his chest and belly, and dribbles covered his fingers.

"Fucking hell, Em. So beautiful. So—"

Emmett brought a messy finger to his lips and sucked it clean. He clenched his ass and chuckled when Tobias's eyes rolled to the back of his head and he was unable to speak anymore.

"*Come* on, baby." At Emmett's gravel-voiced bidding, wrapped in his arms, his legs, Tobias toppled over him and drove into him. With his face tucked into Emmett's neck, he came in a uncoiling rush. Their bodies were made to be together. Safe together.

So good together.

Emmett soothed and kissed and moved them to their sides to relax and unfold. Tobias tangled his legs in Emmett's and covered any skin his lips could touch with soft kisses and warm suckles until they could breathe properly again.

"It's a damned good thing you're *not* broken," Tobias mumbled as he slipped off the condom.

Emmett groaned and stretched his legs out before snuggling back into the crook of Tobias's body, like a contented cat nestling in for his afternoon nap. "Besides the obvious, why?"

"Because if we keep this up, I will be."

"It's that receding hairline, I'm telling you."

"I should kick you out of bed for that."

Emmett pushed back the matted waves at Tobias's brow and kissed his head. "I dare you to try."

◆◆◆

THE PASSAGE OF TIME BLURRED as they attempted to make up for the sexless years between them in one night. After the third round and not enough time between romps, Emmett admitted that maybe, upon further consideration, he *was* broken.

"Fluids. We need fluids," Tobias reasoned. It helped.

Tobias woke first in what he assumed was the morning. The clock read 12:30. Morning was relative. Emmett slept soundly next to him. He was a bit of a bed hog, sprawled out across the mattress on his back, one leg draped over Tobias's, the other bent and peeking out from a slip of sheet. Minus that small swath of thigh, everything else was gloriously exposed.

These were the moments Tobias always wished he could paint. Sculpt like Malik. But he was also grateful to have music to express himself. Words were pointless; only sound and rhythm, harmony and melody could begin to encapsulate the beauty of this man. Of the boy he first loved.

Tobias placed a soft kiss on Emmett's shoulder. Emmett didn't stir.

He grabbed his iPad to check the news, to see if life continued outside these four walls. But his mind wandered with every soft snore, every sleepy twitch next to him, to memories of the beautiful boy and thoughts of how he had healed. And how, sometimes, he hadn't.

Seeing him here now, strong, whole, unbroken—in the truest sense of the word—made the memories so much easier to recall, and granted room for the good ones that had carried their days when everything seemed hopeless.

The summer day Emmett's fixator was removed had been a big day. They had marked it in red circles on their calendars. Tobias rode with Emmett and his mother to the appointment, but Emmett didn't want his mother present for the procedure; they would be speaking of the most intimate parts of his healing.

Emmett was an adult. His decision had been firm. Dr. Cheryl, who had cared for Emmett since the accident, had also insisted that the conversation happen without Emmett's mother. The doctor remained clinical, yet caring. She had respected Tobias as Emmett's boyfriend and addressed the conversation to both of them.

Emmett's injuries had been mostly in the pelvic region. Bladder and bowel function had quickly resumed. Reproductive health most likely would as well, but Dr. Cheryl wanted him to be aware, unafraid. She had assured both of them that Emmett's youth was in his favor, but that it might take time. And practice—this advice had come complete with a very subtle hand gesture.

When she left, Emmett sat silently, as if replaying the conversation over and over in his mind. Tobias waited and was rewarded with the most delightful smile—a rare gift since the accident.

"Did she medically advise me to masturbate?" Emmett asked, pointing to the door Dr. Cheryl had exited.

"I—I believe she did, yes."

Emmett nodded and looked down at his crotch, finally unhindered by the godforsaken rods screwed into his pelvis. And then he smiled again. "And didn't Mom say she wanted to hear everything the doctor told me?"

"Yes. Yes she did," Tobias said. "Demanded it, even."

"Oh, this is going to be a fun afternoon."

They had whispered secret plans in the back of Emmett's mother's minivan as she drove them home: plans for Tobias to "help" Emmett practice. Plans for Emmett to show Tobias what he had learned on his own. By the time they pulled into Tobias's driveway, Tobias had been so worked up he could barely get out of the back seat.

It was a few weeks before they had a chance to act on those whispered plans. In the meantime, Tobias got a breathy phone call from a very excited Emmett announcing that all systems were go. In all of his twenty years, Tobias had never jerked off so hard or so fast. And he did it while on the phone with Emmett, who went for a twofer on his first night back in the game.

The next day, Tobias visited after XACT rehearsal. When he walked in, Emmett was lounging on the couch, grinning like the Cheshire Cat.

"They left. For hours," he said, with a sultriness that defied his young age.

Tobias pulled Emmett from the couch, and they held each other close, swaying to the music in his head that seemed to follow Tobias around whenever he was with this beautiful boy.

Emmett led them upstairs, and, while he tried to hide it, Tobias could still hear the occasional hiss of pain when he put too much weight on his right side.

"Are you sure?"

"I'm sure."

Once they were naked and landed on the bed, the frantic giggles of disrobing and getting tangled in clothing quieted. Emmett's body stretched toward Tobias's touch, his lips, the tender care that guided Emmett to unfurl, limb by limb, from the confines of the coffin he had been trapped in.

"Be on me, Toby."

"Are you—are you sure?" Emmett's pelvis was still bruised and discolored; wounds where the fixator had been screwed into his hips were still healing.

"I need to feel you. I've missed you."

Tobias lowered his weight onto Emmett, fitting with him as if he had been specifically carved to be there. "This okay?"

"Perfect." Emmett spread his legs further. "Your mouth. Toby, please."

Tobias chuckled but slid down his body, peppering it with kisses as he went. "I thought you wanted me on you."

"I do. On me. Over me. Everywhere, God… "

Tobias tamped down his desire to take Emmett hard and fast—it had been months of seeing his broken body, of holding him and being unable to touch him the way they both had so desperately wanted.

He took his time and focused on Emmett's cock, which protruded proudly from his hips. Emmett sighed in relief and sunk his fingers into Tobias's hair; everything was falling right back into place.

Until Emmett lifted his pelvis to meet Tobias's mouth. Emmett hissed, shoved his hand over his hip, held his breath and slowly lowered back onto the bed. The mood had been pierced.

Toby pulled off and worked him with his hand. "It's okay. You're okay."

But Emmett was the master of his own destiny. He softened in Tobias's grip and offered to take care of Tobias anyway. Tobias refused, of course. It was together or not at all.

"I just want to be better. I've worked so hard." Soft, traitorous tears fell down Emmett's cheeks as fast as Toby could brush them away. "You're going away soon."

Tobias kissed the tears away and tucked Emmett's head to his chest to cradle him as his cries became more fervent, from deeper within, tears for everything they couldn't be right then.

"It's not you, you know that, don't you?" Emmett sniffed and hiked up on his elbows, hissing in pain again.

"I've never doubted that. This is your body saying no, not your heart."

"Even when I'm being ugly and shouting at the moon... or at you. I will always want you." Breath shuddered out of Emmett, and he lay down again and twined their legs together. "Always, Toby."

"I know. It'll be okay."

As Tobias looked at Emmett's body now, vulnerable and whole in Tobias's bed, he realized anew that that day, though it was the last time they'd attempted sexual activity in their younger days, was one of the most treasured in his memory. A day that had said, "I love you"—in ways words never could.

Tobias dotted Emmett's chest with soft, dry kisses; he smiled in his sleep, shifted his body in his haze. As on that day long ago, Emmett slowly unfurled—only now it was from the simple confines of sleep.

Now, gently resting between Emmett's legs, Tobias laved Emmett's nipples, one and then the other. He sucked the silky skin into his mouth until Emmett stirred and sunk his fingers into Tobias's hair.

Emmett moaned. "Good morning."

Tobias slid down until he was at eye level with Emmett's tattoo— among other things. "Good afternoon." Tobias licked around the top swirl of the design and sucked a kiss at the puckered scar in the center. "You still haven't told me the story."

"You expect me to talk now?"

Tobias moved to the second swirl and Emmett hiked up onto his elbows. "I do. This is beautiful."

"It's a, um… *ah!*" Tobias had Emmett's hardening cock in his hand, his lips barely grazing the skin over Emmett's hips. "Faerie… healing… " Tobias kissed Emmett's cock and collected the pearled drip from its tip. "Symbol. Fuck."

"You said that already. Earlier." He stroked firmly, steadily, and Emmett swelled in his hand. "What's the matter? Can't concentrate?"

"Fucker." Emmett moaned and flopped back on the pillows.

Tobias decided to give him a break and focus on the task at hand. With great care, steady strokes and tight pulls of his mouth over Emmett's cock, he finished the scene he had recalled from years before. No more discolored skin or ugly scabs, no more winces of pain or insecurities in the faithfulness of Emmett's body.

When Emmett came, Tobias licked him clean, his own orgasm smeared between his skin and the sheets.

"Fuck. Toby, c'mere. Lemme take care—"

Tobias scooted up and sprawled himself across Emmett. "I'm good. Watching you just—I'm good."

Emmett reached for him anyway and chuckled at his softening cock, tacky with spilled come. "Oh. Yes, you are."

It wasn't until after they'd showered and called a local deli for sandwich delivery that Emmett finished his story.

"It was a boyfriend's idea," he said, without any hint of regret or nostalgia.

"Really?" Tobias took a long pull of his soda to weigh his next question. "Please tell me he doesn't have a matching one."

"No. This was all for me. A compromise of sorts."

"Something permanent on your body is a compromise?"

"I thought you liked it." Emmett's smile was wicked and inviting, and if Tobias weren't so damned hungry, he'd drag Emmett back to bed to show him how much he liked it.

"I do. It—it doesn't seem like something you'd do, especially on someone else's whim."

"It wasn't a whim." Emmett flipped through his phone. When he stopped, he smiled fondly at the picture. "This is Derek."

Tobias looked at the picture, gulped and put his sandwich down to take the phone from Emmett. "Derek is a drag queen."

She was dressed in full regalia and had long, flowing black mermaid hair, bright, plum-colored lips with a deeper plum lipliner, exaggerated cheek contouring and highlights and bold, extreme eye shadow in purple, pink and smoky gray. To top it off, she had the most caricature-like eyebrows Tobias had ever seen—even for a drag queen.

"By night, yes. Anita Mann is a drag queen. Derek Moreno really is an investment banker."

It shouldn't have made Tobias laugh—everyone had a secret, after all. Some were more unexpected than others.

"So, you dated a drag queen named Anita, an investment banker, and she convinced you to get a faerie tattoo on your hip."

"See, when you have half of the story, it sounds insane."

"Yeah, but… call me for something stupid. These are the best stories."

Emmett found another picture. "I dated a man named Derek." This photo was of a sharp, good-looking man: tall and well built, with light brown skin; when Tobias looked closely, he saw that this was the face under all of Anita's makeup. Derek was the epitome of tall, dark and handsome.

"I see why he makes a beautiful woman."

"Yes. I met him at Eclipse a few weeks after I moved back home from the Fulton layoff."

"So, out of curiosity, did you meet him as Derek or Anita?"

"Anita. A very bitchy, stressed out Anita. Their sound engineer got sick right before the show and I agreed to take a look at their setup. I'm up there snooping around and she comes stomping across the dance floor—full makeup, wig cap, bustier and heels. Six foot, six inches of drag fury." Emmett slipped into a pissed-off Latina drag queen without batting an eye. "Listen here, *pinche puta*. You will not have me sound like some kind of mousy J-Lo, understand?" Emmett laughed. "Our first encounter was—"

"Memorable. He called you a fucking whore."

"*She* called me a fucking whore. After the show, *he* reintroduced himself and, uh… let's say I'm glad I didn't have a day job at the time."

"Nice."

"He had good timing. I was in the pit of my Epic Days of Discontent and in comes this ray of fucking sunshine, mysticism and, I'm pretty convinced, a little magic."

"So he healed you," Tobias said.

"No. He wanted to do this ceremony thing. Something with healing stones and burned herbs and probably some forest animals chirping in the window. I don't know; it sounded crazy and unnecessary. But he believed in this shit so much. He wanted me to see myself like he saw me. 'Like the spirits see you, *querido*.'" Emmett sighed; this was clearly a fond memory. "Then he found this." Emmett pointed to his hip, shrugged and smiled shyly. "And it meant something."

"He loved you."

"He did. They let him light incense and whisper these chants over me while the guy did the tattoo. It didn't mean anything to me, other than I was important to someone again."

Tobias had to wonder if that sort of admission would get easier. That Emmett had lost so much of himself that—

Emmett took Tobias's hand. "It's okay. It made me want to get better."

"Did you love him?"

"Not like he loved me."

Emmett took a breath to explain further, Tobias supposed, but he really didn't want to hear about Emmett's heart and another man. He stood, dropped to his knees and pulled Emmett's robe apart while Emmett breathlessly tried to finish his thought. "I—I couldn't love him."

Pressing soft kisses to Emmett's chest and belly as gooseflesh spread across his skin, Tobias looked up and smiled into his next kiss. "And what about now? What if he walked through this door right now?"

Emmett combed his fingers through Tobias's hair and moaned before answering. "There's a husband now. He wouldn't be looking for me anyway."

Tobias kept dotting kisses down his abdomen and chuckled as he went. "Pity, that."

"Not really," Emmett said. "He wasn't meant to be permanent."

Tobias stopped kissing. The hair around Emmett's navel tickled his lips as he hovered there.

It's not meant to be permanent.

Those were Tobias's exact words about writing. About the dicking around he'd do at a piano, playing with melody and harmony, rhythm and structure until he'd killed time before his next meeting or exhausted the current conversation.

"Toby?" Emmett's hand was soft on Tobias's cheek, his expression curious and warm.

Tobias shook his head and kissed the tender skin along the waistband of Emmett's shorts. "Nothing… you're just—" He continued to mindlessly lick and suckle while Emmett stroked his head and calmed his mind.

Maybe their time apart really hadn't been all that different. Tobias tinkered with his music, taking gigs as they came without much focus. It was easier than committing to huge shows, than staying in one place and making the most of his talent and his time.

And Emmett, well, he had treated his heart much the same way, though Derek seemed to have been a positive light in Emmett's otherwise darkened world. And, in the midst of all the trials and failures in Tobias's box of clips and chords, there were some quality bits; scraps of workable material in the heap of disjointed musical sorrow.

"I'm just what?" Emmett asked, teasing now, canting his hips enough to let Tobias know what he wanted.

"Delicious." Tobias swallowed thickly and focused on Emmett's hip again, slipping a finger into the band of his boxer-briefs. "Can I? Again?"

"Yeah… "

Tobias rolled the waistband down to expose the triangular sapphire image.

"So, the blue represents water?" Tobias traced one, then the next, then the final swirl.

"Yes. The solid lines are nature." Emmett's belly quivered at Tobias's touch. "Three is a whole number which means… something, and why are you so enamored with it?" The final words rushed out of him as he tugged on Tobias's hair and made him stop.

Tobias looked up at him and blindly traced the scar the tattoo encircled. "It's unexpected. It's—" Tobias kissed the tender skin just above the tattoo. "It's one of my favorite places on you, and it was so… *wrecked.*" He practically worshipped Emmett, with tender kisses across his belly to the other hip. He traced the lines of Emmett's muscles, skimming right over the patch of hair that peeked out of the top of his shorts. "And now you're healed."

Emmett's breath stuttered beneath his touch. His voice was broken and awed when he spoke. "It's just—no one's ever paid much attention. It's a tattoo."

"But it's not. It's—God, Emmett, I missed so much. We missed so much."

Emmett leaned down and kissed Tobias's forehead. It seemed like a blessing, a prayer; good wishes and strength radiating from Emmett's lips to Tobias's cowardly soul. "I'm here now. Let's enjoy now."

Old loves weren't permanent. Unfinished scores weren't permanent. But the tattoo was. Emmett's pronouncement that he had survived would be forever etched into his skin. Into his soul.

Tobias laved over the flesh again, over the dimple of the rounded scar. He had to wonder: Other than the guilt and loss of that day, what did he have of permanence? What did he have that was unwavering and forever etched into his skin?

He had Emmett. Etched into his music. Into his soul. Surely they could come together again.

12

IT WAS THE FOURTH AND final visit to this coffee shop in Boston. Emmett
had grown quite fond of it. The handwritten specials on the chalkboard
menu changed daily, and the oversized bright red mugs were filled to
the brim with some of the best coffee Emmett had ever had. Every
morning, the barista topped each mug with foam art.

Since Emmett had admitted he was flying home, today's image was
a butterfly. Toby got a double heart. And a wink: "I hope he comes
back soon."

Emmett wasn't ready to go home yet. The visit had been much like
this shop, with a bustling schedule that changed every day. And the late
nights had bled into long mornings of warmth and the best lovemaking
Emmett had ever known, complete with thoughtful touches, reminders
of who they were and lessons in who they could be.

Toby insisted on buying a scone to share after their early lunch. He
broke off a corner and offered it to Emmett. "The cinnamon chips in this
are huge." And as Emmett opened his mouth and smiled around Toby's
fingers, Toby blurted out what sounded like an idea he'd had trapped
inside of him all morning. "So. Do you wanna go steady?"

Emmett almost choked. "Go *steady*? Don't you think you should at least take me to the sock hop first?"

Toby laughed and pointed to Emmett's chest, where a crumb had landed from his sputtering. "The man who called cunnilingus 'tipping the velvet' is tormenting *me* for archaic use of language?"

"I was talking about a seventeen-year-old girl. I don't know the code of ethics."

"So, smart-ass, what *are* they calling it now? Dating? Schmoozing? What was it… going together?"

"Going out. They call it—"

"Going out? 'Do you wanna go out?' That's what you do for an evening."

"For a fifteen-year-old, it might last an evening."

Toby nodded and took a bite of scone, smiling almost maniacally as Emmett waited. Emmett cleaned his glasses, drained his coffee and finally, after Toby said nothing more—apparently waiting for Emmett to offer the next nugget of brilliance—he nudged Toby's feet under the table. "What are you doing, Toby?"

Toby grinned and put down the scone. "Mmm. I'm trying to finish the conversation *you* have brought up twice now."

"I've brought up?"

"You've brought up. Twice."

"Yes, twice. You said that. Twice." This is why musicals lasted for three hours, Emmett decided. The stories meandered all over the perimeter and could never get to the fucking point. "How have I—" And then a diminutive young girl with long blonde hair and overzealous blue eyes popped into his memory. "Tori asking if we were boyfriends."

"And before you came up, *you* said you wanted us to label this." Toby offered the last bite of scone and took it when Emmett shook him off. "I'm trying to conclude the debate here."

Toby chewed and swallowed and wadded up his napkin, and sat there as if he had suggested going to a Red Sox game for dime-a-dog night and "Yes, duh," was the only viable answer.

"I'm about to get on a plane, and now you want to—" Emmett sighed, wishing he could hide the persistent grin that poked through his mild irritation. "We never seem to finish things well, do we?"

"I dunno. That was a pretty spectacular finish this morning, when you—"

"Oh my God, shut up. You already traumatized the lady over there by saying 'cunnilingus' a little too loudly."

"Maybe she could learn something."

"Probably. Not the point." Emmett massaged his forehead. "Weren't we having a perfectly reasonable conversation about Starbucks' destruction of independent coffee shops earlier? Let's go back to that."

Toby leaned in and focused so tightly on Emmett it was as if every other diner in the café disappeared. "I'd rather not." The noise seemed muffled in the intensity of Toby's gaze. "I'd rather talk about the fact that I don't want to call the numbers in my little black book when I get to—" Toby blushed and laughed at himself. "I don't know where I'm going next. Minneapolis. I don't want to call the gentleman I know in Minneapolis next week, because I have your number now."

"So you *do* want me to be your traveling fuck buddy?"

"No." Toby didn't blink. He didn't flinch. Emmett wasn't sure he breathed, his answer was so solid and sure. "You're deflecting, and I'm not playing games."

"Right." Emmett swallowed, ashamed of how dry his mouth had become. "You're asking me to give up *my* little black book."

"Yes. I want us to try again."

Emmett had wanted to hear those words for so long, he almost laughed. But he had given up on it ever happening. Given up on ever hearing Toby's voice again. On ever tasting his skin, hearing his laughter. On ever falling into the comfort of their easy affection for one another, an affection that seemed more natural than the constant push and pull he experienced with other men.

"You're thinking too hard," Toby said, leaning back, pulling away from the moment.

"No. Yes. I—"

It was preposterous. Ill-timed. Ill-advised. His flight to Indiana was hours away, but this man made him happier than he had felt in years. Since Derek. And before that and always, there was Toby.

But he was terrified. Everything was still so fragile, so unknown. Their worlds were so far apart. He was not the amazing man Toby seemed to think he was.

"You don't know me, Toby."

"I know every intimate inch of you."

"Yes, but that's not what I—"

"Isn't that reason enough right there?"

"No. Fantastic sex is not enough," Emmett said, not believing it completely. While sex couldn't erase the pain that lingered between them, their intimacy was more than fantastic sex. No one knew him like Toby. He had made sure no man ever would. "I mean that I've seen you three times in the last six months. Let's also consider the fifteen years before that."

"Yeah, so? What's your point?"

"Every time we see each other, I'm on vacation," Emmett said. "And you loosen your schedule to fit me in. I'm a visitor."

"And asking that we consider each other when we're apart won't change that to some degree?"

"You go by a different *name*, Toby. You have no idea what I'm like at home," Emmett said, thinking he might have found a little ground. "You don't know what I do with an unexpected day off."

"Sure I do." Toby sat back and grinned, looking entirely too confident. "Six inches of snow pummels the greater Brighton area and you don't have school. You knew it was coming because you keep an eye on that shit, thinking you can somehow control it."

"I keep an eye on it so I'll know whether I need to run to the store for flour or not."

"Exactly. Because on an unexpected snow day, you bake."

The fucker.

Toby sat up again, on fire and cocky. "You bake and you marathon something on Netflix. Or maybe you work on paperwork, but if it's going to be a few days in, you'll skip it because your obnoxious kids aren't going to be doing homework either."

"What am I baking?"

Toby narrowed his eyes and scrunched his face. "You don't bake cookies anymore—not like you used to, and cupcakes are too cliché."

"Correct on both counts."

Toby studied and Emmett feigned nonchalance, even though he was beginning to get a little creeped out. And then Toby lit up again.

"You've been fooling around with cakes. Those little—" He wiggled his fingers in the air as if to explain himself. "One layer things. With weird shit in 'em like rosemary and basil, but they're sweet. Do they even have a name?"

Emmett stared at him. And blinked, and then checked his mug in hopes of one blessed remaining drop, as cold as it might be. When he found none, he plunked the mug down and stared at Toby again, ignoring the smug look on the man's face. "How in the *hell*?"

"The other night at dinner. You studied that damned olive oil cake like some sort of chef dissecting his next recipe. It was weird."

"It was delicious. I think I need more lemon in mine."

"I know you fine, Emmett."

He did. And if Emmett really considered it, he also knew that on an unexpected day off—a night the power generator blew in the theater, maybe—Toby would grab one of his cast or crew and head out for an extended dinner and drinks. They'd find another show to attend, and he'd weasel his way into the after party, if there was one, and make a few connections that would somehow come to fruition in the form of a new gig.

"What would I be marathoning?" Emmett asked, if only out of curiosity.

"If you were smart, you'd marathon *Firefly* because it never gets old."

"I've never—" Realizing Toby watched it hurt, ridiculous as it was. "I never could watch it. Whedon was *our* thing." Emmett shook his head at himself. "I couldn't do it."

"*Serenity*? *Avengers*?"

Emmett shook his head.

Toby pushed their lunch flotsam aside and took Emmett's hands in his. "We should do that. Take the time. Watch *Buffy* and *Angel* again, catch up on all his movies—"

"This is why, Toby. Right here."

"Right here what?"

"You're planning. Already. Next time. When I'll fly out to another city and visit. And we'll pretend and play like a couple when it's just—it's not our lives."

"I'm not pretending." Toby let go of Emmett's hands. "Have you been pretending?"

"No. Not—no." Emmett took off his glasses and sighed. It was happening again: time to say goodbye, and everything was falling to shit. "I'm not pretending that I love being with you or that something is going on here. I don't understand it or know how to define it, but I am so fucking happy when I'm with you. I'm not pretending that."

"So we're back to me not understanding."

"Come home."

"No."

Toby's answer was sharp and sure, like the falling blade of a guillotine.

"So that's it? You expect me to pack up every few weeks and fly all over the fucking country, step into your life and then back out again as if I don't have a life of my own?"

"Emmett, that's not—" Toby closed his eyes, squeezed a dirty napkin and looked back at Emmett. "I can't, Emmett. I—*can't* go back."

"Then we are clearly not ready for any sort of commitment."

"Wait. You won't agree to—to us—unless I come to Indiana?"

"I won't," Emmett said. "It's all feeling a little one-sided to me, and I'm not okay with that."

"You don't understand."

"I do understand, Toby. I was there for everything that makes you afraid of that place."

"Yes. You were," Toby said, taking Emmett's hand in his. "But my concerns about going back have nothing to do with you."

"Maybe they *should* have something to do with me."

"That's—" Toby pulled his hand away. "That's not fair."

"It really is," Emmett said. He reached across the table for Toby's hand again. "Please?" Toby took his hand and Emmett squeezed, holding on as if he might never let go. "We experienced a great tragedy together. And while Scotty's parents lost their son, no one felt the things we felt. No one else woke up screaming and sweating when we heard the sounds of the crash in our sleep."

"Emmett—"

"No one else knew the fear of maybe never walking again. No one else lost weight and a semester of school because he might get thrown in jail. No one else felt the things we felt together. That's all ours. As much as you want to, you cannot take me out of the equation."

"But, that's just it, Em. I don't want to feel those things again. I cannot walk back into that—that darkness."

Emmett pulled their joined hands to his lips and kissed Toby's knuckles. "You already have. You have been so *enamored*—you've practically spent this entire week making love to my scars. You're there. And it's not so dark anymore."

"No, because you're whole again. You're not broken anymore."

Emmett saw it, then. He saw in the way Toby had almost obsessed over the ridiculous tattoo and Emmett's scars, as if begging for them to also bring him the powers that Derek had wished upon Emmett's body those years ago. He saw it in Toby's insistence that they start all over as if the accident never happened, as if the years of silence weren't strung between them like a rope and plank bridge connecting two separate lands.

So he said it. To give it power. To make it a truth they shared—like their shared tragedy. "And you still are. Broken."

Toby nodded, grasping at Emmett's fingers like a lifeline. "I'm so—" He took a deep, shuddering breath. "I'm so exhausted making sure no one knows."

"Oh, Toby." All the more reason "trying again" was a bad idea. Unready to let go, Emmett kissed Toby's fingers again. "Then come to my home," Emmett offered, trite as it sounded in his own ears. "I've remodeled the master and made a party room in my basement for the kids."

"You've never told me—"

"It's beautiful, really. It's on a couple of acres, and the back of the property is lined with a stream you can hear from the kitchen when the windows are open. It's very peaceful. It sounds like you need some peace."

"You deserve a beautiful life."

"So let me share it with you. At least think about it?"

Toby nodded and began to clean up. "Will you still come see me in San Francisco after school's out?"

"I don't know. I'd really like an answer before I agree to see you again."

"Okay. I'm sorry it's not as easy as it should be."

"I am too, Toby. Being with you was always so easy."

◆◆◆

SAN FRANCISCO—June 2016

Emmett's resolve buckled, and he went to San Francisco a week after school let out. He was also pleasantly surprised that Malik was in town.

Toby was working on a new show, *Thief*. In early stages of development, rehearsals seemed more like rehearsals of rehearsals, and Emmett thought he was in the way. Toby insisted he wasn't. Malik was the easy escape, and joined Emmett on sightseeing expeditions.

On an afternoon together at The Presidio, Emmett learned that Malik and Toby had indeed dated. Briefly. "A couple of dates. A long night in—you know." But Emmett hadn't known. "And by the look on your face," Malik continued, "shit. You weren't supposed to know."

"I can't imagine he kept it from me on purpose. How long ago was this?"

They sat on a bench overlooking the bay. Malik mumbled about what was going on in his life as he calculated the answer: installation at Tobias's first studio, owner was a dick, they saw a couple off-off shows... "I'd guess ten years ago? It wasn't long after we'd met."

"Oh. Pft. That's why I didn't know." Joggers sprinted by them and bicyclists sped past in a blur of activity as Emmett painted mental pictures of the two gorgeous men together. "So, uh… what happened? No chemistry?" He couldn't fathom that.

"Not really. A little, maybe. Mostly, he was still into someone else."

Emmett nodded absentmindedly, still caught up in images of Toby's deft fingers sinking into Malik's long, tight curls as his head bobbed up and—

"Did you hear me, man?"

"Huh? Yeah, yeah. Into someone else. Toby's dated around."

"No. Dude. Stop thinking about him naked and focus here."

Emmett had the decency to blush; Toby's wasn't the only naked body on his mind. "Sorry. I kind of short-circuited there for a minute."

Malik laughed and looked out across the bay before turning to face Emmett. "It was *you*, jackass. I didn't know it at the time. I didn't know you existed, but it was you."

"If you didn't know I existed—"

"I figured it out after you called. That's when he told me about you. Who you were. What happened. And I could see it then—you were the one he never left."

Emmett cracked a sarcastic laugh. "Oh, he left me all right."

"No. He really didn't."

"It sure as shit felt like it," Emmett admitted, with much less vitriol than he used to carry around about it. "What *did* you know? I mean, you've been friends for ten years. That's a pretty important chunk of his life to leave out."

"I knew he was a military brat. That his last place of residence was a small town in Indiana. And that music was a way for him to connect with people." Malik stopped and considered. "And not to connect—he hid behind the piano to keep a distance because he knew he'd be moving again anyway."

Well, at least Toby had been forthcoming about that. "That was it?"

"That was pretty much it. I didn't need much more. He's a nice guy. Funny. Smart. Talented. He helped me when I was confused about my sexuality. Told me to embrace who I was, even if the world wouldn't bother."

That was the Toby Emmett had fallen in love with in high school. The boy who loved him exactly as he was, after years of living with a mother who always wanted him to be something more, someone who reflected her own values and ideals and was not strong enough to have any of his own. Someone more like his sister.

Not wanting to spend another thought on his mother, Emmett checked the time on his phone. "Thank you for telling me, but we'd probably better head back." Emmett stood and unhooked his cane from the back of the bench. "You going to join us for dinner tonight?"

Malik laughed and looped his arm around Emmett's neck as they began to walk. "Nah. I'm thinking you might want to be alone to work out some of those fantasies you had boppin' around your head earlier."

They walked quietly for a few hundred yards, and then Emmett had to ask, "Tell me you at least had a good night together."

"It was good," Malik said. "But I really think he was saving his best for you."

When Emmett and Toby got back to Toby's apartment, Emmett took Malik's advice and fucked Toby up against his apartment door.

Soundly.

And as they cleaned up and Toby sputtered, "What's gotten into you?" and "Can we buy it in bulk?" Emmett took great satisfaction in knowing that ten years ago, Malik—gorgeous, sexy, sweet, kind Malik—had gotten Toby's sloppy seconds.

As he packed his bags to head back to Indiana and begin preparing for the next school year and to appear at a few conferences, Toby stood in the doorway with a cup of coffee and sex-rumpled hair. He was wearing the boxer-briefs he had retrieved from, Emmett believed, the dresser mirror, where they'd miraculously landed after a "Get 'em off, get 'em off" toss an hour before.

"So, Portland?" Toby sipped his coffee and winked over the rim of the mug.

"So, Indiana?"

Toby lowered his mug, unplugged a USB charger Emmett was about to forget and handed it to him with a kiss on his shoulder. He worked his lips to Emmett's neck, and when the warmth of his mouth landed on the soft, tender skin under Emmett's ear, packing was forgotten, Indiana was forgotten, and Emmett almost missed his plane.

◆◆◆

PORTLAND—July 2016

Independence Day fireworks sprayed multicolored confetti over the Willamette River, and, in one sentence, Toby lobbed a bomb of explosive celebration into Emmett's heart as well.

Emmett had almost conceded to the fact that they were going to be visitors in each other's lives—or more specifically, Emmett was going to be a visitor in Toby's life. And while it was far from ideal, it was better than nothing, more than Emmett had imagined. It left him a bit addled every time he returned home, but in time, he reset and carried on with an extra lilt in his step, with a secret in his back pocket.

He hadn't meant his "come to Indiana or forget it" threat to be an empty one. But having Toby there, out of reach, yet just a few calendar swipes away, swathed Emmett in an odd comfort, like a summer single that instantly transported you back in time to the stale jokes and scents of carry-out from the shady Indian place down the block.

Toby was the "Hollaback Girl." B-A-N-A-N-A-S.

Unfortunately, Emmett cracked a laugh at that thought immediately after Toby dropped a significant sentence.

They were leaning back against a tree. Toby's arms were strong and solid around Emmett as the soft "oohs" and "aahs" of fireworks spectators brushed against his ear. During a lull in the explosions and color in the sky, Toby said without fanfare, "So, I realized I haven't seen *Fantasticks* in an age."

And that's when Emmett laughed, with "Ooh, this my shit, this my shit" ringing in his ears.

"What?" Toby asked, rattled. "What's so funny about that?"

"What? Wait? What did you say?" Emmett turned in Toby's arms. Even in the dark, he could see the glimmer of nerves and uncertainty in Toby's eyes. "*Fantasticks*?"

"*Fantasticks*."

Emmett searched his memory for meaning. In an instant, it came back to him. Students at the end of the school year had been scrounging for sheet music from the score: "Soon It's Gonna Rain," "Try to Remember" and "Metaphor."

"XACT is doing that right before summer break is over," Emmett said, as a grin spread across his face.

"I know." Toby leaned in and kissed Emmett's cheek, brushing his nose against his day-old stubble. "Do you think you could get us prime seating, Mr. Henderson?"

Emmett took hold of Toby's shoulders and pulled back to look him straight in the eye. His voice had been so confident, but Emmett saw it in his eyes. This was a hurdle that Toby had been fighting to jump. He wasn't yet sure he could clear it. "Really? You'll come?"

"Only if our seats are close enough that I can keep an eye on the pianist."

"You cannot intimidate the pianist. He's like… eighty years old."

"Then maybe I'd better be ready to fill in, in case he drops de—"

Emmett kissed him, and the fireworks finale began, the whizzes and explosions, piped-in orchestral fanfare and audience roars of glee all silencing to the beating of his heart.

Toby was coming home.

13

MORNINGSIDE—August 2016

The last time Tobias had flown into Brighton Airport was the winter after the accident. His parents had split. They demanded that he come back to the house and pick out anything he wanted; whatever remained would be tossed or sold.

He didn't care if anything would be tossed or sold. They pressed. He caved. Hearing his father say, "Your mother is already upset," one more time might have sent him over the edge. Of course, she was already upset. Her son was being tried for manslaughter, and her marriage was falling apart because of it.

He'd flown in on a Tuesday evening. After sifting through boxes, he had collected an XACT cast photograph from *Anything Goes*, two scores he had accidentally left behind and a jazz band sweatshirt from Xavier High. He ate a late dinner with his mom and found they had very little to talk about. She knew none of his friends in New York. "Emmett started Indiana University in January," was the extent of the local conversation, and he sure as hell didn't want to hear about his dad.

Before his mother woke up the next morning, he had called a cab and waited at the airport for three hours to avoid what he knew would be a morning of visiting people she knew and that he hadn't given a second thought to since he left.

"Everyone asks after you all the time." She had said it at least twice over dinner. He told his mother that his flight had been unexpectedly bumped up.

She was upset. The sky was blue. Grass was green.

It wasn't that he hadn't kept up with the goings-on in Indiana since. Ms. Lipman checked in with him once or twice a year, and had come out to New York to see him direct a small production of *Seussical* in Queens. But an annual phone call about diva drama at the community theater was a far cry from wandering around the Greater Brighton Area to kick up ghosts and demons.

Sure, ghosts and demons were but mere figments of one's imagination. But for Tobias, they might as well have been sitting next to him in first class, stirring roofies into his gin and tonic as they flew over Pennsylvania.

He surfed *The New York Times*. He flipped through *SkyMall*, but when he found himself trying to order a five hundred-dollar audio restoring tape converter, he closed the magazine and swapped it for some financial paperwork. When his mind would not, under any circumstances, add $1,893 to $934, he gave that up as well. His ears popped, and the captain announced the beginning of their descent. His index finger found a mind of its own and tapped nervously on edge of the armrest.

"Nervous flyer?"

"Huh? Oh." Tobias smiled—nervously—at his seatmate. "No. Not at all. I fly all the time."

Her eyes drifted to his finger and lingered there, as if expecting it to pop off his hand and shoot into the seat in front of them.

"I'm, um… I'm meeting someone, and it's been awhile." Tobias huffed a laugh so ridiculously uptight, he laughed again. "I've been an annoying seatmate. I'm terribly sorry."

"Skittish." She smiled at him and patted his wrist. "I'm sure it won't be as bad as you're anticipating."

"His name is Emmett." He closed his eyes and wondered if someone actually had stirred something into his drink. "I'm sorry." He took a deep breath, nestled his head back against his seat and closed his eyes, hoping she would be so freaked out that she would go back to her book.

Her hand touched his wrist again. "Tell me about him." Her eyes were kind. Her touch was maternal.

After Malik, this was the second time Tobias had told the story of Emmett: of their love, of the accident and their lives afterward. Her name was Barb; she said all the right things in all the right places.

When he finished his story with, "I'm still not sure why it's so important to him that I come," and the plane was about to touch down, she placed her hand over his.

"He's made peace with that day. He wants the same for you."

"I have made peace," Tobias said, wanting it to be true.

"Sweetheart, I spent the last two hours sitting next to you. You most certainly are not at peace."

He lost Barb in the midst of the flight attendant's robotic salutations and the crowds meandering through the concourse. He focused on finding Emmett and reliving all the journeys home he'd taken before.

Tobias scanned the crowd as he rode the escalator down to baggage claim. The airport had changed, but the walls of windows, with blue-gray skies melting into the dim, blue-gray color of the room itself, remained the same.

As the escalator planted him on the floor, he spotted Emmett. His hair was windblown, and he bit his lip as his eyes raked over the sparse crowd. When Emmett spotted Tobias, he lit up with bright eyes and a huge smile. With a hop in his step, he snaked his way through the small clusters of people directly into Tobias's arms.

Emmett kissed him, right there in the middle of it all. There was no sneaking into an alcove, as they had done in years past. Emmett kissed him and kissed him, and muttered a rushed, "Oh, God, I'm sorry, excuse me," when he realized they were blocking a main path. And then Emmett pulled him aside and kissed him some more.

Tobias couldn't catch his breath. He didn't want to catch his breath. He soaked in Emmett's joyful energy.

Finally, kisses dissolved into shy smiles. Emmett cupped Tobias's face in his hands and looked at him as if he might possibly be a mirage. "You're here."

"I'm here." The joy in Emmett's eyes began to seep in and soothe Tobias's anxiety.

"You're nervous."

"I'm nervous."

Tobias leaned in for the kiss this time—an assurance, as in years before, that it would all be okay. When they pulled apart, a polite voice broke their spell.

"Excuse me? Um… I'm sorry to interrupt, but—"

"Barb! Hi! I was afraid I'd lost you." Tobias pulled free from Emmett and reached out to bring her into their conversation. "Barb, this is—"

"You must be Emmett."

"I… am? Hi." Emmett shook her extended hand. "Barb?"

"Barb, yes. He told me all about you," she said to Emmett. She blushed and held up a finger to her waiting companion. "And I wanted to meet you. And wish you a lovely visit."

She looked fondly at Tobias, and seeing the look of utter confusion on Emmett's face, he knew he would have to explain. "Thank you," Tobias said. "It was a pleasure to meet you."

She leaned in for a hug and stopped herself, looking at him intently. "I never got your name. How crazy is that?"

Tobias smiled at the sweet guardian angel who had looked out for him as he journeyed back to the place where he hid all of his brokenness. He looked down at Emmett's hand in his, their fingers securely intertwined, and took his first step to becoming whole again.

"I'm Toby. Toby Spence."

"Well, Toby. Emmett—" Barb smiled as she yanked the handle out of her suitcase. "It's been a pleasure. Next time I'm in New York, I'll skim *Playbill* for your name."

"If it's there, come find me in the pit. Say hi."

She smiled, looked at both men and winked before disappearing into a crowd of people.

"Toby, huh?" The green in Emmett's eyes shone brightly and Tobias quickly understood why the blue-gray of the walls was so dull in comparison.

"Yeah. I figure this is as good a place as any to try it on for size again."

THEY STOOD IN FRONT OF a sleek, sexy black sports car that was built for speed. "This is your car?" Toby asked. Of course it was Emmett's car. The trunk had popped with the click of a remote in Emmett's hand. Toby hiked his luggage into the trunk and jumped when Emmett slammed it closed.

Emmett drove a virtual Indy race car knockoff. Naturally.

Toby tried to match Emmett's smile over the top of the car as he got in. As delightful as reliving their old airport reunions had been, Toby now wished he had called a cab.

If Emmett noticed Toby's nerves, he hid it well. He chatted amiably about the car, about the pieces of junk he had driven up until her purchase, like a favorite in college he had not-so-affectionately named Ursula. "She was this huge purple Chrysler. I swore she was out to steal my voice. I missed more lessons, auditions and side gigs because of that piece of shit… "

"Does this one have a name?" Speed Racer? Christine, after the possessed car that mowed down its owner's tormentors?

"She'll only respond to Adele. Anything else is beneath her."

"I should have known." Toby ran his hand along the dash, playing along. "Gotta respect the queen."

Besides, if anyone knew that truth—about respecting the machine—
it was Toby and Emmett. For Toby, respect had morphed into anxiety.
Maybe, if he had hopped "back on the horse," as his father had insisted,
he might not be covering his panic with small talk and a newfound
obsession with the proper place to lay his phone.

As it turned out, Emmett wasn't unaware. He held Toby's hand
without a word and kept the conversation flowing. He pointed out old
landmarks and streets; seeing them was more comforting than Toby
had imagined.

"Ah, Needmore Road. *But… what does it need more of?*" Tobias
teased.

"More cowbell!" They yelped in unison, breaking into a fit of laughter.

Toby wiped his eyes, laughing harder than the joke warranted if only
for a release from his nerves. "God, Scotty always—" He caught himself,
stopped talking and looked out the passenger window at nothing more
than the interstate passing by.

"Do you still watch old *SNL* shows?" Emmett asked.

Toby shook his head, but continued to stare out the window. "I guess
they're my Whedon."

"You know," Emmett said, taking Toby's hand back in his. "Scotty
would be pretty damned happy that whenever he comes up, it's because
of something funny."

"I know." Toby squeezed Emmett's hand, but didn't dare look away
from the window, from his old world speeding past as he sat frozen in
place. "I'm sorry. Now you know why I've never come back."

"You did today."

"I don't want to disappoint you."

"Show's over, Toby," Emmett said. "You don't have to perform for me."

Emmett peeled off the interstate onto another highway, and Toby
pinned his fingers under his shaking thighs. "Mom said I should go to
the cemetery," he finally said.

"Do you want to go?"

"No." And then, "Do you ever go?"

"No. He's not there."

Toby nodded, and they sat in silence again.

"I'm sorry, Toby. I should have called you a cab."

"No." Toby finally broke away from the window and looked at Emmett. Worry wrinkled Emmett's brow, and his finger tapped impatiently on the steering wheel. "It would have been easier for me, yes. But—" Toby reached out ran his fingers through Emmett's hair, through the curl that flipped over the top of his ear. "One of the best things about coming home was knowing you were waiting for me. I didn't want to miss that. No one meets me at the airport anymore."

A smile quirked Emmett's lips. "I always liked that, too." He took Toby's hand again. "We're almost there now."

Toby relaxed in his seat as Emmett exited onto a two-lane, tree-lined road. The houses were set back from the road in small rows with farm-land interspersed. Before long, they turned into a housing development with pristine gardens and manicured lawns.

It was nothing like what Toby would have imagined for Emmett. Nothing like their dreams of what adult life would look like for them.

"A loft in SoHo. No, the Village," Emmett would always start. And then with one more moment's thought, "No, the Upper East Side."

"How about we start in Queens or something?" Toby always reasoned. "Much more affordable."

"Okay, but when we get to Manhattan—"

"The Village, for sure. A walk-up studio big enough for a bed, a two-eye burner and a toilet."

"Shower."

"Well, okay. If you insist."

"I'm not bathing in the toilet, Toby."

And while that vision described his current living situation with almost haunting accuracy, Emmett's home was none of those things. Here were acre-sized properties, two- and three-car garages, riding mowers and street side mailboxes surrounded by colorful perennials. House numbers were painted on the low, sloped curbs, and there was at least one semi-luxury car in every driveway.

Before Toby could say a word, comment on how gorgeous the stone front of Emmett's house was or ask what the large purple flowers were next to his garage, Emmett had him in the house with his tongue slipping between Toby's lips as their luggage and jackets lay in a pile on the floor.

"Would you like a tour?" Emmett's voice came raspy and deep. His eyes implied something more along the lines of a tour of his bedroom.

"Yes. Show me everything."

◆◆◆

THEIR DEAR Ms. LIPMAN HAD been flirting with the idea of retirement. When Emmett mentioned it to Toby in Boston, he had teased that Emmett should take her position. The conversation ended with a perfunctory "No," followed by Emmett shooting a straw wrapper right between Toby's eyes.

What Emmett had kept secret from Toby, was that the show he'd flown in for was Ms. Lipman's last. She didn't want a spectacle for her sendoff. She was dropping her final show in the bucket, taking her final bow and calling curtain on her tenure.

Fantasticks was community theater-perfect, with bumps and blunders, passionate performances by halfway decent actors, and pieces of costumes so old Toby thought he recognized some of them.

At intermission, Toby teased Emmett about the Mortimer role, a character in the play whose specialty was melodramatic, comedic death scenes. "Can you imagine," he said, "if we'd ever done this show? We would have had to put up with Scotty fucking around with that Cockney accent all damned summer."

"Oh God. You know it. Lipman would have given him the role just to irritate us."

"Well, that and he'd have killed it." Emmett was right; it felt good and safe to say his name, to honor his clownishness and good humor.

The story carried parallels with Emmett and Toby's: young love lost, a difficult life apart, a reunion tinted with the idea that they should have never let go in the first place. And as El Gallo, the play's mysterious narrator, sang, Emmett brought Toby's fingers to his lips as he quietly sang along, "Without a hurt, the heart is hollow."

Theater might be fantastical, but it always spoke to Toby's heart.

After the show, they went backstage, and Tori—the production's lovely Luisa—squealed when she saw them.

"I'm so glad I didn't know you were out there!" She hugged Emmett and went to hug Toby, but blushed and shook his hand instead.

He laughed and hugged her. "You proud of your work tonight?"

"I am." Someone caught her attention over Toby's shoulder. "Don't move? I want you to meet someone." She slipped through the gaggle of actors and came back with a very reluctant, but equally adorable young lady.

"Mr. H. Mr. Spence. This is Emily Masters. My. Um… my Emily." Tori beamed and Emily tucked her tall, lanky body behind Tori's very petite one. "She was in the chorus. She has the prettiest alto voice I've ever heard."

After exchanging niceties, Emily escaped any further conversation with a kiss on Tori's cheek and a blushing smile for Toby and Emmett.

Emmett leaned close to Tori. "What happened to Stefan? The third baseman?"

"Left fielder."

"Left fielder. I thought he was—"

"Well!" She stepped back from Emmett's attempt at discretion and spoke so anyone nearby could hear. "He? Made fun of the show. Twice."

"Twice?" Toby said. "Well, that's two times too many."

"It is. I let the first time go because everyone is allowed to be cranky." Tori practically growled. "The second time, I told him not to pick me up for our date the next day. Or ever again."

Emmett grinned and lifted a hand for a high five. "Atta girl. I assume he's off leading a miserable lonely life now?"

"I think he's dating Trinkie McCallister."

"Yeah, but you're dating Emily Masters," Toby said. "So who won?"

Tori beamed. "Hey! You have to come to Dairy Queen after. Like choir concerts."

They agreed, and after the crowd thinned they found themselves standing onstage with Ms. Lipman.

"My boys," she said, taking their hands in hers. "You were always my favorites, you know."

It could have gotten sentimental and tear-stained, but whenever Toby opened his mouth to steer it that direction—because Ms. Lipman deserved all the sentimentality—she would stop him and talk about something specific to the production: "Was it obvious Bellomy was sick?" and, "Maybe by the time they find my replacement, they'll have fixed that left spotlight."

Before they parted, she took their hands again and shot them a mischievous look. "So, um… do you want me to leave you here for a bit?"

"Do you mind? We won't be long," Emmett said.

She didn't mind. She never did. "You remember where the lights are," she said as she kissed them each on the cheek. Before she disappeared backstage, she stopped and said—as she'd done so many times before— "Don't make me regret leaving you two here."

Steel met steel as the backstage door slammed closed behind her, leaving them in stark silence. Without a second thought, Toby wheeled the grand piano upstage and took off the quilted cover.

"It hasn't changed much at all, has it?" Emmett lazily paced through a dance routine that Toby probably could have recognized, had he tried. But he didn't try. He didn't care.

He was at home here. Emmett was at home here. It was their birthplace.

"I think they reupholstered the seats," Toby said. "Weren't they blue?"

"Oh. Yes. I guess—I never noticed."

Toby started playing the tune that was in his blood—the tune that he had been carrying around again for months, had been tinkering and toying with to unearth its hidden magic.

Emmett hummed along, his brow furrowed as he continued to fiddle with the dance routine. "What's—I know that song, don't I?"

"No. Yes. You might. I've played it for years."

Emmett gave up on his defunct dance and approached the piano, hand extended. "Come be my partner."

Toby's fingers fumbled, and he blushed. This place hadn't changed by an inch. Sure, the seats were now burgundy, and it looked as if the floors had been refinished, but it hadn't changed. The pops and cracks of an old building settling into itself were the same. The scents of every theater—of *this* theater—came back to Toby as if he'd never left.

And most essential of all, was Emmett: quiet, contemplative, fluid, poetic Emmett, asking Toby to leave the comfort of the piano for the uneasiness of the stage. "You know I don't dance."

"I know you *do.*" He nodded to his outstretched hand and back at Toby. His voice was soft, with a hint of the song's gentle melody in his voice. "It had to be you… "

Toby couldn't refuse. With a nervous smile, he got up, stepped into Emmett's spin and into his arms. "It had to be you."

Emmett led a fluid foxtrot—slow… slow… quick-quick, slow… slow… quick-quick—as the soft melody played between them, if only in thought.

"Wonder if they fixed that loose board?" Emmett asked with a quarter turn.

"Stage left, wasn't it?"

Emmett led them there, still humming the tune. *With all of your faults*—their quick step on three landed on the creaky board. *I love you still*—they spun away, and Toby closed his eyes to let Emmett take him away.

Instead of Emmett's temple at his cheek, they now stood cheek to cheek, hip to hip; they were a little rusty, with a few more joints popping and hitching enough to slow their step.

But it was perfect, really. Perfect in its imperfections, in the absence of youthful dreams and naïve promises.

Slow... slow... quick-qui—

They bumped into the side of the piano. The spell was broken, but with laughter and Emmett's strong, sure arms pulling him in. "I was afraid we'd never get to do that again," Emmett said as he pressed his lips to Toby's neck.

"Me too."

Their breath fell into rhythm, a small drift back and forth as their song replayed unheard. "We, um… " Emmett pulled back and kissed Toby's cheek. "We should probably head out. You still up to meeting everyone, or do you want to go home?"

Home still seemed like a foreign concept. But if he had to describe it, Toby would describe this: a theater, this man, a quiet moment, an indelible memory. "Let's go get some ice cream—I want to talk to Tori again anyway."

14

EMMETT HAD HOPED TOBY WOULD simply slot into the ordinary joys of Emmett's life as if he belonged, but he didn't dare *expect* it to happen. He was well aware that the act of *coming* to Indiana was an enormous act of faith on Toby's part. And that fact was plenty.

And yet they had barely found a seat at their old Dairy Queen before Toby and Mac began to dance around each other like two male peacocks vying for their potential mate's attention. It had started with Emmett Henderson trivia.

"Oh yeah, do you know what his first lead was at XACT?" Toby had trumpeted, as if having access to Emmett's childhood through awkward family dinners and found baby books was the only way to know the answer.

"John Darling in *Peter Pan,*" Mac answered, bored with the question. "Come on—don't give me that lightweight crap."

It continued with trying to name the best American Broadway composer. Mac claimed it was Leonard Bernstein, while Toby—likely to impress Emmett—vouched for Steven Sondheim.

"You know," Emmett finally said, shoving a spoonful of parfait in Toby's general direction, "they did some of their most well known music *together*, so I'm thinking—"

Mac rallied on, emphasizing Bernstein's vast catalogue of not only musicals, but also ballets and operas, orchestral pieces and chamber music. She listed selections as though she had them memorized. She probably did.

Toby stuttered and pouted when he realized that he had been outwitted with a debate-winning point. Emmett took the opportunity to steal the last scrapings of chocolate at the bottom of their parfait, and hopefully end the ridiculousness.

"That's my favorite part," Toby said. "You hate that part!"

"I hated that part when I was *eighteen*." Emmett licked the spoon with a wicked grin. "When I hit thirty, I decided gelatinous chocolate ooze has its perks."

"Like?"

"Like making you pout like a petulant eight-year-old."

Tori and Emily sat a booth away and shared a sundae. They held up their end of multiple conversations with the adults, who had a tendency to behave more like children, particularly in the presence of soft serve ice cream.

This had been *their* life once upon a time, and while they—like Tori—had so desperately wanted out of it, it was the foundation of who they were, the framework of who Emmett had become. And Toby was fitting back into it, almost as if he'd never left.

As everyone headed out, Toby walked with Tori. They leaned close, pointed back to Emmett, laughed and did it again. Emily tossed a shrug over her shoulder and hung back to stick with Emmett.

"Do I want to know?" Emmett asked her.

She leaned up against Tori's car and smiled. "I don't know enough to answer that. What I do know is that if he was about fifteen years younger, I'd have some tough competition."

"Well, it'd be one-sided, honey. His gate swings one way."

"Ah, well. What she doesn't know... "

"Oh, I think she knows. He's just pretty irresistible."

Emily looked at Toby and scrunched her nose. "Too male for me."

The two deserters joined them again, looking a little more conniving than Emmett was comfortable with. "What? I feel like I'm about to be duped."

"I was asking questions, plotting nothing," Toby said. "Until now. Now I am plotting."

Toby explained his desire to meet with Tori for a little more hands-on assistance in preparing a demo audition tape for college submissions.

"If you offer it for her, the invitation needs to extend to all the interested upperclassmen."

Toby agreed, and they arranged to meet at the high school in two days. Tori began frantically texting anyone who might be interested, and everyone said their goodbyes.

When Toby got in the car, Emmett leaned over his gear shift and kissed Toby so hard and so desperately that Toby laughed when they parted. "So. I take it that means you're not irritated with me for—"

"Oh, I'm irritated all right," Emmett teased.

"I was improvising?"

Emmett turned the key in the ignition and looked back at Toby, who was still flushed and sporting the most ridiculous grin Emmett had ever seen. "Mmm. I still have a lot to say to you, sir... "

"I should have talked to you."

Emmett took Toby's hand and brought it to his lips. "No worries," Emmett said, kissing Toby's knuckles. "I think you'll like my speech." He sucked Toby's index finger into his mouth. "It doesn't have any words."

EMMETT OFFERED A GLASS OF wine, and Toby declined coyly as he ran a finger across the line of Emmett's jaw. "You said you had a speech for me?"

Emmett grinned and eyed the staircase behind him. "Yes," Emmett said, his gaze deep. "Go to my room, please?"

"All right."

Toby left the kitchen, and Emmett waited and took a breath. He needed time to collect his thoughts before stripping himself bare. Toby had been cracking him open, one seam at a time—though his seams had already been weakened from time apart, from bad decisions and, of course, their tragedy.

But having Toby in his home with his jacket draped casually over the kitchen chair where Emmett normally ate breakfast, strands of his blond curls in the bathroom sink, show tunes, Lenny Kravitz and 90s pop drivel—and that confounded *song* Toby was always twiddling with—coming from his piano, made it evident that there was yet more cracking open to do.

Emmett had a speech, all right. A soliloquy without a script.

A hiss of water moving through pipes pulled Emmett into the present moment. A shower was not in his plan. He poured a glass of wine and walked upstairs.

It was time to improvise.

TOBY HAD TURNED BACK THE bed, and his clothes were neatly draped over Emmett's valet in the corner of the room. As Emmett disrobed and added his clothes on top, he considered the hominess of sharing a valet, a bedroom.

He swirled the Zinfandel in the glass, took a drink and joined Toby in the bathroom.

Rivulets of water running down the clear shower door barely distorted the view of Toby under the water. A trail of suds skimmed down his abdomen and legs as he tilted his head back into the stream of water.

Emmett couldn't breathe, barely squeaking out, "I brought wine anyway."

Toby pushed his hair back, and a loud splash of water hit the tile floor before he opened the door. He took a sip of wine and handed the glass back to Emmett with a warm, sweet kiss. "Is this okay?"

"The shower?" Emmett asked stupidly, putting the glass back on the counter. Toby smiled, took Emmett's hand and guided him in and under the water.

Without a word, Toby began bathing Emmett, planted drawn-out kisses on his skin before passing over it with the soapy sponge. There was reverence in his motions, an intention of care that would have normally unnerved Emmett. But with simple commands—"Turn around," "Let's rinse," "Head back"—Emmett could only wonder: is this what improvisation feels like? Letting go of control, yet trusting in unfailing truth? A G-major chord will always sound like a G-major chord; water runs down; Toby's touch soothes.

After spending a few moments laving Emmett's tattoo and kissing his way back up his abdomen, Toby stood in front of him as the water gently cascaded down Emmett's back. Toby was stunning: his hair lay in dark, drenched waves against his head; his eyes glistened in the bright bathroom light; his lips were deep pink and wet.

Yes, Emmett could have been unnerved. He had designed his bathroom to be an oasis for himself; other men weren't welcome. He shared his bedroom openly—too openly—but this room was solely for Emmett, for his own thoughts, his own fantasies.

And now his most vivid fantasy stood in front of him with a hungry smile, the taste of wine and need on his lips.

"Let me—let me wash you," Emmett said, reaching for the sponge.

"I'm good—got started without you."

"You're speedy."

"You were downstairs longer than you realize." Toby smiled, and Emmett stepped into Toby's arms, arms that he trusted were there for him.

And they were, pulling him in, holding him close as they swayed, as so many times before, to unheard music. "I had a great time tonight," Toby said, as his fingers slowly massaged the nape of Emmett's neck.

Emmett answered with an improvised step—slow... slow, quick-quick—a miniature foxtrot in the confines of their cocoon. Toby followed without faltering, chuckling in Emmett's ear as they maneuvered a quarter turn and hit the shower door, popping it open.

Emmett wrapped Toby in his fluffiest bath sheet, hooding him with another towel to squeeze his hair damp-dry. He kissed and tasted Toby's clean skin. And when the air conditioner blew over their damp bodies, Toby was quick to grab another towel from the hook and wrap Emmett in it. They dabbed and snuggled, kissed and patted, and pretended to ignore their growing erections that bobbed into each other.

"You weird about your bed getting wet?"

"No." Emmett grinned at himself. "Yes. Normally. But, no."

With a stolen sip of wine for each, they lost the towels and stumbled out of the bathroom and onto Emmett's bed, kicking away the sheets to feel skin and flesh intertwined with nothing between them, nothing to distract.

Emmett rolled Toby beneath him. Their skin caught on spots of damp and dry as they slowly rutted together. Toby's lips were familiar and steadying on Emmett's. His fingers scratched Emmett's scalp as he combed through his damp hair. Emmett curled his hips into Toby's and pulled away with a smirk. "I still have things to say." He slid down and mouthed over Toby's shoulder and clavicle, dragging his tongue along the valley between. "Are you listening?"

"Yes. God, Em... yes."

Emmett swirled his tongue around a nipple. "Good. Roll over." A drop of water fell from Emmett's hair and onto Toby's chest, and Emmett lapped it up and looked down at him again.

Toby's curls had broken free from the weight of water, lightening as they dried. His eyes were heavy-lidded, and he reached up to cup Emmett's face. "Kiss me again."

The tips of their tongues met first with soft, open lips tasting of a hint of wine. "Roll over," Emmett said again, and Toby did, lifting his ass to meet Emmett's hips. Emmett wrapped an arm around Toby's waist and dotted his back with kisses as the damp curls at the nape of his neck tickled Emmett's nose.

He worked his way down Toby's body, tugging him to the foot of the bed as he stepped off. He nipped and sucked kisses onto Toby's side—the side he had saved for Emmett—while his hand trailed down Toby's spine to the curve of his ass and slipped a finger between his round cheeks. Muscles flexed beneath his fingers, a response to Emmett's mouth, Emmett's touch.

When Emmett parted Toby's cheeks and breathed warmth into the crevice, Toby moaned low and deep, and fell onto his arms.

"Jesus, Toby… " Emmett flicked his tongue over the soft rim of skin and stepped back. He took hold of himself and admired the view for a moment. His breath caught as he studied the strength in Toby's thighs, the curve of his ass, the musculature of Toby's back—and of course, the shock of loose blond curls.

Emmett didn't even know when he had given up the fight, but he knew, without question, that he wanted Toby back, wholly and completely. He wanted Toby, not just any man presenting before him, ready and wanting, not some go-to stress reliever or fly-by-night romance.

Emmett wanted Toby: the real man, the real heart, the one who knew him best.

"I thought you had something to say?" Toby grumbled from his position on the bed. He wiggled his ass and reached out a foot out to tickle Emmett's thigh.

And for once, Emmett *had* something to say. Something to give. It wasn't about shouting at the moon anymore. It wasn't about chasing his youth to see if it still fit. It was about trusting and saying, "Let's live this out together," however they could.

Emmett laughed and rubbed Toby's ass. "Sorry." He knelt down and spread Toby's cheeks apart with his thumbs, breathing warmth onto his skin. "You're distracting." After a soft kiss to each rounded globe, Emmett drew his tongue over the pucker of Toby's hole.

"How can I be distracting—" Emmett lapped at him again and pressed at his rim with his finger, the point of his tongue sloppy and wet. "Fuck."

Emmett worked him over, lost in the clean taste and smell of Toby's skin as he made a wet, slobbery mess. His tongue eased Toby open for a finger to slip in, curl down and tease. Toby whimpered and begged for relief until he finally sucked in a gasp and pled, "Please tell me the lube is within reach."

It wasn't. Of course it wasn't, because that would have required pre-planning—a script—and for once, Emmett had none.

"Need you, Em. Please. Please. Fucking *hell...* "

Emmett slipped a finger in and back out again, slowly and deliberately, before leaving a wanting Toby hanging there for the too-many moments it took him to grab lube and a condom. He apologized and Toby yanked his hand to pull him down for an awkward kiss, dirty and searching— forgiveness with tongue.

He stood and fumbled with the lube and the condom wrapper, a grown man with the constitution of a teenage boy; it was as if he'd never done this before, as if this was the first time for everything.

And maybe it was.

He reached for Toby's ass, moved behind him and slid his lubed finger down Toby's crack and easily in. Two fingers then, tipping forward. Toby arched and bowed his back, cursed and lifted on his elbows.

Yes, Emmett wanted Toby, the boy who ran, who fled, who avoided conflict as if it might poison him or turn him into a troll.

Emmett rubbed his cock up and down Toby's crack, gathering more lube. With one more begging whimper from Toby, Emmett pressed in slowly, waiting, gently holding onto Toby's hips. Toby held still for a moment, and then pushed back and bore down onto Emmett with a deep groan muffled in the pillow he clenched in his arms.

But the boy who ran was the same boy who had stood confidently in his kitchen and said to his disapproving mother, "I love your son. I don't care if you don't like it, but I do." Even after she'd asked him to leave, he told her he'd rather not, his palms sweating and slipping out of Emmett's grip until Emmett's dad stepped in and invited him to stay for dinner.

"Emmett... Em... c'mere. Need you." Toby reached back and flailed for him.

Emmett rubbed Toby's back. "I'm here. It's me." He took hold of Toby's wrist and held it gently at the small of his back as he pushed in, as sweat slicked their thighs and trailed down Emmett's neck. "It's me."

The boy who ran was the same boy who sent flowers from New York to every choir, theater and community performance of Emmett's. The same boy who worked extra jobs in New York so he could afford bus fare to see Emmett after the accident. The boy who bummed rides to see Emmett even when Emmett's mother went out of her way to make him feel unwelcome.

"Let me," Toby gasped and swallowed hard to speak again. "Let me roll over. Let me touch you. Let me... "

When he rolled over, Toby pulled Emmett down for a kiss. He seemed desperate, as if he were afraid Emmett might leave, might thrust once and become a stranger, a little black book one-nighter in Minneapolis. "It's me," Emmett soothed. "Lift up. It's me."

Emmett pushed a pillow under Toby's hips and slid in again, never taking his eyes off of Toby: the cut of his jaw as he tilted his head back when Emmett bottomed out; his hands twisting the sheets, reaching for Emmett's arms, grasping between them for his own cock to tease but not relieve, not yet; the rise and fall of his chest with each deep breath, with each arch of his back.

Emmett's legs tired; his wrists cramped from grasping Toby's thighs. But there was so much more to say. So much time to make up. So few words to begin.

Emmett shifted them, draping Toby's ankles over his shoulders. "Gonna push you back," and in one swift move, he slid Toby closer to the headboard and knelt on the bed. The pillow slipped away and Emmett bent over Toby, folding his thighs back, holding as much of him as he could in his arms.

Toby's hand began to fly over his cock. "God, yes. Em. Come on, please."

Emmett quickened his pace; their sweaty skin slapped together as his orgasm tightened and curled low in his belly. Toby froze and cried out, shooting onto his chest. His ass clenched around Emmett with each pulse. Emmett closed his eyes and his mind to everything but the throbbing heat of Toby around him, his arms holding him, his voice spurring him on.

And this time, *this* time when the images in his mind were of blond curls and brilliant blue eyes, of apple cheeks and the valleys and tendons, pulse points and tender skin of that neck, Emmett opened his eyes to Toby beneath him, gorgeous and spent, love and lust and everything Emmett ever wanted in a man.

Emmett came with one final push, hard and harder still, losing his grip on Toby's legs and yet struggling to hold onto Toby, onto something as his body wrung itself with each surge. Toby's touched soothed again, the unfailing truth he could depend on, as he caught his breath.

"Oh my God." Emmett collapsed onto the bed and quickly took care of the condom, wrapping Toby in his arms again before they chilled. "Why did we shower first again?"

"Um… " Toby giggled and ran his foot up Emmett's leg and down again. "That was supposed to have been a warm-up."

Emmett hiked up on his elbow and traced his finger over the rise of Toby's clavicle, the curve of his neck and shape of his pecs, around each nipple and down to the faint lines of his abs.

"You okay?" Toby took hold of his wrist to still his hand.

"Yeah… yeah, I'm good. Just—" He did have so much more to say; he didn't expect actual words would be involved. But they were here, twisting around without a place to start. "Am I bothering you?"

"No," Toby chuckled and kissed Emmett's fingers, sucking them clean of come from where he'd skimmed his chest. "You usually nap afterwards," he said. "But I like this too."

Emmett changed his focus to Toby's hair and combed through the drying curls, twisting them loosely around his fingers.

"What is it?" Toby tipped Emmett's face up for a soft kiss. "Tell me."

Emmett continued to touch and stare; he probably looked like a crazed buffoon. "I just… " Emmett kissed Toby's cheek and ran a finger across his brow, studying him with the still-present fear that he might disappear again. "I can't believe it's *you*."

A slow smile spread across Toby's face, faint lines pinching at the corners of his eyes. "Of course it's me." He kissed Emmett again. "Who else would it be?"

Emmett fell onto his back and stared at the ceiling. "That's just it. I wished them all to be you. I'd close my eyes—almost every time, Toby." He wiped his face with his hand and sighed. "God, I hate it. I hate that—I'd close my eyes. And almost every time, I'd see you. I'd taste you, I'd feel you under my fingers. All these years, Toby—"

Toby lifted up on his elbow now, worry and hurt etching lines in his face. "Emmett. Sweetheart."

"And it was never you." Emmett rolled his head and looked at Toby. Tears of shame, and fear that he could still never have him, filled his eyes. "It was never you. And now you're here. With my friends. In my house. In my bed, my… " Emmett took a shuddering breath and turned to face Toby, to tangle their legs, to touch and see him. "I love you." A quiet sob slipped from Emmett's throat. "I love you so much."

Toby scooped him up and held him. "Emmett, oh my God. I love—" He pulled Emmett back to cup his face and wiped a tear with his thumb. "I love you. I never stopped. Not for a day. Not for a minute. It's *always* been you."

Emmett curled into his neck and clung tight. "What are we going to do?" He kissed Toby's neck and shoulders, a constant litany of questions clouding his mind. "I don't know how to make—what are we going to do?"

"We're going to lie here until we're too gross to stand it, and then we're going to take another shower."

"We're so stupid. All these years… "

"And then we're going to sleep. Or watch some television. Or… go make some music at the piano."

It was as it had always been: Toby's mind in the now, in the improvisation of the moment, and Emmett back to needing a script, worrying about what was to come next.

"But, you have to leave." It all came back: the visits from New York, the constant battle to enjoy the moment because in a day, in two days, Toby would be gone. "What do we do when you leave? When am I going to see you again?"

"I don't know. But I don't want to spend these next two days worrying about it. We have time. We have freedom we didn't have before." Toby tucked Emmett against his chest and rubbed his scalp. "We'll make it work this time."

And as Emmett rested in the warmth of Toby's arms, all of his questions seemed to fade into assurance.

This time, they would make it work.

15

EMMETT SLID A PLATE UNDER Toby's nose. "Chips are on the table if you want more on top," he said as he kissed Toby's cheek.

"These smell amazing."

It was the morning after. Migas and mimosas, bare toes running up calves under the table, Emmett on his iPad sharing the morning news and Toby, sitting in awe, wondering when his world had shifted into this place of quiet and stillness.

They had worked in tandem preparing their meal as if they'd been through years of culinary school and Toby had been Emmett's sous for decades. Typically, Toby didn't do breakfast with lovers. Emmett said he didn't either.

Of course, Emmett wasn't *just* a lover anymore. Or ever had been, really. Emmett was never "just" anything.

"So, I was thinking," Emmett started, after he'd given up on finding any news worth repeating. "Since you have the meeting with the girls tomorrow and we talked about seeing that new play downtown, do you want to hit Eclipse tonight? It's changed so much since we used to sneak in."

"I'll have you know my fake ID was completely legitimate."

"You got it from that creepy dude who sold bootleg cassettes out of the back of his '74 Catalina."

"Right. A legitimate source for... borderline illegal behavior." Toby grinned. "And he got me that great bootleg of the '93 Glastonbury Music Festival." So, the sound quality was a bit lacking. It was a decent use of thirty dollars, getting to hear Lenny Kravitz "live"—or as live as he could at the time. "My point is, I'd love to go. I'll even bring my real ID."

"And today," Emmett said, his back turned to start washing up. "What about a drive?"

Emmett had asked the same question a couple of times since Toby arrived, and Toby always politely declined and came up with something else. But today he was out of alternative ideas. "No, I'd really rather not."

Emmett's shoulders rose and fell on a long sigh. He shut the water off before turning to Toby. "It's not my driving, is it? I'm trying to be more aware."

"It's not your driving," Toby said. "I just don't like seeing the open road in front of me." Emmett went back to work. "Where did you want to go?"

"I thought it'd be nice to go back into Xavier now that it's daylight. See your old house, the high school... " Emmett gasped and lifted a soapy finger in the air. "I know! We can swing by Mr. O'Day's and see what he's selling!"

"Mmm, maybe he'd have a beat-up VCR so I can watch Lenny again."

"You know, I'm pretty sure you can find Lenny on Amazon now."

"Yeah, but it won't have the tracking problems and the muffled cussing from when that drunk dude knocked into the idiot recording it."

"We could—" Emmett leered. "Skip the sale and head to our old make-out spot."

Toby was running out of excuses. With a steadying kiss, he tried to say, "It's all going to be okay, even if we don't go."

And then, as he got lost in the softness of Emmett's lips, "We don't need... " Toby mumbled against Emmett's mouth, "to hide... from your mother anymore."

"No," Emmett conceded, chasing Toby's lips as he stepped away. "Maybe we should go park in her driveway. I haven't pissed her off in a few months."

Toby laughed and took to the task of drying. "As fun as that sounds... I don't want to go out there, okay?"

"Sure." Emmett rinsed a plate and put it into the rack with more force than necessary. "You have something else in mind?"

"No. Stop." Toby turned off the water and waited until Emmett looked at him. "You're upset."

"Disappointed," Emmett said.

"Why is it so important to you? You've asked me this every day."

"I thought you were feeling better about... everything." Emmett turned the water back on. "You're more relaxed in the car, and we had such a great time last night at the theater."

"I'm sorry," Toby said. "I don't see what good driving down my old street is going to do. I never liked that house anyway."

"What?" Emmett slipped the glass in his hands back into the water. "I loved that house."

Toby loved *Emmett* in that house. So many firsts were shared there. And it was where Toby first came home from XACT rehearsals and tried to write music—real music—to express how he felt about the enchanting tenor who not only won his audition, but also a permanent spot in Toby's heart.

"I'm not asking that we go to the *cemetery*," Emmett said, his voice broken as if on the edge of tears. "I thought going to your old neighborhood would be nice. That pizza joint—where they'd give us free beer if you promised your parents weren't home? It's still in business."

"Vick's. They had the best calzones too."

"We could try lunch there?"

"Emmett, honey. Stop." He took Emmett's hands in his. "I still have those memories. I don't need to go out there to make them come alive again."

"You prefer they remain dead?" Emmett yanked his hands out of Toby's and drained the sink, sloppily spraying water as he spritzed the stubborn suds.

"Em, you're the one that wanted to move forward, not relive our past."

Emmett dropped the spray nozzle back into its slot and stared into the stainless steel sink. "I'm sorry; I'm not trying to push you."

"I know. And maybe one day we'll go." Although Toby couldn't imagine when. "But right now, I'm not ready."

"TOBY, ARE YOU SURE YOU want to do this? You've been quiet all day."

"It's been a quiet day." It was true. They had taken walks around a park close to Emmett's home and thrown together a picnic lunch complete with cheap wine in plastic cups. They had run errands in Brighton.

It was an everyday sort of quiet—exactly what Toby needed to calm the lingering frustrations of that morning's argument. But tonight they were at Eclipse, and Toby couldn't think of a better thing to do than soak up a hot, sweaty, writhing Emmett—in public.

The club had remodeled since his days of nervously passing off a fake ID. The entrance of years past was dark, if not sinister: black walls and dim lights that swayed from outdated wiring. But now the walls screamed a bright pink. A welcoming committee of a drag queen and twinky boys with brightly colored hair, wearing glow-in-the-dark jewelry, sold raffle tickets for a riverboat gambling weekend in Belterra.

Before Toby knew what hit him, Emmett had pressed him up against a wall in a swift, possessive kiss. He pulled back with a dark-eyed gaze and rolled his hips into Toby's.

"Shit. Em. What was that for?"

"It can get crazy in here. I don't want you to think I'll forget who I'm here with."

Toby took hold of the back of Emmett's neck and kissed him, dragging his teeth across his bottom lip as they parted. "I won't let you forget."

The pulsating bass lured them past the long line at the bar and deeper into the heart of the building. They found a corner of the dance floor to call their own, and it wasn't long before it became clear that Emmett was more than a regular. He knew virtually *everyone* here.

He would nod at this hot guy and that dopey-looking dude across the floor. Some worked their way to him, where they casually danced and shouted gossip or life happenings into each other's ears. Toby could have sworn that the short guy with almond eyes and a shock of coal-black hair drooping over his forehead had said he was going to be an uncle.

But Emmett made good on his promise. He was there with Toby. If his arms weren't in the air, letting the music take him away, they were around Toby, draped over his shoulders, hands at Toby's hips as they moved together with the never-ending pulse of music rippling through the club. It was obvious to anyone watching that if they hadn't arrived together, they most certainly were going home together.

A drag queen in a voluminous orange wig sauntered out onto the stage. She wore a sequined dress with tabby cat stripes, a long tail, matching tights and glittering pierced cat ears propped in the mass of synthetic hair.

"Why do I feel like her name is Kitty?" Toby shouted into Emmett's ear.

"Kitten Kabooty." Emmett smacked Toby's ass. "Wanna get drinks?"

Kitten introduced a few more queens who would be dancing onstage throughout the night, collecting tips and, of course, making raunchy, off-color jokes whenever the music broke enough for them to be heard. In other words, minus the new entrance, little had changed at Eclipse since Toby's days of sneaking in.

Not long after they found a table, a man practically ran toward them, calling out Emmett's name. "I thought you'd left us forever!" He was short but model handsome, with dark hair and darker bedroom eyes.

"I was here a few weeks ago, Gino." Emmett offered his cheek for a kiss and fussed at his shiny silver shirt collar. "Did you dress in the dark?"

"Dressed *and* undressed." Gino winked and looked around, as if making sure everyone's eyes were on him. He bopped around to the music and helped himself to a sip of Emmett's drink. Within thirty seconds, Toby was exhausted by him.

"Come dance with me, baby. I miss you." He tugged at Emmett's hand and pulled him off of his stool.

Emmett stood firm and yanked back. "No. Thank you." He looked at Toby, apology in his eyes. "If you'd pay attention for thirty seconds, you'd see I'm here with someone. Gino—this is Toby."

"Oh. Oh! I'm sorry. I didn't see you there." Gino stuck his hand out, waggled his eyebrows and licked his lips before introducing himself. "Gino Agostini. You're darling."

"And you're... Gino."

"Have you been here before?"

"Years ago. Back in the Honey Suckle days."

"Ahh! Honey Suckle!" Emmett practically screeched. "Oh God, she was the *best*!" Emmett sat back on his stool and talked directly to Toby, hands flapping in excitement. "Remember when she did, oh... that Shania Twain number. With the hot as *fuck* models behind her."

"It was 'Man I Feel Like A Woman,' wasn't it?" Toby said, while Gino looked him up and down as if suddenly he was competition. Toby smiled and pretended Gino wasn't there. "Wasn't that the first time you had the balls to go up and tip her?"

"I thought I would die. She was *glorious*." Emmett finally included Gino in the conversation, although from the pursed lips and occasional check of his purple painted nails, he wasn't all that interested. "Bitch licked my dollar, winked at me and shoved it in the waistband of one of the models, remember that?"

"I wasn't sure you were going to be able to walk out of there on your own that night," Toby said, laughing at the memory but mostly at how put out Gino was.

Emmett grabbed his drink and took a long pull from the cocktail straw. "God. I still don't know where the hell she got that many gorgeous men to back her—in Brighton."

"Yeah. So. She sounds… fun," Gino said, shooting a look at Toby that clearly said *go away.* "I was going to ask if you wanted to come backstage and… " He glanced at Toby again, who smiled. Barely. It was more of a pinched, I-just-smelled-something grimace. And then Gino leaned in to Emmett and tried to whisper, "My date cancelled."

Toby slammed back the rest of his drink to avoid laughing.

"So, I'm second string."

"Oh, don't be a bitter bitch with me while you have another girl on your arm. You're probably fourth."

"We'll pass, thanks." Emmett peeled his drink out of Gino's hand again and waved as he flounced off to, Toby suspected, spin someone else's evening into a flurry of self-absorbed idiocy.

"Well," Toby huffed. "He's entertaining."

"He's an ass. And he has boundary issues. I'm sorry he was rude to you."

"I think I can take it, Em." Toby stood and pulled Emmett up with him. "He doesn't seem quite your type." He shook his empty glass to suggest a refill.

"He's not." Emmett looked at him, and all the noise and commotion around them seemed to silence in Emmett's gaze. "He's the polar opposite of you."

"So is that the attraction?" Jealousy tasted sour in Toby's mouth. He couldn't help it.

Emmett looked out into the crowd, up onto the stage and back at Toby, apology again in his eyes. "This is what I meant when I said you don't know me," Emmett said. "You run; I do really stupid things."

After refills and a few more moments watching the crowd move, they headed back onto the dance floor. Toby tugged Emmett to the middle, cupped the back of Emmett's neck and brought him as close as possible so they were eye to eye, chests pressed together. Emmett gasped and smiled as they danced, eye-fucking, lips almost touching, their breath a kiss.

Toby wanted to chant, "Mine, mine, mine," but "*he has boundary issues*" still rang in his ear. He slid his hand down onto Emmett's right hip and whispered, "You okay still? Hip good?"

Emmett nodded against his lips and stepped to straddle Toby's thigh. "I'm so sorry," Emmett said. "I feel like he put a cramp in our evening." He held onto Toby's ass as they danced; his head was heavy on Toby's shoulder and his lips were hot and searching when Toby turned into his neck.

"It's okay. It's just us now, all right? It's okay."

"Take me home, Toby." Emmett's voice was deep and tired, his arms heavy on Toby's shoulders as they started to wind down from the long night of much dancing and little drinking.

"I—I can't do that, sweetheart."

Emmett pulled back with a lazy grin. "You know what I mean." Emmett combed his fingers through Toby's sweaty hair, soothing and seductive. "Take me *home*."

And while Emmett drove them there, Toby took Emmett home.

He prepared a warm bath, where they soaked and lazily sponged off the funk of the club. He led Emmett to bed and mapped every inch of Emmett's body with his hands, with his mouth, with the fullness of his body. Emmett writhed and begged, cried out until they both collapsed, satiated and blissfully exhausted. Toby cleaned them off and prepared a plate of cheese and crackers and a glass of wine to share before dimming the lights for sleep.

And in the dark, as they lay there together, sharing soft kisses and gentle brushes of feet against feet, after strings of "I love you, I love you, I love you," while Toby brought Emmett home, Toby couldn't shake the feeling he had carried around all day: Everything was still so very fragile.

"I have no right to say this," Toby confessed. "I don't like that you've been with him."

"Gino?" Emmett turned in Toby's arms, denying nothing. "He's nothing to me. I haven't been with him in months."

"You deserve better," Toby said speaking more about himself than of Gino.

"I have better. I have you."

Toby took Emmett's hand that had been caressing his shoulder. "I love you," he said with full confidence. Of all things, he was most sure of this. He kissed Emmett's knuckles and curled their held hands together between them. "Please don't ever forget that."

"Toby... what's wrong?"

"I think I'm missing you already. One more day." It was mostly true.

"Yes." Emmett rolled them and pinned their clasped hands over Toby's head. "And two more nights."

"Mmm, indeed." Toby spread his legs to let Emmett rest between them, to let him quiet his unsteady heart. "Should probably take advantage of that."

"Yes. Yes we should."

TOBY COULDN'T SLEEP. HE SPENT most of the night in that horrible place between wakefulness and sleep, never sure which side of consciousness he was on.

Where Scotty called his name again and again. Where Emmett cried out to him as Toby walked out of his life. Where he heard his parents fight over money and court costs. Where Emmett's mother scowled at him as if he was some sort of hungry predator. Where flashes of dreams never achieved and failures frequently endured cut through his vision like bolts of hot, blinding lightning.

And tonight, it was also where he questioned every good thing that had come from this trip. Where he replayed the conversations about visiting their old stomping grounds and questioned Emmett's motives for going, his promises to not bother him about it again.

By 2:07 a.m., he had decided Emmett would never let it go. And why should he? People with a shared history revisited it. They celebrated their memories by retracing the ground from which they came. But Toby couldn't offer Emmett that courtesy, a courtesy he deserved.

At 4:28 a.m., he finally understood Emmett's reluctance to be a "visitor" in Toby's life. Toby didn't belong here. He was an intruder in a life that would never be his own. As much as he wanted quiet in his life, this is what happened when he had it.

He stirred and wrestled in the silence, and then slipped out of the bedroom and tried to tire himself out with his iPad, email and backed-up correspondence.

At 6:14 a.m., he gave up and got in the shower, hoping he wouldn't wake Emmett. Solid, strong, secure Emmett, who knew his own past, was secure in his present and had a grip on his future. These were the things that had always attracted Toby to Emmett, but as he stood under the water, he knew it was exactly what would continue to be the wedge between them.

Toby would always leave; Emmett would always stay.

"Toby?"

Fucking hell.

"In here." Toby opened the bathroom door a crack and peeked out. "Morning."

"You were restless last night," Emmett said from the bed, his voice raspy from sleep.

"Yeah—I didn't wake you, did I?" Toby wet his toothbrush and shut off the water, irritated that he had been too noisy after all.

"You didn't. I sort of—" Emmett stopped talking for a moment. Toby heard him shuffling around the room. "Is everything okay?"

Toby kept brushing his teeth, and Emmett quietly knocked on the bathroom door. "Toby?"

Toby dropped his toothbrush, swore and opened the door without looking up. "You need to use the—I can get out of your way."

"You're fine." Through the mirror, Toby glanced at Emmett, sleep-mussed, boxers crooked and low on his waist. Emmett looked at the bathroom counter; it had been cluttered with Toby's toiletries, but his travel kit now sat there, open and filled with his belongings.

Toby rinsed his mouth. His heart raced. He wished for it to be an hour later so that what was coming would already be over

"What's going on?" Emmett's breathing was shallow, his eyes now huge with fear and worry.

Toby quickly applied deodorant and tossed it into the black bag. "I, uh… " He glanced at Emmett's reflection in the mirror and went about putting product in his hair. "I'm sorry, Em," he said, hardly believing it himself. "I rearranged my flight. I'm going back."

16

EMMETT HADN'T SAID A WORD. He couldn't be sure he had taken a breath as Toby's words and nonchalant movements to get dressed flushed through his body. Icy panic froze him. Toby wasn't just leaving Indiana. Toby was leaving Emmett.

Toby casually glanced at Emmett in the mirror, as if he hadn't dropped a bomb in the middle of Emmett's house.

"Why?" Emmett could only catch shallow breaths as his mind replayed every moment together in an attempt to grasp a reason for the absence of Toby's things on his counter. For the burning heat searing at his chest. "I thought things—" He swallowed and willed words to come out where thoughts could not. "Did I do something? Was it Gino?"

"You didn't do anything, Emmett." Toby wouldn't look directly at him. He turned toward the walk-in closet and rolled out his suitcase, packed but for his toiletry bag. Toby slipped the bag in and zipped the case closed. "It's me. It's—" Toby finally looked at Emmett. His eyes were dark from lack of sleep; his face reddened from the hot shower and maybe, Emmett hoped, from fighting off tears. "It's always me."

Toby grabbed his carry-on at Emmett's feet and brushed past him. A biting cold penetrated Emmett's bones as he walked by. He flushed hot, then clammy as he stood frozen in place. It felt as if Toby was already a ghost.

Toby's suitcase wheels whirred a deep rumble on the tile floor and changed pitch on the hardwood of his bedroom and with each bumped step downstairs. Emmett grabbed his bathrobe, deaf to all but a whispered, *Stop, stop, stop, stop* in his own head.

"Stop!" Emmett jogged down the stairs while fighting with the sleeves of his robe. Toby stopped and turned just as Emmett slipped on a step and landed awkwardly on his right foot. Pain shot to his hip, but he kept going, ignoring Toby's gasp and outstretched hand. "At least give me an explanation this time. You owe me that much."

With the same guilt in his eyes that had greeted Emmett in the Davenport Theater parking lot all those months ago, Toby stared at Emmett's hip and not him.

Emmett's fists clenched. He wanted to throw something. He wanted to slam something. "I'm up here, god*dammit.*" Toby finally looked him in the eye. "You owe me an explanation."

Toby pulled out his phone and checked the time. He swore and looked around the foyer and hallway, avoiding Emmett's gaze with every flick of his eyes.

"You weren't expecting me to drive you to the airport, were you?"

"I got a cab."

"Of course you did," Emmett said. "Were you going to say goodbye?"

Toby checked his phone again, closed his eyes and sighed.

"Do you know how hard it is to wake up to yourself?" Toby started. There was an exhaustion about him that Emmett could not understand. "And all you can see is what you could have been instead of what you've actually become?"

Emmett stared in disbelief. "You know I do."

"What did you do?"

If Emmett was supposed to feel sympathy for Toby's emotional state, he accepted failure. It all felt so old. So tired. So past due.

"I faced my shit," Emmett said, seething. "I fixed my shit. I got a flaky tattoo and almost fell in love with a tacky drag queen." He stopped, hoping he would wake up from the nightmare. Toby still stood there with his suitcase at his side, with his eyes dark with guilt and his hand shoved in his pocket. "I didn't handle it with grace and dignity, and I still fuck it up pretty regularly, but I handled it."

Toby put his hand on the doorknob, and Emmett's anger cracked into desperate fear with its rattle. "Toby, no."

"That's because you're stronger than me. You always have been." Toby looked around again, and his eyes rested on the photos of Emmett's family and friends lining the hall. "You have a community, a real life, this beautiful home, and I'm just—" Toby looked down at himself and over to his suitcase. "I'm just this."

"You're all I want," Emmett said. It was as simple as saying water is wet. Babies cry. Music speaks unspeakable words.

"You deserve someone who's here, Em. Someone who's solid, like you. Who doesn't rely on memories we'll never get back—who loves you with everything they have."

"Did you lie when you told me you love me?"

"That has never been—it will never be a lie."

"Then why isn't that enough?" Emmett's breath pulsed in panic. He was grasping for anything. Anger felt wasteful. He just needed to get him to stay. "Just for one more day? Just one more day, Toby?"

"Don't you get it, Em? You don't need to waste your time with someone who's afraid to go to a pizza joint because of imaginary ghosts."

"You were fine at the theater. We—we danced again. Please, Toby."

"I'm at home in the theater. It's The Great Pretend." Toby grabbed at his suitcase. "I'm not so great at real life."

Seeing the defeat on Toby's face, hearing it in his voice, every fear Emmett had had about making a go of it with this man again finally fell into place. The niggling suspicion that Tori really shouldn't depend on him for—"Tori. What about my girls? Fuck me, leave me, whatever. I'll pick myself up again. But they—"

"Can you tell them? You don't need me to help them; you know what they need."

"What am I supposed to say? Do you not understand how much Tori is counting on you? Do you think of *anyone* outside of—" Emmett stomped back down the hall, took his phone from the charger and shook it in the air as he stalked back. "*You* tell her!"

Toby slipped his carry-on bag over his head. "Seems you haven't changed much either, have you?"

"What? You're surprised I'm angry? You're too fragile for it?" He tossed the phone at Toby's feet. "You promised her. You call her."

Toby let the phone slide past him, tilted his suitcase and opened the door.

Emmett huffed and retrieved his phone. "Well, you didn't disappoint, anyway."

Toby stopped and closed the door. "What?"

"This is exactly what I was afraid would happen." Emmett swallowed his nausea, knowing that no matter what he said next, Toby was going to walk out that door. "I should never have trusted you."

"Maybe you never did. I had to come out here to prove something to you. To prove that I'm strong enough to be yours." Toby stared at Emmett as the truth fell on both of them. "Maybe you never did trust me."

"And here you are, ready to walk out on me, on my girls." Emmett covered his mouth to hide the sob that had been threatening to escape since he woke to an empty bed. "I was right. I can't trust you."

Toby stood, stunned and immovable, as if the arrow of Emmett's truth paralyzed him. His voice shook when he spoke. "I guess that says it all then, doesn't it?" Toby looked out the door again. "My car's here."

He pulled his case outside, and Emmett charged for the door. He grabbed Toby's arm, but Toby yanked it away and glared at him with a heat Emmett had only seen from Toby once before. This time, Emmett was on his feet and ready to fight.

"Did *you* lie when you told me you love me?" Toby asked, his voice shaking.

"No. I have always loved you. I can't not love you, Toby."

"Yet here we are. An encore performance."

The driver honked his horn and they both glared at him. "You're the fucking improviser," Emmett said. "Change the ending."

"Why should I do that? You don't trust me. I don't deserve your trust anyway. What's there to stick around for?"

"If you can't stay for me, at least stay for Tori." Toby didn't say anything, but he made no move to walk off the porch. "But—I want you to stay for me. For us. I want to know we're important enough to you. I think we can fix this."

Toby looked out at the cab and back at Emmett.

"You came out here, so I know you have some fight in you," Emmett said, desperate now. His voice rose in pitch, and he took a deep breath to tamp it down. "That means so much to me."

"Obviously not enough."

"Because you keep running away!" Toby didn't move. The cabbie honked his horn again. "So there it is, Toby. Fight or flight. I'm ready to fight. But if you walk away this time, I'm done. I can't do this again. I won't. I will not chase you again."

"I understand. I'm sorry."

As Emmett stood frozen in his doorway, silently pleading *no, please*, tears streaming down his face, Toby rolled his case to the car, waved off the driver's offer to throw it in the trunk and got in. The car backed into the turnaround and rumbled down the drive, into the street and out of sight.

EMMETT DIDN'T KNOW HOW LONG he'd been sitting in his bathrobe, slumped against the wall in his hallway. His eyes were burning and swollen and his nose felt as if he had endured the latest round of Morningside bubonic plague. After getting up and pressing a cold cloth to his eyes, he looked around his house. Toby was still gone.

His remnants were here: a bottle of mouthwash on the back of the commode, a piece of scrap paper that listed potential songs for the other girls—the girls he didn't know as well as he knew Tori—in his pointed and messy, yet somehow legible handwriting. More wads of tissue in the trash than usual told of pleasures and promises that already rang like distant memories.

But Toby was gone.

And this time, Emmett was determined to not let it break him. His first order of business was to phone Tori.

"Mr. H! I'm glad you called. Lena and Paige were wondering if you were going to record this thing today so we could go back over it like we do in class, or if you were coming too, or—" She took a deep breath. "We are *so* excited!"

Of course they were. "Unfortunately, Mr. Spence can't meet with you today. He had to fly back unexpectedly." Emmett's entire body clenched as he willed his voice to remain unwavering and professional.

The silence on the other end of the phone cut through Emmett's pain, so razor sharp that he could only see Tori's disappointment. "I'd be happy to work with you girls today anyway," he offered. "It wouldn't hurt to get a jump on this before the school year gets too crazy."

"I, um… " Tori sniffed and shifted, and told whoever was in the room with her that their plans were off for the day. "I'm sure he's very busy. Do you—do you think he'll be back and we could do it later?" She gasped a little, and her voice brightened. "Are we going to New York like last year? I mean, it'll be pushing it with time, but maybe we could meet with him then?"

"No, honey. We're not going to New York this fall, remember? We do a big trip every other year." As though Emmett could hear Tori's shoulders slump, he sat up more firmly himself. "I promise we'll get you guys set first week of school. We'd have done it this way anyway."

"Well, yeah, except now it won't be—" Tori was silent for a split second and then gasped again. "Did you two have a fight?"

"Tori, I really don't think that's any of your—"

"You did. Oh my God. My teacher's love life is going to keep me from getting into college."

"That's enough. My offer stands. If you change your mind and want to meet—or if Paige and Lena do—you have my number."

"Don't count on it. We're going to the lake." She shuffled the phone, and, in the background, Emmett could clearly hear Paige say, "Do *not* hang up on him, Tori, oh my God."

And then—"So. See you next week in class. Bye."

Emmett said, "I'm sorry," to a dead line.

He tossed his phone on the counter and took a shower in his guest bathroom. When he retrieved his phone again, there was a message from his mother. And before he could verbalize "no" and "fucking" and "way" in a less offensive fashion, he found himself standing inside her foyer while she kissed and cooed at his face as if he'd lost his best friend in a fatal car accident.

Again.

He finally took her wrists in his hands and stepped away. "Stop. I'll be fine."

"I was trying, Emmett. I did call to invite you both over."

"Yes, I'm aware." Emmett flicked at his dad's newspaper, perpetually lifted in front of his face whenever his mom went on one of her frequent I-know-better-than-you tears. "Hey, Dad."

"Staying for dinner?" Cliff asked.

"To be determined."

Emmett finally took a seat on the couch; his mother sat in her rocking chair. The slick metal slide of her knitting needles cut through the awkward silence. "So," his mother started. "What happened?"

Emmett grabbed the remote and flipped through a couple of channels to stall. The clicking needles stopped. "I really don't want to talk about it; he took off a day early."

"Typical." Miriam checked her pattern and began again. "You're not going to see him again, are you?"

"No." Emmett got up and wandered into the kitchen. "Did you make potato salad?"

"Ellie Shaffer in the garden club—she has a nice single son."

Emmett found a beer in the fridge and wagged it in front of his dad for permission as he walked back by him and unscrewed the top. His mother hissed.

"Isn't Ellie eighty years old?" Emmett smiled at his scowling mother around the lip of the bottle as he took a pull.

"What does that have to—"

"Her son has to be in his late fifties." Another pull. "I'm fine alone. Been alone my entire adult life."

"And miserable. Drinking away your sorrows… "

"No, see, that's *your* perception of my life. If you'd look at the world as it is instead of how you want it to be, you'd see that you're the one who's miserable. The rest of us are living our lives."

"Miriam?" His dad smacked his paper down on the ottoman before heading to the kitchen. "Did you make potato salad?" This family might disagree about most things, but potato salad was not one of them. No one made it like Miriam.

Emmett sat back and worked on his beer as Miriam slammed her knitting into its bag and stormed into the kitchen. "What about that handsome butcher at the grocery in Xavier?" she asked, her voice pinched and obviously friendlier in tone than she was feeling. "Linda down the road says—"

"Stop!" Emmett went to the kitchen and tossed his empty bottle into the recycling bin. His mother retrieved it with her thumb and forefinger and gingerly carried it to the sink to rinse it out as if it were contaminated with nuclear waste. "I did not come here—" Emmett grabbed the bottle and finished the job. "I did not come here to participate in the dating game."

"I want you happy, Em. I don't understand why you'd settle for… for *that boy*."

While Emmett was plenty angry at *that boy*, he was angrier that he couldn't have a simple cookout with his parents without thinking he was damaging his mother's neighborhood reputation by remaining painfully single. At least Toby owned his faults and didn't project them as expectations onto other people.

"That *boy* has a name," Emmett said. "And he has a great capacity to love, in a way you never could."

"What? Don't talk to me of love. You have no idea—"

"He has never expected me to be anything other than what I am in that moment—even if it's awful."

"I have never—"

"You have. You do. You just did. I never measure up."

Cliff looked at Emmett and sighed. Without a word, he got out a plastic storage container and lid and started scooping up potato salad. Emmett was not staying for dinner. But he was going to finish his point—a point that was becoming clear as he spouted it off.

"The problem with Toby isn't Toby so much as it's people like you, Mom."

"Me?"

"Your words of judgment and condemnation, said as he stood by my bed and helped me to heal, still ring in his ears. And now? He doesn't believe he *can* love anymore."

"Surely you're not going to blame me for—"

"Toby's responsible for his own behavior, and so am I. But it would be a real benefit to all of us if you'd spend less time trying to fix my life and more time appreciating what I've made of it on my own."

Emmett grabbed the dish of salad from his dad and caught his gaze. "So, that's a no on dinner. We'll do lunch? After I—" Emmett flapped his hand around trying to make sense of his day. "After I have some time to myself."

"That would be nice." Cliff patted Emmett's arm and kissed his forehead.

Emmett sighed and kissed his mother's cheek. "I shouldn't have come over. I'm sorry."

"I shouldn't let you take that home, the way you spoke to me." But her eyes glimmered with a hint of forgiveness.

"Tell Ellie to introduce her son to the butcher in Xavier. He's sort of an asshole? Needs an older man to whip him into shape." Emmett snapped an imaginary whip, complete with sound effects, and left before he could hear his mother scold.

◆◆◆

THREE NIGHTS LATER, AFTER GIVING up trying to beat Final Fantasy XV, Emmett was home alone, lost to a marathon do-it-yourself show. It featured a buff carpenter, a sassy gay interior designer—*how original*—and a spokesmodel so lithe and vacant that they wouldn't put a crack in a wall of sheetrock if they threw her at it. After listening to her voice for four solid hours, though, throwing her at something sounded like a decent option.

Emmett was surrounded by an empty bottle of rum and two dishes of melted ice cream now hardening in their bowls. Oh, and a glass of what he thought was pop, but remembered was actually watered-down rum. And pop.

The obvious thing to do at this point was to text Gino.

EMMETT: Hey. Whatcha donnig?

GINO: You never text me. What's wrong?

EMMETT: I'm not allowed to txt u?

GINO: I also don't imagine you're a typo texter or a shortcut texter. What's wrong?

EMMETT: I'm lonely.

GINO: Where's Blond and Beautiful?

EMMETT: Bolted.

GINO: Bummer.

EMMETT: Blue balls. Whatcha doing? I got it right that time.

GINO: You're drunk. I'll pick you up. Headed to Eclipse. Do you stink?

Emmett sniffed his armpits and smiled, dropped his phone and picked up his remote instead. The renovation project on his screen was of a kitchen similar to his. He belched, sat back and watched.

After what seemed like no more than thirty seconds, a persistent ringing woke him up. His doorbell.

"What the *fuck*, bitch? I thought you were dead." Gino pushed past Emmett, who wobbled a little and sniffed his armpit again, catching up to the conversation they'd had earlier.

"I am not dead." He didn't recognize his own voice. "I probably should have some water, though."

"And change. And brush your hair. Put some concealer on. They can see your blotches on Saturn."

"Shut the fuck up." Emmett went upstairs, looked in the mirror and grimaced. If he had concealer, tonight would be the night to break it out. But he didn't, so he didn't. He changed, did something less sloppy-drunk to his hair, grabbed a water bottle and they were on their way.

"This is probably a bad idea," Emmett said as he turned down the volume of the electronic music pounding through Gino's car. "You have horrible taste in music."

"All I'm saying is, you puke in my car over that—who is he, anyway?"

"High school sweetheart."

Emmett never moved his gaze from the front window, but he could feel the heat of Gino's glare, and his disbelief running through the car like a tidal wave of disgust. "You got drunk over your high school sweetheart? God, you're an idiot."

"It's not that simple. I don't expect you to understand."

"Try me."

"Just drive, Gino. I'm not explaining anything to you."

It was a bad idea. Emmett spent his first hour nursing glasses of water with lemon and finally accepted an invitation to come sit at the sound booth with his old friend Jake Lester, so he wouldn't look so publicly forlorn.

When he decided a cab ride back to his empty house would be better than the situation as it was, Gino popped up at the top of the stairs with the shittiest of grins.

"What? Did Kitten finally agree to go home with you?"

Gino pulled up a chair next to Emmett and rubbed his hands together. "Oh it's better. I had to come up and sit with you so I could see your face."

"What?"

Gino nodded to the stage. "Wait. You'll see."

Kitten Kabooty came out in her typical regalia, welcomed the crowd and pointed up to the sound booth. "I need a beat fit only for the best!" Jake cranked up the volume of the generic electronica house music and Kitten went on. "Ladies and Bears, back from her hiatus of discontent, give it up for... Anita Mann!"

Gino was on his feet before Emmett could register what was happening. "That'll cure what ails ya', sister." Gino tugged on Emmett's hand and pushed him to the front of the booth. "Some nice, hot Latino ass."

Emmett couldn't deny it. For a married investment banker in drag... Derek looked *good*.

17

NEW YORK CITY—September 2016

Toby couldn't decide if industry parties belonged in the eighth ring of hell—which, if his memory of lit class served, was fraud—or in the ninth ring: treachery. Of course, the amount of time he had been standing at the catering table nibbling on fingerling potatoes and aioli while offering up bits of small talk to this producer and that actress, this musician and that director, might qualify the whole thing for the gluttonous ring of hell, number six.

Regardless, Toby was in hell. He had pretty much been in hell since the sleepless night before he left Indiana. And now, two weeks later, his life was approaching a state of limbo, which, come to think of it, was the *first* ring of hell. That could make slipping out of this party a little easier.

But limbo: He was to leave for a show in Chicago in a few days and, once home from there, he had blocked out some time on his calendar. He planned to work on his score—to fix his shit, as Emmett had so eloquently put it.

The biggest tangible pile of shit in Toby's life, besides his perpetual disaster of an office, was the box of musical scraps he had recently begun to call "It." For example: "I need to spend some more time with

It," and "It still wakens me at night with fresh ideas," and "I'll never be satisfied until I finish It, even if no one ever hears It."

Which is why he was here, in a conference room at the Marriott Marquis, nodding his head and smiling as someone from the Schubert Organization rambled on about upcoming projects. He needed to listen to that sort of chatter to help him decide what to do.

Was there a playwright who might need a specific kind of score? Was there a developing show that needed Toby? Was selling the piece an option he even wanted to pursue?

He had gleaned a few phone numbers and a business card for a friend of a person who knew a donkey who lived in Kiev who might be able to hook him up with a trunk monkey who wrote plays for a ramshackle theater in Dixon, Montana—population 203. It might have been a friend of a neighbor, but by that point he was into his twenty-eighth fingerling and could not be expected to soak in every last detail of the guy's long-winded vitae.

Now Toby stood half listening to a group of people he had very little interest in. He finished his drink, excused himself, found the hostess and took his leave.

He emerged in Times Square and growled. The gentle murmurings of the cocktail party had made him forget the pandemonium just outside its doors. He hastily made his way to Eighth Avenue, head down, destination in sight. He grunted and then glared at a persistent Spiderman with a fake French accent before he could finally slip by him.

Emmett would have laughed at that. In his exuberant love for the city, he would make the Spiderman take *their* picture and probably would have given the fool a tip.

"He's just trying to make a living, Toby," he would say.

Needing to get away from the cacophony of Times Square, Toby grabbed a cab for the nine short blocks to his office. He went directly upstairs, closed his door, pushed the scores littering his keyboard onto the floor and smacked the old, yellowed spiral notebook onto the music rack. He dug into his workbag for a new notebook and a package of mechanical pencils.

"Everything old is new again," he sang to himself. "I can do this."

No more tinkering. No more fidgeting and fighting and fussing. He was going to get down something concrete, a melody, an overture—*something* to show for himself, to remind himself who he used to be, who he once believed he could be. Who he truly was.

Without opening either notebook, he began to play. The beginning had been forming nicely. He knew it upside down and sideways: the piano mimicked staccato strings, a chipper tone of youth and carefree happiness. Enter the exposition—a melodic line—softly, as if from a distance. The staccato rhythm slowed to match it until it stopped completely.

The lyric melody took over then, lush and gentle, a lilt of flirtatious high tones as if to taunt the crisp rhythm to come back and play.

In a perfect duet, it did come back, a give and take of rhythm and harmony, melody and structure. Flashes of his more recent days and nights with Emmett colored the harmonies: a sapphire-blue swirl, a hitched gait, sandalwood and cardamom, a Boston tea party and disco strobe lights all played into the musical lines.

Until Toby's memory stopped. Until Toby stopped. He looped back a few bars, tried again, and ran into a musical roadblock. He opened the old notebook and flipped through pages for a hint, a lick, a phrase, that could propel his transition into his second theme.

Nothing.

This is where it always stopped. He had bits further on. He had a satisfactory finale—but *only* satisfactory. Key elements were missing, elements that remained out of his reach.

Grumbling, Toby retrieved the box of musical parts and secrets, visions and dreams put to song. He looked into the mess, sighed and dropped the notebooks and pencils inside.

This called for a change of scenery.

"What the—are you moving out?"

Toby heard Malik's voice before he saw him. He peered into Malik's studio, where a floor-to-ceiling figure of metal and clay stood, undefined in its form, a dusty and splotched work in progress. "What makes you think I'm moving?"

Malik stepped out from behind his sculpture and grinned. His skin was as dusty as his sculpture, and one dreadlock draped down the center of his head and onto his nose. "The box. It's usually a good first sign."

"Not moving. Adjusting."

"That and you're acting weird. You've been here every day for two straight weeks, holed up in that disgusting office of yours, and have had no show to speak of."

"I leave for Chicago in a few days. Just—" Toby hiked the box up for a better grip. "I'm headed down to the theater. Walk with me. This is awkward."

Malik took off his apron and grabbed two bottles of water from the small fridge in the corner of his studio. "Trade," he said as he held them out to swap Toby for the box.

"I don't need you to carry my schoolbooks, big guy."

"Suit yourself."

Once downstairs, Toby began pulling paper items from the box. Napkins, hotel stationery, manuscript scraps and his two notebooks.

"So, adjusting," Malik said, as he pulled a stool over to the piano. "What does that mean, exactly?"

Toby sat down at the piano, mindlessly played a few chord progressions and shrugged. "I have no idea. It feels like that's what's happening."

"This has something to do with Emmett."

Sometimes Toby hated Malik. He began the piece anew; the crisp rhythm of the keys echoed through the empty theater. "Your wisdom is enviable." Toby shook off Malik's offer of water and nodded at the papers on the lid of the piano. "This is what I really wanted to do with my life."

Malik looked over the mess strewn there. "Why didn't you?"

Toby started playing again, the lyrical theme that he knew in his sleep—that anyone who knew him knew, because that was what came out first when his fingers touched the keys of a piano: the cream that rose to the top. "I tried. Studied composition in college until—" He abruptly changed course and struck descending, diminished chords. He chuckled to himself, envisioning a maiden tied to train tracks in a silent film.

Malik smiled, sadness and understanding in his eyes. "The Accident."

"The Accident." Toby broke his final chord into a tremolo and ended with a sharp strike of the keys. "The accident. The accident, the accident." He flung his hands toward the lid of the piano. "My shit."

"And Emmett plays into this how, exactly?"

"It's all one big pile of shit, isn't it?"

Malik took a swig of water and waited. And, just as happened with Barb on the plane, Toby started talking.

"I was always fooling around with writing until I met Emmett. He was the first person I ever invested in. He gave me a focus." Toby played the melodic line, one line, two simple phrases, and looked at Malik. "I guess he was my—" Toby chuckled and dropped his hand from the keys. "It's ridiculous."

"He was your muse. He *is* your muse."

"Which is the stupidest thing ever. That's what bloviating romances and Jane Austen novels are for."

"Excuse me. Inspiration is not stupid. You cannot create in a vacuum."

Toby got up and grabbed a small stack of notes, pages from a pad he'd taken from a Hilton in Phoenix that were filled with scratched-out chord progressions. At night, when the sessions for a since-forgotten conference were over, and the prospect of finding anyone to bring to his room for the night had grown thin, he went back to his room alone and jotted down the musical notes that had struck him during the day.

He started to play through them, but now they had little musical value. Like lost entries from a diary found far from its original bound pages—*I went to the market today; the vegetables are so plentiful I couldn't decide what to choose*—they remained disconnected memories.

Toby stared at the sheets in front of him, knowing much of what he had was just like this: lost entries, unbound, disconnected not only from one another, but from their original purpose.

The definition of his life lay sprawled out over a grand piano, in scraps.

"Does Emmett know about this?" Malik's voice was gentle. Kind.

"No. He's heard pieces of it—the stuff I always play—but he has no idea what it is."

"Tell him."

"No." Toby started to collect the scraps and put them back in the box. "Especially now. It would be inappropriate." Toby took a deep breath, hoping the air of the theater would calm his racing heart. He had shared too much. His legs itched to run from the room. "You understand. Like your piece upstairs. It's not ready to give away yet."

"Because keeping it for yourself is working so well for you."

"What am I supposed to do, Malik?"

"Well for starters, I wouldn't disconnect from the one thing that inspires me."

Toby grunted and continued to gather the remnants of years of longing. Because that's what it had boiled down to. Not desire. Not love or affection. It was longing for something he knew deep in his heart he could never have, should never have. "He doesn't trust me anyway."

"Because you keep walking out when you're uncomfortable." Toby kept packing until he felt Malik's hand on his wrist, felt his dark-eyed gaze burning his skin. "You know, if you'd stick around, if you'd let him help you carry your shit—Mister I Don't Need You to Carry My Schoolbooks—maybe you'd both come out of it not only together, but whole."

"How am I supposed to do that?"

"Let him love you. Because he does, you know."

"I know. And I keep hurting him."

"Let him love you so much it hurts *you*. You have to let it hurt again, man. That's where it broke. You have to go back there."

"I think I've hurt quite enough, thank you."

"*With* him. Go through it with him. You never grieved together." Toby put another stack of scraps into the box, and Malik pulled them back out. "Do you know how diamonds are made?"

"What?"

"Diamonds. One of the most sought after, hardest, most impermeable gems."

"I know what diamonds are, you ass." Toby put the stack back in the box and sat back down. He was growing impatient and frustrated. "They're mined, I know that."

"Carbon, heat and pressure." Malik counted the three necessary elements on his fingers. "And dude, if you keep running from the heat and pressure, you're just going to be left with a pile of—"

"Of shit."

Malik smirked. "Take this music. Take that man. Walk through that muck and shit you carry on your back every day—with him."

"What if he won't—"

"Shut up. Stop making excuses. Stop answering for him. I'm telling you, Toby—you will have rare gemstones of music."

Toby lowered the fallboard over the keys and shook his head. "Rare gemstones. You're crazy, you know that?"

"I am not! People dream of love like this." Malik took to the stage now and Toby couldn't help but laugh as he started pacing, flailing his arms to make his point. His big dramatic finish. "Bigger than time and distance. Bigger than loss and tragedy. This is the shit that makes losers like me sculpt. Paint. Write." He came close to Toby and lifted a hand to touch his face but then pulled back, speaking silently of intimacy they once shared. "And you have it right at your fingertips, but you're so busy feeling sorry for yourself you're missing it."

After further consideration, Toby didn't hate Malik. Not one little bit. "You'll keep on me? When I get back from Chicago?"

"If that's what you want. But I think you can do it without my bullshit."

Toby smiled and kissed Malik's cheek. "I've grown quite accustomed to your bullshit."

◆◆◆

TWO DAYS LATER, TOBY WAS picking up some last-minute items for his trip to Chicago when Emmett called.

Toby flushed hot, put his phone on his desk and continued searching for his score while the Schoenberg concerto faded into an unanswered phone call. He went to lunch and tossed an extra bag of chips to the receptionist, who was apparently feeling blue: his eye shadow matched his blue quiff with almost scientific precision.

On his way out for the week, his phone rang again as he passed Malik's studio. "I swear to God, Toby. If you do not change that ringtone or start answering your—"

Toby lifted the phone and mouthed, "Emmett."

"Answer it, you jackass." Malik tossed a clay-covered cloth into the air and disappeared behind his sculpture, mumbling something Toby was happy he couldn't hear.

"Hey." In spite of his attempted short, casual yet non-committal tone, Toby thought his heart might leap into his throat and straight onto the piss-yellow laminate floor.

"Hi," Emmett said, not as casually. He definitely sounded non-committal, however. "Did I catch you—you sound out of breath."

"No. Getting ready to head out. How are—"

"No. Stop. This isn't me calling you."

"It sure sounds like you," Toby said, as he went back into his office and closed the door. "And it's your phone number, so unless you've been taken over by some kidnapping ventriloquist… "

"Please stop." Emmett cleared his throat and took an audible breath. "This is, um… this is Tori Graham's high school choir director, from Morningside." The Great Pretend, indeed—with added melodrama. He loved this son of a bitch so much it did hurt. "You had implied to her at some point that you would be sending her files or music for 'Glitter and Be Gay.' Some sort of special arrangement, or… "

"Yes. I have a nice audition-length arrangement."

"That must be it. She's, um—she's not speaking to me much at the moment, so I was having trouble—"

Toby decided to try again. "Also, hi."

"No. I mean it. No 'hi' from you. I'm calling about Tori. Period."

"Right. Business call. I apologize, Mr. *Henderson*. It must have gotten lost in the—" Toby exhaled loudly as he unshouldered his bag and sat down. "In the—" *Fucking hell.* "Wait. She's not speaking to you?"

"Not unless necessary. Can you send that file to me as soon as possible? Apparently all *five* arrangements I have are unsuitable."

Toby bit back a laugh and thought maybe, possibly, he heard a slight chuckle on the other end. "Why don't you bring her to Chicago—isn't there a three-day weekend coming up? We can exchange the music, and I can make up the missed session with her."

"Stop it." Emmett sucked in air again. Toby imagined him sitting up straighter, planting his feet more firmly onto the ground. "You have my email. Send me the files or a link so I can get them myself."

"Would it be easier for you if I spoke with her directly?"

"That's not remotely necessary."

Toby booted his laptop, giving up the notion that maybe Emmett would sway a little to familiar warmth. "I'll send it now. I'm sorry I didn't sooner."

"Thank you," Emmett said. "Have—have a safe trip."

"Sure. It was nice—"

The line went dead, and someone knocked on his door. "Malik… not right—" But Malik ignored him and opened the door anyway.

"You okay?"

"Not even a little." He eyed his box. The Box. The Accident. Toby's life had diminished to Article plus Subject.

"What are you thinking?" Malik asked.

Toby sent the email and opened a blank document. "You have any packing tape?"

"I do. What are you doing?"

Toby got up and retrieved the box. "I think it's time for me to let this go."

18

MORNINGSIDE—September 2016

"Hey, Punky Puss. This came for you." Mac plopped a box that had seen better days onto Emmett's desk. She grabbed her mail from the top and read the return address. "520 Eighth Avenue, Suite 825, New York. Find a new music distributor you're going to tell me all about?"

"Five-twenty?" Emmett stood from his crouched position with a folder of music in his hand. He could feel the blood draining from his head. "That's Toby's office."

"So. Should I leave, or do you want me to stay?"

Dumping the folder on the table, Emmett approached the box as if Toby might jump out of it himself. "I think I'll be—" He looked at Mac and smiled at his own trepidation. "Go on. I know where to find you."

She closed the door, and Emmett stared at the box. He considered ignoring it—return to sender. But curiosity had him digging in his desk drawer for a pair of scissors.

With three swipes, the musty scent of Toby's office hit Emmett's nose. He put aside an envelope with his name and pulled out the contents: flash drives, CDs in paper sleeves, cassette tapes and floppy disks, all banded together by format. At the bottom was a manila envelope filled with all sorts of scraps covered in Toby's handwriting, his minimalist manuscript on hand-drawn staves, frenzied notations that used every inch of paper real estate he had.

"What the hell, Toby?" Emmett plopped down into his chair and grabbed the envelope with his name on it. His heart raced as he opened the typed note with his and Toby's names hastily scratched at the beginning and end.

Emmett,

We've always said that rehearsal is the best part of the project— when the show belongs to the creators and performers—when it still belongs to us.

This is something I've been "rehearsing" since the first time I heard you sing. The first day you smiled at me. The first day I ever really connected to anyone. You've heard bits of it before; I've played around with it again and again and could never go anywhere with it. In time, it became more about me than about its intended—you. Like so much else, I finally quit trying.

I pulled it out again after you visited me last fall and have tried piecing it together. As you can see, it's in shambles. So I'm asking for something I have no right to: I'm asking for your expertise. Your touch. Your technical and digital skills, to help me pull this thing together. I'd love to hear it onstage one day, and that will never happen unless it's finished.

It started with you at its heart. It is my heart—the one thing that has kept me connected to you through the years. It seems time to let that go, to put it in your hands for a while.

For now, if you have the inclination, give it a listen. If you're interested, we can talk further about what I have in mind.

Love always, Toby

"Always" was underlined. Toby's voice echoed in Emmett's mind. Emmett folded the letter and put it back in the envelope. And then he pulled it out and read it again.

He must have been at it—reading and re-reading, staring at the box's contents without actually investigating them—for quite some time. A knock at the door jolted him so severely that he cracked his knee on the underside of his desk.

"I'm headed—are you okay? You're peaked." Mac had her Morningside Band baseball cap on, a whistle around her neck and a clipboard tucked tightly to her chest.

He shook his head as if coming out of a trance and put the letter back in the box, cross-folded the flaps and shoved the box under his worktable. "You need help with marimbas this afternoon? I need to blow off some energy."

"Always. Be out there in five minutes or you're doing laps."

◆◆◆

"Okay, once more from 'Observe how bravely,' please," Emmett said. He took a breath with Tori and began the accompaniment.

She was doing well with the piece Toby had suggested for her demo tape. "Glitter and Be Gay" was the most challenging piece any of his students had ever attempted, and she took to it like a pro.

"No, no. No effects yet, Tori." She also got ahead of herself and wanted to add the trills, the flourishes, the highest of optional notes.

"I'm ready—"

"You are not. I am not. We'll do this together. Same spot. 'Observe how'—"

"Bravely, yeah yeah." She rolled her eyes and took in half as much breath as needed.

Emmett didn't play, and she let out her collected breath with a long-winded raspberry. "Do we need to stop for today?" he asked.

"No," she said with a hint of a glare. "I—I'm impatient."

"I'm aware. I'm also trained in vocal technique, so you *might* want to trust me a little bit here."

Tori put her music stand down and leaned back against the piano, reshaping the bun in her hair. "Why is it so hot in here?"

"Because it's ninety degrees outside and your parents don't want to pay more tax money to keep the school properly air-conditioned." Emmett turned on the bench to straddle it. "What's up?"

Tori side-eyed Emmett and scrunched her mouth before confessing. "Emily says I shouldn't be mad at you anymore."

"I like Emily."

Tori blushed. "Thing is, I'm still mad. A little."

"I'm sorry you're still mad at me. I don't always deal well with being let down either."

"What do you usually do?"

"Ah, maybe years down the road when you're a Broadway diva, I'll fill you in."

"Mr. H!"

Emmett laughed and pointed to her water bottle. "Fluids. And you're probably about the right age to realize that adults aren't always... grown up."

"I don't want to be mad at you anymore."

"I'd prefer that, too." He began to collect the music spread across the rack. "Would you like to talk to Mr. Spence directly?"

"You never let me."

"I'm offering it now." Her eyes lit up, and maybe it was the stifling heat in the building, but Emmett could swear her bun lifted higher on her head. Emmett remembered a time when the thought of talking to Toby could light him up like that. "I'll give him your contact information, so it's on his time."

"I understand. I won't bother him, I promise."

"You do know he's who you should be angry with, correct?"

"I do," she admitted. "But he's so—I'm sure he's very busy."

"He is. He's also not your ticket out of here."

Her shoulders slumped, and she began to clean up her belongings. "What if—what if I don't get out of here, Mr. H?"

"Well, for one, it's not the worst place to be."

"But I don't want—"

"And more importantly, I'm going to do everything in my power to help you."

Tori grinned and started toward the door, then stopped when Emmett interrupted her with an "Ah-ah-ah!"

"Stand. Right. Sorry." She put the music stand where it belonged and hugged him. "You're the best, Mr. H."

"Yeah, yeah. Remember that next time you're not getting your way."

Tori skipped out the door, and Emmett pulled out his phone.

EMMETT: Tori's email: tgrahamcracker99@gmail.com

An hour later, Emmett got a reply.

TOBY: Thank you. I'll check in with her soon.

The marching band came in from rehearsals so loudly it was as if there weren't concrete walls separating Emmett's room from the hallway. They shouted and moaned and groaned about the heat, about Mac's dictatorship—this, obviously, from a freshman who had not yet learned—and about how ignorant the trombone section was. That was chronic; if Emmett recalled his high school days correctly, it went with the instrument.

He closed his classroom door and his office door, and stared at the box beneath his worktable. Turning his back on it, he checked on some music shipments that seemed to be taking forever to arrive. Except they weren't. He felt the box staring at him, and—*Christ*—finally spun around and grabbed the thing.

He read the letter again. *It is my heart—the one thing that has kept me connected to you… It seems time to let that go, to put it in your hands for a while.*

Emptying the box and arranging everything on his worktable, he noticed a post-it on one of the banded-together flash drives: *Start Here.* He plugged the drive into his laptop and opened the only file on it, entitled "Opening."

Within a few short moments, Emmett could imagine a small chamber ensemble playing, spiccato strings opening with plucked, bouncing notes as if someone were skipping through a meadow on a spring day. The first melodic theme joined in, and Emmett gasped and hit pause as if the sound might burn him.

"Oh shit." He hit play again and instantly hummed along, tentatively here, confident there. He covered his mouth with his hand in disbelief, "Oh my God" whispered between phrases. He stopped the recording again and stared at the drive, then the letter.

This is something I've been "rehearsing" since the first time I heard you sing. The first day you smiled at me. The first day I ever really connected to anyone.

He started the track again, his heart in his throat as a smile forced its way through the rush of emotions. "That's Toby," he said, as he picked up the vague melodic line of the plucked pitches. And then, the melody: "And that's me. Oh God."

Emmett sat back in his chair and let the file play—it took only four minutes—and then he started it again. And again.

"Hey. Knock, knock?"

Emmett jolted his attention to the door and paused the track. "Derek! Hi! Hi. I, uh—" The music continued, and he tried again, this time successfully turning off the sound. "Hi. What, uh—wow. Hi!" He flushed as if he had been cheating, caught with his pants around his ankles.

While he and Derek had gone home together the night Anita returned to Eclipse, he owed him no faithfulness. The only nakedness that night was in the unveiling of their respective sob stories. Emmett's heartbreak felt like a stupid repeat offense, while Derek's was raw and jagged and involved betrayal and the withering of a sweet, magical, mystical friend into a normal guy with a broken heart.

"That was beautiful." Derek sat down and nodded toward Emmett's monitor. "What is it?"

"It's, um—" Emmett spied the partially folded letter and quickly shoved it back into its envelope. "It's from—" He stopped, smiled and pulled the flash drive out of the computer. "I have no fucking idea what it is, to be honest. What brings you here?"

"You."

"Well, I didn't think you were here for sweaty adolescent percussionists."

"Oh, honey. You didn't know me in high school, did you?" Derek winked and bit his bottom lip. "Tell me you didn't like a good drummer now and then."

"Was always partial to the boys behind the keys." Emmett shut down his laptop. "So, really. Why are you here?"

Derek plopped his elbow on the desk and leaned in. "This. You."

"What *this*?"

Derek sat back with a huge grin, looking more at ease than he had since his arrival back in town. "I have a proposal."

"Oh, honey no." Emmett eyed Derek carefully. The last time he accepted one of Derek's proposals, he had ended up with a faerie tattoo on his hip.

"Stop. I want to take you out tonight. On a date. When's the last time you went on a date?" Derek asked.

Emmett hated the answer. "I was eighteen."

"And that's not right. So. I've made reservations for that new bistro on the west side. We can go take a walk along the river, or I'm sure we could get last-minute seats to a play in the district." Derek stood and pulled Emmett up, slinking his hands around Emmett's waist and pressing him close. "We could sit outside on your back patio and count fireflies and drink wine for all I care. But only after dinner."

It would be easy, in the spell of Derek's bedroom eyes, his curled accent and sexy sway. Ridiculously easy. "What are you doing?"

"I'm asking you on a date."

"Yes, I hear you. But what are you *doing*?" Emmett peeled Derek's hands off of him and sat back down. "You are in no condition to be dating—" And then he remembered. Divorce court. Property settlement. "What happened today?"

Derek sighed, loosened his tie and sat down. "He got the house."

"How did that happen?"

"No idea, but I'd like that to be the last we speak of it. So. Dinner. A walk. Fireflies and wine, yes?"

"No."

"No?"

"No," Emmett repeated. "What's going to happen after the wine?"

Derrek narrowed his eyes and growled. "You *know* what happens after the wine, *querido*."

"Yeah, no. And no more *querido*, either. I'm not your lover. I'm not your sweetheart."

"You could be." When Emmett didn't blink, Derek cracked his hand on Emmett's desk and resorted to whining. "Oh come *on*. Are you paying me back for when I first turned you down because you were such a fucking mess?"

"No, I'm thanking you. Don't do this; you don't want it."

Derek slipped into his Anita pout, his accent thickened and exaggerated as if flipped on by a switch. "You don't get to tell me what I want."

Emmett simply laughed. "Put Anita back in her wig box, you big baby. I'm not talking to her." Derek rearranged himself and had the sense to roll his eyes. "Look, go home. Burn some incense, stab a voodoo doll, go count the fucking fireflies if you want. Just… take care of you. He's not worth it."

Derek sighed and squeezed Emmett's hand before standing to go.

"Is lunch still on for Tuesday?" Emmett asked, because losing Derek's friendship would be divorce fallout to fight against.

Derek smiled, sadness still in his eyes, and looked at Emmett's monitor, at the envelope with Emmett's name scratched on it. "I wasn't kidding, you know? Toby's music is stunning." Emmett blushed and didn't even try to deny it. "I'll see you Tuesday."

◆◆◆

THE NEXT DAY, THE BELL rang ending Emmett's Music Theory II class. Most of the students there had mixed choir the following period, so the short time between classes became a quick, quiet recess for everyone.

Emmett was known to champion the Inter-Choir Paper Wad Basketball Tournaments. This year, his toughest competition was the soprano section and a rogue science nerd who loved the mathematics behind music. He was about to make a fantastic three-point shot when Mac's voice cracked through the intercom system.

"Mr. Henderson?"

"Yes… " He lifted his arms and lofted the wad of paper. It kissed the edge of the can and fell to the floor.

"I'd like to see you in my office, if you have a moment."

"Ooohh! Mac's gonna get you!" The only thing different about a student versus a teacher getting summoned from an intercom is that a teacher can boss around the little shits who are mocking.

"Kyle, do you have the iPads out for warm-ups yet?"

"No. We were—" Kyle pointed at the trash can. "I'll get on that."

"Warm up number E-four today, please. I'll be right back."

What didn't change from high school to adulthood, however, was the trepidation of walking into the office to which you had been summoned. Mac should not be intimidating to Emmett, and yet her firm posture as seen from the back spoke of irritation. Emmett cleared his throat. "What's up?"

"Sit down, Emmett."

She didn't turn around. He thought about walking away; this was beginning to feel a bit out of line. But he sat, because he respected her enough to let her cross that line from time to time. It was usually for his own good, anyway.

Mac spun around and smiled at him, the kind of maternal smile one sees before one gets his ass handed to him. "I'm about to nose into your business," she said.

"I had a hunch. And not to be rude, but I do have class in three minutes."

"You raise leaders in there. They'll take care of themselves." She smiled again and patted his thigh. "Who was that dark-haired man in your office yesterday?" At Emmett's raised eyebrow, she explained. "I came in to call you outside. The marimbas finally got that lick you'd worked on with them the other day."

"Ah. His name is Derek."

"What are you doing, Emmett?"

"Sitting in your office feeling like I've broken some sort of rule by having a man visit me after work."

"There is a boy in New York who sent, as literally as humanly possible, his *heart* to you, and you've let it sit in a box under a table without so much as a thought."

"Okay. Stop. First, Derek is just a friend."

"Oh." Mac sat back and pursed her lips. "My apologies. It—it seemed very intimate."

"It was. He's going through some shit, and I'm choosing to spend some time alone."

"Probably wise."

"Second, you have no idea what I've done with that box or its contents. Just because it sits under that table does not mean I haven't listened. It doesn't mean—"

Emmett stopped, sucked in air and looked into Mac's eyes: caring, soft, protective, accepting of any stupid thing that was about to come out of his mouth even if he might earn a lecture for it. Mac gave Emmett the kind of care he never got from his own mother. He shouldn't be fighting her the way he fought his own mother.

He sat back and pinched the bridge of his nose, tossing off his glasses when they fell askew. "What am I supposed to do, Mac?"

She didn't say anything, but the heat seemed to rise in her tiny office.

"This is—he has resources for this sort of crap at his fingertips," Emmett continued. "He stretches me like a rubber band and then—" Tears stung at Emmett's eyes and he blinked angrily, letting one drip down his cheek. "It's gorgeous, the music. I don't know what he wants from me."

"I should have done this after school, Emmett. I'm sorry." She handed him a tissue that he waved away. "Let me go check in on your kids. You sit."

Before he could argue, she was gone. He decided to compose himself by looking through pictures on his phone. Considering they were most recently of Toby and sights they had seen together, it was a bad decision.

"Okay, student teacher is getting his first taste of a choir. We'll traumatize everyone in one fell swoop." She apologized again before picking up where they left off. "He wants your help. It's really that simple."

"But why me? He disappears for fifteen years, I call and suddenly he wants to jump back in like nothing happened—"

"I'm going to stop you right there. Listen to yourself, Emmett. This is not about you."

"I didn't say it was."

"You are so worked up about how he left you, how he let Tori down, how he's dumped this ridiculously bizarre request in your lap. You fail to see that every time he runs, he's not running from you. He's running from himself."

It was so obvious, really. So obvious that Emmett had missed it. "Just like I used to."

"And what helped you isn't going to help him."

"No. I needed roots. He needs wings." Emmett needed a script; Toby had to improvise. It really was that simple.

"And he needs a safe place to land once he realizes he's running from imaginary ghosts. But until he has a safe place—"

"What if he never feels safe?"

Mac pointed toward Emmett's room. "That's why he sent that. It's his home. He needs you to help figure out what's missing so you can be safe together."

"I'm an asshole."

"You are my *friend*, and my friends are not assholes. You are also so nauseatingly in love I can't digest my lunch properly." She handed him a tissue for the tears he was unsuccessfully demanding should remain unshed. "And you had a horrible thing happen before you were old enough to know how to balance a checkbook. No one in their right mind would have expected you to handle it perfectly."

"My mother did."

"Your mother can suck a rock. She's half the reason you pushed that boy away to begin with."

Emmett smiled then. "I do love annoying her."

"All the more reason… "

"Thank you." Emmett stood, laughing at the clock. "I wasn't in the mood for mixed choir today anyway."

"Come out and hear the marimbas this afternoon. I might have to hire you as an assistant."

"Oh hell no. I will not do marching band."

"Wimp."

"When you're ready to lead a soprano sectional, we'll talk."

Silence. As expected.

BRUSHSTROKES OF WARM AND COOL colors swept across the sky, and a golden glow fell across the yellowing cornfields, anticipating the autumn to come. It had rained most of the day; it was as if one last wash of summer made way for a new season, and the sunset was its crowning touch.

It was a perfect evening for a drive.

After his meeting with Mac, Emmett had visited the school's computer advisor to have her transfer the floppy disks of Toby's music to a flash drive. Now he grabbed all the drives and disks from the box and pointed his car toward Xavier and Ridgewood with his windows down, a random disk shoved into his never-used CD player and a thrum of energy under his skin.

Even though Toby had primitively recorded from a piano or, as time progressed and the piece had more depth, an electronic keyboard, Emmett could hear orchestration in his head: the brass swells of emotion, the high woodwinds' flutters of fancy, the strings' melodies of splendor.

After passing old hangouts in Xavier, Emmett headed northeast toward Ridgewood, where his only stop was the cemetery. It had been years since he'd been, never having felt the need or inclination, but tonight a visit was fitting. He slowed, remembering where to turn and where to stay the course until he saw the three-foot stone that read "Cox."

It wasn't Scotty's, but Emmett and his sister had always laughed at its location. Scotty's was next to it; a flat stone marked his plot. If Scotty knew he lay forever next to "Cox," he'd live out eternity in laughter.

Emmett turned Toby's music up a hair's breadth and got out to sit, to pick at the grass, to trace Scotty's name on the headstone. He hadn't brought flowers or a note to rest against the stone. He'd brought the music from Toby's heart and a hope that somehow, some way, it would weave everything broken back together again.

19

MORNINGSIDE—October 2016

"You ready?"

Toby looked at Mac as she walked him down the hall, so grateful she had been a steady presence in Emmett's life all these years—and so grateful for her willingness to help him out on this particular day.

It was almost a year to the day since Emmett first called, and his life—a life of tight schedules and monthly changes of scenery, of surface relationships and mediocre music—was blissfully jolted out of its shambles.

It was also about six weeks since he had sent away the meager representation of his life's creative work to no response. He wasn't chasing a response; he even wasn't going to ask for one. But Toby was going to follow through on his promises to a teenage girl with big dreams, little means and an entire county's worth of talent—even if his heart raced and his palms sweated.

He might also have to deal with Emmett in the process. The afternoon could go in a any number of directions.

Mac's hand rested on his back as he turned the knob to the choir room door. "Ready as I'll ever be." A ridiculous response every time it was uttered—one could always, *always* be more prepared. He stepped inside, on the far edge of the spacious choir room.

Rehearsal was in full swing, and no one noticed Toby walk through the door. Emmett was in full command of the thirty-five-voice a cappella group, the same group he had brought to New York. His cane rested against the side of the piano and his waistcoat was draped across the corner of his music stand.

If his musical memory served, the group was working on "She Walks in Beauty," a monstrously difficult number for the most advanced groups. And, judging by the use of solfège—do-re-mi—in place of lyrics, they were in early stages of rehearsal.

"Okay, altos…" Emmett began after he had stopped a questionable phrase execution.

"We know, we know," one of the girls whined. "It sucks."

"If it sounds like that next week, it'll suck. Right now, it needs work." Emmett snapped the tempo as he spoke. "Speak the solfège, starting at *dark*, three, four."

The altos followed his direction, only to be interrupted by a gasp from the soprano section.

Toby lifted a finger to his lips.

Emmett continued to work with the altos on the peculiar notes in their harmonic line, but more and more students noticed Toby. Finally, the choir was rattled enough for Emmett to stop. "Is there a good reason why you cannot wait patiently while I work with the girls? Tenors, surely you can give them half the time they give you."

"It's just that—Mr. H?"

But Emmett was back with the alto section, and Toby waited until the appropriate time to interrupt. "Altos, again. Do-mi-mi-fi," Emmett directed, and sang the line. He pointed his thumb up to help them get the lift of the unexpected final pitch. They nailed it, but the choir continued to fidget.

"Since you all seem to think you know your parts, let's have all voices please. Beat three, measure five. What's the unison note?"

"G-sharp," they chanted in unison.

"Pitch, please."

A student Toby didn't know tried to blow air through the pitch pipe but laughed instead, making it honk. Emmett's head snapped around, the choir laughed and Toby stepped forward to—he hoped—save the entire group from detention.

"I think, Mr. Henderson, that maybe the lyrics of this song are a bit—"

Emmett spun on his heel. His face was unreadable, but *it's so good to see you* was definitely not what it expressed.

"Are a bit juvenile? Do, re, mi?" Toby tried a smile, while his eyes begged for a little leniency in light of the public setting.

At Emmett's silence, the choir silenced. Without moving his gaze from Toby, Emmett directed his class to sit in place, adding a perfunctory "please." He blinked and turned back to them. "Upperclassmen, help the freshmen get the rest of this song labeled in solfège."

The students seemed almost relieved by the direction. They scurried into their folders for pencils and began to work. "Kyle Trentnor," Emmett warned, before turning back to Toby. "In *pencil*. You are a senior, for God's sake."

Kyle looked Toby square in the eye and smirked, as if Toby might be in on the joke too. Toby remained firm, though he bit back laughter; he would have been "that kid."

Toby continued to brace himself as Emmett approached him with a beautiful combination of contained fury, professional composure and, if Toby was completely honest, dark-eyed arousal. But when he spoke, only the contained fury came through.

"Now that you have interrupted my class, can I help you?"

Toby, testing to see if the wall would break, held Emmett's gaze tightly. "I have a two o'clock appointment with Tori and a couple other girls."

Emmett shot a look at Tori, who waved with a guilty grin. Emmett grunted. "Tori is in class until 2:37." He looked back at Toby, closed his eyes and took a deep breath. "You are welcome to stay here while we rehearse. You can wait in my office, or Mac's office is—"

"Down the hall. Yes, I've already seen her."

Emmett's smile was not friendly. "Of course you have."

"Because the office wouldn't allow me to see Tori without being on her registered visitor's list, and I had a feeling you wouldn't respond to my call for assistance."

Emmett narrowed his eyes. "Right." He took in a more deliberate breath. "Those are the best options to wait. She'll be free in about forty minutes."

"I'll wait here," he said. "You know how I enjoy rehearsal."

Emmett's eyes twitched in further irritation, and his voice was but a whisper. "Don't." He turned toward his students, squared his shoulders and got back in position. "Choir, let's put this away to revisit. How about we show Mr. Spence what got us that superior rating at the state contest last spring, huh?"

"Can we do 'Una Caritas,' Mr. H?" The suggestion, obviously a favorite, elicited enthusiasm around the room.

"Yes. Freshmen, you'll find it in your folders. Feel free to try to sight-read along with us in a quiet hum, or listen."

He set their pitches on the piano, took his place at the music stand "podium" and they began.

Toby found a lone chair and closed his eyes to let their gorgeous music seep in. If there really was a heaven—this is what the angel choirs would sound like.

It wasn't as if Toby had never dealt with Emmett's iciness before. He knew full well that an extra change of emotional clothes was an occasional need in living with and loving that man.

But still, Toby had chilled to the bone when he returned to Emmett's office after his time with the girls to find it empty and dark, with a note taped to the door specifically written to Tori—*Tori, please lock my office door behind you. Have a good weekend. Mr. H.*

Now, he finished the mediocre delivery dinner he had eaten alone in his hotel room, turned off the droning weather channel and dialed Emmett.

"Hey," Emmett answered without much emotion.

Well, it wasn't "fuck off," so maybe he had warmed a little.

"Hi. I, uh—I was hoping I'd see you after I met with the girls. It went really well. Tori's definitely ready to go."

Emmett was silent, and then: "I'm not sure 'thank you' is relevant here. I mean, it is my job to prepare my students for college auditions." Toby braced himself for the "fuck you" that might be coming after all. "I'm not sure why you felt the need—"

"Because I'd broken a promise. And I had the time, which I still have." Toby hated that he had created this, and he hated that Emmett took the bait in such a gloriously Emmett sort of way. "We need to talk."

"I have plans this evening. I'm assuming you're leaving tomorrow morning?"

"You assume incorrectly," Toby said. "I don't have a return flight yet."

After another long pause, Emmett asked if Toby was going to see the girls again over the weekend. He was not. He left it there. He might have been the one who walked out, but if anyone was keeping score, the volley really was in Emmett's court.

"I'm, um." Emmett's voice cracked. He cleared his throat and tried again. "I'm headed to the football game tonight. Would you like to join me?"

With that simple invitation, Toby felt every muscle relax. "Who are they playing?"

"East Central. You missed homecoming by a week."

Maybe he hadn't—not really. "Do they still start at seven-thirty? I'll arrange a cab."

Emmett insisted on picking him up; Toby met him in the hotel lobby. They barely spoke on the way, outside of an update on Xavier's lack of successes this season, including Morningside's unceremonious destruction of them on their own turf a few weeks before. "Really, Toby. It was sort of epic in its disaster."

"Hater. You're nothing more than a hater."

At least Emmett had laughed. He bought Toby the nachos with the melted nuclear-orange cheese-flavored chemicals and snuck a few for himself—just as he used to do.

By the end of the third quarter, Morningside was far enough ahead that Emmett had had his fill. "Can I make a weird request?" he asked, as they worked their way through packs of teens and the visiting band that wandered around the concessions as if they'd lost their leader.

Even though the air between them was warming, Emmett kept a distance as they walked. They didn't bump shoulders, didn't knock elbows and most definitely did not lock arms to enjoy a little body heat and fend off the first good bites of autumn air.

Toby held the door for Emmett as they entered the music hall. "It's not, of course, but this seems more like mutual turf. Safer," he explained.

Toby smirked. He had seen Emmett's eyes raking over his body when he picked him up for the game. "Safer. I get it." He grinned in the hope that Emmett might relax a little more and play along.

Emmett tried. He fought to smile, but eventually his stubbornness did win. "Toby—" He chuckled and gathered it back in as if it was too telling. "Stop. I mean, I get it. The flirtation. But you have to understand." He unlocked his office and motioned for Toby to go in first as the fluorescent lights flickered to life. Emmett shut the door and leaned back against it, staring at Toby so intently it seemed as if the air was being sucked out of the room. "I haven't been able to *breathe* since I saw you standing in my room this afternoon."

Toby unbuttoned his coat, finding it difficult to breathe himself. "I'm sorry."

"I know you are. I know that's not what you were trying to do, but—" Emmett's expression was so intense that Toby sensed the swirl of words Emmett was sifting through to say the right thing. "It's unnerving having you here in my space. Without any warning." He put his cane on the worktable and shook off his coat. "In a twisted way, I'm still really glad you came."

A high-pitched squeal rang through the cement block walls. "What the—"

"Band. Game must be over already."

Within seconds, the music hall was filled with raucous band kids. Slammed instrument lockers and honks and squawks from various instruments echoed through the entire wing.

"It'll quiet down soon," Emmett said, hanging their coats on his rack. "It's like a tornado—scary quiet to utter chaos and back to scary quiet before you know what hit."

"I can't believe I'm not hearing Mac."

"She rules with a glare on Friday nights." Emmett grabbed a few pieces of scrap paper. "That or detention slips. She silently passes them over without a word." He demonstrated, handing one to Toby with a very stern "your life is basically over" look over his glasses.

"God, I love that woman."

As they sat to wait it out, Toby caught a glimpse of his box under the worktable. It looked practically untouched. All the good energy in the room evaporated.

But Emmett caught his gaze and dug into his jeans pocket. He tossed a plain flash drive onto the desk. "Before we talk about this," Emmett said, "tell me how long you're going to be here."

"It, um." Toby stared at the flash drive. "It depends on—is that everything?"

"Everything recorded, yes. I put it in some semblance of order based on your file names, vague guessing and a random crapshoot, but it's all there. I saved it in a few different formats, depending on what device and program you'll be using. It's also on a cloud account—the link's on the drive."

"That's more than I could have asked for. Thank you."

"Don't get excited yet. You know as well as I do—this is just scratching at the surface."

And now, more than ever, Toby understood what it meant to be unnerved. Emmett had listened. He had manipulated and reformatted and *listened* to these scattered pieces of himself. And he was being so businesslike, Toby didn't know how to process it.

"What are you doing, Toby?"

"Sort of freaking out at the moment."

"No." Emmett rested his hand on Toby's forearm, and Toby wished for summer days when it would have been skin on skin contact. "Here. With unlimited time to sit in my office and cheer for a high school football team in which you have no investment, and pretend there is nothing unusual going on."

"I'm starting to cut my schedule back a bit. But I *have* to be back in New York a week from Monday—probably sooner. We're rehearsing for a reading. I go to Denver after that, and in between I'm trying—" He looked up at Emmett before he realized he wasn't really answering Emmett's question. He wasn't sure he understood it.

"How do you not fly away, Toby? You're everywhere and you're nowhere and you're trying to collate this—this *thing*. How do you not catch air and take off?"

Toby pointed to the flash drive. "I do this. You always kept me tied to the ground. When I don't have you—" Toby looked up at Emmett and almost lost his train of thought. "I have this."

"And you've worked on it all these years?"

"Most of them. Sometimes I'd play familiar licks over and over, every time I sat down."

"Like a meditation?"

"Yeah, I suppose so. It helped me think. Remember who I was and—when I let myself—who *we* were. No matter where I was, it always came back to you."

"Maybe it should have been more about *you*."

"It is. You. Me." Emmett's businesslike demeanor had been melting before Toby's eyes. His glasses had come off, and he had rolled his chair from his desk to face Toby. "And then this became a flighty mess."

"It's not." Emmett side-eyed his inbox and pulled out the manila envelope of Toby's paper scraps. "This? Is a flighty mess," he said as he handed it to Toby. "Can I give you an assignment?'

"Are you a fair grader?" Toby asked.

"Strict, but fair."

"As expected. What's my assignment, teach?"

"I want you to record what you think is still useful here. Some of it you've already done—toss the paper version of it for now."

"So does this mean you're going to work with me?"

"As best I can from here. I'm not traveling to you, Toby. I'm not ready."

"I understand." Toby stood to fetch his coat and pulled out his phone.

"Where are you going?"

"I should probably get back. See if I can get a flight tomorrow morning."

"No. That's not what I—" Emmett scrubbed his hand over his face. "I wasn't kidding; I am not going to beg for you to stay again."

Toby sat back down.

"You were going to be here a few days. Let's get started while you're here. I have a keyboard at home, there's one here at school if you stay past the weekend... "

Toby shoved his phone back in his pocket. "You think this is worth it?"

"I think it's exquisite, Toby. You have something here, but it's going to take time."

"And stillness."

Emmett stood with him and grabbed their coats. "Loads of it."

◆◆◆

THE NEXT MORNING, TOBY TOOK a cab to Emmett's house. The kitchen smelled not like any ordinary coffee, but like the roast he loved so much from Seattle. And when Emmett slid his mug across the table along with a plate of various breakfast pastries, he knew it was just that.

"Where did you get this?" Toby asked.

"I order it online." Toby caught his eye quickly enough for Emmett to skitter away and fetch butter from the fridge. "Indiana sucks at coffee."

Emmett's blush wasn't missed, however. He might not "be ready," but Toby took an odd delight in the way his presence unnerved Emmett. "So," Toby started—this was supposed to be a business meeting—"let's go back to those undergrad days a bit."

"I'd just as soon not."

"They couldn't have been that bad."

"I made do."

Toby resisted the urge to apologize and surged forward. "You sat through a piano recital and you have to critique it for a grade. The final performance was my... " What was the flash drive and scrap paper pile of music anyway? It barely qualified as much at all. "Composition, as it were. What do you say in your paper?"

"I used the word 'exquisite' last night and I meant it."

"But?"

"No, not 'but.'" Emmett smiled into his mug of coffee. "Yet." He winked. Toby sat back, willing to listen to Emmett talk about this, about the weather, about raccoons in his trash all damned day. "It's exquisite. I can *see* lush meadows and romantic spring rains and coffee shops and soft intimacy. It's easy, and bright, and…" Emmett chuckled at himself. "It's a gossamer-clouded fairy tale."

"You wrote some damned descriptive recital reports."

"That's because I didn't go to half of them. There were six of us. Half would go and bring the programs for the other half so we could write a critique. And then we'd switch."

"I'm not sure whether to be impressed or insulted that you're using your bullshit language on me."

"Oh, don't act so superior. I know you did so much theory homework because you traded completed homework for recital credits."

Toby laughed. "We were both little shits in college, weren't we?"

"Yeah, we were," Emmett said. "And you should be impressed with my flowery language. Your music is about all I've listened to this past week."

"I don't think I've really thanked you for that."

"You're still here." Toby got lost in Emmett's eyes for a moment, and then another, until Emmett shoved Toby's plate closer to him. "You're not eating."

"I'm—" He pulled off a piece of his Danish. "I'm nervous."

"Please don't be. I'm still sorting through everything, but—" Emmett let out a breath. "Can we focus on the music now?"

"It's why I'm here." That was partially true.

"Right. So." Emmett waved at Toby's plate again, more like his mother than he would ever admit. "Tell me how you want to see this onstage. Do you want it to be a concert piece for an orchestra? Do you want to partner up with a librettist?"

"No, I'm thinking a play. I know that means it will be tweaked and rejiggered a bit, but that's okay. Music is fluid; theater is fluid. I just want to be involved in the process."

"Okay. So, the second part of my critique—"

"*Now* it's time for the 'but.'"

Emmett grinned. "It's always time for the butt."

"Yeah, you've been hanging around teenagers too long."

"I have." Emmett's eyes softened, and Toby couldn't breathe. "I really hate how much I've missed you this time."

Toby held his gaze as long as Emmett would allow. "Maybe that feeling will help with this?" Toby took a swallow of his cooling coffee to avoid pressing his lips to Emmett's. "But, you were talking about butts."

"Yes. *But.* There's no musical tension. There's no wringing of hands, no heartbreak. If you want this to accompany a play, then the music has to follow the flow of storytelling, yes?"

"Yes, to a degree it does."

"And right now it's all first kisses and tiptoes through tulip patches. Which is absolutely necessary. But without dissonance and some sort of musical conflict, you only have a beautiful love letter."

Toby nodded, unsure if they were talking about the music or each other. "I know."

"You have an outstanding love letter, Toby. The harmonies are rich, the rhythmic patterns you have going on—with just the piano—are amazing. But if you want to tell a love *story*, you have to include all of it."

"That's where I'm blocking. Like plowing straight into a brick wall."

"It's the ugly stuff. It's the hard stuff. It's—it's the stuff that makes you run."

"That's why I sent it to you." Toby pushed aside his plate and coffee and scooted closer to take Emmett's hand in his. "Can we not work on it this morning? Directly?"

"This is your lead, Toby. Whatever you need."

Toby took a shuddering breath. "Can we, um—can we take a drive today?"

"Oh God. Are you sure?"

No. "Y—yeah. Let's take a drive."

20

Emmett clicked his seatbelt and backed out of the garage. "Okay. Where are we headed?"

"Flowers," Toby said without any hesitation.

Emmett hesitated. The car stuttered, and he finally stopped before his back tires hit the road. "Are you—do you want to go to the cemetery?"

"I don't know. Maybe? It seems like something I should do, I suppose." Toby shook his head and waved at the gearshift. "Just—go. Flowers. We'll start there."

"You know," Emmett said as he backed out into the street, "we don't have to do this."

"Yes, we do."

"Let me rephrase. We don't have to do this *now*. Or today."

"Yes. Yes, we really do." Toby reached over and draped his hand over Emmett's on the gearshift. "I really do."

Emmett took him to his favorite floral shop, where Toby chose a simple bunch of fall flowers, tied in a ribbon that matched Scotty's hair. "That's not creepy, is it?"

"It's October," Emmett said. "Orange works all month."

Toby was quiet as they drove into Xavier. Emmett didn't try to pull conversation from him. He kept the music at a soft murmur and pointed out little details that had changed over the years.

"Let's go by my old house first," Toby suggested.

Now that Emmett had taken the time to think, it made sense that Toby didn't have much of an emotional connection to the house. He had lived there full-time for his senior year and then was off to New York. But whenever Toby had come back into town, it was home to both of them.

Toby's house was one of the things Emmett missed during his recovery from the accident: Toby's bedroom and the million firsts they experienced there; Toby's kitchen, where they would find his mother's stash of Oreo cookies and steal a few so she wouldn't notice—until she did and finally bought another bag for them.

"Wait until you see the tree in front," Emmett said. "It grew *fast*."

"Oh God. Dad almost broke his back putting in that damned sapling. Refused any help. If he didn't kill himself with it, I thought Mom was going to." They wound around the neighborhood, and Emmett slowed as they approached. Toby was quiet until—"Someone painted it. It was green, right?"

"Yeah, a few years ago. I think I prefer the green," Emmett said. "That brown blends in with the trees in back."

"The little tree's as high as my bedroom window now. Pretty landscaping."

"I could have climbed it and snuck in your window!"

Toby laughed tightly. "I don't think you'd have remained Mom's favorite."

"Wait. She had favorites? How many boyfriends did you have?"

Toby turned. "Only you. Always." He squeezed Emmett's hand in his. "Maybe we can drive by the high school and Mr. O'Day's?"

"Do you want to go on to Ridgewood?"

"Yeah." And then Toby smiled, big, bright and genuine. "Let's go see your mom."

"You've lost your mind." Emmett started toward Xavier High School, and then out of town toward Mr. O'Day's house. "Are you in need of a porcelain doll leg for any particular reason?"

"I thought it'd be a nice conversation piece on that shelf in my apartment. Next to the stuffed gingerbread man from *Shrek*."

While Mr. O'Day's didn't appear to be any more cleaned up, there was no yard sale sign or visible doll parts. Emmett teased and pretended to turn into the hidden drive that took them to their favorite make-out spot.

"One day, Em—we really should," Toby said. His body had been relaxing with each mile.

"We'd get shot."

"Maybe, but it would be an adventure."

"Might give you the tension you need in your composition."

Emmett couldn't remember when he had enjoyed a simple drive as much. A soft breeze blew through the cracked-open back windows, scents of the last night's trash fires and bonfires still pinched the air. The bright blue sky was a perfect backdrop for the early hints of autumn colors teasing the tree tops.

"Were you serious about seeing Mom? This is where we need to decide."

When Toby flashed Emmett another huge grin, Emmett conceded. They stopped by Emmett's high school first and shuffled through the leaves in the center courtyard.

"They finally took down that sycamore tree," Toby said, looking a little discombobulated.

"I came home from college one summer break, and it was gone." Emmett tossed up a few stray whirligigs and watched them flutter and spin. "I cried. Mom got mad."

"Because you cried over a tree?"

"No." Emmett tossed one last whirligig in the air. It caught a breeze and floated away before wobbling to the ground. "Because I still loved you."

Toby took Emmett's hand as they went back to the car, skirting the edge of Ridgewood College. It was a preferred performance college, where Emmett's mother always wanted him to attend, but Emmett needed space. If he couldn't get to New York, he would at least get away.

Until he had no choice but to come back.

"You okay?" Toby asked over Emmett's car as they got in. "I'm the one that's supposed to be stressing out."

"Mom gives me stress. I never know what I'm going to get."

"Well, hopefully she has her Neighborhood Volunteer face on today and will behave."

Emmett snorted. "You know her too well."

Miriam seemed pleasantly surprised by the unexpected visit, and more so to see Toby. Emmett couldn't get a read on her sincerity. Toby got a "Call me Miriam" and a kiss on the cheek, and before Emmett could catch his breath, she had whisked Toby off into the guest room to, according to her, show him something she'd unearthed while cleaning out the closet. "I can't *believe* your timing, Toby."

Toby. As if Toby had happened upon her doorstep on a random Saturday in October. Which he had, but that wasn't the point.

His dad sat in his easy chair, engrossed in his paper. Emmett could swear he heard a snort from behind the Arts and Leisure section. With great care, Emmett curled his fingers around the top of the page and peeled it down to reveal a very self-satisfied man.

"I was reading that," Cliff said.

"No you weren't. You're smirking. Your amusement concerns me."

Emmett's dad smiled, folded his paper and motioned for Emmett to sit on the couch. "Beer?"

"Do I need one?"

Cliff considered and got up. "I do. I'll bring two."

Emmett could hear his mother cooing over something in the other room, but his curiosity was more piqued by his dad's peculiar behavior than his mother's. It kept him planted on the couch.

Cliff returned, gave Emmett a bottle and said nothing. They sipped at the same time, and Cliff avoided eye contact. Emmett considered cracking his bottle up against the side table to get his attention. "So, did she finally agree to take Xanax, or—"

"Don't be rude."

"Then stop being elusive. Why is my mother suddenly in love with Toby Spence?"

"Your last visit left a bit of a mark."

Emmett lowered his bottle from his lips without taking a drink. "I was an asshole."

"Maybe a little," Cliff said with a grin. "I might have helped."

"With the asshole part, or the leaving a mark bit?"

Cliff set down his drink and stared at Emmett's until he did the same. "I invited her to do what you said—to stop projecting her wishes on everyone and see them for who they are."

"I bet that went over well."

"Not at first. But I reminded her of the boy who came home from theater practice and his feet couldn't touch the ground because the '*so hot* piano player' asked him out. And the boy who did the entire family's laundry for three months—including his sister's underwear—just to earn enough money to go visit that same piano player in New York.

"I reminded her of the colorless boy in a hospital bed, broken, in pieces, who wanted to see one person because that is who he knew would heal him."

"The hot piano player." Emmett could barely breathe; his dad so rarely showed that he noticed Emmett's personal life. He'd been watching from behind that blasted newspaper all along.

"One and the same. You love him. You have always loved him. And if my sixty years on this planet have taught me anything, it's that you will never stop loving him. And if your mother loves you—and you know full well she does—she had better start getting used to the idea."

Toby's laugh cut through the walls and into the living room, and all Emmett could do was sit back and blink out the tears that had been pooling in his eyes. "I love him so much, Dad. Things are messed up, but he's here. He's trying."

"And so is she. So let her, okay? Don't be snarky. Let her screw it up, because we both know she's going to." Cliff picked up his beer and handed Emmett's back to him. "That grace you keep affording Toby? Might want to extend a little bit to her too."

"She and I are more alike than I thought, aren't we?"

Cliff's answer came from his silence, as he grabbed his newspaper and flapped it open in front of his face.

When Toby and his mom came out of the guest room, Toby looked no worse for wear. Emmett's mother skittered around the kitchen, preparing some pumpkin bread for them to take home. All attempts to get Toby to at least *hint* at what she had shown him in the guest room were unsuccessful.

They got into the car, and Emmett looked over at Toby, who was peeling the cling wrap back from the bread. "What the hell happened in there?"

Toby shrugged, pulled off a corner of bread and ate it. The bastard didn't even offer him a bite. "I dunno, but this is some damned good pumpkin bread."

"Share?"

"Later. I'm ready to go to Scotty's house."

WHILE EMMETT WAS IN COLLEGE, Scotty's family downsized from their large home on many acres to a smaller home on the west side of Brighton. Not only had they lost their son; their life had turned into a fishbowl of nosy neighbors who watched the Barnes' every move to make sure they were grieving their son properly.

Despite various owners, the house hadn't changed much. The shutters were a different color and the driveway had been widened to accommodate a camper, but otherwise it looked as if Scotty might barge out of the side door at any moment, throwing on his coat as he fell into the car.

"I wonder if that tree's still in back," Toby said.

"You mean the one with the broken branch because you thought it would hold your weight, Tarzan?" Emmett rolled the car forward a bit to see if they could tell, to no avail.

"I wasn't swinging from the branches—I was trying to climb it."

"Tarzan also climbed trees. That's how he got up there to swing from the branches."

"Either way, my back hurt for *weeks* after that," Toby said.

"You're lucky you didn't break it."

"Hey now. I was trying to show you how virile I was."

"I was leaning more toward 'stupid,' but they do sort of go hand in hand." Emmett rolled forward a bit more. "You ready or do you want to stay a bit longer?"

"No, I'm good."

Emmett drove to the next driveway and pulled in to get turned back toward the highway.

"Where are you going?" Toby asked as he dug into the bread again, offering a chunk this time.

"Home?"

"No. Not yet." Toby pointed the direction they had been heading. "Keep going that way."

The way to get back, from here, was to not only cross the intersection of the accident, but to approach it from the same direction—something Emmett didn't think Toby would ever want to do. "Are you sure?"

"No. But do it anyway. Unless *you* don't—"

"No, I'm fine. I used to go home this way all the time to—" To what, exactly? To desensitize? To see if there was any way it could have happened differently? To see if maybe, by some fucked up *Field of Dreams* twist, Scotty would walk out of the cornfield? For years Emmett drove through the area, sometimes circling to do it more than once. "Yeah. I'm fine."

Toby nodded, turned his attention out his side window and fell silent. Emmett turned right on Liberty Road. Toby took an audible breath and refocused on the road in front of them.

"You okay?"

Toby nodded and stared straight ahead. His breath quickened, and he reached out for Emmett's hand.

Emmett remembered his first time past the scene. His mom had always refused to make this journey, but after physical therapy one afternoon, his dad had agreed. As they approached, Emmett had held his breath, closed his eyes as they crossed and hyperventilated as soon as they made it through.

The first time he drove through it himself hadn't gone much more smoothly—although he did keep his eyes open. He was alone that day, and floored it the rest of the way on Liberty until he could turn off and head back home. He sent a good thought to Scotty.

It got easier every time.

They passed a stop sign alert—a sign Emmett had forgotten existed until Toby pointed it out, his voice quiet, as if not to rouse any lurking demons. "Has that always been there?"

"No." It went up not long after their accident. That didn't need to be said—Toby knew.

Emmett slowed. Toby's hand was clammy; the color had drained from his face. "Toby?"

"Can we—can we pull over for a minute?"

They were fifty yards away at most, but Emmett pulled over and waited. "We don't have to—"

"Yes. We do. I just—God, I feel so stupid."

"You're not stupid. How about if we walk it? Would that be easier?"

Toby finally broke his gaze out the front window. "That's ridiculous." He grabbed at his door handle and looked at Emmett. "Maybe after we walk it, it'll be easier."

So they walked. Emmett let Toby lead and didn't take his hand, as desperately as he wanted to. Didn't speak a word, as much as he wanted to. Loose gravel crunched under their shoes as they walked. A combine fired up in a field across the road.

Toby looked behind them and took Emmett's hand, leading them to the middle of the road. "Okay?"

"Whatever you need to do."

And then with great purpose, Toby walked the last few yards to the stop sign. He stopped, looked both ways and walked to the center of the crossroads. And then he breathed, let go of Emmett's hand and looked around: at the corner from which they'd come, the one across on the left and the one on the right and then, to his left—the corner where the car had landed after impact.

A small white wooden cross protruded from the stubble of harvested corn. Toby turned his back to it and looked at Emmett. "It's just an intersection."

"To most people."

"Could I put my flowers there?" He looked at the cross again. "Do people still do that?"

"Mostly on his birthday—anniversary of the accident, but yeah. Do you want me to get them?"

"I'll come with you."

They brought the small bouquet and a grave vase to the cross, stepping gingerly over the swampy corner of the field. Toby plopped on the ground. He resembled a young child sitting on his carpet square for story time with his legs splayed out in front of him and dandelions picked for his mom carelessly flopped between his thighs.

"Where did we land?" he asked.

Emmett sat with him and surveyed the field, trying to remember from the few pictures his dad had of the scene. "I think more south. I remember seeing that tree when they wheeled me to the LifeFlight."

"What do you remember?" Toby's eyes were huge and his breath came in quick puffs, as if a deep inhalation might stab him with the pain of that day all over again.

Emmett desperately wanted to tell him to let it go, to scream, cry, throw something, hit him, *anything*, but the fact that they were here talking—it was the first time they had spoken of those frightful moments in any detail—was an amazing feat of its own.

"I remember Scotty calling your name, and then nothing. And I heard Lenny singing, and in my fog I wanted to laugh because it was ridiculous that your damned stereo kept working."

"And the band played on," Toby sang in a cracked, just barely audible voice.

"I remember your hand in my hair, and that I tried to move my leg when you looked for your phone. And then that tree—" Emmett stopped and searched deeper. The few flashes of memory had faded over the years. "Did you come to the gurney before I got in the helicopter?"

"Yeah, I did."

"I wasn't sure if that was real or a dream." Emmett reached for Toby, for his beautiful face with the tears softly streaming down, matching Emmett's. His eyes filled with more, as if once the crying started it would never end. "And then nothing until the hospital."

"I'm so sorry. I'm so fucking—" Years of pain, of agony, guilt and pent-up sorrow broke free into a wail like Emmett had never heard. Emmett scooped Toby into his arms as best he could as sharp points of the sheared stalks of corn dug into his legs.

Emmett didn't tell Toby it was okay. He didn't tell him there was nothing to be sorry for. He didn't tell Toby that this would all have been easier if he had faced it so many years earlier, and he didn't tell him, as his cries got louder and then faded into sniffling sobs, that had he let

Emmett help him carry the burden, they both would have come out much more whole, balanced men.

They sat until Toby quieted. He pulled back to fuss about getting snot on Emmett's coat and Emmett told him to shut the fuck up and kissed his forehead. This time when Toby said, "I'm sorry," Emmett responded with what he probably should have said all those years before and since.

"I know you are." He kissed his head again. "I know you are."

Toby remembered the flowers and fluffed them out a bit. "We don't have water."

"I'll bring some tomorrow. They'll be okay today."

"You'll come collect them before they die?"

"Of course."

Toby tied the ribbon around the dingy green vase and stuck the pins protruding from its bottom into the ground next to the cross. Emmett sat to let Toby settle between his legs and rest against his chest. They stared at the huge maple tree while the breeze blew through its orange and yellow leaves.

"I should have come here years ago," Toby said on a sigh.

"You've carried it all far too long."

"Malik was right, the fucker," Toby said, a faint smile in his voice. "Said I didn't need to carry it alone."

"You're not, anymore." Emmett kissed Toby's temple and combed through his hair as the breeze lifted the loose curls into his fingers. "I like your hair longer like this."

Toby chuckled deeply with his stuffy nose, his voice wrecked from the tears. "Yeah, let's talk about long hair, huh?"

"What?" And then Emmett remembered. And realized. And, if it weren't for the solemnity of the moment, he would have jumped back into his car to go and at least glare really deeply at his mother. "She showed you pictures of me in college, didn't she?"

Toby's chuckle broke into a laugh; his shoulders shook against Emmett's. "Oh, yes. Yes, she did. That little David Beckham ponytail flopping at your crown?" He got up on his knees and turned around to face Emmett. His face was blotchy, and his wet eyelashes highlighted the dark circles under his eyes.

He was radiant.

He traced Emmett's jawline with his finger. "You were still the most beautiful man I've ever seen." Emmett closed his eyes and sensed Toby approach, only to kiss his cheek. "And I told your mom as much."

Emmett jerked back. "What'd she say?"

"She agreed with me. Inside and out." He sat back on his haunches and looked at the cross, at their makeshift memorial. "I think I'm ready to go." He kissed his fingers, pressed them to the cross and stood, reaching out a hand to help Emmett up. "You didn't bring your cane."

Emmett looked at Toby's hand waiting for him, like the day Toby walked away. The scar running down the length of his finger was fainter, and, for the first time, Emmett reached out to purposely touch it, to feel the imperfection of Toby's musical fingers.

Toby didn't pull back, only waited for Emmett to take his hand. And he did with a firm grip as he smiled into Toby's eyes and let him pull him up.

"I didn't need my cane. I have you."

21

"Hey. We're home."

Toby reached through the sleepy murkiness of his mind to the voice—to Emmett's voice, his favorite voice. He willed his eyes open and closed them again as a smile spread across his face. Emmett was his favorite sight, as well. "Hey. I fell asleep."

"You did. In the car, no less."

He snapped his eyes open and, sure enough, there was a black dash in front of him, a plate of pumpkin bread at his feet and Emmett peeking into the door, waiting for him to wake up enough to move. "Holy shit." He stretched his neck and accepted Emmett's hand to get out of the car. "I don't think I've done that since I was a kid."

"I didn't know what you wanted to do, so I brought you back to my place. Did you want to go to the hotel?"

"No. No, this is fine." He smacked his lips. "That garlic bread at Vick's was, um… garlicky."

Emmett laughed and fluffed Toby's hair. "I have extra toothbrushes. Come on, little boy. Let's get you inside before you start whining for your afternoon snack."

Toby's limbs were heavy with sleep and something he couldn't quite define. Drained—he felt completely drained… of *everything*.

After they had gotten back into the car at the site of the accident, Toby had asked if they could drive through it. It was, as Toby had said, just an intersection. Emmett had honored it with a rolling stop, as everyone did there, and they had journeyed back to Xavier for a memorial stop at Vick's Pizza.

The jukebox hadn't been updated since their early days. Neither had the pizza recipe, the garlic bread with cheese or the just-shy-of-too-old lettuce in the iceberg and pink-tomato salad. They played Britney Spears, Backstreet Boys and Matchbox Twenty. Toby would have won the battle for Creed—just to be annoying—until Emmett threatened to make him walk home if he did.

Some institutions aren't called institutions because of their quality—they're called institutions because of the memories they hold.

And now Toby stood in Emmett's kitchen with a glass of water he didn't remember taking.

"What can I do for you, Toby?"

Toby blinked. People didn't take care of him. He didn't need it, and when he did, he never gave any indication that he might. Buck up. Charge forward. Move on.

And now he couldn't move from the spot where he stood. "I think I want to lie down."

Emmett took his hand and led him upstairs to his guest room. He pulled back the bed, fluffed the pillows and brought him a pair of lounge pants. He asked no questions. He demanded no feedback on how Toby was feeling or why he needed another nap, or how long he might hang out in his home. He simply provided.

It was overwhelming.

Toby took off his jeans and slipped into the bed. The sheets were crisp, the mattress a pillow-top with a firm base. The groan he emitted would have been embarrassing if he gave a damn about anything other than the way the pillow sank under the weight of his head. It smelled of lavender and pine.

Emmett tugged the curtains closed. "Is there anything else? Do you want me to wake you or let you sleep?"

"Can you—" Toby spun in his cocoon of blankets so he faced the side of the bed. "Rub my head? Like I used to—"

"For me. God, yes." He stripped off his jeans and climbed in, adjusting until Toby moaned softly under his touch. "That good?"

"Perfect. Thank you."

"I'm so sorry, Toby."

Toby wanted to ask what for, but before the words came to him, he let the luxury of the bed and the comfort of Emmett's fingers in his hair take him to sleep.

WHEN TOBY WOKE, EMMETT WAS gone, but a towel and washcloth rested on the foot of the bed alongside the lounge pants. A small clock radio played softly from his nightstand, and his water had been refreshed.

Toby showered and showered and showered, vowing to contribute to Emmett's water bill to pay for it. He cried again under the pounding stream, bent over with the agony of it all, with the years and years of guilt and shame and *crap* he had been carrying around.

Emmett never asked. Never pushed. When Toby went downstairs, Emmett was waiting for him with warm cider and a freshly baked spice cake. "What about your mom's pumpkin bread?" Toby asked.

"I wanted to bake."

They ate cake and made sandwiches and finally, after all the promises that they would, they watched *Firefly* until Emmett fell asleep and spilled his beer.

Emmett offered to let Toby stay the night, but Toby insisted on going back to the hotel. "You wanted us to take our time. As much as I want to—" And God, did he want to. "We've had a full day." He slept that night as he hadn't slept in years, possibly since college—the first night after each semester's finals.

The next day, itching to get at the keyboard, Toby took a cab to Emmett's house. As he had readied himself for the day, melodies had circled his brain that made no sense until he could get his hands on the black and white keys, where they translated into something beyond himself.

And when he sat down to play, his fingers sang. He skipped Emmett's suggestion of fussing with the scratch papers of notes, and instead wrote new ones. He recorded and re-recorded passages and phrases, rhythmic foundations that could be partnered later.

It was still a mess, but messes could be tidied. He played and jotted. He tried and failed and tried again before the idea of failing ever reached his psyche. Emmett brought him lunch and a kiss. He hummed the melodies and finally brought his own work into the room to sit with Toby. He quietly gave feedback, and refreshed his coffee so that Toby wasn't slugging down cold, grainy crap as he so often did in New York.

They broke for dinner that Emmett had snuck downstairs to prepare. And Emmett dared to poke a little, gently, kindly, with such beautiful patience Toby almost didn't recognize him.

"You doing okay?" It wasn't about the music, but right now that's what Toby had to offer in return.

"Yeah, I am. I feel good." He went on to report what he'd accomplished: a second theme that would interplay with the first better than the jottings from years before, a counterpoint that seemed to be working well. He talked of recording it all and taking it back to New York so he could get it in manuscript form and see the whole of it better.

"I have the software here," Emmett offered. "You don't have to go back for that."

"Do you want me to stay?"

"Do *you* want to stay?"

Toby put down his fork and looked at Emmett. Emmett's gaze was peaceful now, not pleading, "Don't leave, please don't leave me," but asking, "What do you need?" All he could offer in response was the truth.

"I can't imagine going back," he said. The thought of his empty apartment, his messy office, the huge gaping city screaming and flashing his loneliness right in his face, was enough for him to happily live in a third-rate hotel with three changes of clothes and ramen noodles warmed in the breakfast buffet's microwave. "But I have to. I was thinking I might try and get a flight out tomorrow."

Emmett went back to his food. "Will you let me know when, so I can take you?"

"You have school."

"I get days off," Emmett said and looked back at Toby again. "I want to take you this time."

When Emmett dropped Toby off at his hotel that night, Toby hesitated before getting out of the car. "I'm sorry I commandeered your weekend."

Emmett dropped his hand from the steering wheel and looked at Toby. "This was one of my favorite weekends."

Toby let go of the door handle and sat back in his seat. Some of their best conversations had happened in the dark, sitting in someone's driveway, pushing the limits of time and parental leniency. Even without a curfew hanging over their heads, the seclusion begged for more time. "Where did you learn to take care of someone like that?"

Emmett took a moment before answering. "Someone took care of me when I needed it."

"Derek."

"Yes," Emmett said. "He's back in town, by the way. He left his husband." Emmett picked at his steering wheel. "I'm not sure why I'm telling you, except that if you come back Gino will try to turn it into something sordid."

Toby couldn't decide whether to be relieved that Emmett wasn't alone or sick that Emmett... wasn't alone. "Why isn't it sordid? Might be fun."

"A lot of reasons. But mostly, because of you," he said simply.

"Oh."

"Yeah, 'oh.'" Emmett's smile teased at the corner of his lips. "It took me thirty-four years to figure out it's not all about me."

"That's all right. We're always going to learn new things."

The next day at the airport, Emmett escorted Toby inside, waited for check-in and sat with him until it was time to go through security. Toby ate some airport-brand chicken nuggets while Emmett curled his lips in disgust until Toby shoved one into his mouth. He conceded, with regret, that it was not only edible, but damned fucking good.

"Better with ranch. Want another bite?"

"No. Thank you. Let's not tempt fate."

At the unspoken appointed time, they walked toward security, their pace a steady crawl to the point where Emmett would walk one way and Toby the other. They stopped at the side of the queue, and Emmett ran his finger down the strap on Toby's bag.

"Even if you block again, don't stop," Emmett said. "What you have here is amazing. "

"I won't. I can send things to you as I go?"

"You'd better." Emmett kissed him so tenderly it would have hurt if not for the promise within it.

"I'll let you know when I land." Toby kissed him again and one more time, a laugh puffing between them as they parted. "I'm an idiot."

"You are not—"

"I am. This is so much easier than running off."

Emmett laughed, then, bright and clear, and pulled him in for another kiss with Toby's face firmly cupped in his strong hands, announcing to the world that indeed, this was not a goodbye. "Get in line before I keep you."

When Toby landed, the city didn't seem quite as lonely anymore.

◆◆◆

NEW YORK CITY—November 2016

Toby was in line for coffee when it hit him. The harmonic tension, the dissonance of the descending chords, the crack of the rhythmic structure. He stepped away from the queue and sang the leading line of it into his phone as best as he could. He dug in his pocket for his earbuds and tried tapping a quick chord progression into his phone app.

This had happened a few times since his return to New York, and on this day, before he left for Denver, he was chomping at the bit to get back to his office and get it down. He wasn't sure where it came from; he never was anymore. Maybe it was the coffee shop, and a flash of Scotty's doppelgänger in that Seattle coffeehouse as the smell of a good roast hit his nose.

But the piece was coming together. He had trashed some; he had tweaked much. He had re-recorded what he believed in and made it flow in a way that opened the floodgate to more and more ideas.

The rehearsals and readings he led in the city were already a blur. He had to stop and think about what show he was directing in Denver, which probably didn't bode well for the poor people who had entrusted their next few weeks to him.

Once back at his office, he tossed his coat aside, spilled cream on his desk while preparing his coffee and got to it. An hour later, his coffee was cold and untouched. Unbeknownst to him, Malik stood in his doorway.

"That is *sick*."

Toby nodded. *Almost there, almost, an added ninth to this chord maybe... no. Not quite.* "Now it is."

"No, seriously. Is that your—whatever it is you're working on?"

"Yeah." Toby fiddled with the last chord again and grimaced. "Sick, huh?"

"Well, that little doodad is just sad," Malik chuckled.

"I'll get it."

"I know you will."

Malik disappeared again, reappeared with fresh coffee and closed the door behind him as he left. In thirty minutes, Toby had the lick down. In another hour, he had it recorded and uploaded to the cloud account Emmett had set up. In two hours he was home, packing and on the phone with Emmett before leaving for Denver.

"Don't listen to it yet," he told Emmett. "I'm not ready for you to hear it."

"Not until you tell me. Even though you're making it very tempting."

"It feels good. It feels right. And I've got a couple of producers sniffing around."

"Don't let them have it 'til you're done."

"Nope. Mine." Toby grinned and tossed his notebook into his bag. "Ours." He didn't push any sort of conversation about what they were right now. They just were. Present. The first call at a joy or setback. The last call, if at all possible, before shutting down the day. The stability in those simple constants became the assurance Toby needed to believe he could do this. He could complete this.

He went to Denver feeling more confident in his day-to-day work than he had in years. He made sure to play bits and pieces of his composition during down times, testing reactions, talking about it as much as possible, making sure he left a card if anyone of importance seemed curious. Most were friendly and polite, but what he had told Emmett was true. There were nibbles. There was interest.

By the time he was back in New York, Thanksgiving had passed, the average temperature in the city had dropped a good fifteen degrees and the city had lost every ounce of color. The holiday decorations seemed too early, too eager.

Toby spent his days in his office, or slipped down to the theater for a nuanced environment in which to play with sound. He tweaked and recorded, he killed Malik at racquetball every Thursday and, before he knew what he was doing, he was making a phone call he had wanted to make for years.

Emmett sounded groggy that night, as he told Toby about the holiday program set for the following evening. He had rehearsed every group after school. He had put up sound shells and risers in the auditorium, wired up a recording system and tested microphones for proper mix and balance. This was not only the holiday program, he had explained, but also the preparation for large-group competitions in the winter. These recordings would form the backbone of his entire school year.

Toby listened to every detail as Emmett wound up from his sleepy start. Eventually, Emmett wound down again and uttered a relieved sigh. Toby pictured him in his family room, a fire burning low, a glass of deep red wine in his hand, his hair mussed from excitement and frustration. His glasses would be resting on the arm of his easy chair and his socked feet would be propped up on the ugly ottoman his mother had insisted he take with him so she wouldn't have to dispose of it.

And then, in a sleepy voice that made Toby want to jump through the phone and kiss him, Emmett said, "You said you had good news. I totally monopolized. Tell me everything."

"I think I have a good rough draft. I have to smooth the edges down a bit, but—do you want to hear it?"

"I don't know… " Emmett said, his voice waking up.

Toby's mind tumbled. They had the cloud account. He wanted feedback.

"I think maybe it would be better in person," Emmett added.

Toby could fly out, he supposed, although timing would be tricky. He had a little two-night gig at a jazz club in Chelsea and then another short stint at a theater in Queens, but—

"Did I cross a line?" Emmett's voice broke Toby out of his calculations.

He quickly recovered with a genius-like, "What? Huh? No. No, you didn't. I'm trying to see when—"

Emmett chuckled as Toby kept rambling about his December calendar. "Toby?"

"Yeah, I'm trying here. My calendar—"

"As you so kindly reminded me last year, teachers get two weeks off in December."

"Right. I still have that thing in Queens. Well, that's after Christmas, so maybe—"

"Can I come see you?"

"Can you come—what? Oh. Oh!" Toby put the bottle of beer he'd grabbed back into his refrigerator. He didn't need help relaxing anymore. "I, uh… " He laughed at himself, at missing the flirtation in Emmett's voice. And then he put a lilt of it in his own. "I thought you said you weren't going to chase me."

"You know, if you stand still for a hot second? I won't need to chase you."

"Right." Toby grabbed the beer again. Celebrating might be nice. "Please tell me you're not just coming for the music."

"I'm not just coming for the music."

"Then I'll be here. Right where you can find me."

22

Emmett didn't expect Toby to literally "be right here," of course. So when he got off the plane, he turned on his phone, expecting a text from the driver Toby sent. Instead, messages from his mother, holiday greetings from Derek and a few of the other guys from the club, a raunchy holiday joke from Mac and a weather alert for Brighton lit up his screen.

He turned onto the escalator to descend into baggage claim and quickly scanned for his name on the tablets and clipboards held in front of drivers' chests: B. Green, Thrower, Grissom, Dunlap, Winchel.

He hated waiting, especially at LaGuardia.

Emmett grabbed his phone again, and a shock of blond hair caught his eye. He looked up: There stood Toby, staring directly at him, a cocky smile spreading across his face.

"Toby!"

Emmett grabbed his cane, hooked on his arm and stepped down a few stairs of the slow-moving escalator. He got caught behind a large family and then an elderly man and could have sworn that the escalator had grown by fifty steps and five stories.

Finally, finally he landed, and in three long steps was enveloped in Toby's arms. Emmett's bag and cane smacked against Toby's legs, and his fedora popped off the back of his head. He didn't care that it might get kicked away. He couldn't speak. He couldn't pull back enough for a kiss, but was content to hold tight to what he had almost lost, time and again—to what he would never lose again, if he could help it.

A baggage carousel buzzed, and Emmett broke away long enough to read the monitor overhead. "That's me."

But Toby held him still and pressed a soft kiss to his lips. "I thought you'd never get here."

"I thought you were sending a car."

"I did," Toby said as he took Emmett's bag and grabbed his hat off the floor. "I rode along with it."

On the way into the city, they fell into a contented silence while Toby held his hand. It all seemed new and fresh, yet filled with a history Emmett never wanted to forget, like the rides out to dinner with Emmett's family, where holding hands was the only acceptable form of affectionate display. They held hands with gusto then, stroking each other's fingers with a clear sexual message and tracing the creases of one another's palms until it tickled.

"The traffic is terrible, Mr. Spence," the driver said in a thick, nondescript accent. "It would be faster if I went via the tunnel."

"Bridge, please."

"But it's—"

"Bridge, please. It's a beautiful day. Let's see it."

"Yes, sir."

Toby turned to Emmett and stole another kiss. "What do you want to do?"

There weren't words for all Emmett wanted to do. "Everything." All Emmett wanted to say. "Nothing at all."

Toby held his gaze; a faint smile curled at his lips as his eyes darkened in understanding. "Do you want to start at my office and, um… get that over with?"

"No," Emmett said, unblinking. "I have ten days. I'm not in a hurry."

"No. Of course not."

Emmett kissed Toby again and sat back, leaning as far into the center of the Town Car as he could. "Do you have wine at the apartment?"

"Not much. Half a bottle, maybe."

"Let's get some? Maybe… some cheese too? Some fruit?"

Traffic broke and stalled, on again and off, until finally they were in the Village. And then they were in Toby's apartment, where Emmett's suitcase, cane, coat, hat and bag fell to the floor with a crashing *THWUMP*.

Urgent and frenzied, Emmett moved to make up for years past, and for the most recent months. He pawed at Toby's clothes, uselessly fingering buttons, giving up when enough of Toby's neck was exposed. Toby tried to talk between kisses, between buttons, and Emmett laughed at him, at his desperation.

"I know you said you're not in a hurry, but—" Toby mumbled, as Emmett's hand slipped between them to cup Toby in his pants. "Fuck! But I sort of—Christ, Em—maybe we could—"

"Shut the fuck up, Toby," Emmett laughed, and then had them both unzipped and in his hands, making Toby do just that.

Emmett pulled them to the floor, tumbling and grunting, finally giving up on any purpose other than friction and release. He rolled his hips into Toby, his half-clothed cock sliding alongside Toby's with not-quite-perfect pressure.

"You okay? Your hip?"

Emmett ignored his concern. "Lube? Condom? Tell me you can pull a condom out of this floorboard."

"Um… "

Emmett remembered his bag nearby. Toby pushed his pants off, and tugged off Emmett's. Emmett got Toby sheathed and reached back around himself with lubed fingers, not wasting another moment.

"Fucking hell, Em."

"Want you." He straddled Toby's hips and bent for a kiss, tonguing Toby's bitten lips. "Need you." Emmett inched forward and took hold of Toby's cock, teasing the tip at his rim, and closed his eyes in the simple pleasure, in the almost. He played there, smiling down at Toby, at this man he had so foolishly and unknowingly blamed for things that had been beyond their control.

This was the man who filled his heart to the brim; his unapologetic love for Emmett had been announced when they were young men and told again and again in the quiet of his life through a song he could not yet sing.

Emmett closed his eyes again and eased down until his body gave in to the welcome, necessary intrusion. Toby held him there, his fingers digging into Emmett's hips, and with slight thrusts into Emmett, gasped a desperate "I love you."

Emmett didn't answer. "I love you" seemed trite, scripted. He danced over Toby slowly, undulating around him, filled with him. His waistcoat and dress shirt were still half buttoned, dragging over his cock as he moved. When he started to take them off, Toby stopped him with a rasped, desperate plea. "Leave them on."

"Dirty boy."

Toby pulled Emmett down by the back of his neck. Kisses, hot breath and curses echoed through the room, skin slapping skin as Toby worked up into him. Emmett met his pace, his cock smacking Toby's belly, the friction of skin and clothes and sweat just shy of enough.

Toby's scratched into Emmett's hair and down his back. His breath was hot at Emmett's ear, cursing with each thrust, and it was then, when Emmett's entire body was on and around and holding and cradling this man, *this* man, when nothing else mattered but them in this moment, that Emmett said the trite, the scripted, the most honest of all utterances: "I love you. I love you." His orgasm washed through him, a slow, powerful release of pleasure, until he could catch his breath and say it again. "I love you."

With a whimpered cry, Toby's body stilled and then jerked, his fingers squeezing Emmett's ass as he pushed hard into him with one final pulse of his own orgasm. They spot-cleaned quickly and Emmett was back on Toby, straddling him, every inch of their bodies reconnecting. They tasted and explored each other's mouths and necks, nipping at earlobes and stopping to hold, to be near, to let the world fade away, to make this moment last and last.

"I'm crushing you," Emmett finally mumbled into the crook of Toby's neck.

"Maybe a little."

Emmett sat up, still on Toby's thighs, and looked down between them. "Well, that's not so hot anymore." He picked at his shirt and his vest and grimaced. "I'm assuming there's a decent dry cleaner in the Village."

"Yes, but they won't touch jizz stains."

For a split second, Emmett believed him. Sense hit him too late; Toby was already laughing.

"Come on," he said as he tapped at Emmett's leg and tried to wiggle up. "I want wine. And cheese. And fruit." He kissed Emmett, mostly with his tongue. "And more of this." Toby groaned as he sat up and cracked his neck. "And maybe a mattress. We're too fucking old for this floor shit."

WHILE IN BED WITH THE wine and cheese, and possibly some juice of the fruit all over Toby's sheets, they'd made a perfect plan for their near future. First, for the next ten days, they would never leave the bed. Toby would call in a substitute for his jazz gig. And, ten days of delivery would not, by an edict that Toby made up while standing naked on the bed, make their arteries block and their valves weaken.

Reason rested somewhere in the midst of the rumpled sheets and silliness, but in this moment, while the setting sun shone golden light over Toby's room, and Toby was warm against Emmett, pliant from the wine and the sex, reason was not something to worry about. "I want to thank you," Emmett said in the quiet. "For giving me some time to get my head straight."

Toby breathed deeply and pulled himself closer. "Did it help?"

"I'm here, aren't I?"

"You are definitely here," Toby teased with a thrust of his hips into Emmett's thigh. But then he hiked up and kissed Emmett's cheek with a faint wrinkle furrowing his brow. "I don't want to end up on two sides of the same fucking door again."

"We both know you're going to leave again." Toby started to protest, but Emmett stopped him. "It's who you are. It's who you were before I ever met you. But now I know I'll be okay. I won't fall apart without you."

"You know I'll always come back to you."

"Yeah. You never leave me behind. Not really."

Toby bent for a kiss; His breath was wine-sweet between them as he asked his next question—as if he were too afraid to look Emmett in the eye. "What happens when—I mean, just because I finally had a day of reckoning—" He pulled back and looked at Emmett with an embarrassed smile. "Does it all still freak you out now and then? Scotty?" Toby trailed his hand down Emmett's abdomen and traced the scars on his hips with his thumbs. "All of it?"

"Two weeks ago, Mac found me on the verge of tears in my office."

"You didn't tell me this… "

"Remember the YouTube video I sent of the kitten on the Roomba? What did I say with it?"

"Um, something like, 'Some days it feels like you go nowhere and everywhere all at the same time.'"

"That was me telling you."

"What happened?"

"The weather had been shit. Cold and rainy and colder and rainier, and I felt like I'd been on my feet for months. My hip was screaming at me about it. My tension was exacerbating it and I got pissed. Pissed at my body and pissed at Scotty for distracting you and you for letting him. Pissed at not insisting I drive that day and then, since I stayed pissed long enough, I got scared."

"They do go hand in hand, don't they?"

"I'm always afraid I'm going to need a damned hip replaced before I'm forty, and then another at sixty, and if I do it right I'll need two more, because I am never dying."

"Emmett."

"No. No pity face. That's what I mean. Freakouts happen. It's going to fuck with us for the rest of our lives. And I want you to know that you can fly when you need to fly."

"And you need kitten videos when you need to fight."

Emmett still couldn't believe it was Toby. Here. In love with him. Believing in him. Holding him accountable by virtue of loving him exactly as he was in the moment. In this moment. In any moment, Emmett was always enough.

"I'm fond of sea lions too," Emmett confessed. "For the record." They snuggled into the blankets again, this time with Emmett tucked into Toby's arm. "Promise me something."

"Anything."

"Tell me when you need to fly," Emmett said. "Don't just take off."

"Maybe sometimes I can take you with me."

"Hmm. I've never been to Italy."

"When we go to Italy, it will be because we want to go. Not because I need to take a spin on the anxiety Tilt-a-Whirl."

"You're taking me to Italy?"

"Emmett, I will take you wherever you want to go."

"I'm good right now," Emmett said as his eyes drifted shut. "Here is good."

◆◆◆

MORNINGSIDE—March 2017

When Emmett went back to Indiana, he dove into the winter season with new vigor. This year's senior class was one of his best ever; Tori was only one of the many bright lights that had been with him from freshman year until now, dutifully helping to rebuild the program into one that other schools envied.

While walking from the office of Regent High School during a large-group competition, Emmett overheard a few students from another high school lamenting the performance schedule.

"Oh God. Oh God, we're doomed, someone tell Mrs. White. We're after Morningside. The judges are going to pack up and go home after them."

And they should. Really. While groups competed against themselves, not each other, comparisons happened. Morningside was on top of their game as they had never been before.

Now it was mid-March, and Emmett had stayed late to remix a few rehearsal tapes for the next week's lessons. No student had been seen in the building for a few hours, so when he heard his steel choir door slam shut, he startled and lost his grip on an iPad.

"Oh! Mr. H!" Tori rushed to his side, almost before he had bumbled the device back onto the music stand. "I didn't mean to scare you." Rosy cheeked from the cold and a coy grin curling her lips, she stood there with two envelopes.

"What's up? You look dangerous."

She said nothing, but handed him the envelopes, one from the University of Cincinnati, the other from Ball State.

"These are addressed to you," he said, understanding and tamping down his own joy so it could belong to her first.

"I know. I've opened them. And now I'm sharing them with you." She bounced on her toes. "Open them already oh my God you are worse than my father!" This came out as one word.

Emmett slowed his movements as he turned the envelopes in his hands. The University of Cincinnati was especially exciting; they welcomed just eighteen people into their program every year—with nationwide auditions. He opened Ball State first.

Of course, it was a welcome letter to the conservatory there. Ball State was another select college with a great history of New York agent sign-ups post-grad. "Congratulations."

She beamed and nodded at the second envelope. "Two?" he asked. He quickly skimmed Cincinnati's acceptance letter and lowered it, not fighting his tears. "Come here."

Tori threw herself into Emmett's arms. "Thank you, Mr. H. Thank you so much. I've been a royal pain in the ass—butt—and I know it and I know my senioritis is at epic levels, and my dad won't stop crying, and it's all because of you."

"You're a royal pain in the ass because of me?"

"Well, you do sort of have that skill down, you know."

"You know who else would be proud of you?" Tori's eyes lit up even more. "Do you have a minute? Wanna give him a call?"

They found Toby in his office in New York. Emmett whispered a hello when his face came into view on the computer screen.

"Hi, beautiful," Toby smiled back. "How's your Tuesday?"

"Oh my God, you guys are so gross and cute—" Tori slapped her hand over her mouth. Her presence was *supposed* to be a surprise.

Emmett looked at her. "I bet you're fun before surprise parties."

"I suck at them." She scooted her chair next to Emmett's and peeked at the monitor. "Hi, Mr. Spence. Is it gray and ugly in New York too?"

"The grayest. I'm about to write up a petition to move Broadway to Jamaica. You think I'll find enough signatures?"

"You won't know until you try!" She bounced in her chair, and Emmett could do nothing but laugh.

"Out with it, young lady. You're going to explode all over my office."

Emmett moved out of the way, and Tori broke her news, adding that she was still waiting to hear from Indiana University.

"Congratulations. You deserve it all, sweetheart."

"I couldn't have done it without you, Mr. Spence. My demo got me an audition, and I knew what to expect, and Mr. H is—" she reached for him, and he gave her his hand. "Thank you both so much for helping me not be an idiot."

"You did all the hard work," Toby said. "I expect to play for you onstage one day."

"Maybe you could direct? That would be fun. Or… Mr. H. says you're writing. Maybe you could write a song for me one day."

"I'd be honored." Toby said. "Knowing you, though, I'll be writing an entire show for you before I retire."

"I'll hold you to it, Mr. Spence." She stood and plopped her hat onto her head. "I have to run. Mom's going to think I'm dead in a ditch somewhere." She looked at the screen and blew a kiss. "Thank you, Mr. Spence." She turned to Emmett and smiled through more tears. "Thank you, Mr. H. You've made high school fun and… I wish I could take you with me."

"Oh, no. College and Mr. H. do not do well together. You go and be smarter than I was, and we'll call it a deal."

She flew out his office door and ran back to close it before he could correct her. Then the slam of the choir room door cracked through the empty hall. By her energy alone, Tori was going to conquer the world.

Emmett turned his attention to the screen, to the man who had his heart. "Thank you. I'm sorry I doubted you."

"I'd given you few reasons not to." Toby sipped his coffee. "I was going to call you this evening anyway."

"You call me almost every evening."

"Well, with a purpose this time."

"Oh? Let's save the 'what are you wearing' conversation for after work, huh?"

Toby didn't smile back, not really. His eyes crinkled, but he pressed on. "I think I'm done, Emmett. It feels complete."

"Are you serious? Have you sent it anywhere?"

"No. It needs… " Toby pushed away from the range of his laptop camera and started playing his keyboard, talking over it loudly enough for Emmett to hear. "It needs you, though. A bit more of you."

"What can I do?" Emmett listened to him play. The second theme was so rich and harmonic he still got gooseflesh whenever he heard it.

"I don't need your help necessarily, but I'd love your input with some of the orchestral arrangement. I'm hearing vocal type things, but with strings." He demonstrated the section: choral, almost hymnodic, a musical prayer. "I can do it, of course, but—"

"Anything. Anything you need. Send it in, Toby. It's time to let it go."

Toby stopped playing and slid into Emmett's view. Emmett almost whined when the music silenced. "It won't be ours anymore, Em."

"It's okay," Emmett said. "We don't need it anymore."

23

MORNINGSIDE—April 2017

Toby stood outside the choir room door. He was early. Four days early, which probably made this less a visit and more a surprise. After his last attempt at a surprise visit during rehearsal, Toby proceeded with caution.

The a cappella group's rehearsal was muffled through the concrete walls and steel doors. Toby couldn't resist. He slowly turned the knob, prayed for a non-squeaking door and let himself into the back of the room, as he had so many months before.

The kids were fully focused on Emmett. It was run-through time. "Just like the real thing," as he always told them. No stops. All eyes on Emmett. Leave your problems at the door.

They were preparing for the spring concert—a respite from the high-intensity contest season. They sang "Linus and Lucy," an a cappella version of the piano solo theme song to all the Charlie Brown television shows that everyone knew, regardless of age.

A few students spotted him as they sang, but smiled with their eyes and continued singing. Emmett cut them off from their final *dah-daht*—the only words in the song—and Toby stepped forward with generous applause.

This time when Emmett spun around, it was more like meeting him at the airport. His eyes lit up, his feet lifted from the ground, and while the class laughed behind him, he walked—not ran, that would be entirely *too* unprofessional—right into Toby's arms. "You're early!"

"A little." Emmett stepped back, and Toby could see the arguments flying across his face. *Kiss him. Don't kiss him. You're the teacher; they'll tell the principal Mr. H. was making out during class. These are the good kids, they'll do no such thing.* Toby finally solved the problem by kissing his cheek and turning him back to his class. "I really think you need to work on lyrics, though. Every time I show up it's 'doh' this and 'dah' that. Good lyrics can really sell a tune."

Emmett showed his students off: state contest numbers, the sight-reading selection they had loved so much that they perfected it just for the fun of it, and the numbers for the spring concert that were still rough around the edges.

The bell rang, and the choir actually whined; they still wanted to sing, and they lingered in the room until Emmett reminded them of buses and waiting parents. "You idiots have prom tomorrow night. Get out."

Before they all left, Toby congratulated Tori in person and learned that she had chosen the University of Cincinnati. And that Emily was wearing the prettiest gray tuxedo to prom.

As soon as they were alone, Toby greeted Emmett with a kiss that would have gotten them a long series of detentions in high school. And all Emmett could say when they broke was, "You're early."

"We covered that," Toby said. Emmett kissed him again and then picked up the scraps of paper that teenagers seemed to drop like shedding dogs' chunks of fur. "Would you rather I leave and come back?"

Emmett stood, huffed and kissed him on the way to the trash. "It's just—this weekend is nuts. I have to meet with chaperones here in… " He looked up at the clock and groaned. "Less than an hour, and there's senior brunch tomorrow morning and prom's tomorrow night, and—I thought I told you all of this." Emmett unplugged his recording microphones and wound them around his arm. "How did I get on the fucking prom committee anyway?"

"You mentioned something about Gino."

"Oh yeah. Right. Payback for missing Derek's last show. Narcissistic idiot."

"Who? Derek or Gino?"

"Gino. Obviously. Derek's lovely. Oh. He said good luck on selling your music, and he'll burn some… smelly something-or-other on your behalf. It's a compliment."

"Thank you?"

"Yes, thank you is good. He's flaky, but he's kind." Emmett hadn't stopped moving since the kids left. Toby tried to help, but Emmett would grab whatever he had in his hand and tend to it himself. Toby wasn't sure Emmett was aware he'd been doing it.

"Can you, maybe—" Toby sat down at the piano and started playing. It was nothing, really. Not his composition, although a few chord progressions slipped in because they were so ingrained in his head. Like Pavlov's dog, Emmett stopped, closed his eyes and walked to the piano, putty in Toby's hands. "Do I have your attention now?"

Emmett leaned on the grand piano with his elbows. "My full attention."

"Good." Toby wound his song up to the highest range, so that tinkling raindrop notes fell as he spoke. "About this prom thing." With finesse that impressed even himself, Toby spun the song into the opening theme of his work. Their work. "You and I… we never got to prom."

Emmett smiled; a blush tinted his cheeks. "No. No we did not."

"And I was thinking about it. About how I never went to prom anywhere because I never felt that attached to my school, but you did. And you—you couldn't go."

"Toby…"

Toby continued to play with his left hand while he reached into his jacket pocket with his right. He pulled out a small box and laid it to the side of the music shelf. He nodded at it while he kept playing.

Emmett's mouth fell open. "No way. Toby, are these—" He grabbed the box and opened it, gasped and looked at Toby. "How did you—are these *mine*?" He lifted one of the Fenrir cufflinks out as if it was solid gold.

"They are, actually." With a quick, arpeggiated chord, Toby ended the piece and stood with Emmett.

"You've had them all this time?"

"Mom did for a while, but yeah. I've had them for years. I sort of forgot until I was cleaning out shit from under my bed." He was cleaning shit out from under his bed because his lease was up. Because he was moving. To Emmett. To Indiana. The damned place was going to be home after all.

"Where were they?"

Toby reminded Emmett of the night *before* the accident. The night that Toby had surprised him, arriving a day early. The cufflinks had come in the mail, and he took them to Toby's house to show them off. He couldn't stay; his mother insisted he be home for dinner, but—"We sort of got distracted," Toby said.

"Oh God, did we get distracted."

They shared another school-inappropriate kiss, and Toby continued. "You left them on my bedside stand."

"And after? I mean, surely you saw them?"

"Well, you know what a mess my room was, so no. I didn't. Until I was packing to go back to New York. You were never over anymore, and I just—"

"Yeah... " Nothing was the same. Except Toby's love for this man.

"So, I found them and couldn't bring myself to show you. Mom kept them and she sent them after they moved."

Emmett rolled down his shirtsleeves and popped one cufflink into the button hole, holding the other buttoned side to it. "God, these are clunky."

"I think I tried to tell you that, but—"

"Oh, hush. I was eighteen and knew everything."

Toby kissed Emmett's cheek and took the link out of Emmett's sleeve. "It'd be a shame to let them go to waste."

"It would," Emmett conceded. "What will you wear?"

"I brought a tux."

"You did not bring a tux."

"I… brought a tux," Toby said. "It's very Broadway. Smells like greasepaint."

"Do you have a tight curfew?"

"Oh no, sweetheart. There's no curfew for grown-up prom."

"Blue delphiniums make gorgeous boutonnières."

"I'll buy two."

◆◆◆

TOBY HAD TO GIVE IT to Emmett; he was trying. He was trying to let Toby be mysterious and vague and strange in preparation for their years-tardy prom night. He told Emmett he had errands and to trust him. He told Emmett he knew what he was doing and to trust him. He told him to stop being such a fucking control freak and to trust him.

"I do trust you," Emmett assured him, every time. And Toby believed him. In the truest sense of the word, Toby knew that Emmett trusted him. He just didn't appear too confident in Toby's ability to get back to the house so they could get to dinner and then prom on time.

"This is sort of my job tonight, Toby. I can't be fucking around—" Toby shut him up with a kiss, a hand down the back of his pajama pants and a firm squeeze. "You have things to do. I will be home in time for dinner. *Trust me.*"

He finally got to the door, where a cab waited, and Emmett called from upstairs. "My cufflinks! Where did you—"

"On the tray of your valet." He waited for Emmett's "Got 'em!" before he left.

He ended at Mac's house, where they finalized details of the recording sessions that were to take place after school the following week. Toby had decided he wanted to use a live orchestra rather than the digital replications of his keyboard for his demo tapes. He wanted to offer the piece as close to stage-ready as possible. With Emmett's recording expertise and Mac's award-winning instrumental program, he was set.

Besides, the experience it provided the students would be immeasurable.

Mac fed him lunch, and they talked for hours. She lovingly lectured him on how slow and painful a death he would endure should he ever hurt Emmett again. He thanked her for being such an important person in Emmett's life while he was busy being an idiot. She never argued the "idiot" point, but did give him a sloppy kiss on the cheek when he left.

And, as promised, Toby was in the driveway of Emmett's house at the appointed time. He had changed at Mac's, ridiculous in Emmett's eyes—*"This isn't really our prom, Toby"*—but important for the final surprise he had in store.

He got out of the car, put on his jacket and buttoned it. Before ringing the bell, he checked his reflection in the storm door as best he could: too old for prom. Not too old for a fun date.

When Emmett answered, he hadn't yet tied his bow tie or fastened the straps of his backless vest. His shirt was unbuttoned at the collar and his glasses were in his teeth.

Maybe Toby was early again. Maybe they could start after-prom early, too.

"You're early. Again."

"My apologies. You, um… " Toby swallowed thickly. "You look like someone I'd like to keep safe at home."

"Mmm. A man with taste. I like that." Emmett yanked him in the door and started to kiss him, but stopped. He eyed the car in the driveway. "Is this what the big surprise was? You got us a Town Car?"

"Well. Yes. And no." Toby did the opposite of what he really wanted to do, and started buttoning Emmett's shirt. Emmett closed the door and let him; a peaceful smile lit his whole face when their eyes met.

"Lemme get your—" He tied Emmett's tie and spun him around to fasten his vest. "Where's your jacket? You need your cane?"

Jacket on and boutonnière pinned, they checked themselves in the hallway mirror and headed out.

Toby tried to act nonchalant as they approached the car. But Emmett stopped before he got to the black sedan. "Toby?"

Toby rushed ahead of him and opened the passenger door. "Your ride."

Emmett stared at him. "Toby?"

Toby pulled a set of keys out of his pocket, flipped them in his hand and grinned. "I know it's more formal to hire a driver, but I uh—I thought I could be our driver tonight."

Emmett peeked inside the car and back out at Toby, his eyes round in shock. "You got your license?" And then—"In the *city?*"

Toby laughed, then, finally able to breathe and rev up the nerve to actually do this with an audience other than his instructor. "No. I went to Jersey a couple times a week. I'm not that crazy."

Emmett gave him a wet, off-center kiss. His cane fell to the ground, and he looked at Toby in disbelief before kissing him again and again, until they were standing in the middle of Emmett's driveway making out like two horny teenagers. Emmett combed through the curls over Toby's ear with his fingers. "You didn't have to do this."

"Yes. I really did. For me. It's never going to be my favorite thing to do, but… yes. I had to do this. And I wanted to."

"Well." Emmett stood straight, grabbed his cane and unbuttoned his jacket. "Then I guess I'd better get in."

Toby closed the door and took five huge breaths before getting into the driver's seat. He looked over to Emmett, his passenger, his partner, his everything, and started the engine.

"Full circle, huh?" Emmett said as he put his seatbelt on and met Toby's gaze.

"Round and round she goes."

Xavier Native Pays it Forward
New play to premiere at Xavier Area Community Theater

XAVIER—Xavier's own Tobias Spence, award-winning musical director of numerous Broadway and regional shows including *Candide, Cinderella, Chicago* and *Rent,* will be returning to his roots to premiere the play *Diamonds from Dust* on Friday and Saturday, October 19 and 20.

Spence composed the score for the play, and will conduct Morningside High School's chamber orchestra in the two-night-only production showing at Xavier Area Community Theater. The play will be entirely cast with XACT's talented and experienced roster of thespians, including Victoria Graham, who is currently studying musical theater at the University of Cincinnati. Ms. Isabelle Lipman will temporarily leave retirement from a thirty-six-year career at XACT to direct.

The play has been successfully workshopped in New York City, starring previous Tony Award nominee Anthony Harkness. After its two-night run in Xavier, it will premiere in Chicago at the Raven Theater beginning November 27.

Tickets are $75 general admission and can be purchased at all Ticketlist outlets or at XACT's box office. All proceeds for *Diamonds from Dust* go to the Scotty Barnes Foundation, providing scholarships for Wayne County athletes who choose to pursue the performing arts in college.

Spence graduated from Xavier High School in 1998, and was the driver in the tragic automobile accident that killed Barnes in April of 2000. When he's not directing or writing his own productions, Spence lives a quiet life with his husband, Emmett Henderson—originally from Ridgewood, and also injured in the accident—in Morningside. Mr. Henderson conducts seminars around the region on the use of technology in the classroom, and has led the Morningside High School choirs for eight award-winning years.

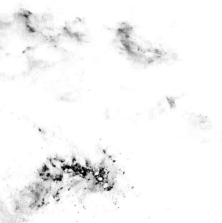

FIN.

ACKNOWLEDGMENTS

THE SEEDS AND WITHERED ATTEMPTS at this story sat in various hard drives for a number of years. It was my first writing attempt after years of drought and would still be in those digital closets if it weren't for the direct, and often indirect, support of some amazing people.

To the team at Interlude Press, my bottomless gratitude for giving me not one, but two opportunities to fulfill a dream I barely allowed myself to dream. I look forward to many more years together. To Lex especially, you always wished for us to simply keep writing good stories. I will. I promise.

To my family and friends who probably thought I was lying when I said I was still working on this book, and yes I wanted to get together, but no I could not do that now... thank you for waiting. For cheering me on anyway. For giving me free reign to create in my twisted, tangled, occasionally tear-filled way. A special thank you to A—for making me cry in the back of a cab. It still took time, but that moment set this on the right course. I'm always a better writer and a better person after speaking with you.

And finally, to the teachers that taught me more than the subject at hand, that loved me when I became impatient, that weren't afraid to play and work and make mistakes all in name of helping me be the best I could be. Above all, JT—even though I'm no longer in music, you continue to guide my way in everything I do.

ABOUT THE AUTHOR

LYNN CHARLES' LOVE OF WRITING dates back to her childhood, but continued into adulthood filling books upon books of journals long before journaling was cool. She lives in central Ohio, and while she now considers herself a rusty musician, music has always been a driving force in her life, through earning her degree in music education and many years performing and directing choral music. When she's not writing, she can be found strolling local farmers markets in search of ingredients for new recipes and falling into the google rabbit hole researching for her next writing project.

Her novel *Chef's Table* was published December 2014 by Interlude Press.

Connect with Lynn at lynncharles.net.

For a reader's guide to Black Dust and book club prompts, please visit interludepress.com

also from lynn **charles**

"...sweet contemporary debut... a delightful pair of protagonists."
—*Publishers Weekly*

CHEF'S TABLE

LYNN CHARLES

Chef Evan Stanford steadily climbed New York City's culinary ladder, earning himself the Rising Star James Beard award and an executive chef position at an acclaimed restaurant. But in his quest to build his reputation, he forgot what got him there: the lessons on food—and life—from a loving hometown neighbor.

Patrick Sullivan is contented keeping the memory of his grandmother's Irish cooking alive through the food he prepares in a Brooklyn diner. But when Chef Stanford walks in for a meal, Patrick is swept up by his drive, forcing him to reconsider if a contented life is a fulfilled one. The two men begin a journey through their culinary histories, falling into an easy friendship. But even with the joys of their burgeoning love, can they tap into that secret recipe of great love, great food and transcendent joy?

ISBN (print) 978-1-941530-17-7 | ISBN (eBook) 978-1-941530-20-7

interlude press™
you may also like...

Sweet by Alysia Constantine

Alone and lonely since the death of his partner, a West Village pastry chef gradually reclaims his life through an unconventional courtship with an unfulfilled accountant that involves magical food, online flirtation, and a dog named Andy. *Sweet* is also the story of how we tell love stories. The narrator is on to you, Reader, and wants to give you a love story that doesn't always fit the bill.

ISBN (print) 978-1-941530-61-0 | ISBN (eBook) 978-1-941530-62-7

What It Takes by Jude Sierra

Milo met Andrew moments after moving to Cape Cod—launching a lifelong friendship of deep bonds, secret forts and plans for the future. When Milo goes home for his father's funeral, he and Andrew finally act on their attraction—but doubtful of his worth, Milo severs ties. They meet again years later, and their long-held feelings will not be denied. Will they have what it takes to find lasting love?

ISBN (print) 978-1-941530-59-7 | ISBN (eBook) 978-1-941530-60-3

The Bones of You by Laura Stone

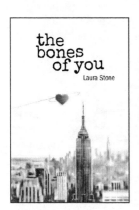

Oliver Andrews is wholly focused on the final stages of his education at Cambridge University when a well meaning friend upends his world with a simple email attachment: a video from a U.S. morning show. The moment he watches the video of his one-time love Seth Larsen, now a Broadway star, Oliver must begin making a series of choices that could lead him back to love—or break his heart.

The Bones of You is full of laughter and tears, with a collection of irritable Hungarians, flirtatious Irishwomen and actors abusing Shakespeare coloring Oliver and Seth's attempts at reconciliation.

ISBN (print) 978-1-941530-16-0 | ISBN (ebook) 978-1-941530-24-5

interlude press™

One **story**

can change

everything.

interlude**press**.com

CPSIA information can be obtained
at www.ICGtesting.com
Printed in the USA
FFOW02n2329130416
23179FF